HOT FLASH!

"We have received a flash alert, Lieutenant."

War? Esmay's stomach clenched.

"Lord Thornbuckle's daughter has been taken captive by an unknown force which threatens reprisals against Familias should any action be taken to rescue her. She has been mutilated—"

"Not . . . Brun!?" Esmay could feel the blood draining from her head; she put out a hand to the hatch coaming.

"Yes." Solis shook his head as if to clear it, and gave Esmay another long challenging look. "You don't seem pleased that your prophecy that she would come to grief has been fulfilled—"

For a moment she could not believe what he had said. "Of course not," she said, then, "It has nothing to do with it. I never wanted anything bad to happen—

"Y ou had best hope, then, that she is recovered quickly, alive and healthy, Solis said, because otherwise . . . as I'm sure her father . . . drawed her out and she . . . her Mountain in a temper. . . realize, Lieutenant Su . . . Space S . . . t this m . . .

BAEN BOOKS by Elizabeth Moon

Hunting Party
Sporting Chance
Winning Colors
Once a Hero
Rules of Engagement
Change of Command (forthcoming)

Sheepfarmer's Daughter
Divided Allegiance
Oath of Gold
The Deed of Paksenarrion
Liar's Oath
The Legacy of Gird

Remnant Population

Phases

Sassinak
(with Anne McCaffrey)

Generation Warriors
(with Anne McCaffrey)

RULES OF ENGAGEMENT

ELIZABETH MOON

Rules of Engagement

This is a work of fiction. All the characters and events portrayed in this book are fictional, and any resemblance to real people or incidents is purely coincidental.

Copyright © 1998 by Elizabeth Moon

A Baen Books Original

Baen Publishing Enterprises
P.O. Box 1403
Riverdale, NY 10471

ISBN: 0-671-57841-3

Cover art by Gary Ruddell

First paperback printing, November 1999

Library of Congress Catalog Number: 98-39189

Distributed by Simon & Schuster
1230 Avenue of the Americas
New York, NY 10020

Typeset by Windhaven Press, Auburn, NH
Printed in the United States of America

Dedication

In memory of the victims of the
Jarrell, Texas, tornado, May 27, 1997,
and especially Brandi Nicole Smith and
Stacy Renee Smith, and their mother,
Cynthia L. Smith.

Acknowledgements

The usual suspects (you know who you are . . .), with special thanks to Ellen McLean and Mary Morell for helping with the psychology behind the pathology. Mary managed to read the first draft and make intelligent comments even as the rain poured down, the roof leaked, and a dead mouse turned up in the guest room. This is heroic manuscript help. Diann Thornley let me pick her brain about what kinds of things are taught in junior officers' leadership courses. Ruta Duhon helped me think through one of the final bits of excitement over lunch one day, probably because she was tired of hearing me complain that I was stuck. Anna Larsen and Toni Weisskopf each contributed a specific nudge to the emotional side of the plot. Kathleen Jones and David Watson took on the task of "cold reading" the final draft aloud, and did it in just a few days. Their comments markedly improved the *new* final draft. Debbie Kirk, as always, found more typos than anyone else and gently nudged my erratic spelling back toward consistency. Certain anecdotes contributed by persons who asked not to be named added grit to the fictional reality.

Special mention must be made of the bits of Texana which decorate this story. Some are real (other Texans know which), some are fictional, some are Texas mythology of the future. The misappropriation and distortion of Texas history and traditions by characters in the book does not in any way represent my attitude towards that history or those traditions. Readers with a knowledge of history and a sense of irony may be amused by the juxtaposition of certain characters' surnames; the intended references all predate the 20th century. (It was tempting, but not *that* tempting, to play in contemporary Texas politics.) Any coincidence of name is purely accidental. The movements mentioned as ancient history in the text are, however unfortunately, alive and sick in the 20th century; it would be not only useless but dishonest to pretend that the New Texas Godfearing Militia did not derive its nature from elements all too close to home, in Waco, Fort Davis, and even Oklahoma City.

CHAPTER ONE

**Regular Space Service Training Command,
Copper Mountain Base**

Halfway up the cliff, Brun realized that someone was trying to kill her. She had already shifted weight from her left foot to her right foot when the thought penetrated, and she completed the movement, ending with her left foot on the tiny ledge almost at her crotch, before she gave her brain a "message received" signal.

Instantly, her hands slicked with sweat, and she lost the grip of her weaker left hand on the little knob. She dipped it into her chalk, and reached for the knob again, then chalked her right hand and refound that hold. That much was mechanical, after these days in training . . . so someone was trying to kill you, you didn't have to help them by doing something stupid.

She argued with herself, while pushing up, releasing her right leg for the next move. Of course, in a general way, someone was trying to kill her, or any other trainee. She had known that coming in.

Better to lose trainees here than half-trained personnel in the field, where their failure would endanger others. Her breath eased, as she talked herself into a sensible frame of mind. Right foot *there*, and then the arms moving, finding the next holds, and then the left leg . . . she had enjoyed climbing almost from the first day of training.

A roar in her ears and the sudden sting on her hand: she was falling before she had time to recognize the noise and the pain. A shot. Someone had shot at her . . . hit her? Not enough pain—must've been rock splinters—then she hit the end of her rope, and swung into the cliff face with a force that knocked the breath out of her. Reflexively, her hands and feet caught at the rock, sought grips, found them, took her weight off the climbing harness. Her head rang, still; she shook it and the halves of her climbing helmet slid down to hang from the straps like the wing cases of a crushed beetle.

Damn . . . she thought. Reason be damned, someone was trying to kill her—her in particular—and plastered to a cliff in plain sight was not her idea of a good place to be when someone was shooting at her. She glanced around quickly. Up—too far, too slow, too exposed. Down—150 feet of falling in a predictable vertical line, whether free or on the rope. To the right, nothing but open rock. To the left, a narrow vertical crack. They had been told not to use it this time, but she'd climbed in it before, learning about cracks and chimneys. If she could get there . . .

She pushed off, and the next shot hit the cliff where her head had been, between head and right hand. Splinters of rock sprayed her hand, the right side of her face. She did not fall. She lunged for the next hold, not in a panic but with the controlled speed of someone who knew just where each hold would be. Whoever it was had some reason not to fire on automatic, at full speed. But now they knew which way she was going. They could adjust their aim . . . she took a chance, and her foot slipped on one hold. For an instant, she hung from her arms, feet scrabbling . . . then she found the hold, and the next. The sheltering crevice was just ahead—this time it was her left hand that slipped, when she reached too far, and even as she cursed, the next shot shattered the hold for which she'd reached, loosing a shower of rock.

She didn't hesitate. The breakage offered new holds; in a second she was into the crevice, yanking hard on the rope for more, for enough to move into deeper cover. What she hoped the shooter didn't know was alignment of the crevice. Here, she was as vulnerable as on the cliff face, apparently held in a vertical groove. But the forces which had made the crevice had produced an almost spiral fracture. Not ten feet above she could be safely hidden from the shooter.

The rope from below dragged at her. No more slack. They hadn't understood . . . or were they part of the plot? She yanked again, unsuccessfully.

Our Texas, formerly Kurzawa-Yahr
Joint Investment Colony

Mitchell Langston Pardue, Ranger Bowie of the New Texas Godfearing Militia on Our Texas, sat in his heavy carved chair and waited for the Captain to finish reading his report. He stroked the carving on the right arm—supposed to resemble the Old Texas animal called a dilla, whatever that had been—and thought how he could imply that the Captain was an idiot without actually saying so.

"Mitch, you payin' attention?" Pete Robertson, Ranger Travis and Captain of Rangers, had a querulous waver in his voice that made Mitch want to slap him upside the head with something heavy. He was getting old, with a wattled neck like a turkey gobbler.

"You bet, Captain," he said. "You say we need about thirty more of them nukes from Familias Regnant's space fleet, in order to top up the first depot. Your timetable for hittin' the Guernesi is runnin' behind a little . . ."

"It's stopped in its tracks like a mule in a swamp," the Captain said. "An' if we wait too long, they won't make the connection we want." The Guernesi had reacted with vigor to the theft of a shipload of tourists, and had gotten them back, though with casualties. Then they'd imposed a trade embargo, and blown up a couple of ships to make their point that they held a grudge about the ones who had died. "We've gotta get more weapons. And there's somethin' wrong with our main agent at their space fleet headquarters—the last signal we got from him makes no sense."

"He's gettin' old, though," Sam Dubois, Ranger Austin said. "He's had one of them proscribed procedures . . ."

"He was rejuvenated," Mitch said, using the correct term. "They started rejuvenating their most senior NCOs about ten, fifteen years ago, and he's one of 'em. If they hadn't, likely we wouldn't have got anythin' from him."

"But it's an abomination," Sam said. Stubborn as rock, Sam was, and tighter than a tick to Parson Wells.

"Yes, it's an abomination," Mitch said. "I'm not sayin' it's right. But the devil takes care of his own, sometimes, and them rejuvenations have been working awhile now. The man's only eighty; his mind should be fine even if he hadn't had the drugs."

"But it's not," the Captain said, with a triumphant look at Mitch. "Look at this here." He passed down a sheet of paper.

Mitch looked at it. "Gobbledegook," he said after a glance. "Did he change ciphers or something?"

"No. I think he's taken to some heathen practice— or that rejuvenation is eating his brain. I've heard about that." His next glance at Mitch was calculating.

"Could be," Mitch said. Everyone knew he had read more widely in the dangerous literature of biomodification than was strictly approved by the parsons. The Captain was trying to trap him into a discussion that would prove his contamination, but Mitch was smarter than that. Instead, he had his own plan.

"Well?" Sam said.

"Captain," Mitch said formally. "I'd like to make a proposal."

"Sure," the Captain said. His gaze didn't waver. Mitch could have laughed; the idiot still thought Mitch would incriminate himself.

"You know you gave me permission 'way last year to do some work in the Familias myself—"

"Yeah—"

"Well, sir, I cast bread on the waters and let me tell you, there are hungry souls out there all athirst for the true word of God." Now the others all nodded, leaning forward. "I found us some agents here and there—in big trading firms, and one in a regional weapons depot, an assistant station master—and we've been getting a nice little flow of illicits in here for about six months."

Mitch pulled out his own report and passed it around. "More'n that, gentlemen, any time we want an entire cargo hold loaded with nukes or anything else, I've got just the person to do it. What I thought was, I'd go on and tell 'em to load up, and then go get us a transport as well as the weapons. There's this ship that takes a shortcut through a deserted system— a fine place for an ambush."

"Ah—and you want our help, Ranger Bowie?"

"No sir, I don't. With all respect, sir, there's too much goin' on to pull resources from the rest of our people. What I thought was, I'd take all of the Bowies, and take care of this little chore—and that should put us back on track for knocking the Guernesi flat on their tails."

Silence, during which the others digested this, and looked for ways to profit from it. Mitch made himself sit still, and observed.

"What about the crew?" the Captain asked finally.

Mitch shrugged. "Our usual rules. We still need more females, if we can find some that aren't too badly contaminated."

"You know, we've had to mute damn near every foreign female we've brought in," Sam said. "And I worry about their effect on our women."

Mitch smiled. "We're real men; we can control our women." The others quickly nodded; nobody wanted to admit to having a problem in that area. "Besides, we know God approves, because the imported women have strong, healthy babies, fewer of 'em born with defects." That, too, was unarguable. A child's defects reflected parental sin; if healthy children came from women brought up in sin, then it must be because God celebrated their release from the abominations of the ungodly.

"If Parson Wells will bless your mission, Ranger Bowie, you have my approval," the Captain said formally.

Just wait until he, Ranger Bowie, was Captain of Rangers, and then see if he rolled over like that for anyone. Mitch nodded, and when the parson came in he explained the proposed mission again. Parson Wells pursed his lips, but finally nodded. "Just be sure to avoid contamination, Ranger Bowie."

Mitch smiled. "Yes, sir, Parson. I got no intention of going heathen." He had every intention of coming back with weapons, women, wealth—and every intention of making it to the captaincy before he was many years older.

✧   ✧   ✧

R.S.S. Training Command, Copper Mountain

Lieutenant Esmay Suiza arrived at Training Command's Copper Mountain Base with high hopes only to find herself waiting her turn for security clearance in a big echoing reception hall with two of the ugliest murals she'd ever seen. On the right, over the com booths, a scene of ships in combat in space. They looked nothing like ships as Esmay had seen them from the outside. Realism would have been dull at best, but she couldn't help an internal smirk at the astronomical decorations . . . stars, comets, spiral galaxies. On the left, over the luggage dumps, a scene depicting ground combat, which looked even less realistic than the space one . . . for one thing, nobody's uniform ever stayed that clean. For another, the artist had only a shaky grasp of anatomy and perspective; all the figures looked squashed sideways.

Esmay tried to get her mind back to her own high hopes. A change in track, from technical to command, and she was finally pursuing her destiny, using her best talents. Certainly her commanders thought so. She had made friends, including Barin Serrano who was—if she was honest with herself—much more than a friend. In his admiration, she felt herself more capable; in his concern, she felt herself loved. That still made her uncomfortable: she had never really thought about love, about being loved, and she could hardly believe it had happened, or that it might last. But she still felt the touch of his hands on her face— she pulled herself back from that memory and made herself consider what came next.

She glanced at the space combat scene again and could not help shaking her head.

"Gruesome, aren't they, sir?" asked the sergeant at the first security station. "Supposed to be very old and valuable, but really—it looks like something done by a half-gifted amateur."

"That's probably what they got," Esmay said, grinning. She presented her orders and identification.

"New rules, Lieutenant, require a full med-ID scan before you receive station tags. If you'll follow the yellow line to the next station, they'll get started."

Security had been tighter all the way across Familias Space, a natural result of all that had happened in the past quarter year. Still, she hadn't expected the level of confirmation required here, at a training base whose only access was through a Fleet-controlled orbital station. Where were intruders supposed to be coming from?

An hour later she was waiting outside yet another security checkpoint. It was ridiculous. How long did it take to do a retinal check, even a full neuroscan? Her stomach growled, reminding her that she'd broken one of the great rules of military life—eat whenever you get a chance. She could have grabbed a snack before leaving the transport, but (her memory mocked her) it was only supposed to be a couple of hours down to Copper Mountain.

In for the retinal check at last. "Just follow the yellow line, Lieutenant . . ." said the voice behind the screen.

"But can't you just—"

"Follow the yellow line."

Which ended in another bench to wait on until her name was called. Ahead of her was a whole squad of neuro-enhanced combat troops . . . she'd heard of these but never seen any up close. They looked like anyone else who happened to be carrying about twice the muscle and half the fat of anyone else. They had been chatting, but fell silent as she came up to the bench. She felt fragile beside them.

"Excuse me, Lieutenant—" She looked up to see that they had reshuffled themselves to put one of the women next to her.

"Yes?"

"Are you the Lieutenant Suiza who was on *Despite* and then *Koskiusko*?"

Esmay nodded.

"Lieutenant, I'm really glad to meet you. I—we've always wondered what it's like outside during FTL flight. Would you mind telling us about it? They tell us the debriefing sims won't be out for another six months."

"It's . . . really odd," Esmay said. "First, the starfield disappears—" She was about to go on when the clerk called her name.

"If we don't take you now, you'll be here for hours," the clerk said. "These neuro-enhanced jobs take forever."

Esmay felt a wave of cold dislike rise from the seated squad, and hoped they were aiming it at the clerk, and not her. "Excuse me," she said to them all.

"Of course, Lieutenant," said the woman who had asked her the question. She had green eyes, startling in her dark face. Then she looked beyond Esmay to the clerk, and Esmay was not surprised to hear the clerk's breath catch.

She hadn't had a full neuroscan since she entered the Academy, and it was still as boring as ever, being stuck in the dark maw of the machine following orders to think of this, or that, or imagine moving her left little finger . . .

Finally it was done, and the last yellow line led her back to the desk where her duffel lay waiting for her, along with a handful of ID tags she would need for the facilities she was authorized to enter.

"Junior officers' quarters and mess that way, sir," the sergeant said, and gave a crisp salute as he passed her through. Esmay returned it and stepped onto the indicated walkway. She had missed out on command training, once she'd chosen technical track, so now she would be taking back-to-back courses—more school! Her own fault, she reminded herself, and yet not a fault to spend much time on. Her Altiplano conscience worried about the quickness with which her retrained neurons pushed away that momentary pang of guilt, and she grinned mentally at it. Her Altiplano conscience, like her Altiplano family, could stay where it belonged . . . on Altiplano.

She signed into the officers' quarters and the officers' mess, showing her clearance tags each time, picked up a duty roster, then a class schedule. She slung her gear into 235-H, one anonymous cubicle in a row of anonymous cubicles, and then headed for the mess. Even if it was between mealtimes for the school, they should have something for officers arriving from different time zones.

The dining room was almost empty; when she walked in, a mess steward peered out from the galleys and then came toward her.

"Lieutenant?"

"I just came in," Esmay said. "Our ship was on . . ."

"Fleet Standard. I understand Lieutenant . . . you're overdue for . . . midday, right? Do you want a full meal or a snack?"

"Just a snack." She would get herself on the planet's schedule faster this way, but she felt hollow as a new-built hull at the moment.

He seated her at a table a discreet distance from the two that were occupied, and left to bring the food. Esmay glanced casually at the others, wondering if they would be in her class. A young woman in fatigues without insignia, her curly blonde hair cropped short, sat hunched over what looked like a bowl of soup. Beside her, an older man in a lieutenant commander's uniform who, from his posture, was laying down the law about something.

Esmay looked away. Unusual to chew someone out while they were eating, but it would be rude to observe. Could this be father and daughter? At the other table, three young men wearing exercise clothes who were, she realized, watching *her*. She met their gaze coolly, and they looked away, not as if they were embarrassed, but as if they had seen all they wanted. Their gaze wandered the room steadily; they ignored the litter of plates and cups before them.

The steward brought out a platter of sandwiches, pastries, and raw vegetable slices arranged in a fan-shaped pattern. Esmay ate a sandwich of thinly sliced cattleope spread with horseradish sauce, several carrot sticks, and was considering one of the curly pastry things which smelled so deliciously of cinnamon and hot apples when the blonde woman erupted.

"I'm *not* quitting!" she said, loudly enough that Esmay could not fail to hear. She was sitting upright now, her face flushed slightly. With that flush Esmay could spot the irregular patches of fresh healing . . . she had been in a regen tank to repair some kind of injury to her face and—Esmay could not help look-ing—hands and arms.

The older man, with a cautionary glance at Esmay, rumbled something she could not hear.

"No!" the blonde said. "It's something else—something important. I know—" Then she too looked around, met Esmay's eyes, and fell silent for a moment.

Some instinct prompted Esmay to look not merely down, but—under lowered lids—across at the other table. The three men there now made sense . . . their dismissive assessment of her, their constant surveil-lance of the room. These were the bodyguards of someone who hired the best—or to whom the best were, by custom, assigned.

Whom were they guarding? Surely not the young

woman . . . if they had been, they had failed in some way or she would not have been hurt. A lieutenant commander? Hardly . . . unless he were not a lieutenant commander at all.

She glanced back at the young woman, and surprised by an expression on both faces so alike that it had to imply a relationship. Her eye, trained on a planet where families mattered, and where she had been expected to recognize even the most distant Suiza cousin, picked out now the similarities of bone and proportion, as well as behavioral quirks like the sudden lift of eyebrow that both older man and younger woman showed at that moment.

"Brun . . ." That carried, in part because the tone was so like the pleading tone her own father had used. Her mind caught on the unusual word. Brun. Wasn't that—? She clamped her mouth shut on the apple tart. If that was the blonde girl who had been involved in the Xavier affair, then her father was the present Speaker of the Grand Council . . . the most powerful man in the Familias Regnant. What could they be doing here?

Speculation having outrun data, she munched steadily through the tart, studiously ignoring the argument which continued, in lower voices, at the other table. She struggled to remember all the snippets of rumor she'd heard about Thornbuckle's wild youngest daughter . . . a spoiled beauty, a hotheaded fool who had plunged into the thick of intrigue with no training, an idiot who'd ended up dead drunk and naked in a rockhopper's pod in the aftermath of a battle. But also something about being, in some obscure way, Admiral Vida Serrano's protégé, because of her services to the Familias and—most particularly—to Admiral Serrano's niece Heris.

"Excuse me," someone said. Esmay swallowed the last bite of tart, and looked up. She had been concentrating so hard on not noticing what she shouldn't

notice that she hadn't noticed anyone approaching her
table.

It was one of the bodyguards. He had no rank
insignia on his exercise clothes, but from his face he
was older than she.

"Yes?"

"You're Lieutenant Suiza, aren't you?"

Despite the therapy, her gut tightened. "Yes, that's
right."

"Lieutenant Commander . . . Smith . . . would like
to meet you."

"Lieutenant Commander Smith?"

He nodded his head toward the other table.
"Smith," he said firmly. "And his daughter."

For a moment Esmay wished that she had just
lived with her hunger until the next scheduled main
meal. She had no desire to get involved in whatever
was going on, whether it was a matter of father-
daughter dissension or some plot against the Familias.

"Of course," she said, and rose from the table.

The older man and the young woman watched her
approach with, Esmay thought, the wrong sort of
interest. The older man had the sort of face which
might have been pleasant, but presently had locked
into a tight mask of concern. The young woman
looked both annoyed and afraid.

"Commander Smith," Esmay said, "I'm Lieutenant
Suiza."

"Have a seat," the man said. Although his uniform
fitted his tall, lanky body perfectly, she was sure it
did not fit his spirit . . . it would have needed stars
on the shoulders, and plenty of them.

"This is an unexpected honor," the man went on.
"I had heard about you, of course, from Admiral
Serrano, after Xavier—and now this recent busi-
ness—"

This, for instance, was not the way a real lieutenant
commander would have brought it up. Esmay

wondered whether to relieve him of the need for faking a military identity, and had her mouth open when the young woman spoke.

"Dad! Stop it!"

"Brun, I'm merely—"

Now almost whispering, but still angrily, the young woman continued. "You're *not* really a lieutenant commander and it's not fair." She turned to Esmay. "I'm Brun Meager, Lord Thornbuckle's daughter, and this is my father."

"I'm pleased to meet Commander Smith," Esmay said, "under the circumstances."

His face relaxed a bit, and his mouth quirked. "Well, one of you young ladies has a bit of discretion."

"I'm not being indiscreet," Brun said. "She could see you weren't really a Fleet officer, and I could see the wheels going around in her head as she tried to figure out how to handle it."

"One allows prominent people to introduce themselves as they choose," Esmay said. "One's private curiosity never intrudes."

Brun blinked. "Where are you from?"

"Altiplano," Esmay said. "Where, on occasion, senior officials may choose to appear in borrowed identities."

"And where good manners seem to have penetrated more than in some other places," Lord Thornbuckle said pointedly. Brun flushed again.

"I don't like deception."

"Oh, really? That's why you so carefully avoided using your own name when you were coming back to Rockhouse—"

"That was different," Brun said. "There was a good reason—"

"There's a good reason *now*, Brun, and if you can't see that I'll go back to calling you Bubbles with reason." For all his low, even voice and quiet face, Lord Thornbuckle was seriously angry. Esmay wished she were on the other side of the planet. Father-daughter conflict raised ghosts she wanted laid to rest. Brun subsided, but Esmay had the feeling she was not really subdued.

"Perhaps we could continue this in another location," Lord Thornbuckle said. Esmay could think of no polite way to refuse, and she wasn't sure where her duty lay, as an R.S.S. officer. But she would have to report to class at 0800 local time the next morning, and she had a lot to do in the meantime. Still . . . he was who he was, and even who he wasn't out-ranked her.

"Of course, sir," Esmay said.

Thornbuckle nodded to the men at the other table, who stood up. "I'm afraid we will have an escort."

That didn't bother Esmay; what bothered her was landing in the middle of whatever mess this was. She noticed that the escort split up, two going ahead and one trailing behind. Were they Fleet? She couldn't tell. She felt she should be able to tell; the civilians aboard *Kos* had been obvious enough. These didn't look like civilians, but they didn't quite fit Fleet, either. Private guards?

The conference room they finally entered was small, centered with a table large enough for only eight or so to surround. It had a display console at one end, but Lord Thornbuckle ignored that. He waited until his escort nodded, then sat at one end of the table. Habit, Esmay supposed.

"Sit down, and I'll make this as brief as possible. You haven't been here long, have you?"

"Just got off the shuttle, sir," Esmay said. "I'm here for the command courses I missed earlier, and then the standard junior officers' course." The one that would qualify her to command a ship in combat, according to the Board of Inquiry which had recommended it. Of course, not being qualified hadn't stopped her yet—but she put that out of mind and prepared to focus on whatever Lord Thornbuckle had to say.

"My daughter wanted to take some training with Fleet experts," Thornbuckle said. "I agreed, in part because she'd gotten herself in so much trouble without training . . . it seemed the risk-taking genes had all come together in her."

"And the lucky genes," Brun said. "I know they're not enough, but they're also not negligible. That's what Captain—Commander—Serrano said. And her aunt admiral."

The thought of anyone calling Vida Serrano "aunt admiral"—even a niece—shocked Esmay. For this girl—for Brun was clearly younger than she was—to do so would have been unthinkable except that Brun had just done it.

"But there've been incidents," Thornbuckle went on, ignoring what Brun had just said. "I thought she'd be safer here, on a Fleet training facility—"

"I *am* safer," Brun said.

"Brun, face the facts: someone shot at you. Tried to kill you."

Esmay managed not to say what she was thinking, that a Fleet training facility was not, in the nature of things, the safest place in the universe. Live fire exercises, for instance. Was this what the girl had gotten into?

"It wasn't anywhere near a live fire exercise," Thornbuckle went on. "That was my first thought, of course. Military training is dangerous; it has to be. But we—and by 'we' I mean not only myself, but others who've seen Brun in action—thought it would be less dangerous than turning her loose on the universe untrained." He spread his hands. "No—this has been different. I suppose we were just careless. We knew there were traitors in Fleet; that mess with Xavier proved it. But it didn't dawn on me that there might be traitors here, in a training base, until

Admiral Serrano pointed it out. We knew that Brun might be at special risk, but we didn't react fast enough."

"I'm alive," Brun said.

"You survived with your usual flair," her father said. "But you also had to spend a day in the regen tank, which is not what I call coming out unscathed. Too close for comfort is my analysis. You have to have more protection, or you have to leave."

Brun's shoulders twitched. "I'll be careful," she said.

"Not good enough. You have to sleep sometime."

"Have you identified the nature of the threat?" Esmay asked, to forestall another round of useless argument.

"No. Not . . . precisely. And the worst of it is that I can see a variety of threats. The Benignity's not happy with their loss at Xavier, and we are sure they have other agents in Fleet. Some have been identified, others haven't. They consider assassination a political tool. The Bloodhorde . . . well, you can imagine how they would like to have my daughter in their control. Then there are my personal enemies among the Familias. A few years ago, I would not have believed any of the Families would make war on personal relations, but now—things have changed."

"And you—or your advisors—think your daughter should leave this facility?"

"It would be easier to protect her at home, or even on Castle Rock."

"I would go crazy," Brun muttered. "I'm not a child, and I can't just sit around doing nothing."

"Do you want to join Fleet?" Esmay asked. She couldn't really imagine this obvious rebel wanting to join anything with discipline, but if she hadn't understood . . .

"I did at one time," Brun said, eyeing her father. "Now—I'm not sure."

"She doesn't want to get stuck doing boring things," Thornbuckle said. Brun flushed.

"It's not that—!"

"Isn't it? When Captain Serrano pointed out how much of her time was spent on boring routine, you said you didn't much like that prospect."

"I don't, but that's part of any life. I do understand that, just as I understand that the exciting bits are dangerous. You seem to think—"

Esmay jumped in again, as much for her own comfort as for the hope of getting useful information. "Perhaps you could tell me what you think I might do to help?"

"She needs a"—Thornbuckle paused, and Esmay was sure he was thinking of the word *keeper*— "Mentor," he said instead. "If she's going to stay here, I need to know that someone of her—" Another pause, during which Esmay could almost hear the unspoken, discarded choices: *social standing, rank, type, ability* . . . "Someone she might respect and listen to, anyway, will be near her. She's been chattering about you and your exploits—"

"I do not chatter," Brun said, through her teeth.

"So I thought maybe you—"

"She has her own responsibilities," Brun said. "And there are the . . . guards." In that gap was some epithet Esmay was glad the guards had not heard.

"Are you telling me now that you *will* accept the security procedures we talked about?"

"Rather than bother Lieutenant Suiza, yes." Brun gave Esmay a challenging look. "She will be busy with her own courses here; they don't exactly give officers time off to play nursemaid to rich girls."

Esmay interpreted this as having more to do with Brun's determination not to have a nursemaid than any consideration of her own convenience.

Thornbuckle looked from one to the other of them. "I have seen more cooperative senior ministers of state," he said. "Whatever gene sculpting we did on you, Brun, is not going to be repeated again."

"I didn't ask for it," Brun said. Again Esmay sensed old arguments lurking below the surface.

"No—but life gives you a lot you didn't ask for. Now—if you promise me that you will cooperate with the new security procedures—"

"All right," Brun said, not quite sulkily. "I'll cooperate."

"Then, Lieutenant Suiza, I'm very sorry to have wasted your time. And I must thank you for your recent actions; you well deserve your recent award." He nodded at the new ribbon on her uniform.

"Thank you," Esmay said, wondering if she was just supposed to leave and forget the conversation had ever happened. She turned to Brun and supressed an almost wistful expression on her face. "If we end up in the same class, I'll be glad to share notes with you. I'm glad to have met you."

Brun nodded; Esmay got up when Thornbuckle did, and he walked her to the door. "I'm officially still Smith," he said quietly.

"I understand, sir." She understood more than she wanted to, or than he expected. She was glad to get back to her own quarters, where she could deal with her memories of her father in privacy. There, she found a stack of study cubes in the delivery bin, and racked them into the cube reader's storage. Some looked much more promising than others; *Leadership for Junior Officers* made sense, but why did she have to study *Administrative Procedures for Junior Staff*? She didn't want anything to do with administration.

✧   ✧   ✧

Brun curled up on her bunk under her very non-regulation afghan and pretended to nap until her security detail had finished whatever it was doing and gone to stand outside. As if she were a prisoner. As

if she were a naughty child. As if being shot at were
her fault.

Her father had done it again. She would have been
fine, if he had only been somewhere else, if only she
had had time to get well before he showed up. But
no. He had to come here, still unsure she should be
doing things like this, and embarrass her in front of
a roomful of professionals . . .

In front of Esmay Suiza.

She rolled over, and picked up her remote, then
flicked on her cube reader, cycling through the
selections until she found the one she wanted.

Back on Xavier, while she herself was drunk and
incapable (as her father had mentioned more than
once), Esmay Suiza had survived the treachery of her
captain, the mutiny that followed, and then saved
everyone—including Brun—by blowing up the enemy
flagship. Brun had followed the court-martial of
Despite's crew in the news; she had wondered over
and over how that calm young woman with the
flyaway hair managed to do it. She didn't look that
special—but something in the expression, in the eyes
that never wavered, caught at her.

And then the same young woman had been a hero
again, in an adventure that seemed like something out
of a storycube series . . . she had been outside a ship
during FTL flight and survived; she had defeated
another enemy. Once more her image filled the news
viewers, and once more Brun had imagined meeting
her . . . talking to her . . . becoming—she was sure
they could become—friends.

When she'd learned that Esmay Suiza was coming here, to Copper Mountain—that she might even
be in the same classes—she had been so certain that
her luck was running true. Here at last was the
woman who could help her be like that, help her
combine her uncooperative past experiences into the
self she wanted to be.

And now her father had ruined it. He had treated Suiza as a professional, worthy of respect; he had made it clear he thought Brun was a headstrong child. What would Esmay Suiza think now—what *could* she think, when the Speaker of the Grand Council, her own father, had presented her that way? It was impossible that Suiza could see her as a competent adult.

She would not let it be impossible. She would not let this chance go by. There had to be some way to convince Suiza that she was more than a silly fluffhead. Fluffhead made her think of Suiza's hair, which could certainly use some attention . . . maybe Suiza would be approachable on a girl-to-girl level first, and then she could prove what else she could do. . . .

✧   ✧   ✧

At the next main meal, a few hours later, Esmay returned to the mess, and sat with a tableful of jigs and lieutenants who had arrived the day before. She remembered a few of them from the Academy, but had not served with any of them. They knew of her recent exploits and were eager to discuss them.

"What's it like to fly a Bloodhorde raider?" asked Vericour, another lieutenant. In the six years since their graduation, he had gained several kilos and now sported a crisp red mustache.

"Fun," said Esmay, knowing the expected response. "Goes like a bat, even if you don't redline it."

"Shielding?"

"None to speak of. And the weapons systems are amazing for its size. The interior's mostly weapons, very little crew space."

"They must have lousy shooting, if they missed you—"

"They didn't shoot at us first," Esmay said. "After all, I was in *their* ship. They let us get close, and— poof."

"Yeah . . . that's the way. What're you here for?"

"A whole string of things," Esmay said. "I'm changing to command track—"

"You mean you *weren't*?"

"No." How to explain this one?

Vericour shrugged. "That's Fleet Personnel for you. Take someone with a flair like yours and shove her into technical, just because they need more techs. They ought to recruit techs, if they want more."

Esmay opened her mouth to explain it hadn't been Fleet's fault, considered the difficulty of the subsequent explanations, and nodded instead. "Yup. So now they've let me into command track, and I have to play catch-up. All the stuff I missed—"

"They're not going to drag *you* through command psychology, and all that dorf?"

Esmay nodded.

"When you've actually commanded ships in battle? That's ridiculous."

In sardonic chorus, everyone else at the table said "No, that's regulations!" Vericour laughed, and Esmay along with him. She was enjoying herself, she realized, with people who were almost strangers, even without Barin. The discovery that she could enjoy herself like this was new enough that it still surprised her when it happened.

"You know, I heard the Speaker's daughter's here," Anton Livadhi said, in a lower tone.

"Well, she's run through the whole of the Royal Space Service," Vericour said. "I suppose she's looking for new blood."

Esmay said nothing; she could not say anything without revealing knowledge she wasn't supposed to have.

"Is it true she was floating around in a rockhopper's pod stark naked at Xavier?" Livadhi asked.

"Alone?" asked someone else Esmay didn't know.

"That's the story," Livadhi said. "My cousin—you

know Liam, Esmay; he was on *Despite*—he said he heard from a buddy on the flagship that she got stewed and somehow ended up out there all alone. But Liam's a bit inventive; I figured Esmay would know if it really happened."

"Why?" asked Esmay, buying time.

"Because they'd have put a young female officer with her, afterwards," Livadhi said. "I figured that would be you."

"Not me," Esmay said. "I was busy doing scutwork on *Despite*. Never even saw her." Until now, but that was another thing she couldn't tell them.

When she left the table, she glanced around but did not see Brun. Did the girl have meals alone somewhere? She pushed aside the thought that the girl might be lonesome. Brun Meager was not her problem . . . this course was.

CHAPTER TWO

At 0500 local time the next morning, Esmay shivered in the chill predawn breeze, much cooler than ship standard. The air smelled of growing things, and distance—sharply different from ship air. Some of the others sneezed, but Esmay sniffed appreciatively—it wasn't home, but some of the smells were the same.

Her shivering didn't last long once the exercise started. Esmay grinned to herself—she had always worked out faithfully, but some of these people had not, judging by the sounds they made. She was sweaty, but not exhausted, after an hour and a half; she had surprised herself by coming in fourth in the final run around the drillfield. In the distance, she had seen the irregular cliffs for which Copper Mountain was named emerge from predawn dimness to show the oranges and reds and ochres, when the sun hit them. Vericour was complaining loudly, but good-naturedly; she suspected it was mostly for effect. He didn't seem to be breathing any harder than she was, and it took breath to complain.

"When's your first class?" he asked, as they jogged back to quarters.

"Not class—testing," Esmay said. "They think I can test out of some things, to make room for others." She hoped so; otherwise her schedule would be impossible.

They parted with a wave, and Esmay went in to shower thinking how different he was from Barin. He was older; he was her peer; he was pleasant and handsome . . . and about as exciting as a bowl of porridge.

That first day passed in a blur of activity. She tested out of some sections—she'd been told she probably would—Scan, as she expected, and Hull and Architecture, which she had not. She must've picked up more of that on *Koskiusko* than she'd thought. The military law segment concentrated on treason, mutiny, and conduct unbecoming . . . giving her an unfair advantage, she thought, but she wasn't going to complain. Administrative Procedures, though, was her downfall, along with tables of organization and command chains in areas where she'd never served.

"Your schedule's going to be all over the place," the testing officer said, frowning. "If you actually took both courses, back to back, you'd be here five standard months. You've placed out of about half the lower course, and a tenth of the upper . . . let's see now." He finally produced a schedule that looked impossible for the first two weeks—though he claimed that two of the classes were no-brainers—and merely difficult for the next seven.

She had a few choices, and picked Search and Rescue Basic, and Escape and Evasion; they sounded more active than the optional staff support and administrative methods courses. Besides, she knew they were practical. She didn't want to end up in Barin's situation.

By the end of the first five days, Esmay felt settled in the academic routine. She was carrying about half again as many hours as her classmates, but the pace of instruction was much slower than it had been at the Academy. Early morning PT woke her up for the day's classes, and she didn't have to stay up too late to get all the work completed. Already some of the others had established a habit of going into Q-town when classes let out, eating there instead of in the mess hall. She was almost glad that her extra classes made that impossible for her; she had never socialized off-ship with other officers, and felt shy about it now. Many did not go into town every evening, and whenever she emerged from her room for a break, she would find someone ready to chat or play a quick game in one of the rec rooms.

Administrative Procedures was as dull as she'd feared, though she understood the importance of the course. She tackled it as she had tackled technical data in Scan or Hull Architecture, and found she could remember all the niggling little details even if she was bored by them.

Professional Ethics for Military Officers was another matter. She had started in eagerly, expecting—she wasn't quite sure what, but not what she got. Three lectures on personal relationships left her feeling unsure and guilty about her . . . friendship . . . with Barin Serrano. Example after example where a senior officer's pursuit had damaged, if not ruined, a junior's career. Examples of apparently innocent liaisons, which ended in grief for all concerned. She wondered if he was talking about one of her Academy class-mates, a stunning blonde from the Crescent Worlds. She hadn't seen Casea since graduation, but she had heard that she had moved on from classmates to more senior officers.

And yet—the instructor had insisted—Fleet had neither the desire nor the power to prohibit close friendships and even marriage between officers. The standards governing such relationships were, according to the instructor, perfectly clear and reasonable.

Esmay could recite them forwards and backwards, without knowing for sure if she and Barin had done anything wrong, or if going where they had talked about going was forbidden. She wished she had someone to ask about it.

To her relief, her Tactical Analysis class did not consider either the action at Xavier or the *Koskiusko* defense; along with her classmates, she plunged instead into a comparison of Familias and Benignity small-ship capabilities and battle performance.

"Lies, damn lies, and statistics," muttered Vericour, her assigned partner. "I hate statistical analyses of battles. It's more than just so many tons throw-weight—"

"Mmm . . ." said Esmay, extracting another set of figures from the archives. "Did you know that the Benignity had better battle performance out of *Pierrot* than we did, after they captured her?"

"No! That's got to be wrong—none of their tacticians use maneuver the way we do—"

"Yup. Renamed *Valutis*, confirmed from salvage . . . their commander got five hits on *Tarngeld*, at extreme range."

"Says who?" Vericour leaned over to look. "Uh . . . you trust that scan data from *Tarngeld*?"

"Well . . . it's embarrassing to have to admit you were clobbered by a ship a third your mass, which used to be on your side, so I'd bet on its being accurate. Besides, according to the post-battle plot, nothing else was in that direction. My question is, what did they do to *Pierrot-Valutis* to make her that effective, and are they doing that to their other ships?"

"Wouldn't think so. They didn't at Xavier, did they?"

"Not that I know of, but . . . they had *Pierrot* for three years before she showed up in their lines."

"Well, someone must've noticed that . . ."

"Yes, but did they apply it?" Esmay handed over

the relevant bits. "If the Benignity does whatever it did to that ship to others of the same size, we've got a new element to worry about."

"Maybe. But if they could, they'd have used it at Xavier, wouldn't they?"

"I wish I knew what it was . . . it matters if it was some one-time thing that depended on some of our architecture—"

"One really good scan tech? Weapons tech?"

"Maybe," Esmay said again. "But if they've got one that good they might have more. I think we ought to make this one of the main points of our presentation."

"I'm not going to argue with the hero of Xavier and the *Kos,*" Vericour said, with a grin that took the sting out of it. "It's not something I would have thought of. Maybe you are that smart."

"I do my best," Esmay said, grinning back. He wasn't Barin, but he was comfortable.

She was still thinking that when Vericour reached out and touched her hair. Esmay managed not to flinch, but she moved smoothly away.

"Sorry," he said. "I just . . . thought you might like it."

So Barin wasn't the only man who could find her attractive . . . she didn't know whether she found that reassuring or just bothersome. At least she knew for sure that another lieutenant was within the limits allowed by regulations and the ethics class.

"I'm . . . not in the mood," she said. She couldn't explain about Barin, or claim a preexisting relationship, not yet.

"If you ever are in the mood, just let me know," Vericour said. "I'll even swear on whatever you like that it's not just hero worship."

She chuckled, surprising herself. "I didn't think it was," she said.

He grinned back, but made no more advances.

That's what the manuals all said was supposed to happen, but she'd never had to deal with it before. She felt a small burst of surprise that the manuals were right.

A few days later, their presentation gained the highest rating in the class. Afterwards Vericour suggested a celebratory drink in Q-town, the little cluster of commercial establishments just outside the gates. "You're certainly good luck," he said. "I hope we're on the same team for E and E. They say no one ever makes it all the way through the field exercise without getting captured, but you might be able to pull it off."

"I doubt it," Esmay said. "The instructors know the terrain backwards and forwards. Just like natives."

"Well—it would be more fun with you, anyway. So—will you come?"

"No—remember I'm taking extra classes, and I have a final in Admin Procedures tomorrow."

"My sympathies." Vericour bowed elaborately, and Esmay laughed. So he was no Barin—he was still fun to be around. She went back to her quarters and tore into the Admin Procedures material until long past her usual bedtime.

The next morning, she was surprised to see Brun Meager lining up for PT with the others. During the run, she moved up beside Esmay.

"Hi—I hardly ever see you." She didn't sound out of breath at all.

"I've got a heavy schedule," Esmay said. Unlike many, she actually enjoyed the run, but one of the things she enjoyed about it was sinking into a meditative state.

"So I noticed. This was the only thing I could take right now where we'd overlap, but I'm going to be in your Escape and Evasion course."

"You?" Esmay glanced at her. Brun was taller; she

loped along as if she could run forever, like one of the endurance horses.

"Well—if people are out to get me, I need to learn to get away."

"I suppose." She could also learn to let her security personnel guard her the way they were supposed to, and quit putting herself into dangerous situations. But that was for someone else to say.

"And I wanted to ask you—if we get a choice— I'd like to be on your team."

Great. Just what she needed, a spoiled rich girl on her team. Esmay glanced at her again, and scolded herself. Brun might be spoiled but she was willing to work and learn—not every rich girl would pile out of bed at that hour to do PT with a lot of grumpy soldiers. Admiral Serrano had sponsored her; that had to be worth something. Rumor had it she didn't ask any favors in her classes, either.

"I don't know if we get a choice," Esmay said. "But if it's possible, it's all right with me."

"If you ever wanted, we could go into Q-town together," Brun said, an almost wistful note in her voice.

"No time," Esmay said. Q-town held no attraction for her; if she wouldn't go with Vericour, she certainly wasn't going with a civilian.

"You don't ever go?"

Esmay shrugged. "No—they have good steaks in the mess."

"Um. And good steaks constitute your definition of entertainment?" That had a slight edge to it.

"No—but I wouldn't expect you to find much entertainment there either."

"Well . . . I like a drink with friends now and then," Brun said. "Or a meal outside, just because it is outside." They ran on a ways, and then she said. "That redheaded lieutenant—Vericour. He's a friend of yours?"

"We were classmates," Esmay said. "And we've been assigned some problems together."

"But you like him?"

"He's nice," Esmay said. She couldn't figure out what Brun was driving at. Did she want an introduction? "He goes to Q-town fairly often."

"I know," Brun said. "I've seen him there with friends—I wondered why you didn't go."

"Schedule." It was harder to talk when she was used to solitude in the mornings. "I've got a final this morning," she said, hoping Brun would take the hint.

"What in?" Brun asked. As if she were really interested, which seemed unlikely.

"Administrative Procedures," Esmay said.

"Sounds dull," Brun said. "But I guess I should let you review it in your head."

That would have been nice, but they were almost back to the starting point. Esmay was glad she'd spent the extra hours the night before.

"There's going to be an ensign in our class," Vericour said, as they headed toward the first of the Escape and Evasion classes.

"An ensign?" Esmay hoped her face didn't reveal anything. Barin had left a message saying he was down, but she hadn't seen him yet; she had back-to-back classes. "So?"

"Well . . . this is a bit upper-level for an ensign, don't you think? But I hear he's a Serrano; that probably explains it."

"Says he was on *Koskiusko*," Vericour said. Esmay finally realized he was fishing, and what he was fishing for. She wanted to strangle him.

"Let me see," she said, and stopped at the next dataport to suck the class list. "Oh . . . yes. Barin Serrano. I know him." She hoped that was sufficiently casual. Her eye ran on down the list and got snagged on Brunhilde Meager. She had hoped someone would talk the girl out of this; the class was known to be dangerous, but there she was.

"And . . . ?"

She gave Vericour a glance that moved him back a half step. Good. "And he's a fine junior officer— what more do you want?"

"Was he on your crew on the Bloodhorde ship?"

"No." And she was not going to tell Barin's secrets, either; Vericour could find out for himself.

In the classroom, she saw Brun first; the tall blonde was leaning on a desk, surrounded by male officers, while her bodyguards stood by the wall, looking as blank as robots. She had, Esmay had to admit, an infectious laugh and a smile that lit up the room. Esmay moved to a seat midway up on the left side, and then spotted Barin, front row right, already seated and looking compact and composed.

Should she go up there? But she was already in her seat, and Vericour was in the next . . . it would be obvious if she moved. Barin turned, as if her glance were a warm hand on his neck, and spotted her. He smiled, nodded; she nodded in return. Enough for now; they could talk later. Although . . . certain paragraphs in the professional ethics lectures came back to her. They would have to be careful. They were not presently in the same chain of command, but she was senior enough that the relationship would be called "not recommended."

At the chime, the instructor came in; he looked as if he'd been slow-dried over a fire . . . the color of jerky and not any more extra fat. Lieutenant Commander Uhlis, his name was.

"Escape and evasion," he said, without preamble. "If you're lucky, you'll never need this course, but if you need it and haven't mastered it . . . you'll be dead. Or worse." He glanced around the room, then his gaze rested on Barin.

"I understand that Ensign Serrano already has

experience as a captive," Lieutenant Commander Uhlis said. "But none at all in escape." Esmay gave him a sharp look. His tone was ambiguous, edged in some way she could not yet determine.

Barin said nothing; the others had turned to look at him.

"It is the duty of a captured officer to attempt to escape, is it not, Serrano?" The edge was sharper, sarcasm at the least.

"Yes, sir."

"Yet . . . you did not."

"I did not escape, sir."

"Did you even *try*?" Contempt now. Esmay could feel the tension in the room.

"Not effectively," Barin said. "Sir."

"I would have thought a *Serrano* the equal of a few Bloodhorde thugs," Uhlis said. "Would you care to explain to the class your mistakes?" Put that way, it was not a request.

"Sir, I was careless. I thought the person I saw in the inventory bay, wearing a Fleet uniform with Fleet patches, was Fleet personnel."

"Ah. You expected the Bloodhorde to be fur-clad barbarians carrying swords—"

"No, sir. But I didn't expect them to be laying an ambush in the inventory bay. As I said, sir, my carelessness."

"And precisely how did they capture you, Ensign?"

Esmay could tell from the quality of Barin's voice that he was both angry and shamed. "I was climbing an inventory rack—the Deep Space Repair has automated inventory racks some twenty meters tall, but the machinery had been shut off. Ship regulations required using safety harness and line, so I was clipped into the ladder I was climbing. The parts trays were far enough apart that someone could lie flat in them; when I climbed up that far, I found a gun to my head."

"And did you struggle?"

"Yes, sir. But between the harness and the ones who grabbed my legs, and getting knocked unconscious, not effectively."

"I see." Uhlis eyed the rest of the class. "The lesson here is that a moment's inattention—a brief lapse of caution—can and someday will result in your capture. The ensign thought that he was safe, aboard a Fleet vessel, even though he knew intruders had penetrated the ordinary defenses. He saw nothing, heard nothing, smelled nothing, felt nothing—and no doubt convinced himself that anything out of the ordinary was the result of the overall emergency situation. Someone else would take care of it. He is lucky to be alive, presumably only because his captors thought he might be useful that way."

Uhlis paused, long enough that a discreet rustle indicated uncertainty among the other students. "But the ensign did something right. Two things, in fact. He stayed alive, when it might have been easier to die. And he worked through his post-capture trauma properly, as his reactions just now proved."

A hand shot up on the far side of the room. "Sir— I don't understand."

"Lieutenant Marden, I presume?"

"Yes, sir."

"Kindly identify yourself next time. And haste, in this course, can get you killed. When you don't understand, *wait*. Be still. Listen. You might learn something that will save your life."

Everyone was very still; Esmay found it hard to breathe. Even Brun had gone immobile, she noticed.

"But since I was going to explain anyway, I will now. Ensign Serrano could, no doubt, have changed his captors' decision to keep him alive, by being too much trouble, while not able to escape. From my understanding, having reviewed his debrief, he had no real opportunity to escape. Therefore, his duty was to stay alive, if possible, by not driving his captors to kill him. This he did, enduring physical abuse without losing control, making no threats, being as passive as possible. Second, he cooperated fully with remedial therapy. Some rescued captives cannot face what they consider the shame of such therapy; although they cannot evade a minimum requirement, they do not cooperate, and do not receive the benefit of it. Ensign Serrano, by all reports—and of course most of this is confidential, so I have only the output summary—cooperated completely, and his therapists were convinced that he had no residual psychological deficits." Another pause, which no one interrupted.

"Some of you, no doubt, thought I was being rough on Ensign Serrano—sarcastic, critical. I was. I was testing for myself the validity of the therapists' report, before putting him through the trauma of this course, where any unresolved issues might make him a danger to himself and others. He passed *my* test. The rest of you . . . we'll just have to see about." Uhlis turned to Barin. "Ensign Serrano."

"Sir." The back of Barin's neck was no longer flushed.

"Congratulations."

"Sir." Barin's neck reddened again.

"I presume you've all read the introductory material for this class," Uhlis said. His gaze scanned the classroom. Esmay had, as usual, read beyond the introductory assignment, but she judged from the uneasy shifting of some classmates that they had not. Uhlis glanced down at his display. "Lieutenant Taras, please explain the legal difference between military capture and hostile seizure."

Taras had been one of the wigglers, seated two down from Esmay. She rose to her feet. "Sir, military capture is when a unit surrenders, and hostile seizure is when they're caught off-guard."

"And the legal situation?"

"Well . . . one is surrender and one is—being caught."

"Inadequate. I assume you did not read the assignment, is that correct?"

"Yes, sir." Taras looked deservedly wretched.

Uhlis looked along the row. "Lieutenant Vericour?"

Vericour stood. "Sir, I read it, but I am not sure I understand—I mean, it's clear when someone is kidnapped from a space station while they're on leave or something, as compared with the surrender of personnel from a damaged ship."

"Suppose you were sure that you were facing a situation of hostile seizure: what would be your legal position?"

"Sir, the Code says that I am to attempt escape by any means possible, assisting others to escape—"

"Yes . . . and what obligation do your captors have toward you?"

"If they're signatories to the Otopki Conference, which the Benignity of the Compassionate Hand and the Guernese Republic are, but the Bloodhorde are not, they are obliged to provide adequate life support and medical care . . ."

"Well enough. Lieutenant Suiza—" Vericour sat down, and Esmay rose. "Please define Ensign Serrano's situation in terms of the legal issue I've raised."

"Sir, although Ensign Serrano was captured on board a Fleet vessel, his situation is more like a hostile seizure than military surrender. Since the Bloodhorde are not signatories to the Otopki Conference, they acknowledge no obligation to captives under any circumstances, but Familias law still holds them responsible."

"Very well." Uhlis nodded; Esmay sat down, and he turned his attention to someone else. In a few minutes, he had determined exactly who had read the assignment, and who had not—and who was inclined to be hasty or foolish. Brun was one of the latter, not to Esmay's surprise. Uhlis had just called on her, and found that she had not read the assignment either, and had told her it was even more important for her than for the others.

"I don't see why," Brun said. Uhlis looked at her, a long considering look.

"Even a civilian, Ms. Meager, is expected to abide by the basic courtesies of the class. Please request permission to speak, and identify yourself, before blurting out your ignorance. Better still, listen a little longer and see if you can learn on your own."

Brun's neck reddened, and Esmay could see the tension in her shoulders. But she said nothing more, and Uhlis turned to someone else. Esmay could not relax no matter whose behavior was under his harrow; she almost regretted choosing this class, except that Barin was in it.

Esmay's next class was just down the hall. Barin was there when she came out of the door. "Lieutenant—good to see you again." His eyes said more. Esmay felt a warm glow, as if she'd stepped into a spotlight.

"Morning, Ensign," she said, being just as formal. She could feel Vericour's interested gaze on her back. "Glad to be off old *Kos*?"

Barin grinned. "They tell me they'll put me on a line ship after this—assuming I pass all the courses." In his tone was the confidence of someone who always passed his courses.

"You passed the hardest, back on *Kos*," Esmay said seriously. "And Uhlis knows it."

"I would have preferred things in the opposite order," Barin said. "Training before performance— though you did the same trick with command, only better."

Brun appeared suddenly at Esmay's side. "Hi

there—introduce me, Lieutenant Suiza, to this most attractive young ensign. Unless, that is, you're keeping him for yourself."

Barin flushed, and Esmay could feel her own ears heating up. With an effort, she forced a smile onto her face and said, "This is Ensign Serrano . . . Ensign, this is Brun Meager." She didn't have to give a pedigree; everyone knew it.

"You must be Admiral Serrano's grandson," Brun said, practically shoving in front of Esmay. "I heard a lot about you—do you have a few minutes?"

Esmay didn't—it was time for her next class. She ignored the desperate look Barin gave her and abandoned him to his fate. If he couldn't handle one dizzy blonde . . .

But she had trouble concentrating on tactics, for the first time in her life. Brun was beautiful, in a way she had never been beautiful, and she had that ability to attract almost anyone. Even Esmay had liked her, in spite of disapproving; it was impossible, it seemed, to stay distant from her. Naturally she would like Barin—charming, handsome, talented—and naturally Barin . . . she yanked her mind back to the lecture, and realized that Vericour had noticed her distraction, which made it even worse.

She made it through class after class, dragging her attention back again and again from the thought of Barin and Brun. If this was what love did, she told herself grimly, no wonder they cautioned officers against it. Back on *Kos* it had seemed simple: her feeling for Barin made her stronger, more confident, happier—and her performance had soared. But that was the first burst of feeling . . . this was something else, not helpful at all. Was he having the same problem? Would loving her destroy his chances to be the officer he could be? She tried to think what her therapist would have said, but none of the phrases she remembered helped at all.

At the evening meal, she was hunched morosely over her tray when a chair scraped at her side.

"Lieutenant?" It was Barin. She felt something clench and release in her chest.

"Ensign," she said. She felt like crying; she choked that feeling back. "Barin—how was your first day?"

"Interesting," Barin said. He was grinning at her in obvious delight. "You're looking good. When Uhlis started in on me, I wasn't sure what to do—but then I figured out what he was driving at."

"I could have clobbered him," Esmay said, startling herself with the fierceness of that. Hunger returned, and she took a bite of bread as if it were Uhlis's flesh.

"No—" Barin paused for a spoonful of soup. "He was right, and I did make an interesting demonstration for the class. I would bet they don't have someone like me in every class—unless they import them especially." He looked thoughtful a moment. "I wonder if that's why I got this course. It's just devious enough—" He shook his head. "But you—I hear you've been taking one course on top of another. Are you getting any sleep at all?"

She felt her ears going hot, even though she knew it was an innocent inquiry into her health. "I'm doing fine, as long as I don't do much but study."

"Oh, I wasn't going to interrupt you," Barin said. "I know this is important to you. I just hoped—"

"I know," Esmay said, into her roast beef. "I'm just—you know it's been awhile."

"Ah." Barin ate some peas, then something orange that had probably started life in the squash family. "I saw you yesterday, when I came in. Going to some class—seems like you're getting along well with the other officers."

"Trying to," Esmay said. "All that you told me about the difference in cultures—it helps. Though I still catch myself about to apologize or explain far too often."

"Glad to be of service," Barin said. "I was going to ask—"

"Well," said a voice from overhead. "I hoped to find my favorite ensign for a dinner companion, but he's already engaged—"

Esmay nearly choked; Barin turned. "Hello, Sera Meager . . ."

"Brun. Nobody calls me Sera Meager or Ms. Meager but people who want to keep me from doing things. You don't mind if I join you, do you? I promise my watchdogs will keep a respectful distance."

"Of course," Barin said; he stood while Brun found a seat across from Esmay, exactly where Esmay did not want those clear blue eyes.

"How did the exam go?" Brun asked Esmay, with apparently genuine interest. "Administrative Procedures, wasn't it? Sounds deadly boring to me. Forms-filling, isn't it?"

"A bit more than that," Esmay heard herself say, with unmistakeable coolness in her voice. She cleared her throat and tried again. "Forms-filling is part of it, but then you have the decisions of which form, and to what office it should be sent. Filling it out correctly doesn't help if you've sent the wrong level of form, or sent the right form to the wrong office."

"Deadly boring. My sympathies. I hope my heckling you that morning didn't hurt your performance."

"No," Esmay said. "I did all right."

"All right being number one in the class. Don't hide your light, Lieutenant," Barin said.

"Good for you," Brun said. "Though I can't see you as a forms-filler, I suppose into every life a few forms must fall."

Esmay could not stay annoyed, not with that combination of interest and goodwill beaming at her from across the table. "I thought it was boring," she said. "But—it was a requirement."

"So you topped out. What I'd expect. Are you sure you won't come into Q-town, the both of you, and celebrate?"

"I can't," Esmay said. "The Tactics final is in two days, and our workgroup is studying tonight and tomorrow night."

"Well, then, Ensign—do you have a final coming up?"

"No, but—"

"Then you can come, surely? If you're not in Lieutenant Suiza's Tactics class, then she's not going to be spending time with you—not that she'd cradle-rob anyway."

"I'm hardly an infant, Brun," Barin said, before Esmay could say anything. "But yes, I'll be your escort . . . since your watchdogs will be along to ensure my good behavior."

Esmay watched them go with feelings not so much mixed as churned. She did have a Tactics study group meeting, but she had hoped for a few more minutes with Barin, in which she could ask him about his interpretation of the rules governing personal relationships between officers not of the same rank, or in the same chain of command. He had grown up in Fleet; he was used to the rules. If he thought there was nothing wrong, there probably wasn't anything wrong.

✧   ✧   ✧

Barin eyed the Speaker's daughter as they walked through to the base gates. Dangerous waters, he told himself. Professional officers did not mix with Families; the shadowy aura of Undue Influence brooded over any such liaison. Still, common courtesy to a guest of the Fleet demanded that he accompany her . . . and her security detail.

He would much rather have talked to Esmay. They had things to discuss . . . and anyway, she looked tired, strained, and he wanted to help her, ease that strain. She had been trying so hard for so long; she was on the right track now, but . . . his fingers twitched, imagining the softness of her hair, the way he could soothe the tension from her neck.

"So . . . you knew Lieutenant Suiza on the *Koskiusko*?" Brun asked.

"Yes," Barin said, brought back abruptly from his reverie.

"Is she always so . . . stiff?"

"Stiff? She's hardworking, professional—"

"Dull," Brun said. But her mouth quirked.

"You can't mean that," Barin said.

She grinned at him. "No, I don't mean that. But I wanted to meet her, talk to her, and she's always so . . . so upright and formal. Not to mention that she never seems to stop studying. She's at the top in just about every class—what more does she want?"

"What any of us wants," Barin said. "To be the best." He was aware of his spine growing slightly more rigid, and wondered why.

"It's so different," Brun said, in a thoughtful tone. "I've been around Royal Space Service officers for years, and they're not like all of you."

Because they weren't really military, but that was not something to say when Brun was being trailed by six of the Royal Security's finest.

"I don't know why all this is necessary," Brun went on. "Professional competence I can understand, but the rules are ridiculous."

Barin managed not to snort. "What rules are these?" he asked instead.

"Oh, you know. All this formality in class—standing when the instructor enters, and saluting all the time, and everything divided by rank."

"There are reasons," Barin said vaguely; he didn't feel like explaining millenia of military tradition to a privileged civilian who was in a mood to dislike it anyway. "But if you don't like it, why did you come?"

"Admiral Serrano recommended it. Over my father's objections, in fact. She said I would benefit from the chance to develop my special talents in a controlled environment."

"That sounds like a quote," Barin said.

"You know Admiral—oh, that's right, you are a Serrano. So you also know Heris, I'd imagine?"

"Admiral Serrano is my grandmother; Commander Serrano is one of my cousins." No need to go into that.

"Well, then, we'll be friends," Brun said, taking his arm in a way that made him distinctly uncomfortable. "Now let's go have some fun."

Barin thought longingly of Esmay, hard at work no doubt in her quarters.

CHAPTER THREE

Brun had developed a habit of stopping by Esmay's quarters every day or so, for what she termed "a friendly chat." Esmay did her best to be polite, though she resented the time it cost her, and even more the fact that Brun seemed to consider herself qualified to comment on everything in Esmay's life.

"Your hair," she said, on one of her first visits. "Have you ever considered having it rerooted?"

Her hair had been an issue since childhood; before she could stop herself, she had run a hand over it trying to smooth it down. "No," Esmay said.

"Well, it would probably help," Brun said, cocking her own gold head to one side. "You've got quite nice bones . . ."

"I have quite a nice lot of work to do, too," Esmay said. "If you don't mind." And was not sure which was worse, the insults or the casual way Brun slouched out, apparently not the least offended.

One evening, she arrived with Barin, who made some excuse and left, casting a lingering glance that Esmay wished she knew how to interpret.

"He's nice," Brun said, settling herself on Esmay's bunk as if she owned it.

"More than nice," Esmay said, trying unsuccessfully not to resent Brun's proprietary tone. Just what had Barin and Brun been doing?

"Handsome, courteous, clever," Brun went on. "Too bad he's only an ensign—if he were your rank, he'd be perfect for you. You could fall for him—"

"I don't want to 'fall for' anyone in that sense," Esmay said. She was uneasily aware that her ears felt warm. "We're colleagues—"

Brun cocked an eyebrow. "Is Altiplano one of those places where no one can talk about sex?"

Her ears felt more than warm; her whole face burned. "One can," she said between clenched teeth. "Polite people, however, do not."

"Sorry," Brun said. She didn't look, or sound, very sorry. "But it must make it hard to talk about people, and to people. How do you indicate . . . preference?"

"I had none," Esmay said. That sounded bad, even to her. "I left my home world quite young," she added. That wasn't much better, but she couldn't think of anything that would help.

"Mmm. So when you met attractive young men— or women—you had only instinct to help you." Brun buffed her fingernails on her vest, and examined them critically. "And they say the men are the inarticulate ones."

"You—that's—rude."

"Is it?" Brun didn't sound concerned; she sounded arrogant. "If it seemed so to you, I'm sorry. I didn't intend it that way. We don't have the same rules, you see."

"You must have some," Esmay said. Whatever they were, they didn't match Fleet's—or Altiplano's.

"Well . . . it would be rude to discuss the grittier bits with someone who was not a friend—or while eating."

Despite herself, Esmay wondered what Brun might mean by "grittier bits."

"And," Brun went on, "it would be rude to comment on someone's genetic makeup as revealed in their—I'm not sure what term wouldn't offend you. Body parts? Equipment?"

"Genetic makeup!" This was not what she had expected; curiosity overcame outrage.

"Whether they're a Registered Embryo or not, and what the code is."

"You mean that's . . . visible?"

"Of course," Brun said, still in the superior tone that was raking Esmay's patience. "There's the registration mark, and the code number. How else are you going to be sure—? Oh. You don't do that."

"Well, I certainly don't have any registration marks or numbers on me," Esmay said. The thought made her skin twitch, but curiosity was a worse torment. "Where—?"

"Lower left abdomen," Brun said promptly. "Want to see?"

"No!" Esmay said, with more force than she intended.

"I didn't mean that," Brun said, not specifying. "But surely you *have*—I mean, you're older than I am."

"What I do is none of your business," Esmay said. "And I plan to keep it that way."

Brun opened her mouth and shut it again, then gave a little shrug that irritated Esmay as much as anything she might have said. She fished in one of her pockets and brought up a tangle of wire with a few plastic beads on it. "Here—know what this is?"

"Haven't a clue," Esmay said, glad to be off the topic of Barin.

"According to Ty, it's a good-luck charm. I thought it was a chunk of obsolete electronics."

"Mmm." Esmay gave the little object a better look, then grinned.

"What?" Brun asked.

"Well . . . it's a good-luck charm only under certain circumstances. That is—this is the sort of thing they gave us when we started the senior scan course. You were supposed to hang it up—did Ty mention that?"

"Yes—above my desk, from the lamp bracket."

"Uh huh. What it is, underneath the distractions of bent wire and pretty beads, is a scan device. Along about week six, if you were doing your work, you would suddenly realize that it had been transmitting everything you did and said . . . and you'd look up—everyone did—and that picture of your sudden revelation went into the class scrapbook. The earlier, the better luck . . . they'd calculated the mean, and if you beat the mean, you got extra points, depending on how early you were."

"You mean it's . . . spying on me?"

"Well, you knew you were under surveillance."

"I hate it!" Brun flung herself down, in a gesture that reminded Esmay of a child's petulant flounce. Esmay was not moved.

"So? You agreed—"

"I agreed to have the stupid bodyguards around, not to have them putting illicit scan devices in my room. Damn them!"

Esmay felt much older than this spoiled girl. "They're doing their job . . . and you're not making it easier."

"Why should I?"

"Grow up!" It wasn't what she'd meant to say, but she had been thinking it, and she couldn't hold it back any longer. To her surprise, Brun whitened as if Esmay had hit her.

"I'm very sorry to have bothered you." She was up and out the door before Esmay could say anything. Esmay stared at the shut door a long moment. Should she apologize? Altiplano manners demanding apology for almost everything quarrelled with Serrano advice not to apologize too much; she wished she could talk to Barin about it, but she had to finish the calculations for a project in support planning. She forced herself to concentrate on the work, with the consoling thought that perhaps Brun would no longer want to be on her team.

But that hope disappeared when the study team assignments came out. Brun had managed, by whatever means the daughter of the Speaker of the Grand Council could use, to get herself assigned to Esmay's team in the Escape and Evasion course. Esmay told herself that was unfair; it might not have taken any deviousness at all. Perhaps she'd just asked, and they'd given. Brun's demeanor gave no clue; she gave her usual impression of complete unconcern.

"Your problem today is to assess the security problem associated with moving a high-risk individual from this room"—Uhlis pointed at it on the diagram—"to the shuttle port, which is here." A map graphic came up on the screen. "You have available the materials in the box on your table; you are briefing the head of the security detail in forty-five minutes. Go."

The first thing to do, the class rules declared, was to open the envelope in the box and find out who was commanding this exercise. To Esmay's relief, it was neither Brun nor herself. Lieutenant Marden—who had, though hastily, at least read the first assignment—seemed to have a basic grasp of the topic so far, as he handed out the materials to Esmay, Brun, and Vericour. They all set to work, and their presentation won a passing grade, though not a high one. Brun's failure to recognize a potential threat dropped their score, and Uhlis was unforgiving.

"The point of working as a team is for all of you to combine skills and knowledge, not to hide in your own narrow area of responsibility. Any of the rest of

you could have noticed that Sera Meager had ignored
the possibility of an aerial attack on the motor route—
and should have."

Esmay felt the sting of that. She *had* wondered why
Brun didn't mention it—and she had said nothing,
since she was trying to arrange the resources she supposedly had, none of which included anything she
knew could take out aircars. But Uhlis's greatest scorn
fell on Lieutenant Marden, as their commander. By
the time he was through, Esmay was afraid Marden
would be in shreds on the floor . . . as it was, he
disappeared rapidly after the lab, and showed up again
only at dinner. Esmay took her tray to his table.

"I should've said something," she said. "I did
wonder about air, but since I didn't have any
resources to deal with an air attack—"

"That was in my packet," Marden said. "If and only
if someone mentioned it, I could call for reinforcements. I thought that meant I couldn't mention it
myself, but—as you heard—that's not what it meant
at all." He stared at his plate. "I'm not really hungry.
Sorry to lower your ratings average, though."

"Don't worry about that," Esmay said. "I think we
were all too worried about stepping on each other's
territory. Wonder if all the other groups had the same
problem."

"Well, from what I hear, no one got a satisfactory,
let alone a commended. But I feel really stupid."

"I don't think—" began Esmay. But Vericour
appeared at the table.

"Do you think we'll have the same teams for the
field exercise?" He sat down before either of them
answered. "I hope not—getting the Speaker's daughter
through it safely is going to make it harder on us." He
turned to Esmay. "Harder on you, in particular."

Esmay felt moved to defend Brun. "I don't know—
she has no military background, but she is smart and
willing."

"And just about demonstrates rashness, from what I hear." Vericour reached for the condiment tray, and sprinkled galis sauce generously over his entire plate. Esmay sneezed as the sharp fumes went up her nose. "Sorry—I forget what this can do to sensitive noses. Mine went years ago."

"She is the Speaker's daughter," Marden said, in a lower voice than Vericour had used.

"Well, yes. She's also a celebrity in her own right, so she can't expect not to be talked about. She's always on some newsflash or other. You know they have a team here covering her training."

"She can't help that," Esmay said. "They're always after prominent people, and she is good-looking—"

"She's spectacular," Vericour said. "But I can't see her sneaking across anything unobserved, can you?"

"She got from Rotterdam back to Rockhouse Major—" Marden said.

"Yes, back when no one imagined a girl like that would work her passage on an ag ship. Now they know—and you can bet she won't do that again." He turned back to Esmay. "Do you follow the news-flashes, Esmay?"

"No," Esmay said. She had never paid much attention to the gossipy newsflashes, with their emphasis on fashion and celebrity.

"Well . . . if you had, you'd have seen Brun Meager in everything from formal gowns to skinsuits, posing elegantly on a horse or lounging by a picturesque beach. Flatpics of her are probably in more lockers than anyone but actual storycube stars."

Great. Someone else who thought she was astound-ingly beautiful. Esmay could picture every flaw in that face and body—not that there were many.

"But except for the daring rescue of the most noble Lady Cecelia"—that sounded like a quote from someone's purple prose—"nothing I've read suggests she had any real sense. So now we're stuck with her . . ."

"If the teams are the same," Marden said. "Maybe they aren't."

"Maybe they aren't, but I'll bet Esmay ends up on the same team. They'll want to put another woman on her team, and who else would they put? Taras? Don't make me laugh. Taras wouldn't have a chance with Brun Meager. No, they'll put the best they have, and that's you, m'dear." Vericour bowed, grinning. Esmay felt embarrassed. How could she deal with this? It did not help that Brun chose that moment to appear at their table.

"Won't do you any good to flirt with Suiza," she said to Vericour, apparently apropos of the bow. "But you could always flirt with me."

Vericour spread his hands, rolled his eyes, and then mimed a swoon; everyone laughed but Esmay. It was funny, but she was too conscious of the vivid intensity next to her to enjoy it.

"Could I talk to you a bit?" Brun said, turning to her with a more serious expression than usual. Under the eyes of the others, Esmay had to say yes.

"I know I did something wrong, but not what . . . how could I arrange air cover when we didn't have any resources? And why should I have worried about it, when the information we were given didn't mention any such threat?"

A technical problem she could answer; Esmay quickly outlined the logic behind their low score. Brun nodded, apparently paying attention, and Esmay warmed to her again.

"So . . . even if there's no evidence to indicate a certain kind of threat, you still have to counter it?"

"You have to assume your intelligence is incomplete," Marden put in. "It always is."

"But if you're too cautious, you can't get anything

done," Brun said. "You have to act, even before you know everything—"

"Yes, but with an awareness of what you don't know, and its implications," Esmay said.

"And it's not so much what you don't know, as what you think you do know—that's wrong—that will get you killed," Vericour said. "It's the assumptions—that no mention of an aerial threat means no aerial threat, or no mention of piracy in a sector means there are no pirates."

"I see," Brun said. "I'll try to do better next time, but I have to say I'm better at reacting quickly than seeing invisible possibilities."

When Esmay got up to leave, Brun trailed along instead of heading for the ball courts with the others, and Esmay sighed internally. She was tired already, and had at least four hours of studying to do; if Brun insisted on talking to her, she would be up late again, and her energy was running out.

"I know you're busy," Brun said, as they got to Esmay's quarters. "But this shouldn't take long, and I really don't know where else to go."

This appeal cut through Esmay's worry about her classes. "Come on in," she said. "What's wrong?"

"There's something wrong with Master Chief Vecchi," Brun said.

"Wrong? What kind of wrong?" Esmay, her mind on their previous conversation, had been expecting a question about Fleet manners.

"Well . . . right in the middle of the lecture today, he suddenly didn't make sense. He was telling us how to secure a line on a derelict in zero gravity, and he got it backwards."

"How would *you* know?"

Brun had the grace to blush. "I read the book," she said. "His book, actually. *Safety Techniques in Space Rescue.*"

"It slipped his mind," Esmay said. "Everyone makes mistakes sometimes."

"But he didn't know it. I mean, he went right on, explaining things wrong. When one of the jigs asked if he was sure, Vecchi blew up . . . then got very red, walked out, and when he came back, he said he had a headache."

"Maybe—"

"It's not the first time," Brun said. "A week ago, he actually inserted a Briggs pin upside down."

"Testing you?"

"No—it was his own line, and he was about to move on it when one of the junior instructors—Kim something. Tough little woman, about half my size but can haul me up one-handed. She did. Anyway, she noticed Vecchi's mistake and fixed it."

"Um." Esmay couldn't think why this was her problem, except that anything that bothered Brun was her problem.

"It bothered her, I could tell. She watched everything else he did, checked it all. Not the usual cross-checks, but as if he were a student."

"How old is Vecchi?"

"What, are you thinking he's just gotten old? He's rejuved, I know that. One of the first enlisted rejuvs."

"When?"

Brun looked disgusted. "I don't have his medical records—how would I know?"

"I just wondered . . . maybe it's wearing off."

"It doesn't work that way," Brun said. Esmay raised her eyebrows and waited. "My father," Brun went on. "He's rejuved, so is Mother. Their friends . . . so I naturally know how it works."

"And?" Esmay prompted.

"Well, the usual reason for repeating a rejuv is physical. The people I know who've had more than one certainly didn't have any mental problems. Their personalities don't change, and they're just as alert."

"But wasn't that earlier kind of rejuvenation associated with mental degeneration?"

"Only if you tried to repeat it." Brun made a face. "Mother's second cousin or something did that, and it was horrible. Mother tried to keep me away from her, but you know little kids . . . I thought there must be something special in that suite if they wanted me out of it, so I sneaked in."

"So . . . is Vecchi anything like your mother's cousin?"

"Not . . . exactly. Not as severe, anyway. You don't suppose they made a mistake and gave him the wrong kind of rejuv procedure, do you?"

"I don't know. It would help if we knew more about rejuvenation, and also about the procedure used on Vecchi."

"I thought you could do something, since you're in Fleet."

Esmay snorted. "Not dig into his personnel and medical records—I have no reason to see them, and it's against regulations to snoop."

"Not even . . . unofficially?"

"No." She would stop this right here. "I'm not going to ruin my career to satisfy your curiosity. If Vecchi is impaired, someone in his chain of command will notice. If I observe something myself, I can report it. But I cannot—and will not—attempt to snoop in his records. You can report it, to—oh—whoever's commanding over there. Who's the senior instructor?"

"A Commander Priallo, but she's on leave somewhere."

"Well, find someone else—whoever is her junior—"

"I'd think you'd care," Brun said.

"I care—" If anything at all was wrong, but this was only Brun's word. "But I have no right to intervene; this needs to go to his commander. I suppose you could tell the Commandant."

"Maybe I will," Brun said, and after a moment sighed and went out. Esmay put Brun's worries out of her mind and tackled her assignments.

When the field exercise team assignments came out the next day, she found Vericour was right. Brun was on her team, and she had the smallest team of all—because her security would have to come along. How would that work? Would they really let her be roughed up? Or would they interfere in the exercise? And what would that do to the scoring?

Meanwhile, Brun maintained an indecent level of energy and enthusiasm. She learned content as fast as anyone Esmay had ever known—Esmay wondered if her intellectual capacity had ever been pushed near its limit. She did not, however, seem able to learn the attitudes that were by now second nature to those young officers for whom they were not first nature. Reprimands slid off her impenetrable confidence; suggestion and example alike had no effect.

"She's a dilettante," Vericour said, in another of those mealtime discussions. "Though what else could we expect from someone of her background? But she takes nothing seriously, least of all Fleet culture."

Anton Livadhi, a cousin of the Livadhi with whom Esmay had served on *Despite*, shook his head. "She takes us seriously enough . . . but she's not one of us, and she knows it. She wants us to be serious, while she has fun." He had his own team for the field exercise, and they were well up the chart on the evaluations for the preliminary exercises. Esmay's team performance was only middling; Brun fluctuated between brilliant and maddening, and her security could not commit emotionally as team members were supposed to do, and still be guards. They had taken almost twice as long as the fastest team in several exercises.

Esmay began to dread the field exercise itself, four

days of intense and dangerous work in the badlands west of the base. She was reasonably sure that Brun's guards wouldn't let her be killed, but that left her and Jig Medars to do the work of an entire team. Two days before the exercise, she left a lecture on ship systems maintenance and found a message on her personal comunit: Lieutenant Commander Uhlis wanted to see her at her earliest convenience. Since she had an hour between classes, that meant right now.

She could hear the angry voices from ten meters down the corridor; Uhlis's door was ajar.

"You have to see that it's impossible." Uhlis sounded annoyed.

"Why?" Brun sounded more than annoyed; Esmay paused, wishing the door had shut firmly.

"Because you're already the target of assassins. The field exercise is by nature dangerous, and it's also impossible to secure. All it would take is one person—just one, with the right skills—to pick you off."

"You mean to tell me that on a base covered with Fleet personnel, you can't even let me do a simple field exercise?" Scorn in that, as if Brun expected to shame Uhlis into changing his mind. That wouldn't work.

"I mean we will not approve it. Nor will your father; I have already forwarded our decision, and our reasons for it, to him. He agreed."

"That's—that's—the stupidest thing I ever heard!" Brun's voice had gone up another notch. "If I'm a target for terrorists, then it's perfectly clear that escape and evasion is exactly what I need to know. What am I supposed to do if I get kidnapped and need to escape?"

"The escape segment will be available—at least the urban end . . ."

"Fine. So I've broken out of some provincial jail somewhere and have to cover a hundred kilometers to a safe haven, and I have no training?"

"According to your father, you have had ample training in the basics of survival and navigation in the field, both on Sirialis and on Castle Rock. Your field skills are, in his opinion and those of our instructors who reviewed the recordings, equivalent to those of most graduates. So the escape segments should fill out your skills very well."

Silence for a moment. Esmay wondered if she could just walk past the door now, but even as she moved, Brun stormed out, silent but obviously in a rage. She broke stride when she saw Esmay.

"You will not believe—!" she began.

"Excuse me," Esmay said, not wanting to hear it all again. "I overheard a little, and I have an appointment." Brun's eyes widened, but she moved aside. Esmay edged past Brun and into the office, where a grim-faced Commander Uhlis looked ready to melt bulkheads with his glare. "Sir, Lieutenant Suiza reporting—"

"Close the door," he said.

"Yes, sir." Esmay shut the door firmly, aware of Brun hovering outside.

Uhlis took a deep breath, then another, and then looked at her with less intensity. "I wanted to talk to you about your team assignment," he said. "If you overheard much of that"—he nodded at the door— "then you know we have concerns about security. Up until last night, we still had orders to accommodate Meager and include her in all the courses, including the field exercise. However, since we now have permission from the highest levels to exclude her and her bodyguards, we need to rearrange team assignments. We're going to split the exercise, and you'll be assigned to a new team, acting commander." He gave her a dangerous smile. "I understand you do very well at motivating strangers, Lieutenant."

So the camaraderie she'd built up with her team over the past week would be no use to her—and the team she went to might well resent losing its familiar commander. But at least she wouldn't have Brun to worry about.

"Thank you, sir," she said.

"Thank me afterwards," he said. "If you can. Remember, your score depends on not only your own successful evasion, but how many of your team make it."

Her new team waited for her in the afternoon skills exercise. They had a bored, wary look . . . they were, she realized, the team that Anton Livadhi had led. And Anton had remarked, just too audibly, that he had his doubts about the source of Suiza's success. "Serrano pet" was a phrase she'd been meant to overhear; she had ignored it, but these people hadn't. Two other women, four men; she ran the names over quickly in her mind. All but one had been in her class in the Academy, but she hadn't seen any of them for years, and she hadn't been close to them even then.

That afternoon's exercise was deceptively simple. From a scatter of raw materials, improvise a way to cross a series of "natural" barriers. Each obstacle required not only teamwork but also innovative think-ing . . . none of the poles were long enough, none of the ropes strong enough, none of the assorted other objects were obviously meant for the tasks at hand. Esmay tried being forthright and cheerful, as recom-mended in the leadership manual, but only some of her new team responded. Lieutenant Taras was inclined to be pettish if her ideas were not accepted the first time; Lieutenant Paradh and Jig Bearlin could always think of ways for things not to work. By the time the period was over, they had completed only four of the five obstacles. Esmay was aware of the frowning instructor, ticking off points on his chart. This team had been ranked first or second in every exercise; now they wouldn't be.

It was possible to request overtime, though it was

rarely done because it imposed a twenty percent penalty on the entire score. Esmay raised her hand; Taras made a sound that might have been a groan. Esmay rounded on her. "We are going to finish this, Lieutenant, if we have to stay here all night—"

"We can't *win*," Bearlin said. "We might as well take the eighty percent we've got—"

"And when you need that other twenty percent of experience, where are you planning to get it?" Esmay asked. "We're completing this exercise, and we're doing it now."

She expected more resistance, but despite some sidelong grumpy looks, they tackled the final obstacle with more energy than they had any of the others. Five minutes later, they had solved the problem—and although Esmay halfway expected them to dump her in the mud, they got her over the pit with the same care they expended on each other.

"Good choice," the instructor told them afterwards. "You wouldn't have got eighty percent before—you were about as effective as a jug of eelworms—but you've got it now."

By the time they got back to the mess hall, Esmay felt she had a chance with this group—a slim chance, but a real one. If only she'd had a few more days before the field exercise.

The next day's prelims went better; her new team seemed willing to work together again, and they were back up to third in the daily ratings. Esmay went to her quarters to pack her gear for the field exercise, and try to snatch a few hours of sleep before time to leave.

She had everything laid out on her bunk when her doorchime rang. Stifling a curse, she went to open it. Barin might have stopped by, though she'd hardly seen him for days, except with Brun. She hoped it was Barin. But instead it was Brun, and a very angry Brun at that.

"I suppose you're proud of yourself!" Brun said first.

"Excuse me?" What was the girl talking about?

"You never did want me on your team; you haven't liked me from the beginning."

"I—"

"And now you've made sure I can't do the field exercise, so you can take over a top team . . ."

"I did not," Esmay said, beginning a slow burn. "They just assigned me—"

"Oh, don't be stupid," Brun said, flopping onto the bunk and making a mess of Esmay's careful arrangement. "You're the heroic Lieutenant Suiza—they want you to shine, and they've arranged it. Never mind what it does to other people's plans . . ."

"Like yours?" Esmay said. She could feel her pulse speeding up.

"Like mine. Like Anton's. Like Barin's."

"Barin's!"

"You know, he's really quite fond of you," Brun said, idly prodding a stack of concentrate bars until they collapsed. Two slid off onto the floor. Esmay gritted her teeth and picked them up without comment. She did not want this. "I was trying to find out why you're such a cold fish, and I thought he might know—and I'll bet you didn't even know the poor boy's half in love with you."

Didn't she . . . ? Esmay contemplated for a moment the probable result of pulling out Brun's tousled gold curls by the roots.

"Of course, such an upright professional as yourself would never stoop to dally with mere ensigns," Brun went on, in a tone that could have removed several layers of paint from a bulkhead. "He, like the rest of us, is far beneath your notice—unless someone gets in your way." This time she picked up a water bottle and opened and shut the spout.

"That is not fair," Esmay said. "I didn't have

anything to do with your being taken out of the field exercise—"

"I suppose you want me to believe you support me?"

"No, but that's not the same thing. It wasn't my decision to make."

"But if it had been—" Brun gave her a challenging glare.

"It wasn't. What might have been doesn't matter."

"So true. You *might have been* a friend; you *might have been* Barin's lover; instead—"

"What do you mean 'might have been' someone's lover?" Even as angry as she was, she could not say Barin's name in that context. Not to this woman.

"You don't expect him to hang around worshipping your footsteps forever, do you? Just in case you might come down from your pinnacle and notice him? Even a bad case of hero worship yields at last to time."

This was her worst fear, right here and now. Had it been only hero worship? Was it . . . over?

"And you, of course, were right there to help him over this unwarranted fixation . . . ?"

"I did my part," Brun said, flipping out the gold curls with a gesture that left no doubt what she meant. Esmay had an instant vision of them strewn about the room, little gold tufts of hair like fleece on the shed floor after shearing. "He's intelligent, witty, fun, not to mention incredibly handsome—I'd have thought you'd notice—"

A light of unnatural clarity seemed to illuminate the room; Esmay felt weightless with pure rage. This . . . *this* to be pursuing Barin. *This* to displace her, to ruin her relationship with Barin. A young woman who boasted openly of her sexual conquests, who refused to abide by any rules, who claimed to be unafraid of rape because "it's just mechanics; and aside from that, no one can make me pregnant." She was like Casea

Ferradi, without Ferradi's excuse of a colonial background.

Hardly conscious of what she was doing, she reached out and lifted Brun off the bunk, and set her against the wall, as easily as she could have picked up a small child.

"You . . ." She could not say the words she was really thinking; she struggled to find something hurtful enough. "You playgirl," she said finally. "You come bouncing in here, all full of your genetically engineered brains and beauty, showing it all off, playing with us—*playing* with the people who are risking their lives to keep you and your wonderful family alive and safe."

Brun opened her mouth, but Esmay gave her no chance; the words she had longed to say came pouring out.

"You wanted to be friends, you said—what did you ever do but get in my way, take up my time, and go lusting after anyone who caught your fancy? It never occurred to you that some of us have a job to do here—that people's lives, not just ours, will depend on how we do it. No. You want to go play in Q-town, someone should go with you . . . it doesn't matter to you if that means learning less. After all, what does it matter if you pass a course or flunk it? It's not your life on the line. You don't care whether you ruin Barin's career or not—" Not the way she herself cared; not the way she agonized over it. "You think your money and your family make it right for you to have anyone you want."

Brun was white to the lips. Esmay didn't care. Her anxiety about the next day, her exhaustion from weeks of extra work—all had vanished, in righteous rage. "You have the morality of a mare in heat; you have no more spiritual depth than a water drop on a window. And someday you will need that, and I promise you—I promise you, Miss Rich and Famous—you will wish you had it, and you will know I'm right. Now get out, and stay out. I have work to do."

With that, Esmay yanked the door open; she was ready to shove Brun out, but Brun stalked past her, under the eyes of her waiting security, who carefully looked at neither of them. The doors were not made to slam, or Esmay would have slammed hers. As it was, she restacked her gear with shaking hands, packed it, set it aside, then lay unsleeping on her bunk to wait for the alarm.

CHAPTER FOUR

Brun stalked along the streets of Q-town trying to push her anger back down her throat. That sanctimonious little prig . . . that prissy backcountry *chit* . . . her family probably slopped hogs in their bare feet. Just because she herself had grown up rich, just because she could talk about sex without squinching her face up—!

In one corner of her mind, she knew this was unfair. Esmay was not an ignorant girl, but an accomplished older woman. Not much older, but an Academy graduate, a Fleet officer, a combat veteran—Brun would have been glad to have Esmay's experience. She wanted Esmay's respect.

But not enough to turn into a frumpy, tight-buttoned, sexless, joyless . . .

Esmay wasn't joyless, though.

Brun didn't want to be fair. She wanted to be angry, righteously angry. Esmay had had no right to ream her out like that, no right to say she had no moral sense. Of course she had moral sense. She had rescued Lady Cecelia, for one thing. Even Esmay granted that. Aside from the requisite helling around that all the people in her set went through in adolescence, no one had ever accused her of being immoral.

She hunted through her past, finding one instance after another in which she had acted in ways she was sure Esmay would approve . . . not that it was any of her business. She had protected that little Ponsibar girl at school, the one who had arrived so scared and so easy to bully. She had told the truth about the incident in the biology lab, even though it had cost her a month's detention and the friendship of Ottala Morreline. She had been polite to Great-Aunt Trema even when that formidable old lady had regaled guests at the Hunt Ball with tales of "little Bubbles" cavorting naked in the fountain as a toddler. She'd had to fight off entirely too many of her schoolmates' brothers after that one, but she hadn't turned against Aunt Trema. She and Raffa on the island . . . they had saved each others' lives.

She could not, however, find something to plaster over all the accusations. Well . . . so what? Her standards were different; that didn't mean she had none. Just as her inner voices began to talk about that, she decided she was thirsty, and turned into one of the bars that lined the street.

DIAMOND SIMS, the sign read. Brun assumed it referred to fake diamonds, with an implication of world-weariness. Inside, the tables and booths were full of men and women who might as well all have been in uniform as in the mostly-drab shipsuits now the favorite casual wear for the military. The way they sat, their gestures . . . all revealed their profession. A few—less than a third—were in uniform. She didn't see any of the students from the courses here—not that she'd know any but those in her own section, anyway. But she hadn't wanted to see anyone she knew, anyone who would wonder where her bodyguards were. She wanted new faces, and a new start, and new proof that she was who she thought she was.

With that in mind, she edged past crowded tables to the one double seat empty toward the back. She sat down, and touched the order pad on the table—Stenner ale, one of her favorites—and put her credit cube in the debit slot. She glanced around. On the wall to her right were framed pictures of ships and people, and a display of little metal bits arranged in rows. A faded red banner hung up in the far corner; she could not make out the lettering from where she sat.

A waitress deposited her frosted mug and the bottle of ale, and gave her a saucy grin. "What ship, hon?"

Brun shook her head. "I'm on a course." The waitress looked slightly surprised, but nodded and went on her way to deliver the rest of the tray to another table. Brun poured her ale. Behind her, she heard the dim confused sound of voices, and realized that there was another room—apparently private—adjoining the main room. And on her left, the long bar, the same matte black as the stuff covering ships' hulls . . . could it possibly be a section of the same material? Above it, suspended from the high ceiling, were ship models. Brun recognized the odd angular shape of a minesweeper among the more ordinary ovoids of the warships. And behind the bar, the expected mirrors were framed with . . . her eyes widened. She knew enough about ordnance now to recognize that every frame had once been part of a functioning weapon. In a quick glance around the room, she saw more and more . . . it was as if the inside of the bar were made of the salvaged pieces of wrecks.

She felt the hair rising on the back of her neck, on her arms. It wasn't real—it could not be real—no one would really . . . but her eye snagged on a display at the near end of the bar. *Paradox*. That

name—she could not forget that name. And here was
a plate—an ordinary dinner plate, its broad rim
carrying the same dark-blue chain design she'd seen
on all the dinnerware aboard Admiral Serrano's ship,
with the four lozenges that had surrounded the name
Harrier. Here, the design inside the lozenges was
slightly different . . . and the plate, sitting on a stand
she was suddenly sure had been made of other debris,
was brightly lit by a tiny spot that also illuminated
the label, for those who were too far away to see the
lozenges. Beside it was a stack of crockery.

Brun looked at the mug holding her ale, suddenly
feeling almost sick. Had she been drinking from . . . ?
No, it wasn't *Paradox*. But now that its frosting had
melted, she could see it was etched with some design.
She squinted slightly. R.S.S. *Balrog*.

She had been drinking from dead men's cups. She
was sitting on . . . a seat made from salvaged bits . . .
and what bits? Her elbows rested on a table made
of . . . she wasn't sure what, but she was now sure it
was something that had been part of a living ship, and
had been salvaged from a wreck. She looked for
clues—and there, in a dull-finished plaque set into the
tabletop next to the menu screen, she found it. R.S.S.
Forge, enlisted bunk 351. A tiny button to one side
caught her eye; she pressed it.

The menu screen blanked, replaced by a historical
note: R.S.S. *Forge* had been lost thirty-two years
before, in combat with a Benignity strike force; all
hands had died. This fragment had been salved twenty-
eight years ago, and identified by the stamped part
number (still on the underside of the table); at the time
of the ship's death, enlisted bunk 351 had been
assigned to Pivot Lester Green.

The table's pedestal, the note went on, was formed
of a piece of shielded conduit from the same ship;
the two chairs were both from *Forge*, but one was
from the enlisted mess and the other had been that

of the senior weapons tech serving the aft starboard missile battery. The five people who had taken that position during *Forge*'s final battle were all listed: Cpl. Dancy Alcorn, Sgt. Tarik Senit, Cpl. Lurs Ptin, Cpl. Barstow Bohannon, Sgt. Gareth Meharry.

Brun's breath caught. Bad enough that all the names were listed, real people who had lived real lives and died a real death. But Meharry . . . she had known Methlin Meharry . . . was this a relative? A . . . parent? Aunt? Uncle?

Each name was linked, she realized, to some other information. She didn't want it; she didn't want those names to be any more real than they already were. But Meharry—she had to know. She activated the link.

Gareth Meharry had been twenty-six when he died; his family tree, spread across the screen, with Fleet members in blue, was more blue than gray. His parents (both now deceased, one in combat) had been Fleet; of his four sibs, two were active-duty Fleet, and two were married to Fleet members. Methlin Meharry was his sister . . . hard to think of that tough veteran as anyone's sister. One of his nieces—her niece too—was named after her. So there would be another Methlin Meharry someday, and with both parents, and aunts and uncles, in Fleet, there was every chance that she would go into Fleet.

Sudden curiosity—and an escape from the weight of tragedy that was making it hard to concentrate— sent Brun back to the main menu. Sure enough, below the lists of drinks and food, she found data access choices. From this table, she could check on the publicly accessible records of anyone in Fleet.

Esmay—she wondered if there were other Suizas in Fleet. She entered the name and waited. Up on the screen came only one name, and Fleet's choice of data for public consumption. Name . . . she had not known that Esmay's full name was Esmay

Annaluisa Susannah Suiza. Planet of origin: Altiplano. Family background . . . Brun caught her breath. In a few crisp sentences, she was informed that the Suiza family was one of the three most prominent on Altiplano . . . that Esmay's father was one of the four senior military commanders . . . that her uncles were two of the others, and that the fourth was considered to be a Suiza choice. That the military influence on Altiplano's government was "profound."

Brun tried to tell herself that a senior military commander on a backwater planet was nothing special—her father's militia, back on Sirialis, was just a jumped-up police force. Its commander, though given the title "General," had never impressed her as the regulars of Fleet did. But Altiplano . . . she read on . . . had no Seat in Council. It had no Family connections at all. Which meant—she wasn't sure what, but she suspected that a General Suiza had a lot more power than old General Ashworth.

Of Esmay herself, there was little: a list of her decorations, with the citations that went with them. Conspicuous gallantry. Outstanding leadership. Outstanding initiative. A list of the ships she'd served on. Her present assignment, to Training Command's Junior Officer Leadership Course.

Well. Brun sat back, aware of tension in her neck and shoulders, the feeling that she'd got herself in well over her head in more than one way. She returned the screen to its default, and thought of ordering a snack. But it would come on a plate from some wrecked ship. She didn't think she could face that. As it was, she already had tears in her eyes.

"Something wrong?" asked a deep voice behind her. She turned.

He was stocky, heavy shoulders thick with muscle; his bald head, like Oblo's, deeply scarred. His eyes were scarcely higher than hers; he was in a hoverchair. Brun kept her eyes from dropping to see why with an effort—but that gave him a clear look at her face.

Out of the scarred face, brown eyes observed her with more insight than she liked. His wide mouth quirked.

"Lady, you're not Fleet, and you don't know what you've gotten yourself into, do you?"

The "lady" threw her off-stride for a moment. In that pause, he jerked his head toward the farthest angle of the back.

"Come on over here, and let's get you sorted out," he said. She was moving before she realized it, compelled by something in his voice. His hover-chair turned, and slid between the tables; Brun followed.

Two tables away, someone called, "Hey! Sam!" He turned his head slightly—he could not, Brun realized, turn it all the way—and raised a hand but did not answer. Brun followed him and found a half-booth: enclosing bench and table, with space on the other side for his hoverchair.

"Sit," he said. Then, over his shoulder to a waitress, "Get us a pair of Stenners, and some chips." His gaze returned to Brun, as disturbing as ever.

"I'm not really—" Brun began.

"That much I know already," he said, humor in his tone. "But let's see what you are." He ticked off points with a stubby finger that looked as if it had been badly moulded of plastic. "You're Thornbuckle's daughter, according to your credit chip, and according to the class list over there—" He jerked his head in the direction of the Schools. "You're Brun Meager, choosing to use your mother's family name. Target of assassination attempts—" Brun noted the plural and wondered how he knew. "By your instructors' reports, physically agile and strong, bright as a new pin, quick learner, gifted with luck in emergencies. Also emotionally labile, argumentative, arrogant, stubborn, willful, difficult. Not officer material, at least not without a lot of remedial work."

Brun knew her face showed her reaction to that. "And why not?" she asked, trying for a tone of mild academic interest.

He ignored the question and went on. "You're not Fleet; no one in your bloodline's been Fleet for over two hundred forty years. You come from a class where social skills are expected in a normal person your age. Yet you come into a Fleet bar—"

"There's nothing *but* Fleet bars in Q-town," Brun muttered.

"And not only a Fleet bar," he went on, "a bar with special connotations, even for Fleet personnel. Not all of them will come here; not all of them are welcome here. I've seen kids with what you would call no social background at all come through the door and recognize, in one breath, that they don't belong here. Which makes me wonder, Charlotte Brunhilde Meager, about someone like you *not* noticing."

Brun glared at him. He gazed back, a look neither inviting nor hostile. Just . . . looking . . . as if she were an interesting piece of machinery. That look didn't deserve an answer, even if she'd had one, which she didn't. She didn't know why she'd ducked into this doorway instead of another. It was handy; she'd wanted a drink; when the thought of a drink and a doorway offering drinks overlapped, she went in. Put that way it didn't sound as if she were thinking straight, but she didn't want to think about that. Not here; not now.

"You know, we've got security vid outside," the man said, leaning back a little. "When your cube ID popped up on my screen, I ran back the loop. You were stalking along the street like someone with a serious grievance. Then you hitched a step, and turned in here, with just a glance at the sign. Anyone tell you about this place?"

"No." Even to Brun's present mood, that sounded sulky, and she expanded. "I was given a list of places that catered to various specialties, mostly sexual. They have a code of light patterns in the windows, the briefing cube said. Anything else was general entertainment."

"So, just as it seemed on the vid, you were in a rage, thought of getting a drink, and turned into the first bar you saw." His mouth quirked. "Really high-quality thinking for someone of your tested intelligence."

"Even smart people can get mad," Brun said.

"Even smart people can get stupid," he replied. "You're supposed to have a security escort at all times, right? And where are they?"

Brun felt herself flushing again. "They're—" She wanted to say *a royal pain*, but knew that this man would think that childish. Everyone seemed to think it was childish not to want half a dozen people lurking about all the time, looming over private conversations, listening, watching, just . . . being where she didn't want them to be. "Back at the Schools, I suppose," she said.

"You sneaked out," the man said, with no question at all in his voice.

"Yes. I wanted a bit of—"

"Time to yourself. Yes. And so you risk not only your own life, which is your right as an adult, but you risk their safety and their professional future, because you wanted a little time off." Now the scorn she had sensed was obvious in his expression and his tone. Those brown eyes made no excuses, for himself or anyone else. "Do you think your assassin is taking time off, time to have a little relaxation?"

Brun had not thought about her assassin any more than she could help; she had certainly not thought about whether an assassin kept the same hours as a target. "I don't know," she muttered.

"Or what will happen to your guards if you get killed while they're not with you?"

"I got away from them," Brun said. "It wouldn't be their fault."

"Morally, no. Professionally, yes. It is their job to guard you, whether you cooperate or not. If you elude them and are killed, they will be blamed." He paused. Brun could think of nothing to say, and was silent. "So . . . you got mad and barged in here. Ordered. Started looking around. Noticed the decor—"

"Yes. Pieces of ships. It's . . . morbid."

"Now that, young lady, is where you're wrong."

Faced with opposition, Brun felt an urge to argue. "It is. What's the point of keeping bits of dead ships, and—and putting people's names on them, if not morbid fascination with death?"

"Look at me," the man said. Startled, Brun complied. "Really look," the man said. He moved the hoverchair back a little, and pointed to his legs . . . which ended at what would have been mid-thigh. Brun looked, unwillingly but carefully, and saw more and more signs of old and serious injury.

"No regen tanks on an escort," the man said. "It's too small. A buddy stuffed me in an escape pod, and when old *Cutlass* was blown, I was safely away. By the time I was picked up, there was no way to regrow the legs. Or the arm, though I chose a good prosthesis there. They'd have given me leg prostheses too, but I had enough spinal damage that I couldn't manage them. Now the head injuries—" He dipped his head, showing Brun the scars that laced his head. "Those were from another battle, back on *Pelion*, when part of a casing spalled off and sliced me up."

He grinned at her, and she saw the distortion of one side of his mouth. "Now you, young lady, you don't have a clue what using part of *Cutlass*'s hull as my bar means to me. Or to any of the men and women who come here. What it means to have crockery from *Paradox* and *Emerald City* and *Wildcat*, to have cutlery from *Defence* and *Granicus* and *Lancaster*, to have everything in this place made of the remnants of ships we served on, fought on, and survived."

"I still think it's morbid," Brun said, through stiff lips.

"You ever killed anyone?" he asked.

"Yes. As a matter of fact, I have."

"Tell me about it."

She could not believe this conversation. Tell him about the island, about Lepescu? But his eyes waited, and his scars, and his assumptions about her ignorance. Which of these finally drove her to speak, she could not have said.

"We—some friends and I—had taken an aircar to an island on Sirialis. It's a planet my father owns." She didn't like the sound of that, now; she wasn't boasting, but it sounded like it. He didn't react. "We didn't know that there were . . . intruders. A man—he was a Fleet officer—"

"Who?"

She felt a reluctance to answer, but could think of no way to avoid it. "Admiral Lepescu." Was there a reaction? She couldn't tell. "He and some friends—at least, I was told they were friends—had transported criminals . . . well, not really criminals, but that's what they said . . ." He shifted, with impatience she could almost feel. "Anyway," she said, hurrying now, "he and his friends transported these people to the island, to hunt. To hunt them, the supposed criminals. Lepescu and his friend stayed on a nearby island, which had a fishing lodge on it, and flew over every day to hunt. The hunted had cobbled together some kind of weapon, and shot down our aircar, thinking we were Lepescu. They captured us. When they realized their mistake, we realized that we would all be hunted; Lepescu would try to cover up his crimes."

"And no one knew he was on this planet?" The man's voice conveyed his disbelief.

"Dad found out later that one of his station commanders had been bribed. There was so much traffic in the system—it was the height of hunting season, with lots of guests coming and going—that the others had not noticed an extra ship at one station."

"Umph." Disbelief still in that, but a sharp nod made Brun go on with her story.

"So Raffa and I went off to an old hideout I remembered from childhood," Brun said. She felt herself tense, felt the fine sweat springing out on her skin. She didn't like thinking about that night or the next days. She rattled through the story as fast as possible: how she and Raffa had each killed one of the intruders and acquired their weapons, the discovery that the intruders had poisoned the water, their flight to the cave, and the final confrontation in the cave when Lepescu had been killed by Heris Serrano.

The man's expression changed at the mention of Serrano, but he said only, "So you yourself actually killed someone who was trying to kill you . . ."

"Yes."

"And did you enjoy it?"

"No!" That came out with more force than she intended.

"You were scared?"

"Of course, I was scared. I'm not a . . . a . . ." *Military freak* hovered on her tongue, but she was able to choke it back.

"Militarist crazy?" he asked. Brun stared. Mindreading was impossible, wasn't it? Then he sighed. "I do wish that somewhere in history people would quit diminishing courage in military personnel by assuming they aren't subject to normal emotions."

"Lepescu didn't seem to have any," Brun said.

"Lepescu was a serious problem," the man said. "He damn near ruined the Serrano family, through

Heris; he was probably responsible for more deaths than the enemy in any engagement he had to do with. But he was hardly typical. Even in his own family, there are good officers, not that any of 'em will have a career now."

He took a long swallow of his ale, then put the mug down and gave her another straight look.

"So . . . back to you. What put you in a rage?"

"An argument."

"With whom?"

"Esmay Suiza," Brun said. Anger burst out again. "She was like you—she thinks I'm just a spoiled rich girl helling around the universe having fun. She had the nerve—the gall—to tell me I had no moral structure to my life."

"Do you?"

"Of course I do!"

"What, then, do you conceive as the purpose of your life? What is it that you do, to justify your existence? What are you here for?"

Put that way, in his easy voice that carried neither praise nor blame, Brun found the answers that floated into her mind clearly inadequate. She was her father's daughter; she existed to . . . to be her father's daughter. No. She didn't want to be just her father's daughter, but she had found nothing else.

"I've helped people," she said lamely.

"That's nice," he said. She wasn't sure if sarcasm edged his tone or not. "Most people have, at one time or another. You saved your friend's life on that island. That's a point for you. Is that your mission, saving peoples' lives by killing those who want to kill them? If so, I must say you're woefully undertrained for that and overtrained for other things."

"I . . . don't know." Brun took another sip of her ale.

"Mmm. You're in your mid-twenties now, right? By your age, most young people without your . . .

advantages . . . are showing more sense of direction. Consider the officer you quarrelled with. By your age, she had chosen a profession, left home against some resistance to pursue it, and performed capably in her choice. She was not flitting around having adventures."

"Just because I'm rich—"

"Don't try that," he said; this time contempt laced his voice. "It has nothing to do with wealth; your father, for instance, shows every sign of being an honorable, hard-working man whose service to the Familias—and his own family—are his mission. Your sister Clemmie, even before she married, had chosen to work in an area of medicine where her skills and ability actually served someone else. You, on the other hand, while willing to help out friends, have no consistent direction in your life."

"Yes, but—"

"So I would say Lieutenant Suiza has the right of it. You are a fine lady, Brun Meager, but you aren't anything else. And someday, if you haven't developed the spiritual muscle, you're going to find yourself in a situation you can't handle—and with no tools at all to deal with it."

Brun glared at him, unable to think of anything to say.

"All of us here have been in those situations," he said, after a pause. "Brains aren't enough. Physical strength isn't enough. Life will throw things at you that brains and strength can't deal with. Smart people and strong people can both go crazy—or worse, go bad like Lepescu, convinced that whatever they want must be acceptable, or should be acceptable. There must be spiritual strength."

"And you think I don't have any?"

He shrugged. "That's not for me to say. I would have to say you haven't *shown* any yet. You haven't shown any ability to see yourself as you really are, for instance—and self-examination is one good clue to an individual's spiritual state. You have the capacity, certainly—anyone does—but you haven't developed it."

"I think you don't know what you're talking about," Brun said. She drained the rest of that mug of Stenner. "You haven't any idea what my life has been like, or what I've done, nor does your wonderful Lieutenant Suiza. You think being rich had nothing to do with it? Let me tell you something . . . the rich learn early on that you can't trust anyone—*anyone*—but the other rich. And you Fleet people are just the same. You don't trust anyone who's not born to Fleet. Nothing I did would make any difference. You all decided I was just a spoiled rich girl, from day one, and there was no hope of changing your minds. What passes for your minds."

She pushed herself away from the table and made her way outside, carefully not meeting anyone's eyes. She had had it; there was no way to do what she wanted to do as long as no one would give her a fair chance. She would leave Copper Mountain; she would figure out for herself what she needed.

By the time she got back to base, she had cooled down enough to be icily polite to her security escort. They were icily polite in return. It was long after midnight; she could hear the snarling of the transports picking up teams for the field exercise. The exercise she should have been on.

She checked the outbound shuttle and transport schedules. No doubt there would be formalities, but she should be able to get away before Esmay came back. She put her name on the list for an appointment with the Commandant of Schools in the morning, and went back to her quarters to take what rest she could.

When she went in, it was clear that the Commandant already knew something. She could see it in his face, and before she even sat down, he started to apologize.

"Sera Meager, I understand a junior officer acted very inappropriately—"

"You had scan on Lieutenant Suiza?"

He coughed. "On . . . you, Sera Meager. I'm sorry, but for your own safety—"

It was intolerable. She could not even have a quarrel without someone listening in. "Well, I suppose you got an earful."

"Lieutenant Suiza was totally unprofessional; you have my—Fleet's—apology . . ."

"Never mind that. She was rude, yes, but she made it clear I will never be accepted on my own merits. And I'm placing an undue burden on your staff, trying to keep me safe. I'm resigning my place, or whatever you call it."

"Does your father know?"

She could have slugged him, but his question was another proof that she was right. "I am informing him by ansible transmission this morning, sir, as soon as public hours open. I plan to take Fleet transport to the nearest civilian transport nexus—" She could not think of the name. "I will probably lease a vessel from there."

"You need not hurry . . ."

"I would rather be gone before the field exercise is over," Brun said. She was determined not to see Esmay Suiza again. Or Barin Serrano, for that matter—she could just imagine what his grandmother would say.

"I see." His lips compressed. "Again, while I think your decision is probably best under the circumstances, you have my assurance that Lieutenant Suiza's behavior will not go without official rebuke."

Exhaustion rolled over her suddenly like a heavy blanket. She didn't care about Lieutenant Suiza; she just wanted to be away from these people with their punctilious rules, their unbending righteousness.

"I will cooperate with all necessary procedures,"

Brun said, pushing herself up. What she really wanted was a week's sleep; she could get that once she left this miserable place. She put on her public persona to get through the remaining hours; she smiled at the right time, shook the right hands, murmured the right pleasantries, assured everyone that she had taken no offense, harbored no grievances, had simply come to the conclusion that this was not right for her.

By nightfall, her father had replied to her request that he send his personal militia to replace the Royal Space Service security when she reached civilian space. He had agreed—with what enthusiasm she could not judge—to her plan of spending a few months visiting relatives and business contacts before returning to Sirialis for the opening of the hunting season. At local midnight, she boarded the shuttle offplanet . . . and hoped that Esmay Suiza was having a miserable time, wherever she was.

❖   ❖   ❖

Thirty hours into the field exercise, Esmay wondered why she had ever thought this was a good idea for an elective. She had led her team safely through the first third of the course; they had spotted and evaded a number of traps. But they were hungry, thirsty and tired now, and she was fresh out of ideas. Ahead lay grassland—just grassland—to the line of fence that represented safety. They hadn't been spotted in the broken ground, but out there they couldn't hide—and it was too great a distance to cross in a rush. If they stayed where they were, they'd probably be found, and anyway they wouldn't get the extra points for getting to the safehold.

"A tunnel would be handy," Taras said.

She was right, of course, but why were her good ideas so impractical?

"I don't suppose we could find an animal burrow?"

"I doubt it." Briefing had said the native animals were all under five kilos. Of course, briefing had left a lot out. Esmay held them all where they were until dusk, then they began a slow, careful crawl through the grass toward the fenceline.

The hood cut off sight instantly; she struck out uselessly, knowing it was useless. Her blows fell on air, but the blows aimed at her landed . . . knocked her sideways, back, sideways again, until she finally fell, her head slamming into a hummock she had not been able to see. She tasted blood; she'd bitten her tongue in that fall. Before she could react, the assailants grabbed arms and legs, and in seconds she was immobilized like a calf for branding.

Had it been like this for Barin? No, for him it had been real . . . but the harsh voice that promised pain was real now, too. A fist grabbed her hair through the hood, and yanked her head back.

Think of something else, Barin had said. It does help, though you don't believe it at the time. That was in the manual, too, so others had found it useful. As she felt rough hands on the fastening of her clothes, and the cold edge of a blade, and then the tug as her clothes were cut away, her mind slid back toward that other time, in childhood.

No. She would not go there. She would think of something that made her feel strong.

What came into her head was the argument with Brun. In her head, in this pain-filled dark, she could think of much more to say than she had said. As the hours passed—hours she could not count—she elaborated on the argument and its causes, all the way back to that first meeting with Brun, and imagined herself and Brun and Barin. What each said, what each was thinking, what each thought the other was thinking. The verbal assaults of her captors became the things Brun had said, or would have said if she'd thought of them. The blows they dealt were the blows Brun would have dealt if she had dared fight openly.

But in the story she was telling herself, she gave as good as she got—better, in fact. For Brun's attacks, she now had the right counterattacks. For Brun's invincible arrogance, she now had a response that brought Brun to her knees, that forced her to acknowledge Esmay's position, skills, knowedge . . . In her mind, at least, she could triumph.

She was vaguely conscious that her captors were considerably annoyed with her for some reason, but nothing mattered as much as Brun's appropriation of Barin, and her own determination to defend—not territory, exactly, but her chance at—

As suddenly as it began, it ended. She didn't notice at first, though as she came back to real space and time, she was aware that her mind had noticed, and had begun pulling her back from the story she'd been writing in her mind. She felt the cool blunt snout of a hypospray against her arm, then a wave of returning clarity. When she opened her eyes, a medic smiled at her, and gave the code phrase that meant the exercise was over. And Lieutenant Commander Uhlis, looking no grimmer than usual, reached out a hand to help her up.

"Suiza, you're tougher than I thought. Whatever you were doing inside your head worked—keep it in mind in case you need it."

She felt shaky when she stood, and only then noticed that her hands were bandaged. He nodded at them. "You'll need an hour or so in the regen tank. The team kept thinking they could get to you in just another little bit. But it's all within regs." Now she could feel the pain, working its way past the restorative drug. Uhlis put out his arm again. "Better take hold—we'll get you into the transport. You're the last here—"

"The team?" she asked.

"You all passed," he said. "Even Taras. I don't know how you got her through it, but you did."

"She did," Esmay said. She felt distinctly odd, with the combination of stimulant and residual imagination, but managed not to throw up or fall down. Once in the transport, she tried to let herself relax, but she couldn't quite. It could still be a trick . . . it could still be . . .

She woke briefly back at the base, when the medics were easing her into the regen tank; one glimpse of her hands was enough. She didn't fight the sedative they gave her, but slid into unconsciousness.

By the time she got back to her quarters, she was more than ready for solitude and sleep. The pain was gone, and there were no visible bruises, but her body insisted that something traumatic had happened. The medics said she'd feel much better in the morning, that tank healing often left people feeling slightly disoriented and peculiar.

She had just decided not to bother with undressing, when her comunit chimed.

"The Commandant wishes to see you at your earliest convenience," the voice in her ear said. "He will expect you within ten minutes."

She tried to shake herself awake, staggered into the shower, and into a clean uniform. What could the Commandant possibly want? Some administrative matter, no doubt, but why the hurry?

CHAPTER FIVE

The Commandant did not look as if this were just an administrative matter. Esmay came to attention and waited. Finally he spoke.

"I understand you had an . . . er . . . disagreement with the Speaker's daughter, Brun Meager."

As if she didn't know who it was; as if she did not know with whom she had quarrelled. And could this be what it was about? A simple quarrel?

"Yes, sir."

"The . . . er . . . surveillance recordings indicate that you criticized Sera Meager on grounds of her moral failings . . ."

"Sir." Certain phrases came back to her memory for the first time in days, as if highlighted in flame.

"Do you really think that was appropriate professional demeanor, Lieutenant?"

"If you have the tapes, you know why I said what I said," Esmay said. She wished she'd been more tactful, but it was petty of Brun to have reported their argument.

"Let me put it another way, Lieutenant." The voice was a shade cooler; Esmay felt it on her skin, like a cold breeze stiffening the hairs of her arms. "Whatever the provocation, do you think it is appropriate for a Fleet officer to lecture a civilian—a prominent civilian—as if they were rival fishwives?" Before Esmay could think of anything to say, he went on. "Because, Lieutenant, I can tell you that I do *not* consider it appropriate. I consider it an embarrassment, and I am quite seriously disappointed in your performance. Allowances have been made for your background—"

Esmay stirred, but he held up a warning hand and went on.

"Your background, as I said, would be some excuse, if you were not from a prominent family on Altiplano, and if you had not previously commented on the greater formality of manners there. I hardly think you would have spoken to a civilian guest of your father's in such terms as you used to Sera Meager."

"No, sir." She wouldn't, because no young woman of family would have behaved like Brun Meager. She tried to think of an equivalent crime, and couldn't. But no use explaining . . . that never did any good.

"And then to make comments where someone in the media could hear you—!"

"Sir?" She had no idea what that was about.

"Don't tell me you don't know about that!" He glared at her.

"Sir, after the argument with Brun, I finished packing and then left on the field exercise. I didn't talk to anyone else about anything at all; I didn't talk to anyone about her during the exercise, and I just got back from medical . . . I'm sorry, sir, but I *don't* know what you're talking about."

He looked slightly taken aback, someone in a righteous rage who had stumbled over an inconvenient contrary fact.

"You spoke to no one?"

"No one, sir."

"Well, you must've been loud enough for someone to overhear, because it certainly made the news."

There would have been no media on a military installation on Altiplano. It wasn't fair to blame her because they'd let media follow Brun around and poke into every cranny.

"You of all people should know that Fleet is under great suspicion at this time—between the mutinies and the Lepescu affair—and the last thing we need is some wild-eyed young officer accusing the Speaker's daughter of immorality. That does us no good with the Grand Council, or for that matter with the populace at large. Do you understand?"

"Yes, sir."

"I wonder. You are an intelligent officer, and supposedly talented in tactics, but . . . in all my years, I don't think I've ever seen as egregious an example of bad judgement. You've embarrassed me, and you've embarrassed the Regular Space Service. If you didn't have such a good record previously, I would seriously consider having you up for conduct unbecoming an officer."

All she had done was tell a rich spoiled brat the plain truth . . . but clearly some unpleasant truths were not to be told. Brun was the one who had done wrong, and now *she* was in trouble. Her head was pounding again.

"Let me tell you what you're going to do, Lieutenant. You are going to avoid any interviews on any topic whatsoever. You are going to make no comments whatever about Sera Meager, to anyone. If asked, you will say you lost your temper—which clearly is the case—and you have no more to say. I would have you apologize to Sera Meager, except that she chose to leave this facility—and no wonder—and I doubt she wants to hear from you anyway. Is all that clear?"

"Yes, sir."

"Dismissed."

Esmay saluted and withdrew, angry with both herself and Brun. She shouldn't have said what she said—all right, she could admit she'd been too angry to think straight. But Brun had taken advantage of her, time and again—and to go complain to authority was . . . was another proof of her childishness.

She was supposed to meet Barin—he'd left word on her comunit—but she really wanted to crawl into her bunk and sleep another twelve hours. At least, she thought, he wouldn't waste their time talking about Brun.

Brun was the first topic he brought up. "You were pretty hard on her," Barin said, after mentioning that he'd seen the newsflash along with everyone else in the class. "She's not as bad as all that . . ."

"She is," Esmay said. It was too much; she was not going to let Brun get away with ruining this, too. She saw his face change, his expression harden against her. Sorrow cut through her, but her anger pushed her on, forcing her against the blade of his disapproval. "She had no right to come after you; if she had one scrap of morality—"

"That's not fair," Barin said. "She does. It's just that—that someone like that—"

"The richest girl in the Familias Regnant? The rules are different for the rich, is that what you're saying?"

"No—yes, but not the way you mean it." The slight emphasis he put on "you" stung; he had meant it to, Esmay was sure.

"The way I mean it is that people who have her advantages ought to have used them for something more than personal pleasure."

"Well, had you told her that we were . . . anything to each other?"

"No, I did not." Esmay could feel her own face getting stiff. "It was none of her business. It has nothing to do with me and you; it has to do with her assumption that anyone she wants should climb in bed with her . . ."

"Anyone!" Barin looked startled, then amused, then alarmed. "She didn't try to get you—?"

"No!" Esmay shook her head, which was beginning to throb in the old way. "She didn't, of course she didn't. It's just that she went after you, and you're an officer of Fleet, and younger than she is—" Too late she remembered that she herself could not be simultaneously older than Brun and co-equal with Barin. Her voice wavered; she gulped and went on. "It was—was—unseemly. Chasing junior officers."

"Esmay, please." Barin reached out but drew back his hand before touching her. "It was perfectly natural. And all she did was ask. When I said no, she didn't bother me. Perfectly polite, perfectly within the bounds of courtesy."

"You said no?" Esmay managed to get out around a dry lump in her throat.

"Of course I said no. What do you think?" His heavy Serrano brows drew together. "You thought I *slept* with her? How could you think that?" Now he was angry, black eyes flashing and a flush coming up in his face.

Esmay felt panic rising in her. He hadn't slept with Brun? Had Livadhi lied? Misunderstood? Not known? She could say nothing. Barin, glaring at her, nodded sharply as if her silence confirmed some dire suspicion.

"You thought I did. You thought just because I shared a few meals with her while you were busy, just because we talked, just because she's a rich girl, that I'd leap into her bed like a tame puppy. Well, I'm no one's pet, Esmay. Not hers, and not yours. If you really cared for me, you'd know that. I'm sorry you understand so little, but if you want to succeed in Fleet, you'd better get off your moral high horse and start dealing with reality."

He was gone before she could say anything, and long before anyone could have suspected what she had once worried they might suspect. She made it to her quarters at last, and spent another night not sleeping, staring at the ceiling over her bunk.

When they met in class the next day, Esmay could do nothing but stare miserably at the back of Barin's head. He did not turn to look at her. When called on, he gave his answers in his familiar crisp voice; she found that she could do the same, though she wasn't at all sure how her brain could keep working when her heart was lying in a sodden heap somewhere below her navel.

She had never been in love before. She had heard others describe similar symptoms, but had thought they exaggerated. They did not exaggerate, she decided; in fact, they had not begun to describe the misery she felt. They had all lived through it; she supposed she would too, but she wasn't sure she wanted to.

To her surprise, she received a high score on her field exercise. It did not make her feel better, though her subdued acceptance of the certificate seemed to please Lieutenant Commander Uhlis. She could feel the subtle withdrawal of her classmates, even those like Vericour who had been friendly all along.

Anonymity had been a lot easier than disgrace.

On the day Barin was due to leave, she made her way to the exit area; she felt she had to make some contact with him, or she might as well jump off a tower. Her hands were icy; she could feel her heart pounding as she spotted him across the room.

"Barin—"

"Lieutenant." He was coolly polite. She didn't want coolly polite.

"Barin, I'm sorry. I didn't mean to insult you." That came out in a rush, almost all one word.

"No apologies necessary," he said, almost formally. She thought she saw a bit of warmth in his eye, but nothing more. He wasn't going to reach out for her, not here in public, and he showed no signs of wanting a more private conversation.

"I just—don't want us to be enemies," Esmay said.

"Never!" He took a breath. "Never enemies, Lieutenant, even if we can't agree." A long pause, during which Esmay heard what he did not say aloud—or what she imagined he was saying. She didn't know which. "Goodbye, Lieutenant, and good luck on your first assignment in command track. You'll do fine."

"Thank you," Esmay said. "And good luck to you." Her throat closed on the rest of what she wanted to say: We could stay in touch. We could plan . . . No. She had ruined what they had, and that was it.

They shook hands, formally, and then saluted, formally, and then he moved over to the line forming for his shuttle. Esmay did not wait to see if he would turn around and wave. She was sure he wouldn't.

She had not been outside the gates of the facility before, but now she found herself wandering out to Q-town in the kind of numb misery she thought she'd never feel again. She didn't want to see anyone from her class in the mess hall, but she had to eat before leaving, or she'd throw up. Someone had said—who was it? She couldn't recall, someone on *Koskiusko*—that while she was on Copper Mountain, she'd have to visit Diamond Sims. She spotted the sign down the street, and made for it.

"Lieutenant Suiza!" The man in the hoverchair called to her almost as soon as she cleared the door. "I'm glad you came. I'm Sam—I run this place."

Someone was glad to see her? She glanced around, recognizing with a strange shock what this bar was about, and made her way toward the back.

"We're honored you came by," the man said. "Major Pitak said you might, if you had time."

"Sorry it took me so long," Esmay said. "I was doubling courses—"

"Yeah—we keep track of people at the school, so I knew you were busy. Didn't expect you before now, and didn't know if you'd have time. When's your shuttle?"

"About five hours." Esmay took the seat he indicated.

"You in trouble about that Meager woman?" he asked.

Brun again. Esmay managed a nod, and hoped that would indicate she didn't want to talk about it.

"It's partly my fault," the man said. "She came in here hopping mad that night, and shot off her mouth in front of the whole room. We think what happened is that one of the newsies on her tail got it with a spike-mike from out on the street. Least, nobody that was here will admit to telling it."

"It's—not worth worrying about," Esmay said. "It happened; I can't change it now."

"You sound like someone who needs a steak," the man said. He raised his hand, and a waitress appeared. He glanced at Esmay. "Steak all right? Onions?"

"No onions, thanks." Not with a shuttle liftoff. But she nodded to the rest of his suggestions, and soon the sizzling platter appeared.

When she had started eating, the man went on chatting. "She's a pretty thing, but stubborn as a stump. A good argument against letting civilians train at our facilities, no matter whose children they are. It does no good to mix with the Families. They employ us; they cannot *be* us."

For some reason—perhaps the energy imparted by the steak—Esmay was moved to argue. "She had a lot of talents we could use—"

"Oh, certainly, if she had any discipline at all . . ."

"She did pull off some good stuff I heard about," Esmay said. "Helping that old lady—she worked hard on that."

His eyes twinkled. "You'd make a silk purse out of any sow's ear, would you, Lieutenant? A good attitude for a young officer, but you'll find some of 'em smell of pig no matter what you do. So where are you going now?"

"I'm not sure," Esmay said. "They're supposed to have my assignment ready by the time I get to sector HQ. They may bury me in paperwork—"

"No, I don't think so," the man said. "Even if you're in trouble now, it will pass, and they're not going to waste a young officer with real combat ability."

"I hope not," Esmay said.

Junior Officer Assignment Section, Regular Space Service HQ

"We're going to have to find something else," the admiral said. "I know what we thought we were going to do with Lieutenant Suiza, but we certainly cannot reward her performance with a plum assignment."

"We needed her the way she was—" the commander said.

"The way we thought she was. Thank any deity you like that we brought her in for training before assigning her permanently to command track. Imagine the mess she could've caused as a cruiser captain, if all this had slid by."

"I still find it hard to understand. There was nothing—*nothing*—in her record to indicate that kind of character flaw, rather the opposite."

"There was nothing in her record to indicate her ability in combat until Xavier," the admiral said. "If she could hide that kind of talent, and she did, then this is no more difficult. And after all, she'd never been in contact with any of the Families before—Altiplano has no Seat in Council."

"There is that." The commander looked thoughtful. "I wish we knew whether there was anything more to it."

"More? Verbal assault on the Speaker's daughter isn't enough?"

"Well . . . is it just personal, or is it political? Is she the spearpoint for something?"

"I don't know, and at the moment I don't care. We've wasted entirely too much money and time on this young woman, and we're going to have to figure out a way to get repaid without risking the welfare of the Fleet." The admiral looked around the table. "Someone had better have an idea how."

Down at the far end, a lieutenant commander raised her hand. "Sir, she's elected to take both the basic level Search and Rescue as well as Escape and Evasion, right?"

"Yes . . ."

"SAR is chronically short of junior officers for both ship XOs and SAR team leaders, and those are command track billets. There are at least three openings for lieutenants in Sector VII alone."

The admiral thought a moment. "Relatively small ships, elite crew, operating independently for the most part—yes. She'd be under really close supervision; if she messes up, or tries to foment some kind of action, her captain would know for sure. Good. What have you got?"

"*Shrike*, I thought. Podaly Solis is commanding it, and his exec just applied for family leave."

"Mmm. I don't know about having her second in command . . ."

"My thought was, it puts her more directly under the captain's supervision than she would be as a team leader. And we have no doubts about Solis; he helped us clean out that mess at Sector HQ, as I'm sure the admiral recalls."

"Yes, that's true. Probably the best we can do. Blast the girl; why couldn't she have been as good as she seemed?"

Sector VII HQ, Aragon Station

Esmay arrived at *Shrike*'s dock area to find it in perfect order; the guard saluted crisply and checked her orders.

"I'll just let the captain know—we didn't expect you until early next shift."

"*Gossamer* came in early," Esmay said.

She wondered what her father would think now, both about her promotion and the trouble she was in. She was sure he'd followed her career as best he could from Altiplano; her promotions and awards were matters of public record, and the news media had covered the *Koskiusko* affair. Her thoughts drifted to her great-grandmother—so fragile, so embedded in her culture's past. What would she think? For an instant, she wished she could sit beside that low chair, and pour out the whole story. Surely her great-grandmother would understand about Barin; surely she would feel the same way about Brun.

Captain Solis greeted her with reserve; she did not know whether it was his habitual mood, or whether he had been informed of the trouble she was in.

"You're quite inexperienced to be taking over as number two," he said. "I understand you have a distinguished combat record, especially considering that you were not in command track at the time. But the executive officer of an SAR—that's asking rather a lot of you."

"I'll do my best, sir," Esmay said.

"I'm sure you will. Your experience on a DSR will be some use, and I see you stood well in your classes in both search and rescue and escape and evasion. Still, it will be a stretch, and you might as well be prepared." He gave her a long look. "Now, about this other problem—your quarrel with the Speaker's daughter." He shook his head. "If I'd been your CO, I'd have had you up for conduct unbecoming. He didn't, and so far you have no record here, but I warn you—I will not tolerate disrespect for the civil government of the Familias Regnant. Officers do not play politics. We serve; we do not interfere."

Esmay wanted to say that Brun was not her father, and had no official position of her own, but she knew she must not. Why did they keep thinking that her opinion of Brun's behavior had anything to do with her loyalty to the Fleet? "Yes, sir," she said.

"You will find no support for any Family games on my ship," he went on. "And no room for grand-standing, either. You do your job, and do it well, and you'll get the appropriate credit in your fitness reports. Nothing more, nothing less."

"Yes, sir."

"I'll expect you back here in two hours for a briefing. Dismissed."

It was cold comfort that her duffel was all in her compartment when she got there. At least her new position ensured a compartment, even on so small a ship. She glanced around. Bunk, storage lockers, desk, cube reader, and—to her surprise—a row of display screens above the desk. Esmay inserted her datawand into the slot, and these screens flashed to life. One displayed the orders of the day; another gave the status of the two SAR teams and their vehicles; yet another listed stores, crosslinked to consumption rates.

Esmay stowed her gear in the lockers—she had nothing to put in two of them—and changed into a clean uniform. She did not look forward to the next meeting with her captain.

He was, however, slightly more affable. "I hate losing Colin," he said. "But his wife was killed in a traffic accident while she was downside arranging for their children to change fosterage. It's going to take him quite a while to sort everything out . . . the kids have outgrown the grandparents, and the retired uncle who was going to take them was killed in the same accident." He shook his head, then smiled at Esmay. "You'll find we have good teams, Lieutenant. And a tour on an SAR is always interesting. We deal with problems that the big boys ignore—everything from private yachts stranded by jump-drive blowouts, to collisions. You will learn a lot. And since we didn't expect you until tomorrow, you're not on the watch list yet, which gives you time to poke around and start learning your job."

"All I've had was the basic SAR course, sir," Esmay said. "They assigned me before I had time for the advanced . . ."

"Better than nothing," he said. "And if you know you don't know, you'll ask questions instead of blundering around causing trouble. Now—the duties of exec on this ship are different than on line ships. That's because our mission is different. There's the basic stuff, of course—but I'd like you to look at this—" He handed over a data cube. "And of course you'll want to meet everyone—we'd planned a get-together this evening, at 1900—"

"That's fine, sir," Esmay said. "I can get unpacked, have a chance to look this over . . . unless you have something now."

"No, that's fine. We're not kicking out of here until day after tomorrow anyway. There's a meeting tomorrow, which you'll have to attend as my representative—you haven't been with the ship quite long enough to take over full prep."

Alone in her cabin—her name was already on the door, she noticed, with the permanent engraving EXECUTIVE OFFICER underneath—she inserted the cube the captain had given her into the reader. She knew what an exec did—or thought she did. Run the ship, basically, under the captain's command. But on a Search and Rescue ship, the exec also had the responsibility of supervising all rescue efforts, while the captain concentrated on ship security—of both this ship and the rescued one. She blinked at the listing for the security detachments—she had not realized that an SAR ship would carry marines, though it made sense. Most of the time when ships needed rescue, it was the result of some deliberate act, and the troublemakers might still be in the area.

And she'd had only the basic course . . . so it was definitely going to be a case of "sergeant, put up that flagpole" if they had a rescue call before she had learned the rest of the stuff she needed. Which meant she had better make friends with the sergeant equivalents.

She scrolled quickly through the headings of her job description to the ship's table of organization, and began to figure out who would do the actual work, while she "supervised." These were the key people she must have on her side. The words in the leadership manuals were fresh in her mind. The five rules of this; the seven principles of that. She reminded herself where the cube of those manuals was. She would review it as soon as she'd finished the captain's cube. She knew she could lead, when she let herself remember it.

Shrike mounted two complete rescue teams, cross-trained in both gravity-field and zero-gravity work. Like most of the smaller SARs, the gravity-field training specialized in low-pressure and vacuum work. Most of their calls would be to space stations or ships in deep space. A forensic team and a lab full of analytical gear suggested that SAR might include something more than accident assistance. And the medical support team was substantially larger than a ship this size normally carried, including both major trauma regen tanks and two surgical theaters, with all that implied. Again, it reminded her of a miniature of *Koskiusko*.

Rescue One was commanded by a lieutenant she remembered from the Academy as a clown of sorts, Tika Briados; he didn't seem clownish now, as he led her around the ready room with its racked suits and equipment. It all seemed a jumble to Esmay, though an orderly one—she recognized only about half the equipment and wondered how long it would take to learn the rest. Rescue Two's commander was a jig she'd never met before, Kim Arek; she was eager and energetic, busily explaining things that Esmay hoped she could remember. She kept nodding, and found herself liking Jig Arek for her single-minded enthusiasm.

Going through both rescue team areas had taken hours, she found when she finally got away from Arek, and she needed to get ready for the meeting with the other officers. She did hope they weren't all going to mention Brun Meager.

The wardroom was crowded when she got there. "Lieutenant Suiza—glad to meet you." The blocky major who thrust out his hand reminded her of Major Pitak. "I'm Gordon Bannon, pathology."

"Officers—" That was Captain Solis, who stood; the others quieted. "This is Lieutenant Esmay Suiza, our new executive officer. Some of you have heard of her—" There were murmurs that Esmay hoped referred to her earlier exploits. "She's fresh out of Copper Mountain, with the basic course in SAR, so

I'm sure you'll all cooperate in educating her into the real world." He sounded friendly enough; this was clearly an old joke, for their chuckle had no edge to it.

After that, the others came up one by one to introduce themselves. Esmay began to relax as she chatted with them; they were clearly more interested in how she might perform here than in anything which had happened in her past.

In the next few days, she threw herself into her work, loading her scheduler with everything she could think of, or that anyone suggested. When *Shrike* left the base, she was just beginning to think she had a handle on her assignments. *Shrike* would patrol alone through the sector, ready to assist in any emergency that fell within its mission statement. According to those who had been aboard longest, days might go by with nothing happening, or disasters might overlap . . . there was no way to predict.

"The ship's a part-container, part-bulk hauler that lost power on insertion . . . the insystem drive's functioning at maybe twenty percent. They say it's fluctuating, and they can't make orbit. We've advised them that there's a registered salvage company in this system; the captain sounds unhappy with that. Says he's had trouble before with salvage companies."

The first emergency since she'd come aboard. Esmay listened to the précis of the problem, and tried to remember which protocol this fell under.

"He wants Fleet assistance." Captain Solis looked at Esmay. "We have a responsibility in such cases, but we must also consider our responsibility to the whole area. So I want an estimate on the time it will take us to skip-jump over there, rig grapples, and put him in tow, then sling him back toward the orbit he wants. He's not an emergency."

"Sir." Esmay ran the numbers quickly. "Sixty hours,

allowing a safety margin for rigging the grapples; he should have standard tug connections, but just in case."

"Well, then . . . let's go catch us a freighter."

Esmay watched the approach plots carefully on the bridge displays. External vid showed a bulbous, almost spherical ship with rings of colored light indicating tug grapple connections.

"Ugly, isn't it?" asked Lieutenant Briados. The Rescue One commander was on the bridge to watch the approach. "You'd think they could design big freighters with some character, but they all look pretty much alike."

"It would hold a lot of soldiers," Esmay said, the first thing that came into her mind.

Briados laughed. "I can tell you're off a warship. Yeah, it could, but it hasn't got insystem maneuverability worth spit. Even with the insystem drive working."

"How do they even know where to mount the drives? What's the drive axis?"

"Well, they want low-speed maneuverability near stations, so they mount two, usually, out near the hull and separated by sixty degrees; the drive axis is the chord perpendicular to the chord between the drives, in the same plane." It took Esmay a moment to work that one out, but she nodded finally.

Captain Solis turned to her. "All right, Suiza—let's see how you handle this. Just pretend you've been doing it for years."

Her stomach churned. She nodded to the com watch, and picked up the headset to talk to the freighter captain, explaining that a team would be boarding.

"We just wanted a tow," the captain said. "I don't see why you want to board."

"It's R.S.S. policy to board all vessels seeking assistance," Esmay said, repeating what Captain Solis had told her. "Just a routine, sir."

"Damned nuisance," the captain said.

"Think of it as practice," Esmay said. "If we didn't practice close-hauling and boarding, we might not be quick enough for someone with a serious emergency. After all, it might be your ship . . ."

"Oh, all right," he said. "Just as long as you're not planning to practice cutting holes in my hull."

Shrike deployed standard tug grapples, backed up by its military-grade tractor. In this instance, the grapples homed neatly on the freighter's signal, and locked on as *Shrike* maintained matching course and velocity. The tractor snugged the SAR ship closer still. Esmay gave the orders that sent Jig Arek and her team across a few hundred meters of vacuum to the other ship.

Rescue Two made its way in and out of all the holds, while *Shrike* boosted the freighter gently on its way, then returned before Solis ordered the grapples retracted.

"Captain—what were they looking for?" Esmay asked.

"Just practicing," Solis said.

She looked at him; finally he grinned at her.

"All right. You might as well know. Sector's concerned about possible shortages in the munitions inventory. We think some stuff's being diverted from Fleet to civilian use. So the admiral says to check every ship that asks us for a boost. It is good practice, including the use of the warhead detection equipment."

"What's missing?" asked Esmay.

Solis spread his hands. "I've been told I don't need to know, but since they specified the equipment we were to use looking for it, I'd say someone's misplaced some of the more effective nukes."

"Ouch."

"Exactly. If our stuff's being transshipped on civilian freighters, it could be going anywhere. To anyone.

Probably not the Benignity—they have their own munitions industry, and plenty in stock. But any of the lesser hostile powers, or domestic malcontents . . ."

"Or simply pirates," Esmay said.

"Yes. Anyone who wants a big bang."

CHAPTER SIX

Elias Madero, owned by the Boros Consortium, followed a five-angled route that had proved lucrative for decades. Olives and wine from Bezaire, jewels mined on Oddlink, livestock embryos from Gullam, commercial-grade organics from Podj, entertainment cubes from Corian, which had FTL traffic from deeper insystem, and the largest population in the area. She was a container hauler, picking up at each port the hold-shaped containers that had been filling since her last visit there. Her crew, most of them permanent, often had no idea what was in the containers. The captain did, presumably, and also the Boros agents at each port. But the containers had no accessible hatches—one advantage of container ships was supposed to be the impossibility of petty pilfering by crews—so they had no idea that the container in Hold 5 which was supposed to be filled with 5832 cube players was actually full of arms stolen from a Fleet stockpile. The other containers in Hold 5, which should have had entertainment cubes to be played in the cube players, contained more illicit weaponry, including thirty-four

Whitsoc 43b11 warheads, their controlling electronics, and the arming keys.

Boros' agent at Bezaire would not have been happy to find the contents of that container, since she had a contract to supply the cube players and the entertainment cubes supposedly filling the rest of Hold 5.

Elias Madero came out of FTL flight, retranslating to normal space, to traverse the real-space distance between two jump points in the same system, colloquially known as Twobits. This shortcut had been marked "questionable" on standard charts for years, because the presence of two jump points in the same system was believed, on theoretical grounds, to lead to spatial instability of the jump points. If the insertion point shifted, an inbound ship might find itself emerging too close to a large mass, with no time to maneuver clear. But the nearest greenlined route meant three more jump point calculations, and added eleven days to the Corian-Bezaire passage. Since jump point temporal coordinates were fuzzy anyway, many commercial haulers used shortcuts to ensure that they met contractual delivery dates . . . while filing flight plans that were all greenlined.

This crew had made the traverse before, many times, without incident. The jump points had not shifted in the past fifty years, while the possibility that they might kept the system uncrowded.

On this trip, system insertion went as smoothly as usual, and the *Elias* transferred to insystem drive without a hitch.

"That's done, then," Captain Lund said to his navigator, clapping a hand on the man's shoulder. "Four days, and we'll be out of here again. I'm going to bed." Custom and regulation both required that a captain be on the bridge during jump point insertions; Lund had been up three shifts running because of a minor engineering problem.

His navigation officer, a transfer from *Sorias Madero*, a sister ship, nodded. "I have the course laid, sir. By my calculations, ninety-seven point two hours."

"Very good."

Captain Lund, balding and stocky, waited until he was in his cabin to take off his jacket and kick off his shoes. He hung the jacket up neatly, set his shoes side by side, laid his trousers, neatly folded, over the back of his chair, with his shirt over them. This was his last cycle . . . when he reached Corian again, he would retire at last. Helen . . . his grandchildren . . . the neat little house set high on a slope above the valley . . . he drifted into sleep, a smile on his face.

The sharp yelp of the emergency alarm woke him. He touched the comunit above his bunk.

"Captain here—what is it?"

"Raiders, sir."

He sat up, ducking automatically from the over-hanging cabinets. "I'm on my way."

Raiders? What kind of raiders would hang around a route where almost no ships went? No ships, really—he'd never found any indication that others used this two-jump transit.

Had they been tailed through FTL? He'd heard rumors that Fleet was developing some kind of scan that worked in FTL. The Benignity? Certainly not Aethar's World, and they were across Familias space anyway.

From the bridge, the situation was clear. Two of them, their weapons systems lighting up the scan board with red threats. On the com screen, a hard-faced man in a uniform he didn't recognize was speaking in accented Standard—an accent he hadn't heard before, with the words pulled out twice as long.

"You surrender your ship, and we'll let the crew off in your lifeboats—"

Captain Lund almost choked. What good would

lifeboats be, in a lifeless system that no one visited because of the paired jump points?

"Wheah's yoah captain? I wanna talk to him."

Lund stepped up to the comunit, and nodded to his exec, who stepped back.

"This is Captain Lund. Who are you and what do you think you're doing?"

"Takin' yoah ship, sir." The man favored him with a tight grin that did not look at all friendly. "In the name of sacred liberty, and the Nutex Militia. We apologize for any . . . ah . . . inconvenience."

"You're pirates!" Lund said. "You have no right—"

"Them's harsh words, sir. We don't like disrespect for our beliefs, sir. Let me put it this way—we have the weapons to blow your ship away, and we're offerin' you a chance to save your crews' lives. Some of 'em, anyway. If you surrender your ship, and allow us to board without resistance, we will swear not to kill any of your legal crew."

Lund felt that he had waked into a nightmare, and his mind refused to work at its normal speed. "Legal crew?"

"Waal . . . yes. We're aware, you see, that you work for a corporation with obscene and unnatural views about moral issues. In our books, there's things that just ain't natural and normal, let alone *right*, and if you have people like that on board, then they'll have to face justice."

Lund glanced around; the faces on the bridge were tense and pale. He thumbed the com control to prevent his words going out in transmission. "Do any of you have the slightest idea who these crazies are? Or what they mean about natural and unnatural?"

The junior scan tech, Innis Seqalin, nodded. "I've heard a little about the Nutex Militia . . . for one thing, they think it's wrong for women to be spacers, and for another, they don't tolerate anything but what they call normal sex."

Lund felt his stomach churn. If they didn't allow women in space, what kind of sex did they think was normal? And why not allow women in space? "Is it . . . something religious?"

"Yes, sir. At least, they say it is."

Lund felt even sicker. Religious nuts . . . he had gone to space to get away from them back on his home world. If these were the same sort . . . he had too many crew at risk.

"I'm warnin' ya," the pirate officer said. "Answer, or we'll blow your holds . . ."

"All right," Lund said, as much to gain time as anything. "I'll send my people to the lifeboats—"

"We'll see a crew list," the man said, smiling unpleasantly. "Right now, afore you can doctor it up. If a lifeboat separates before we've approved the list, we'll blow it."

Lund's mind raced into high gear. The crew list did not mention gender—and certainly not sexual preferences—so if he could just keep the medical records out of their hands . . .

"And the medical records," the man said, "in case you got some of them so-called modern women that don't have good women's names."

He could refuse, but then what? According to scan, he was facing weapons easily capable of blowing his ship. But they wouldn't want to blow his ship . . . they would want the cargo, and perhaps the ship itself, intact.

"Personnel and medical records aren't networked," he said, thanking whatever gods were around, including those he didn't believe in, for the fact that this was standard, and known to be standard.

"Ten minutes," the pirate said, and clicked off.

Ten minutes. What doctoring could he do in ten minutes? And why hadn't he denied the presence of women right away, so that he might have had a chance to pass them off as men? But the ship's tiny medical staff had been listening, and Hansen gave him a call.

"I'm changing the genders, and stripping out all reference to gender-specific medications . . . six minutes for that. What else do you think?"

"Seqalin says they have some weird beliefs about sexual practice—but I don't know which."

"Umm. If they go to space in single-gender ships, maybe they have obligatory homosexuality in space? I could code everyone as male/male preference."

"Yeah, but if we're wrong . . . I don't know."

"And what about the children?"

Elias Madero, like most commercial ships, carried some of its crews' children aboard. Children had been found well worth the extra work and worry, in terms of keeping a crew entertained and cooperative. Right now there were six, four under school age and two taking a work-study tour as junior apprentices.

"We put the kids in the core, where the scans are least likely to find them. Sedate the littles. If they just rob the ship and go on . . . the older ones can come back out and send a message. Got to clear out the nursery, though . . ."

"Do it," Lund said. "But don't code gender preference. Just leave it." How was he going to hide the women? And what would happen to them if they were found?

◇   ◇   ◇

Hazel Takeris, age sixteen, had found her first working trip to be as dull as her father had warned—but she wouldn't have missed it for anything, certainly not another five terms at the Space Dependents Middle School on Oddlink Main Station. So she had willingly performed the routine chores allotted to the apprentices, reminding herself—when enthusiasm for washing dishes or scrubbing the deck flagged—that she could have been listening to Professor Hallas discourse on the history of a planet that lay—to Hazel's mind—in the dim past of human history. A long way away, and very far back, and who really cared which millenium had produced which oddly named king or scientist.

When the alarm came, she was doing inventory of the galley stores, as ordered by the cook. She heard nothing of the ensuing discussion, because Cookie had told her to get back to work, and be sure her count was right. Thirty-eight three-kilo sacks of wheat flour. Six half-kilo boxes of sodium chloride salt, and four of a 50/50 mix of potassium and sodium chlorides. Eight—

"Haze—drop that and listen up." Cookie's face was an odd shade, the rich tan paled and splotchy. "Get four emergency ration kits, and go to Core 32. Hop it!"

"What—?" But apprentices didn't ask questions, not when a crew member looked like that. Hazel grabbed four emergency kits, and as she went past Cookie dumped two more on top of them. She scurried as fast as she could through the corridors, turned into the drop to the Core, and met her dad, who was even paler than Cookie.

"Haze—gimme two of those—now go to 32. We're going to lock you in. I put your suit in there already. Put it on, and wait. Be sure you wait long enough."

She had grown up a spacer's child; she could figure it out. "Raiders," she said, trying to keep her voice steady.

"Yeah. Go on, now. You and Stinky will be awake; we've sedated the littles, and they'll be in Core 57 and 62. Oh—and remember, it's the Nutex Militia."

Hazel fell down the drop, landing easily, feet first, on the pad. Thirty-two was clockwise four; she had known the geography of this ship from early childhood. Thirty-two's hatch was open; she slid in, dumped her rations, pulled the hatch shut, and locked it from inside. Her suit stood slumped in one corner, along with a stack of extra oxygen tanks. She got herself into it, her fingers shaking, fumbling at the catches and seals.

She started to report herself secure, on suit com, and then didn't—what if the raiders were already aboard? No one had told her when to expect boarding; no one had told her when to come out. Wait long enough? How long was that? How was she supposed to know?

In her suit, she could not quite lie down in the compartment, but she propped herself corner-to-corner, so that if she fell asleep, she would not fall and make a noise. She had the helmet open to ambient air—no sense in wasting suit air yet, and the helmet would snap shut automatically at any drop in pressure. She looked at her suit chrono, and marked the time. Wait long enough. She wished she knew how long.

She wished she and Stinky had been in the same compartment so they could talk. As the two apprentices, they had formed a natural alliance. Besides that, they liked each other's parents, and had spent the voyage trying to maneuver her father and his mother into some kind of arrangement. So far the adults had been resistant, but she and Stinky hadn't given up hope. Surely everyone felt the same urge to partner that she and Stinky felt . . . that's how adults came together to have children, after all.

Locked in the empty compartment, it finally occurred to Hazel that the straightforward solution would have been for her and Stinky to partner, and leave the parents alone . . . but she wasn't ready to partner anyone. Not yet. Later . . . she allowed herself a few delicious minutes of imagining what it would be like if Stinky were in the same compartment, without the pressure suits or the adult supervision. She had thoughts like that, even though she had chosen to take the treatment to delay puberty; she might look only ten or eleven, but she was sixteen for true.

She pulled her mind away from that to the littles, locked away in other compartments. Sedated, her dad had said. How long would the sedation last? Brandalyn was always first up in the morning, bouncing around . . . would she come out of sedation first? Had they put her in the same compartment as her sister? Surely they'd thought of that. Stassi was quieter, and very attached to her big sister. The other two littles, Paolo and Dris, were cousins.

She looked at the chrono. Only fifteen minutes had passed. That couldn't be long enough. The raiders might not have boarded yet. She might have to wait hours.

Her suit transmitted nonspecific vibrations that she could not identify—except that they were different from those she knew so well after all these months aboard. One hour, two, three. How long did raiders stay aboard a ship to plunder it? Docked at a regular cargo station, the automated handlers could unload a hold in seven hours and twelve minutes—if nothing went wrong. Would the raiders try to unload an entire hold? All the holds? Would they have the right equipment? How long would it take them?

It would be easier to steal the whole ship; she felt cold as she thought of it. If they did, if they took the entire ship . . . then what would happen to her? To Stinky? To the littles?

She heard noises—nearby noises. It must be the raiders, because no one had unlocked her compartment yet. Shuffling, thumping—then a shriek that stiffened her. Brandy, that would be; they had all joked that she had a scream that would slice steel plates. The child screamed again. Hazel clambered up, clumsy in the suit, and tried to unlock the hatch. She had to stop them—she had to protect the child. She had the lock undone when the hatch was yanked out of her grip, and two big men grabbed her, one for each arm, and pulled her out of the compartment. She could see Brandy kicking and screaming in the grip of another, who was trying to gag her with a length of cloth. Stassi was crying, more quietly, in the grip of another; the two little boys clung to Stinky, who looked as scared as she felt.

"A girl," one of the men said. "The perverts." Brandy's scream choked off; the man holding her had managed to tie the gag. "You take her," he said, shoving Brandy into Hazel's arms. "And bring her along."

She held Brandy to her, trying to comfort the child, who was sobbing into the gag. Stassi clung to one leg and Paolo to the other. Stinky carried Dris. The raiders pushed her along, back up toward the bridge.

The first thing she saw, coming into the bridge, was her dad's body in a pool of blood. She almost dropped Brandy, but the child clung to her, legs and arms fastened tight. There were other bodies, all people she knew—Baris the navigator, and Sig the cargo chief, and—and Stinky's mother, gagged and bound, but glaring furiously. All the women of the crew, she noted, were lying there in a row, bound and gagged. Captain Lund faced the bridge access, bound to his command seat. And all the armed men wearing the same uniform as the ones who had captured her.

The leader turned to Captain Lund. "You lied to us, captain. That wasn't very smart." He drawled the words out, an accent that Hazel had never heard before.

"I . . . wanted to save the children."

"God saves the children, by giving them to those who will bring them up in righteousness." The leader smiled, a smile that made Hazel feel cold inside.

Captain Lund looked at Hazel, then at Stinky. "I'm sorry," he said. The leader slammed his weapon into Captain Lund's head.

"You don't talk, old man. Nobody talks to our children but our family. And you're going to be really sorry that you lied . . ." He turned to his men. "Get goin' now . . . let's check these heathen sluts out, see if any of 'em's worth botherin' with."

Hazel lay in the compartment that had been the spare passenger cabin, trying to hug all the littles at once. Dris was still dozing, and she didn't know if that was the sedative or the lump on his head. Paolo whimpered softly; Stassi had her whole hand in her mouth, sucking furiously. Brandy was out cold, snoring through the gag. Hazel wanted to take it out, but she was afraid of the man with the weapon who stood by the hatch. She was afraid of everything. She had to pretend not to be, because the littles needed her; she was the one person they knew, the one person who could make them feel safe, if anything could after what they'd been through. How could you make someone feel safe if you didn't feel safe yourself?

She still could not believe it was all real. The soreness in her own body was real, and the hunger, and the fear, but—had she really seen all she remembered? The women who had been her aunts, her mentors, since her own mother died, all . . . she didn't even know the words for what had been done to them, except the killing at the end. And poor Captain Lund . . . she had known him since she could remember, a gentle man, a kind man . . . and they had stuffed his mouth with the tongues of the women, and then . . . and then shot him, at the last.

Paolo whimpered a bit louder; the man by the hatch growled. Hazel stroked the child's back. "Easy," she murmured. "Sshh." She wouldn't think about it any more; she would think only of the littles, who needed her.

*   *   *

"These are the rules," the raider said. Hazel sat on the deck, with Brandy in her lap and the others nestled against her. "Look at me," the raider said. Hazel had been looking at the littles, because she'd been slapped already for looking—staring, the man had said—at one of the raiders. Now she looked up, her shoulders hunching. "That's right," the man said. "You look when I tell you to, where I tell you to. Now listen. These are the rules. You don't look at our faces unless you're told to. You don't talk. You—girlie—you can whisper to the babies if you have to, but only if none of us's talkin'. You keep the babies clean and fed; you keep the compartment and all the rest clean; you do whatever you're told. No talkin', no arguin', nothin'. If you want to keep your tongue in your head."

The grown women hadn't believed that, at least not at first. And they had died. She had to keep her tongue, to comfort the littles.

"Now what do you say?" the man said, leaning close. She was too scared to answer; he'd just told her not to talk. He grabbed her hair and yanked her head back. Her eyes watered. "I'll tell you what you say, girlie. Nothing. You bow your head, when you're told what to do, and you say nothing. Women are not to speak before men. Women are to be obedient in silence. You understand?"

Trapped, terrified, she tried to nod against the pull of his hand on her hair. He let go suddenly, and her head bobbed forward.

"That's right," he said. "Bow your head in respect, in obedience." He straightened up and took a step backward; Hazel watched his boots. "Now you get busy, girlie, and get these brats cleaned up."

She needed clothes for them; she needed cleaning supplies. She wanted to ask . . . and she wasn't supposed to talk.

"One of us'll bring you what you need," he said.

"Food and water, as long as you're obedient. Decent clothes for the babies. There's nothin' on this heathen ship fit for you to wear; you'll have to make somethin'. We'll show you pictures. You've got the sink and toilet in there; you'll wash their clothes in that."

She wondered why, when the crew laundry would return the dirtiest clothes clean, dry, and unwrinkled, in only a few minutes. She didn't ask.

The supplies came a short time afterwards. Packets of food, powdered milk to mix with the water in the bathroom, sheets and towels and a sack of children's clothes, soap and shampoo, combs and brushes. Even a few toys: two dolls, blocks, a toy groundcar. Hazel was grateful. She handed each of the littles a sweet-bar, and rummaged through the sack of clothes . . . there was Paolo's tan jumpsuit, Brandy's striped shirt, Stassi's flowered one, Dris's gray jumpsuit. But none of the girls' jumpsuits, nor the shorts they wore with shirts.

The littles were so dirty—she couldn't tell which were smudges and which were bruises. As they finished their sweetbars, she herded them into the bathroom, and used the towels and soap to clean them up. Then she got them all dressed, as much as possible, and folded the rest of the clothes. Four more shirts, four more jumpsuits . . . three sets for each child, if only they'd been complete. And for herself . . . nothing but a long-sleeved pullover that was really Stinky's; it had been in her compartment because she'd traded shirts with him, this last segment. She didn't put it on because she had nothing to wear with it . . . the thought of wearing that on her top, and nothing below, was worse than nothing at all.

She stacked the clothes neatly in one corner, and put the food in another. She let the children sort through the toys. Brandy chose blocks, as always; Stassi hugged her doll to her chest, fiercely. Paolo began handing blocks to Brandy, while Dris put the other doll in the groundcar and rolled it along the floor.

The hatch slammed open, startling her; she almost looked up but remembered in time. The littles did look up, but quickly glanced away, toward her.

"Why aren't you dressed, girlie?"

She must not speak. She didn't know how to answer without speaking. She shook her head, spread her hands.

The boots moved closer, the big hands tossed aside the neat stack she'd made of the clothes, and came up with Stinky's pullover. The man threw it at her. "Put this on, girlie. Now."

She fumbled her way into it. "You wrap yourself in one of them sheets." She hadn't thought of that; she scrambled across the deck, grabbed a sheet, and wrapped it clumsily around her body. How could she make it stay? Something thumped on the deck in front of her—a small canvas bag. "That's a sewing kit—if you can't sew, better learn. Make yourself something decent from the sheets. Cover your arms, everything to the ankles. Don't make the skirt too full. Only decent married women wear full skirts. Make them girl babies skirts too; sew 'em to their shirts." He walked around, stood over the littles.

"What's this?" She didn't look up; didn't answer. "Now girlie, you got to teach these babies right. Girls play with girls; boys play with boys. Girls got dolls; boys got boys' toys. You keep 'em separate, you hear?"

But Brandy and Paolo were friends; they'd played together since infancy. And Brandy always played with blocks and building toys. Hazel crouched, scared and furious both, as the man knocked down Brandy's block tower, and moved her near her sister. "You—take this doll." Brandy took it, but Hazel could see the anger in her eyes, almost enough to overcome the fear. Paolo, left with the scattered blocks, had already picked one up and was reaching toward Brandy. "No!" the man said. "No blocks for girls. Blocks for boys." Paolo looked puzzled, but Brandy let out a furious screech. Casually, the man slapped her against the bulkhead. "Shut up—you better learn now, sissie."

The next days were, if possible, a worse nightmare. The littles could not understand any of the restrictions; Hazel struggled to keep them separated as the raiders demanded, to keep them engaged with "appropriate" toys, to keep the compartment clean enough, herself "decent," and still figure out how to make the garments the raiders demanded she furnish for herself and the girls. She had never sewn anything in her life; she had seen Donya using the sewing machine to create artworks they sold when they stopped at Corian, but clothes came from shops, or—in emergencies—the fabricator. You put in the measurements, dialled the style, and out came clothes. She had no idea how to turn flat cloth into the tubelike garment in the picture the raiders showed her.

It wasn't a practical garment anyway. Snug tubes for the arms, a long one covering her from armpits to ankles . . . no one could sit comfortably, walk comfortably, climb and play and do things in a shape like that. But she didn't argue. She struggled to figure out the odd implements in the sewing kit: dangerous thin sharp bits of metal that had no place around small children, reels of fine thread, scissors, a long tape marked off in sections that corresponded to no measuring system she knew, a short metal strip—also marked in sections—with a sliding part.

Sewing by hand was much harder than it looked, though when she figured out that the tiny cup-shaped thing would fit over her finger and protect it from pricks of the long sharp thing that the thread fit through, she got along better. The fabric seemed to have a mind of its own; it shifted around as she tried to poke through it. But finally she had a long straight skirt attached to the bottom of her pullover, and skirts on the girls' shirts. They hated them, and pulled them up around their waists to play . . . but that, it turned out, was something else forbidden to girls.

"You were reared among heathen," the man said. "We know that, and we make allowances for it. But you're among decent folk now, and you must learn to act like decent folk. It is forbidden for any female to show herself off to men; these girl babies must be decently covered at all times."

Then why, Hazel wanted to scream, won't you let us have underwear? Long pants? And how can you call a toddler playing on the floor a female showing herself off to men? She said nothing, but bobbed her head. She had to protect the littles, and she could do that only by being there—being able to sing them to sleep, to comfort them in a murmur that grew softer day by day.

She had no idea how much time had passed when the daily visitor first took the boys out of the compartment. By then, of course the raiders knew all the children's names. At first, Paolo and Dris hung back . . . but the man simply gathered them up and carried them out. Hazel was terrified—what would they do to the boys? But in the time it took to feed the girls their lunch, the boys were back, grinning from ear to ear. Each held a new toy—Paolo had a toy spaceship, and Dris had a set of brightly colored beads.

"We had fun," Dris said. Hazel shushed him, but Paolo spoke up.

"We can talk. They said so. Boys can talk all they want. It's only girls have to be quiet."

Brandy scowled. "Gimme!"

"No," Paolo said. "This is mine. Girls can't play with boys' toys." Brandy burst into tears.

After that, day by day, the boys were weaned away from the girls. Daily visits outside the compartment—

they returned with glowing reports: they could run up and down the corridors; they could use the swings in the gym; they could use the computer in the schoolroom. The men fed them special foods, treats. The men were teaching them. The men read to them from books, new books, stories about animals and boys and exciting stuff. They were gone hours a day now, returning to the compartment only for baths and bed. Hazel was left with the girls, the two dolls, and the endless sewing.

"You teach those girl babies to sew," Hazel was told. "They're old enough for that."

They didn't want to learn, but that made no difference. Hazel realized that. But . . . no books at all? No vid, no computers, no chance to run and play? She didn't ask. She didn't dare. She didn't even dare tell them stories, the stories they knew, because the compartment was rigged for scan. She had been warned to talk no more than necessary . . . telling them stories would, she knew without asking, be breaking the rules.

The days dragged by. Stassi, though younger, was better with needle and thread than Brandy. Her stitches were ragged and uneven, but she could get them lined up into a sort of row. Brandy, more active by nature, fretted and fumed; her thread kept getting into knots. Hazel tried to find ways to let the child work off her wild energy, but in that small space, and hampered by a long skirt, the child was constantly being frustrated. She cried often, and had screaming tantrums at least once a day.

Hazel would like to have had a screaming tantrum of her own, and only the littles' need for her kept her quiet.

CHAPTER SEVEN

Brun Meager exchanged the squad of Royal Security guards for ten of her father's personal militia from Sirialis with considerable relief. She had known some of these people for years, and although she would rather have travelled alone, this was the next best situation. With them, she visited the Allsystems Leasing office and chose a roomy private yacht for the next stage of her journey. If she was not going to have Fleet's respect anyway, there was no reason to endure discomfort. She chose the highest-priced food and entertainment package, and paid extra for an accelerated load-and-clearance that would get her on her way quickly. Allsystems checked her licenses, and those of the militia who would act as crew, and—in less than 24 hours—she had undocked and headed for her first destination. From now until the Opening Day of the hunt on Sirialis, she was free of schedules and demands, except those she chose for herself.

Since it was handy—relatively—she decided to check out her holdings within the Boros Consortium. It was something her father would approve of, the kind of grownup, mature behavior he claimed she didn't show often enough. And it was a long, long way from Castle Rock.

She spent two days with the accountants at Podj, feeling virtuous and hard-working as she waded through stacks of numbers, and then decided to skip Corian—where there would be more news media, since it was a shipping hub—and go straight to Bezaire. She plotted the course, calculated the times . . . and scowled at the figures. If she went to Bezaire by any of the standard greenlined routes, she wouldn't have time to visit Rotterdam before the start of the hunting season on Sirialis. But she was determined to visit Lady Cecelia and discuss with that other adventurous lady those things which she could not say to her parents. She could skip Bezaire—but she didn't want to skip Bezaire.

She looked at the navigation catalogs again. A caution route would save her five days, but that really wasn't enough. Maybe the Boros pilots that ran the circuit all the time knew of a shortcut . . . she called up their time-on-route stats. Supposedly they all took greenlined routes . . . but the on-time figures were improbably high for the Corian-Bezaire leg of the journey. They had a shortcut; she was sure of it. Now who might be willing to let her in on the secret?

For the rich and beautiful daughter of Lord Thornbuckle, a stockholder, the secret wasn't that hard to find. A double-jump-point system where the two jump points had been stable for over fifty years. Fleet had warnings about systems harboring two jump points, but Fleet had warnings about everything. Brun grinned to herself as she plotted a jump direct from Podj to the first of the double jumps. A nice slow-vee insertion in such a small-mass vessel, and she would be safe as safe—and have plenty of time to visit Lady Cecelia.

*   *   *

Jester slid through the first jump point, and scan cleared. Brun checked the references, and grinned. The second jump point was right where it was supposed to be . . . an easy transit. She was tempted to make a flat run for it—nothing else should be insystem—but checked for beacons anyway.

Four popped up on the screen. Four? She punched the readout, up came *Elias Madero*, which should have cleared the system three days before, and three ships with non-Familias registry.

"Jump us out now!" Barrican said. Brun glanced at him; he was staring at the scan monitor.

"They won't notice us for another few minutes," Brun said. "Whatever's going on, we can find out and—"

"We're scan-delayed too," he said. "They aren't where you see them, whoever they are. And it's trouble—"

"I can see it's trouble," Brun said. "But if we're going to get them help, we need to know what kind—who it is, what's going on."

"It won't help anyone if we're blown away," Calvaro said. He had come up behind her. "This thing can't fight, and we don't know what those are—they might outrun us."

"We're little," Brun said. "They'll never even notice. Flea on the elephant."

"Milady—"

That did it. Her father's men, protecting her father's daughter; they probably thought she would faint at the sight of blood. When would her father realize that she was grown, that she was capable . . .

"We're going to sneak in closer," she said. "And look. Just look. Then we can jump out and tell Fleet what's happened."

"That's foolish, milady," Calvaro said. "What if they—"

"If they're pirates, they'll think we're too small

to bother with." She pushed back memories of that lecture on recent incursions from outlying powers. These were not the Benignity—she had seen Benignity ships on scan. Nor the Bloodhorde, which was all the way across Familias space and probably still licking its wounds after the *Koskiusko* mess. These were common criminals, and common criminals were after the big, easy profit . . . not chasing a small yacht with a few insignificant passengers.

"If you would jump out now, we could be back in range of the Corian ansible in just a few hours—"

"And have nothing much to say. No, we need to record some data, at least the beacon IDs of those other ships—" She grinned at them, and saw the grin have its usual effects. Her father's employees had been putty in her hands since she had convinced the head cook to give her all the chocolate eclairs she could cram into her mouth. Nor had she been sick, which only proved that the stuffier grownups were entirely too cautious.

Sneaking nearer with the insystem drive just nudging them along was dead easy. Brun napped briefly, slightly worried that one of them might figure out the lockout code she'd put on the nav computer so that they couldn't go into jump while she was asleep. But they hadn't. They'd tried—she could see that in their expressions, a mix of guilty and disgruntled—but she'd used a trick she'd learned at Copper Mountain and it held.

Scan delay was down to one minute by then. One of the mystery ships was snugged up to the merchanter, and one was positioned a quarter second away. The third . . . her breath caught. The third had moved . . . on an intercept course.

It couldn't have seen *Jester*. The yacht was too small; they could have spotted the bobble near the jump point, but after that—after that she had laid in a straight course and they could have extrapolated.

She should have jinked about. In the back of her mind, a nagging voice told her that she should have done what Barrican said, and jumped out right away. The pirates could not possibly have caught her then. Now—if they had military-grade scans—she flicked off the lockout. She could jump from here; there were no large masses to worry about. She had no idea where they might come out, jumping this far from the mapped points, but it had to be better.

She set up the commands, and pushed the button. A red warning light came on, and a saccharine voice from the console said "There are no mapped jump points within critical; jump insertion refused. There are no mapped jump points . . ."

Brun felt the blood rush to her face as she slapped the jump master control the other way. A rented yacht, with standard nagivation software . . . she had not thought about that, about the failsafes it would have built in, which she would not have time to bypass. Of course Allsystems Leasing would protect their investment by limiting the mistakes lessees could make.

She looked at the insystem drive controls. The yacht's insystem drive, standard for this model, should be able to outrun anything but Fleet's fastest—but only if she could redline it. She noticed that the control panel stopped well below what she knew was its redline acceleration. Still, it was all she had.

"Milady—" Barrican said softly as she reached out.

"Yes—"

"They might not have seen us, even so. If you don't do anything, they might miss us still."

"And if they don't, we're easy meat," Brun said. "They've got the course; a preschooler could extrapolate our position."

"But if we seem to be unaware of them, they might still consider us unimportant. If you do anything, they'll have to assume you have noticed trouble."

What she had noticed was how stupid she'd been. Someday you'll get into something you can't handle by being bright and pretty and lucky, Sam had told her. She'd assumed someday was a long way away, and here it was.

"We have essentially no weapons," she said softly, though there was no need for quietness. "So our only hope of escape is to get within effective radius of that jump point—unless they do ignore us, and somehow I don't think they will."

On scan, the other ship's projected course curved to parallel theirs. Another of the smaller ships now moved—and moved in the blink-stop way of a warship that could microjump within a system.

"We can't outrun *that*," Brun said, under her breath. "Two of them . . ."

"Just go along as if we had no scans out at all," Barrican advised.

It was good advice. She knew it was good advice. But doing nothing wore on her in a way that action never did. Second by second, *Jester* slid along much more slowly than it had to; second by second the unknown ships closed in. What kind of scan did they have? Koutsoudas had been able to detect activity aboard other ships—could these? Would they believe that a little ship on a simple slow course from jump point to jump point would notice nothing?

Seconds became minutes, became an hour. She had shut down active scan long since; passive scan showed *Elias Madero* and the third unknown in the same relative location, with the other two flanking *Jester*. They were approaching the closest point to the merchanter on their projected course to the second jump point. If they got by, if they weren't stopped, would that mean they were in the clear?

There was no logical alternative. One could always choose certain death . . . but it was amazingly hard to do. So this was what Barin had faced . . . this was what the instructor had been talking about . . . Brun dragged her mind back to the present. The yacht had a self-destruct capability; she could blow it, and herself and her father's loyal men. Or she could force the raiders to blow their way in, and not wear a pressure suit—that would do it. But . . . she made herself look at the faces of the men who surrounded her, who were about to die for her, or with her.

"I was wrong," she said. "No comfort now, but— you were right, and I was wrong. I should have jumped right back out."

"No matter, milady," said Calvaro. "We'll do what we can."

Which was nothing. They could die defending her . . . or be killed without fighting; she did not believe the raiders would spare them.

"I think we should surrender," she said. "Perhaps—"

"Not an option, milady," Calvaro said. "That's not a choice you can make; we're sworn to your father to protect you. Go to your cabin, milady."

She didn't want to. She knew what was coming, and it was not death she feared, but having forced these men into a position where they had to die—would die—in a futile effort to protect her. *I'm not worth it*, she wanted to say . . . to admit . . . and she knew she must not say that. She must not take their honor from them. They thought her father was worth it, or—again Esmay's words rang in her head—they thought *they* were worth it. She said their names, to each of them: Giles Barrican, Hubert Calvaro, Savoy Ardenil, Basil and Seren Verenci, Kaspar and Klara Pronoth, Pirs Slavus, Netenya Biagrin, Charan Devois. She could find no words for them beyond naming them, recognizing their lives. She gave them all she had, a last smile, then went meekly to her cabin as they wished. It wouldn't work; she would die at the end, but . . . they would not have to see her dead or captive. They could die remembering that smile, for all the good it did . . . and she did not even know if they believed in an afterlife where such a memory might be comforting. She wrote their names, over and over, on many scraps of paper and tucked them in places she hoped the raiders would not find. They deserved more, but that was all she could do.

When the cabin hatch gave at last, she faced the intruders with her personal weapons, and the first one to try the opening fell twitching. But the small sphere they tossed in burst in a spray of needles . . . and she felt the fine stinging all up her body. Her hand relaxed, her sidearm fell, she felt her knees sagging, and the deck came up to meet her.

She woke with a feeling of choking, tried to cough loose the obstruction, and then realized it was a wad of cloth tied in her mouth. A gag, like something out of an ancient story. Ridiculous. She blinked, and glared up at the men standing over her. They were in p-suits, helmets dangling in back. Her body still felt heavy and limp, but she could just move her legs when she tried. Then they spoke to each other in an accent so heavy that she could hardly understand it, and reached for her. She tried to struggle, but the drug made it impossible. They dragged her upright, then out through the twisted hatch into the main passage of the yacht . . . over the bodies of her guardsmen . . . through the tube they'd rigged between the yacht and their ship, whatever it was.

They pushed her into a seat and strapped her in, then walked off. Brun wiggled as much as she could. Her arms, then her legs, began to itch, and then tingle. So . . . the drug was wearing off, but she didn't see how she could get away. Yet. *Your first duty is to stay alive.*

Several more men came through the tube . . . was that all? Or had some stayed aboard the yacht, and if so, why? She felt her ears throb as they shut the exterior lock, then the interior lock. They must have cast off the yacht . . . someone would find it. Someday. If another Boros ship came this way, if another Boros ship even noticed a minor bit of space debris . . .

The ship she was on shuddered uneasily—jump?—then steadied again. Three of the men were still back by the airlock. Now they went to work . . . Brun craned her head, trying to see. Her ears popped again. Something clanked; the ship made a noise like a tuning fork dragged on concrete, then stopped. The men moved on into the airlock, and—judging by the sounds—undogged the outer hatch. Colder air gushed in, chilling her ankles. She heard loud voices from the other—ship, it must be—and those men leaving.

The ones who'd originally brought her aboard reappeared, now in some sort of tan uniform instead of p-suits, unstrapped her, and hauled her upright. If she could break loose, while they thought she was still weakened—but three more appeared at the airlock. Too many, her mind decided, even as her body tried to twist. Too much drug, she realized, as her muscles refused to give her the speed she was used to. Well, if she couldn't fight, she could at least observe. Tan uniforms, snug-fitted shirts over slightly looser slacks, over boots. Brown leather boots, she noticed when she looked down. On the collar, insignia of a five-pointed star in a circle.

Once she was through the airlock, she saw the Boros Consortium logo on the bulkhead . . . so she must be on the *Elias Madero*. The men hustled her down the passage—wide enough for a small robot loader—past hatches with symbols and labels she felt she should recognize. Past a galley with its programmable food processor humming, past a gymnasium . . . to the bridge, which reminded her instantly of the bridge where she'd stood when she'd broken the second mate's nose . . .

But the man who stood in the center of the bridge was no merchant captain.

He had to be the commander. He wore the same uniform as the others, but the star-in-circle insignia on his collar was larger, and gold instead of silver. She met his gaze with all the defiance she could muster. He looked past her to her escort.

"Got the papers?" He had the same accent as the others.

"Yep." One of the other men came forward with her ID packet. "She's the one, all right. We checked the retinal scans and everything."

"You done good, boys." The commander glanced at her papers, then at her. "Not a single shred of decency, but what can you expect of that sort?" The other men chuckled. Brun struggled to spit out the gag; she knew exactly what she wanted to say to this . . . this person. The commander came closer. "You're that so-called Speaker's daughter. You're used to having your own way, just like your daddy. Well, all things come to an end." He waited a moment, then went on. "You probably think your daddy will get you out of this, like he's gotten you out of all your other scrapes. You may think he's going to send that *Regular Space Service*"—he made a mockery of Fleet with that tone—"to rescue you. But it ain't gonna happen that way. We don't want your daddy's money. We aren't scared of your daddy's power. They won't find you. No one's gonna find you. You're ours, now."

He grinned past her, and the other men chuckled.

"Your daddy and that Council of Families, they think they got a right to make the laws for everbody, but they don't. They think they got a right to set fees and taxes on everbody comes through their so-called territory, but they don't. Free men don't have to pay any mind to what perverts and women say. That's not the way God made the universe. We're free men, we are, and our laws come from the word of God as set forth by the prophets."

Brun wanted to scream at him: *They will destroy you,* but she could not make a sound. She thought it at him anyway: *You can't do this; you won't get away with it; they will come after me and blow you to bits.*

He reached out to her face, and when she turned away he grabbed her ears with both hands and forced her to face him. "Now your daddy may try—or maybe, because he'll know we've got you, he'll have the good sense to let us alone if he doesn't want to see his little girl in pieces. But he's not gonna get you back. No one is. Your life just changed forever. You're gonna obey, like the prophets said women should, and the sooner you start the easier it will be on you."

Never. She threw that at him with her eyes, with every fiber of her body. Maybe she couldn't do anything now, but now was not forever. She would get free, because she always did come out on top. She was lucky; she had abilities they didn't know about.

But the fear edged closer. Someday, Sam had said, Esmay had said, your luck will run out. Someday you'll be helpless. Someday you'll be stuck. And what will you do then?

The words she had thrown at them sounded thin now, faced with these men. But she had meant them. She would not give up; she would not give in. She was Charlotte Brunhilde . . . named for queens and warriors.

He moved his hands down the sides of her head to her neck. "You don't believe me yet. That's fine . . . doesn't matter." He slid his hands out her shoulders, then curled his fingers into the neck of her jumpsuit. Brun would have curled her lip if she could. Here it came, the predictable move of a storycube male captor. He was going to rip her clothes off. He would be surprised when he tried; she hadn't spent all that money for custom-tailored protective shipsuits for nothing. But he didn't try to rip the suit, just ran his fingers inside the neck, feeling the cloth. "We'll need the slicer, boys." Well, hackneyed, but smarter than dirt, maybe.

The knife the other man handed him was large enough to gut an elephant, Brun thought. He wanted her to be impressed with it—some men always thought bigger was better—but she had seen knives that big before.

"Now the first thing," the man said, sliding the tip of the long blade into the neck of her suit. "Women don't wear men's clothes." *Men's* clothes! How could anyone mistake a custom outfit designed for her body as a man's outfit? With those darts, it wouldn't have fitted any male she'd ever seen. But the man was still talking.

"Women who wear men's clothes are usurping men's authority. We don't put up with that." He made a single rapid slice downward, and the shipsuit opened from neck to crotch. He could just as well have pulled the tab, but he had to make a dramatic thing out of it, ruining an expensive shipsuit.

"Women are not allowed to wear trousers," he said. Brun blinked. What did pants have to do with it? Everyone wore pants if they were doing the kind of work in which pants were more comfortable. But this was probably just an excuse to cut her clothes off. He inserted the tip of the knife into the lower end of the opening, and sliced open the leg of the shipsuit . . . then the other leg. Brun stared ahead. They would want her to react; she wouldn't react. "Women are not allowed to wear men's shoes." At a nod from the commander, two men grabbed her legs and pulled off her boots. Stupid, stupid, stupid.

Custom-made boots, *her* boots, and she was a woman, and therefore those were women's boots, not men's boots. Then they dropped her legs; her bare feet thudded on the cold deck.

Next the commander gestured and someone behind her pulled the ripped sides of her shipsuit behind her. This she'd expected. Her chin lifted. *Take a good look. You'll pay for every leer.* But the commander's frown was not a leer. He was staring at her abdomen, at the Registered Embryo logo with its imprinted genetic data.

"Abomination . . ." breathed one of the other men. "A construct—" He pulled out his own big knife, but the commander's gesture stopped him, just as Brun was sure she would be gutted right there.

"It's true that none of the Faithful can tamper with God's plan for their children, but this woman is the result of tampering. What was done to her was not her responsibility." Brun relaxed muscles she didn't realize she'd tensed. The man leaned over, peering at the mark, then rubbed his finger over it. Brun thought of kneeing him in the face, but there were still too many of them . . . she would have to wait.

"I don't like it," one of the others said. "What perversions have they bred into her . . ."

"None that will survive our training," the commander said. "And she is strong, well-grown. By all reports, she carries genes for intelligence and good health. It would be a waste not to make use of them."

"But—"

"She will be no threat to us." He looked Brun full in the face. "You—you are thinking still that you will be rescued, that you can go back to your abominations and perversions. You do not yet believe that your old life is over. But you will soon. You have already spoken the last words you will ever speak."

What did that mean? Were they going to kill her after all? Brun stared back, defiant.

"You will be used as you deserve . . . and as a mute breeder, you will be no threat, no matter what."

Brun felt a shock as her mind caught up with that. Mute? What was he . . . were they going to cut out her tongue? Only barbarians did things like that . . .

He laughed then, at a change in expression she did not know she'd made. "I see you understand—that much, at least. You're not used to that—not being able to plead and beg and wheedle your way around your weakling father. Or the other men you've whored with. But that's over. The voice of the heathen will be heard no more; yea, the tongues of those who know not God will be silenced. And, as the holy words also say, Women shall keep silence before men, in respect and submission. You were born in sin and abomination, but you will live in the service of God Almighty. When it is time, when *we* choose, you will sleep, and when you awake, you'll have no voice."

Her body jerked, in spite of herself . . . she struggled, as she had not struggled before, knowing it was useless. The men laughed, loud confident laughter. Brun fought herself to stillness, hating the tears that stung her eyes, that ran down her face.

"We'll put you away now, to think about that. I want you to know ahead of time, to understand . . . for this is part of the training you will receive, to learn that you have no power, and no man will listen to you. You are silenced, slut, as women should be silent."

It could not be happening. Not to her, not to the daughter of the Speaker of the Grand Council. Not to a young woman who could rappel down cliffs, who had earned badges in marksmanship, who could ride to hounds, who had never done anything she didn't want to do, with anyone she wanted to do it with. Things like this happened, if they happened, in dull history books, in times long past, or places far away. Not to her. All this, she knew to her shame, was in her eyes, was in the tears, in the shaking of her body, and the men laughed to see it.

"Take her back—be sure you've cuffed her. Start an IV, too. Just saline, for now."

For now. For however long. She believed, suddenly. It was real, it was happening . . . no, it couldn't be! The men holding her moved her firmly along, her bare feet stumbling on all the rough places where her boots had protected her. She was cold, frozen with a fear she had never understood when she saw the storycubes or read the old books in her father's library.

In the compartment, four of them laid her on the bunk, ignoring her struggles, and cuffed her hands to the sides, her feet together. She tried to plead with her eyes: loosen the gag, just for a minute, please, *please*. They chuckled, confident and amused. Another one came, with a little kit, and turned her arm . . . inserting the IV needle deftly. She stared up at the bag of saline hanging from a hook overhead.

"When we're ready," one of them said, "we'll put you to sleep." He grinned. "Welcome to the real world."

She hated them; she writhed with fury. But it was too late for that.

She would go to sleep . . . it would be a dream, when she woke. A bad dream, a scary dream, and she would go tell Esmay about it and apologize for having laughed at Esmay. She would . . .

She woke to a sense of pain, and fought her way to consciousness. No gag in her mouth; she could breathe through it. Had they—? But she could feel her tongue, too large it seemed, scrubbing around in her mouth. So they hadn't. At least not yet. She swallowed. Her throat felt raw and scratchy. She looked around, cautiously. No one . . . she was still cuffed to the bunk, with the IV running in her arm, but no one was there. She took a breath of pure relief . . . ahhh.

And froze in horror. No sound. She tried again. And again. No sound but the rush of air in her throat, which hurt a lot now. She tried to whisper, at least, and realized that she could shape words, she could make hisses and clicks (though moving her tongue made the pain in her throat worse) but she could get no real volume out, hardly enough sound to carry across a small room.

Almost at once, the door slid aside, and the one who had inserted the IV came in.

"You need to drink," the man said. He held a straw to her mouth. "Swallow this."

It was cold, minty. She could swallow . . . but she could not say anything. Her throat hurt as the liquid went down, then eased.

"You've realized what we've done," he said. "Cut your vocal cords, some muscles. Left your tongue— you can eat normally, and swallow, and all the rest of it. But no speech. And no, it won't grow back. Not the way we do it."

It had to be a dream, but she had never felt a dream this real. The cold air on her skin, the ache from being bound in one position too long, the pain in her throat, and . . . and the silence when she tried to speak. She tried to whisper, to mouth words, but at that he put a hand on her mouth.

"Stop that. You don't talk to men, ever. Make faces at us, and you'll be punished."

It wasn't making faces, it was communication. How could he not know that?

"Nothing you have to say is important to us. Later, if you're obedient, you can lipspeak to other women, in the women's quarters. But not now, and never to men. Now—I'm going to examine you. Do as I say."

His examination was clinical and complete, but not brutal; he handled her body with the same smooth competence she had received from doctors in her father's clinics. He spoke the results aloud, for a recorder. Brun learned that she was now catalogued as Captive Female 4, slut, gene-altered, fertile. Her instant satisfaction at the error in that disappeared when he held up her fertility implant, and she realized they had removed it. Through the haze of drugs, she now felt the pain in her left leg, from the incision. She was fertile, then—or soon could be, if they also knew about fertility drugs. She thought they probably would.

When he was through, the man called others; they carried her from that compartment to another, somewhat larger, but empty of anything she could use as a weapon against them or herself. She was still cuffed, this time one arm to the corner of the bunk. Beside her the men left a soft tube of nutrient gel and a carisack of water. She had just dozed off when the commander appeared with the man who had waked her.

"How long?"

"Well, she'll be strong enough in another two or three days, but she won't ovulate for another twelve to fourteen. I gave her the shots, but it takes that long to cycle."

"We'll move her in with Girlie and the babies when she's strong enough. She can start sewing, though I doubt she knows any more about it than Girlie did." He stepped up to the bunk. "Now you know we spoke truth; living among liars as you did, you might have doubted us. Now your next lesson. You aren't who you were. No one will ever call you by that heathen name you used. Where you're going, no one will even know it. Right now you have no name at all. You're a slut, because you aren't a virgin or a wife. Sluts are any man's pleasure. When you've borne your third child, if anyone wants you and if you've been obedient, you'll be available for junior wife."

He left, taking the other man with him, before she even thought to curse him in whispers. Brun wanted to cry, but tears would not come. Instead, despair settled over her like a dark blanket, tucking itself around her mind until she could see nothing else. She struggled against it briefly, but it held her as firmly as the cuff on her arm, and she was so tired.

She slept again, and woke. Her throat hurt; she sucked at the nutrient tube, and the chill gel eased it again. The move to the other compartment had to be better, Brun thought. If she lay there alone she would go crazy. Another human—even women belonging to these men—had to be better.

❖   ❖   ❖

Hazel looked up from the littles only as far as the men's waists . . . she saw the woman's bare legs and almost forgot to keep her gaze down. They had told her about this woman, and Hazel's heart had ached for her . . . but it frightened her, because they had shown Hazel pictures of what they'd done to her, and threatened to do the same to Hazel and the littles if Hazel disobeyed. Now they pushed the woman down onto the pallet along the wall. Hazel pulled the littles back into the corner. The woman was pale, almost as white as milk, and dark bruises stood out on her skin. She had a rough red scar on her leg, and her face . . . Hazel didn't want to look at her face, but the burning blue eyes seemed to reach for hers and demand a response.

"Girlie, you take care of her. Feed her. Make sure she eats and drinks and goes to toilet. Keep her clean. But don't talk to her. Understand?"

Hazel bobbed her head. They'd told her and told her—if she talked to the woman they were bringing in, they'd do the same to her. And to both the littles. She couldn't let that happen.

"You teach her to sew, if she doesn't know how. Make her a decent dress. We'll bring more cloth."

Hazel bobbed her head again. The men left, leaving the strange woman alone. Hazel hitched herself across the deck, being careful not to uncover her legs, and retrieved the food sack. She held out a tube of paste concentrate. The woman put her hand in front of her mouth and turned away. Hazel went back to the littles, who were staring at the woman with wide eyes.

"Who she?" asked Brandy, barely breathing the words.

"Shhh," Hazel said.

"No clothes," breathed Stassi.

"Shh." She handed the littles their dolls, and started them on the dancing game she'd devised.

✧   ✧   ✧

Every word Brun had said to Esmay seemed etched on her skin in acid. Simply a matter of practice, she'd said. Just think of pistons and cylinders, she'd said. Easy . . .

In the silence, in her mind, she apologized again and again, screaming the words she could not say. How could she have been so wrong? So stupid? So arrogant? How could she have thought the universe was set up for her convenience?

Her body ached, raw and sore from waking to sleeping again. They had all used her, over and over, for days . . . how many days she didn't know. Through one cycle, at least, for she had bled heavily. They didn't touch her then, and would not even enter the compartment. Not until she was "clean" again . . . and then it started all over.

When her breasts swelled up, sore to the touch, she winced away from one of them. He stopped. "Slut . . ." he said warningly. Then he prodded her breasts, and moved away. She lay slack, uncaring. If it wasn't hurting right now, that was enough. Another one came . . . the one, she now recognized, who was some kind of medic. He felt her breasts, took her temperature, and sampled her blood. A few minutes later, he grinned.

"You're breeding. Good."

Good? That she was carrying the child of one of these disgusting monsters? He seemed to read her feelings in her face.

"You won't be able to do anything unnatural. If you try, we'll confine you alone. Understand?"

She glared at him, and he slapped her. "You're just pregnant, not injured. You will answer appropriately when I ask you a question. Understand?" Against her will, she nodded. "Get dressed now."

Under his gaze, she fumbled back into the ugly tubelike dress the girl had made for her and tied the tapes that held it closed. She threw the square of cloth that covered her arms around her shoulders. They hadn't figured out yet how to put sleeves in the dress.

"Come along," he said to her, and led her back to the compartment where the girl and the little ones waited. The girl looked at her, then looked away. Brun wasn't sure how old the girl was; she looked very young, perhaps eleven or twelve, but if she'd had an implant to retard puberty, she might be as old as eighteen. If only they could talk—even write notes back and forth . . . But there were no writing materials in the cabin, and the girl refused to talk, looking away when Brun tried to mouth words at her.

Day followed day, unbearable in their sameness. Brun watched the young girl try to quiet and entertain the two little ones, feed them, keep the compartment clean. She was always gentle with the younger girls, always busy in her care for them. The girl accepted Brun's help, but seemed afraid of her. When the girl held out food she had been ordered to give Brun, she looked down or away.

Brun had no way of telling time, except by her

body's growth. When she felt the first vague movement that could not be ignored, she burst into tears.
After a while, she felt someone patting her head
gently, and looked through tear-stuck lashes to see
one of the babies—the one the girl called Stassi. The
child put her head near Brun's.

"Don' cry," she said very softly. "Don' cry."

"Stassi, no!" That was the older girl, pulling the
child away. Brun felt as if she'd been stabbed in a
new way. Did the girl think she would hurt the child?
Was she to have no one to comfort her? She struggled
to hold back the sobs, but couldn't.

To get her mind off herself, she tried to pay more
attention to the others, especially the older girl. The
girl could not be one of them—not originally. She
sewed clumsily, with no real knowledge of how to fit
cloth to human shapes. When the men dropped off
garments to be mended, Brun could see that they had
been made originally with great skill . . . with hand
sewing, like the most expensive "folk" imports, the
stitches subtly imperfect. Surely a girl of their people
would know, by that age, how to do it right. She
glanced at the girl, whose brown hair hung down like
a curtain to either side of her face. She didn't even
know the girl's name . . . the men always called her
Girlie, and the little ones Baby.

If the girl weren't one of theirs, where had she
come from? No clues now . . . the pullover that
formed the top of her dress might have come from
anywhere, one of the millions sold in a midprice shop
at any spaceport. Spaceport? Had she been snatched
off a space station? Or a ship? By the color of her
skin and hair—by her features—she could have come
from any of a hundred planets, off any of a thousand
ships. And yet—she was herself, an individual, just
as Brun was. She had a past; she had hoped for a
future. Ordinary . . . but very real. Brun found herself

imagining a family for the girl, a home . . . wondering
if the little ones were her sisters or just other captured
children. How did the girl stand it?

Tears choked her again; she clenched her hands
to her swelling belly. The girl flashed her a quick look,
wary. Then, for the first time, she reached out a hand,
and patted Brun's. That did it. Brun cried harder,
rocking back and forth.

CHAPTER EIGHT

Some days after boosting the trader on its way, *Shrike* nosed into the spindown military docking collar at Overhold, the larger of the two orbital stations serving Bezaire, as gently as a spider landing on a tree. Esmay carried out the docking sequence under Solis's watchful eye; it was her first docking. Everything went smoothly; Solis nodded as the status lights flicked to green, and then spoke to the Stationmaster. "R.S.S. *Shrike* docked; permission to unseal?"

"Permission to unseal. All personnel leaving ship must be ID'd at the security desk opposite the docking bay."

"Understood, Stationmaster. We anticipate a brief visit, and no station liberty. My quartermaster will be coming out to arrange for some supplies."

"Right, *Shrike*. You do have a hardcopy packet in the tank."

"Thank you, sir." Solis grimaced as he flicked off the screen. "Idiot civilians . . . says that right out on the station com, where anyone with a halfway decent datasuck could get it." He turned to Esmay.

"Lieutenant, you'll take the bridge while I'm on station picking up our mail. I anticipate being gone less than an hour. If I'm delayed, I'll call you."

"Sir." Esmay toggled the internal com. "Security escort to the access for the captain, on the double."

"And . . . I think we'll do a practice scan, as well. Nobody's checked Overhold since Hearne was by, and there's no reason to trust her data. You can set that up while I'm gone."

Nothing showed up on the scan by the time Solis returned, and he sent Esmay off to other routine duties. Half a shift later, Chief Arbuthnot came back from the station in a state of annoyance and reported to the cook while Esmay was in the galley inspecting the sink traps.

"They don't have any Arpetan marmalade in, and we need it for the captain's birthday dinner. I always get it here; it's better quality than out of stores at HQ. They say they don't expect any until the Boros circuit ship comes in. You know how fond he is of Arpetan marmalade, especially the green gingered."

"Odd. Wasn't that ship supposed to be in already?" The cook glanced up at a schedule on the bulkhead. "We usually get here a week or so after her."

"Yes, but she's not. They don't sound very worried, though."

Esmay reported that conversation, minus the specifics of a treat for the captain's birthday, to Captain Solis.

"They don't seem concerned . . . interesting. I think perhaps we'll have a word with the Boros shipping agent here."

The Boros agent, a flat-faced woman of middle age, shrugged off Captain Solis's concern.

"You know yourself, Captain, that ships are not always on time. Captain Lund is getting on a bit— this was to be his last circuit—but we are confident in his honesty."

"It's not his honesty I'm questioning, but his luck. What was his percentage of late arrivals?"

"Lund? He's better than ninety-three percent on time, and in the last five years one hundred percent on time."

"Which you define as . . ."

"Within twenty-four hours, dock to dock."

"On all segments?"

"Well . . . let me check." The woman called up a file and peered at it. "Yes, sir. In fact, on the segment ending here, he's often twelve to twenty-four hours early."

"When would you have reported an overdue ship, if we hadn't asked?"

"Company policy is to wait three days . . . seventy-two hours . . . for any run, and add another day for each scheduled ten days. For *Elias Madero*, on this segment, that would come to ten days altogether. And from day before yesterday, when she was due, that's . . . seven days from now."

Captain Solis said nothing on the way back to the ship, but called Esmay into his office as soon as they arrived.

"You see the problem . . . scheduled transit time is seventy-two days, from Corian to Bezaire, dock to dock . . . most of that time spent on insystem drive. If you consider beacon-to-beacon time, she should have been off-scan only sixteen days."

"What's the scan data from Corian?"

"Normal exit from system. The approved course was like this—" Solis pointed it out on the charts. "That makes the scheduled transit fairly tight . . . if the company really schedules things that tight, then it makes sense to allow some overage. But I'd expect someone on this route to be over the alloted time at least thirty percent of the time. And the *Elias Madero* wasn't. Does that tell you anything?"

"They've been using a shortcut," Esmay said promptly. "They'd have to."

"Right. Now we have to figure out where."

"Someone at Boros should know," Esmay said.

"Yes—but if it's an illegal transit, unmapped or something, they may not want to tell us. Tell me, Lieutenant, who would you recommend for a little quiet questioning?"

The crew list ran through Esmay's mind, unmarked by any helpful notes on deviousness; she hadn't been with them long enough to find out. She fell back on tradition. "I would ask Chief Arbuthnot, sir."

"Good answer. Tell him we need someone who would be confused with a shady character, someone who can get answers out of a rock by persuasion."

Chief Arbuthnot knew exactly what Esmay wanted and promised to send "young Darin" out at once. The answer that finally came back several days later was expected, but not overly helpful.

"A double-jump system," Solis said, when he had taken the data and dismissed the pasty-faced Darin. "Hmm. Let's see if we can get confirmation out of someone at Boros. They probably ran into a shifting jump point."

"Why would someone retiring risk that?" Esmay wondered aloud.

"He probably thought it was stable. Some of those systems are stable for decades, but that doesn't mean they're safe."

Something tickled Esmay's mind. "If . . . they were carrying contraband . . . then the time gained in a shortcut would give them time to offload it. Or if someone knew they had contraband, it'd make a fine spot for an ambush."

"Well . . ." Solis raked a hand through his hair. "We'd better go take a look and see . . . I have to hope it's not a shifting jump point . . ."

By this time, the local Boros agent was quite

willing to list the *Elias Madero* as missing. Even so, it took Solis another two days to locate someone higher in the Boros administration who could confirm not only the existence, but the location of the shortcut.

"There's an off odor about this whole thing," he said to Esmay. "Normally I'd expect reluctance to admit to using a dangerous route, but there's something more. Or less . . . I'm not sure. Now—how would you plot a course to this place?"

It was not, Esmay discovered, a simple matter. The shortest route would have been to reverse what the trader's course would have been, but Fleet charts did not list any insertion data for the outbound jump point.

"Besides," Solis said, "if we go in that way, we'll cross any trail they made. We need to come in the way they did."

"But that'll take much longer."

Solis shrugged, a gesture which did nothing to mitigate the tension of his expression. "Whatever happened has already happened. My guess is that it happened days before we got to Bezaire. So what matters now is to find out what happened, in as much detail as possible. That means approaching the system with all due caution."

All due caution meant spending twenty-three days jumping from Bezaire to Podj to Corian, and from there to the shortcut jump points. Esmay set up each course segment, and each time Solis approved.

Shrike eased its way into the system with what Esmay hoped would be low relative velocity. So it proved . . . and as scan steadied, she could see that the system held no present traffic.

"But over here, Lieutenant, there's some kind of mess—I can't tell if it's distortion from interaction of the two jump points or leftover stuff from ships. If it's ships, it's more than one." The senior scan tech pointed to the display.

"Huh." Esmay looked at the scan herself; ripples and blurs obscured what should have been a steady starfield. "What's the range?"

"Impossible to say right now, Lieutenant. We don't know how large it is, so we can't get a range . . . but to me, the texture looks closer to this than the other jump point." The scan tech glanced at the captain.

"We'll continue on course for two hours, then see what parallax gives us," Solis said.

In two hours, the area of distorted scan was hardly larger.

"Well, Lieutenant," Solis said, "we can risk a micro-jump, run in a few light-seconds, and see what happens . . . or we can sneak up on it. What's your analysis of the relative risk?"

Esmay pointed to the scan display. "Sir . . . this knot in the grav readings ought to be the second jump point, and if it is, it hasn't shifted. Nor has this one. Which suggests that we're definitely looking at transit residue . . . and therefore, unless it's an entire Benignity battle fleet, it's not that big. So . . . it's close, but not within a light minute—we could jump in 15 second increments, and have a safe margin."

"If it's only transit residue, you're right. If it's also debris—it's been expanding from its source—and we don't know the location of its source—at some velocity we also don't know, for at least—I'd say thirty days. Worst-case: *Elias Madero* was carrying the missing weapons, and for some reason they all detonated . . . how much debris, in how big a volume, are we talking about?"

"I don't know, sir," Esmay said, feeding numbers into the calc subunit as fast as she could.

"Nor do I, and that's why we'll jump in *one* second bursts, with the main shields on full."

Solis brought *Shrike* toward the anomaly in repeated small jumps. At twenty-one light-seconds in, the scan was markedly different. Now they could see clearly that more than one ship had been involved.

"Let's just sit here and look at this," Solis said. On insystem drive, *Shrike* was hardly sitting still, but it would still take her hours to reach the distortion. "Do we have any indication at all of an original track?"

"Very attenuated, sir, but this might be the merchanter's original trace—" Scan switched filters and enhancement to pick out, in pale green, a faint, widened trail. "If we take the centerline of that, we get appearance at the incoming jump point, and progress consistent with an insystem drive of its class up to this point—" He pointed to the confusion of stronger traces. "But there's a more recent trace, much smaller."

"So . . . assume for the moment that we have found the merchanter's incoming trace, and it's a perfectly straightforward course toward the second jump point, just as they'd done before. There's no bobble indicating slowdown until the mess?"

"None, Captain, but the traces are so old I can't be sure."

"Right. But I'm assuming that for now. She comes in, she heads for her outbound jump, and . . . runs into a bunch of other ships. Trouble, no doubt. Do we have *any* older traces?"

"No, and from this angle it'd be hard to see 'em."

"Fine, we'll go up and take a look there." Solis put his finger on the chart. "A thirty-two-second jump to these coordinates. I want to be well outside the zone of distortion."

Scan blurred and steadied again. "Now," Solis said, "I want to find out where those other ships came from, and in what order."

Esmay found this tedious, but knew better than to say so. Surely the fastest way to find out what had happened to the *Elias Madero* would be to go in and look. The system was empty—what could be wrong with that?

The scan tech raised his hand. "Captain, the merchanter—or the ship that made the incoming trace—left by the second jump point."

"What!"

"Yes, sir. Look here. There's five outbound traces: three maybe patrol-size craft, one very small—my guess is it's whatever little ship overlay the merchanter's trace on the way in—and the big one, the merchanter itself."

"Then why hasn't it shown up?" Solis muttered.

"They . . . raiders don't steal entire ships, do they?" Esmay asked.

"Not . . . often. But . . . if she was carrying weapons . . . they might. Let's think this through. We have one large ship—we're assuming for now it was the Boros ship—coming in, running into something, and then leaving by the second jump point. One little ship, sometime later, following it in and out—"

"Excuse me, Captain, but the little ship's departure trace is the same age as the others. Within a few minutes, anyway."

"So . . . they had arranged a cleanup? Someone to follow behind and make sure the merchanter went through?" Solis shook his head. "But then we still don't know who the other three ships were. Which way they came in. Any other traces?"

More color shifts on the scan monitor, as the tech cycled through all the enhancement possibilities. Suddenly three pale blue tracks showed up, angling from the second jump point to make a wide circuit and end up positioned along the merchanter's track.

"There they are, sir. Came in by number two . . . and set up an ambush, looks like."

"So I see. Good job, Quin. Well, that seems clear enough. Someone knew the merchanter was coming, and wanted it; someone came in and set up either an ambush or a rendezvous." He grinned at Esmay. "Now, Lieutenant, we'll go in and see what evidence we can pick up."

The first evidence was a scatter of what was clearly debris.

"So the ship blew?" Esmay asked. "Or was blown?"

"No—not enough debris." The scan tech pointed out figures along the side of the screen. "I've been keeping track of the estimated total mass of all fragments, and it's less than would fit into one of the five cargo holds of the freighter we're hunting. Moreover, if it was from an explosion, it would be much more scattered by now. This was dumped from something with very low relative vee, perhaps given just a little push in addition. My guess is that someone captured it and took it." She reset one of the fine-grain scans. "Let's see if we can find any bodies."

Hour after hour, then day after day, the painstaking work went on. The SAR ship located and identified one piece of debris after another, all the while plotting location and vector on a 3-D display. Hundreds, thousands, of items . . . and then, the bodies they had known must be there, that they had both hoped and feared to find. They gathered the bodies into one of the vacuum bays, tagging them with numbers, the order in which they were retrieved. Men, women . . . the men in shipsuits, with their names stenciled on back and chest, as expected; the women . . .

"Their tongues have been cut out," the medic said. "And they're naked." Esmay could hear the strain in his voice. "I can't tell, out here, if it was done before or after death."

"I never heard of the Bloodhorde making it into this sector," someone said.

"This isn't Bloodhorde work . . . they mutilate

males as well, and this isn't their typical mutilation anyway."

Lieutenant Venoya Haral, Major Bannon's assistant, piled the items on the table. Bannon himself was in the morgue, working on the recovered bodies. "All these things were all marked and recorded in place," she said to Esmay. "Now we need to know what they tell us about the crew and the raiders."

"Didn't Boros give us a crew list?"

"Yes, but crew lists aren't always dead accurate. Someone gets sick or drunk and lays off for a circuit, or someone's kid comes along for the ride."

"Children?"

"Usually. Commercial haulers often have children aboard, especially those on stable runs like this. We haven't found any juvenile bodies yet—which doesn't mean anything either way. They're smaller, and less likely to be picked up. We're still missing five adult bodies, including the captain. Let's see." Haral started sorting items into classes. "ID cases . . . put those down at that end. Grooming items. Recording devices . . . a*ha*." She started to pick it up and shook her head. "No . . . do things in order. But I can hope that this recorded something useful."

"Here's a child's toy," Esmay said. It was a stuffed animal, in blue and orange, well chewed by some child. She didn't want to think about the fate of those children on the merchanter. She had to hope they were dead.

"Good. Stick it over there, and anything else that looks like it belongs with children. Where was it found?"

Esmay referred to her list. "In the back pocket of a man whose shipsuit read 'Jules Armitage.'"

"Probably picked it up off the deck where some youngster dropped it. How was he killed?"

Esmay looked back at the list. "Shot in the head. Record doesn't say with what."

"The major will figure that out. Oh, here's something—" Haral held up a handcomp. "We might get some useful data off that, if they used it for anything but figuring the odds on a horse race. Didn't you have background in scan?"

When they had catalogued the items, Haral began examining them. "You don't know how to do this yet," Haral said. "So I'll give you the easy stuff. See if any of those cubes have data on them. They're pretty tough, but the radiation may have fried 'em."

The first cube seemed to be a record of stores' usage by the crew over the past eight voyage segments; it listed purchases and inventory levels, all with dates. The second, also dated, was from environmental, a complete record of the environmental log covering thirty days six months before.

"One of a set," Haral said. "But it gives us some baseline to go on, if you find the one that should've been running when the ship was taken. It suggests they blew the ship, but there's not enough debris."

"It was found in . . . caught in the crevice of a lifeboat seat, the record says."

"Um. Someone tried to take the environmental log aboard a lifeboat, and the lifeboat was blown. That makes sense. They may have put all the logs aboard it."

"What would that be, on a merchanter?"

"Environmental log, automatic. Stores inventory. Captain's log—how the voyage was going, and so on, and might include the cargo data. Accounting, which would definitely include the cargo data, pay information. Crew list, medical—pretty sparse, on a vessel like this with a stable crew. Communications log, but some merchanters put that in the captain's log."

Esmay slotted the next cube into the reader. "This

looks like communications. And the date's recent . . . fits with the ship's last stop. *Elias Madero* to Corian Highside Stationmaster . . . to Traffic Control . . . undock and traffic transmissions and receptions."

"Good. Let me see." Haral came over and peered at the screen. "This is really good . . . we can match this against the records at Corian, and see if anyone tampered with the log. Wish they'd put it in full-record mode, but that does eat up cube capacity. Let's just see how far it goes . . ."

"Elias Madero—you get your captain to the com. You surrender your ship, and we'll let the crew off in your lifeboats." The voice coming out of the cube reader's speakers startled them both.

"What is *that*—" Haral leaned forward. "My God—someone had the sense to turn on full-record mode when the raiders challenged them. No vid yet, but—"

The screen flickered, changing from text to vid. A blurry image formed, of a stern man in tan—Esmay thought it might be a uniform, but she couldn't tell. Then it sharpened suddenly.

"Got the incoming patched directly to the cube recorder, instead of vidding the screen," Haral said. They had missed a few words; now another voice spoke.

"This is Captain Lund. Who are you and what do you think you're doing?" A shift in the picture, to show a stocky balding man who was recognizable from the crew list Boros had supplied. It was definitely Lund. The recording continued, including Lund's off-transmission commands to his crew.

Haral paused the playback, and sat back. "Well, now we know what happened to this ship . . . and we know they had kids, and hid them. Question is, did the raiders find them? Take them?"

"Must have," Esmay said, feeling sick at the thought. Four preschoolers, the age she had been when—she pushed that away but was aware of a deep

rage stirring to action. The person who had had the
sense to put this cube in the lifeboat—who had
thought to switch to full-mode recording—had also
quickly shot vid from the children's records. So they
knew the children's names, and had faces to go with
them. Two girls, sisters. Two boys, cousins.

"The vid quality is good enough that we should be
able to read the insignia on those uniforms, see if intel
has anything on them. Faces—we may have them in
the file somewhere. And that's the most audio we've
ever had from raiders. Interesting accent."

But all Esmay could think about was the children,
the helpless children. She turned the orange and blue
toy over and over in her hands.

One by one, the rescue crews located and retrieved
the bodies.

"We've got too many bodies," the team chief said.
"How many were on the merchanter's crew?"

"So some raiders died," Solis said. "I'm not
grieving."

"These men have been stripped—not like the
others. Would the raiders have stripped and dumped
their own dead?"

"Unlikely. Stripped, you say? Why these men?"

"Dunno, but there's no ID on them at all. We can
take tissue samples, but you know what that's like—"

"No fingerprints, retinals?"

"Nope. All burned. After death, the medic says;
they died of combat wounds."

Solis turned to Esmay. "Ideas, Lieutenant?"

"Unless we've stumbled into some local fighting
ground . . . no, sir."

"The merchanters look like ordinary spacers," the
medic said. "Light-boned, small body mass . . . merchanters nearly always run with low grav because it
feels good. Varying ages—the cook was two years older
than the captain, all the way down to the kid." The

scrawny teenager who'd been in a fight before he was shot. "But these others . . . they could be Fleet, except that they don't have Fleet IDs. Look at the muscular development—and their bone mass indicates regular hard exercise in a substantial field, at least standard G. Even though the raiders burned off the fingerprints, we can see enough callus structure on the hands that's consistent with weapons use . . ."

"Assuming it was the raiders, why wouldn't the raiders want them identified? If their primary target was the merchanter—which seems obvious—and they left the crew identifiable, what was it about these?"

"Don't know. Military, not Fleet . . . a Benignity spyship, maybe? A probe from the Guernesi? But— why would the raiders care if we knew that? Unless they're from the same source—but that would imply that these are *their* people, and we've already said they probably aren't. About all we can be sure of is that they weren't merchanter crew."

"We can't do a genetic scan?"

"Well, we could—if we had one of the big sequencers. The forensic pathology lab at Sector would have one, but that still doesn't tell you much. Maybe a rough guess at which dozen planets the person came from, but the amount of travel going on these days, it's less and less accurate. I'm running the simpler tissue scales here . . . but I don't expect anything to come up. If someone reports missing persons, and has their genome on file, that would do it."

"We're finding less each sweep," Solis said. "Time to move on. This jump point has how many mapped outlets?"

"Five, sir."

"All right. We'll hop to Bezaire, where the merchanter was headed, and report to Boros on what we found. I don't expect to find any trace there—we'd have noticed it when we were there before—so we'll have to let HQ decide if they want us to check each of the other known outlets or send someone else. Prepare a draft report for Sector HQ, and we'll pop that onto the Bezaire ansible when we get there. Include a recommendation to interdict this route, and a request for surveillance of all the outlets . . . not that it will do any good."

Shrike popped out in Bezaire's system, and Esmay oversaw the signal drop to Fleet Sector HQ. Scan reported no traces matching that of the *Elias Madero* . . . no other ship of that mass had been through in over a hundred days, according to the Stationmaster.

"I told you that before."

"Yes, but we have to check."

"The Boros Consortium local agent wants to talk to you."

"No doubt." Solis looked grim. "I want to talk to Boros, as well. We'll need a real-time link."

Bezaire Station, Boros Consortium Offices

"Not . . . *all* of them?" The Boros agent paled.

"I'm sorry," Solis said. "Apparently the ship was captured—there is evidence under imminent threat of heavy weapons—and although the crew had been promised safe exit in a lifeboat, they were instead killed."

"The . . . children?"

"We don't know. We found no children's bodies, and we know the crew had concealed them in one or more core compartments."

"But—but who—?"

"We don't know yet. We've sent the data we have back to headquarters; someone will figure it out, I'm sure. Now, about the deceased—"

The agent drew herself up. "You will of course

release the remains to Boros Consortium, for transmittal to the families—"

"I'm afraid we can't at this time. We have positively identified all adult crew personnel and one apprentice, but it's possible the bodies bear additional evidence of the perpetrators. We must continue to examine them."

"But—but that's outrageous."

"Ma'am, what was done to these people was outrageous. We must find out who did it, so that we don't have more of this—"

"What was done . . . what *was* done?"

"There was . . . mutilation, ma'am. And that's all I care to say until forensics is through with the remains. I can assure you that all due care will be taken to return remains to family members as soon as possible."

❖ ❖ ❖

When the crew remains and the other debris had been transferred to the courier that would take it to sector HQ, *Shrike* went back out on patrol.

"We don't try to pursue?"

"No. Not our job. We can't tangle with three armed ships, and we have no idea where, besides Bezaire, that jump point leads. Someone's going to have to explore it blind. The trail's cold, and growing colder. We did what we could—we have hull signatures on the raiders, or close to, we know what happened to the crew—"

"But not if there were weapons aboard—"

"No. But I'd say it was a fair bet that there were. We'll just have to keep eyes and ears open." He looked at her with what might almost be approval. "You're asking good questions, though, Lieutenant Suiza."

CHAPTER NINE

Barin returned the sentry's salute as he came to the access area for the *Gyrfalcon*. At last, he was going aboard a real warship, to a proper assignment. Not that he would have missed the time on *Koskuisko*, and meeting Esmay. He quickly turned his mind from that painful thought—meeting her was one thing, but their relationship now was something he could have missed quite happily. But this—since he'd been out of the Academy, this was his first regular assignment, and he was more than happy to get it.

As he expected, when he reported aboard he was called to the captain's cabin. Captain Escovar . . . he had looked Simon Escovar up in the Captains' Lists. Escovar was a commander, with combat experience at Patchcock, Dortmuth, and Alvara; he had, besides an impressive array of combat decorations, the discreet jewels that denoted top rank in academic courses ranging from his cadet days at the Academy to the Senior Command and Staff Course.

"Ensign Serrano," he said, in response to Barin's formal greeting. "Always glad to have a Serrano aboard." The twinkle in his gray eyes suggested that he meant it. "I served under your . . . uncle or great-uncle, I suppose. There are too many of you Serranos to keep straight." Barin had heard that before. And the Escovars, though an old Fleet family, had never had as many on active service at one time as the Serranos. "You've had an unusual set of assignments so far, I see. I hope you won't find us too mundane."

"By no means, sir," Barin said. "I'm delighted to be here."

"Good. We have only three other command-track ensigns at the moment, all with a half-standard year on this ship." Which meant they already knew things he would have to scramble to learn. "My exec is Lieutenant Commander Dockery. He has all your initial assignments."

Lieutenant Commander Dockery spent five minutes dissecting Barin's past career and preparation, pointed out that he was a half year behind his peers, and then sent him on to Master Chief Zuckerman to get his shiptags, data cubes, and other necessities. Barin came out of Dockery's office wondering if Zuckerman was another step on the "cut the ensigns down to size" production line.

Master Chief Zuckerman nodded when Barin introduced himself. "I served with Admiral Vida Serrano on the *Delphine*. And you're her grandson, I understand?" Zuckerman was a big man, heavily built, who looked about forty. Rejuv, of course; no one made master chief by forty.

"That's right, Chief."

"Well. How may I help you, sir?" A lifetime's experience with the breed told Barin that the twinkle in Zuckerman's eye was genuine . . . for whatever mysterious reasons senior enlisted sometimes decided to like young officers, Zuckerman had decided to like him.

"Commander Dockery told me to acquaint myself with the starboard watch orders—"

"Yes, sir. Right here." Zuckerman fumbled a cube out of a file. "This has your schematics, your billeting list, your duty stations. Now you can either view it here, or check it out; if you check it out, it's a level-two security incident, and I'll require your signature on the paperwork."

"I'd better check it out," Barin said. "I'm on duty four shifts from now, and I'm supposed to know it by then."

"You'll do fine, sir," Zuckerman said. He rummaged a bit in a drawer and came up with an array of papers. "Captain likes hardcopy on all checkouts of secured documents, so it really is paperwork."

Barin signed on the designated line, initialled in the spaces. "When do I have to have it back?"

"Fourteen hundred tomorrow, sir."

Barin smiled at him. "Thanks, Chief."

"Good to have you aboard, sir."

There were worse ways to start ship duty than by having a master chief for a friend; Barin went off to put his duffel in his quarters considerably cheered. He knew Zuckerman would be as critical—perhaps more critical—than another man; he knew he would have to live up to Zuckerman's standards. But if a master chief took a youngster under his wing, then only a fool would ignore the chance to learn and prosper. It was probably due to his Serrano inheritance—but that worked both ways, and it was pleasant to have it working his way for once.

Young officers in command track were expected to know everything moderately well; ensigns rotated through various systems and sections of the cruiser, learning by doing—or, as often, by making mistakes less critical at their level than later on. The other three ensigns aboard had all started at the bottom—

environmental—and completed their two-month rotation there, so Barin expected his first assignment: unaffectionately known as the "shit scrubber special."

"Your nose is unreliable," he was told by the environmental tech officer he reported to. "You think it stinks—and it does stink—but your nose gets used to it. Use your badges and readouts, and any time you're actually opening units, suit up. This stuff is deadly."

Barin wanted to ask why they weren't all dead then, but he knew better than to joke with someone like Jig Arendy. It was clear from her expression that she took sewage treatment very seriously, and—he suspected—spent every spare moment reading up on new technology.

She led him through the system he would help maintain, explaining every color-coded pipe, every label, every gauge and dial. Then she turned him over to Scrubber Team 3, and told him to do a practice inspection of the system from intake 14 to outputs 12 to 15. "And you can't use that old saw about flagpoles," she warned him. "This is my test team, and they'll do exactly what—and only what—you tell them."

Barin heaved an internal sigh, but started in. He remembered almost everything—he forgot to have them turn off the check-valve between primary feed and the intermediate scrubbers—and Arendy gave him a grudging thumbs-up. Then she spent ten minutes with the flow diagrams explaining exactly why that check-valve should be closed during routine inspections.

In a few days, Barin felt he was fitting in well. All four command-track ensigns bunked together; they were pleasant enough, and genuinely glad that someone else had the scrubber duty for the next two months. Meals in the junior wardroom enabled him to meet the other juniors—jigs and lieutenants—who were his immediate superiors. Jig Arendy, he discovered, could talk about something other than sewage; she turned out to be an avid follower of celebrity newsflashes. She and a handful of others discussed celebrities as if they were family members, endlessly poring over their clothes, their love affairs, their amusements. When she found he'd been at Copper Mountain with Brun Meager, she wanted to know all about it. Was she really as beautiful as her pictures? What kind of clothes did she wear? Had there been many newsflash shooters around?

Barin answered what he could, but luckily it did not occur to Arendy that he himself might have been a target of Brun's attention. When the wardroom discussions of Brun became uncomfortable, he took himself off. He would much rather listen to Zuckerman's tales of the old days in *Delphine*, with his grandmother. She'd never told him about the time a missile hung in the tube with a live warhead.

He mentioned that to Petty-light Harcourt, while they were replacing a section of feeder pipe.

"Zuckerman is . . . well, he's Zuckerman," the petty-light said.

Barin was surprised at the tone. P-lights knew more than he did, and he'd never met one who didn't admire a master chief. But Harcourt sounded unsure. He thought of asking more, but decided against it. Whatever it was, a mere ensign shouldn't be getting involved. If Harcourt had a serious problem, he also had the seniority to feel comfortable taking it to his own commander.

He had come to that decision when Harcourt sighed, an expressive sigh, and went on.

"It's like this, sir . . . Zuckerman's got a fine record, and I'm not saying anything against him. But he's . . . changed, in this last tour. He's not the man he was. We all know it, and we make allowances."

But allowance shouldn't have to be made, not for a master chief. Harcourt was still looking at him, and Barin realized he was expecting a comment.

"Family?" he murmured. It must've been the right thing to say, because Harcourt relaxed.

"I wouldn't bring this up with a junior officer, begging your pardon sir, but you *are* a Serrano, and . . . well . . . the chief's always talking about the time he served with a Serrano on *Delphine*. It's not anything we—I—can understand. It's not all the time. Just sometimes he's . . . it's like he forgets things. The kind of thing you just don't forget, not with his years. We—I—have to have someone check his pressure-suit settings, for instance. One emergency drill, he didn't even have his suit sealed."

He shouldn't be hearing this. Someone considerably senior should be hearing this. Because anything which could make a man like Chief Zuckerman forget to seal his suit was too much for an ensign to handle.

"I did say something to Major Surtsey," Harcourt went on. "He arranged to have the chief called in for a random health survey, but . . . that was one of his good days. And on his good days, he's sharper than I am. And then the major was reassigned, and I . . . I was just . . . I don't quite know how far to take this."

So the sticky problem had just been handed off to a very junior ensign. With the Serrano reputation. No good to tell Harcourt that he didn't feel comfortable with it either . . . the job description for ensigns did not include comfort.

"And you'd like me to take this on upstairs?" Barin asked.

"It's up to you, sir," Harcourt said. "Although . . . if I could make a suggestion . . ."

"Sure," said Barin. Having hooked the ensign, of course the petty-light could play him.

"Commander Dockery is . . . prefers to have . . . all the ducks in a row, sir, if you know what I mean."

"In other words, I should investigate this myself, and have some documentation?"

"Well . . . yes, sir."

He would have to have something, that was certain, something more than the word of a petty-light who might have some grievance Barin didn't know about. "I'll have a look," he said to Harcourt, who looked satisfied with that. He himself had no idea how to go about finding out if a senior NCO was going bonkers for some reason.

He remembered what Brun had said about that man at the Schools . . . what was his name? She'd claimed he was making too many mistakes, but that was right before she and Esmay had the big fight. Barin had no idea what had happened after that, if anyone else had confirmed Brun's suspicions. She was, after all, only a civilian, and she might not have told anyone else.

Still, he paid close attention to Zuckerman every time his own duties took him that way. The man seemed much like every other master chief he'd met, decades of experience providing him with a depth of knowledge and competence far beyond the ability of an ensign to assess. Zuckerman could be missing whole chunks, and he'd never know it. He liked Zuckerman, and Zuckerman seemed to like him; he felt that Zuckerman would have liked almost any Serrano. He hoped he wouldn't find anything to worry about; he worried that he might miss something important.

But most of the time he was too busy to worry, too busy to find time to visit Zuckerman. He had his own work, in an area remote from Zuckerman; he had watches to stand, inspections to take, duties that kept him busy. He had peers, the other ensigns in both command and technical tracks, whose personalities and relationships became ever more important as time went on. Jared and Leah were already engaged; Banet recorded a cube every other day for someone on *Greylag*. Micah had quarreled with Jared over plans for the ship's Commissioning Day festivities, and Leah had blown up at Micah in the junior wardroom in a way that reminded Barin painfully of Esmay.

He tried not to think of Esmay. As time wore on, he could not stay angry, but he remained confused. They had liked each other a lot, back on *Koskiusko*; they had shared secrets neither had told anyone else. He had expected her to welcome his presence at Copper Mountain—and granting that she had been extremely busy and tired, there was still something else different about her, a new reserve, a tension. And then there'd been Brun, always around when he wanted to talk to Esmay, always with time on her hands. Exuberant when Esmay was reserved. Jolly when Esmay was serious. Fun when Esmay was . . . he would not say dull, because to him she was never dull, but . . . busy, tired, not really present when she was sitting right beside him.

Perhaps she never had loved him. Perhaps it had worn off, and she was too kind to say so. That didn't make sense, though, if she was angry because she thought Brun had tolled him into her bed. He thought of sending mail . . . but after all, their quarrel wasn't *his* fault.

As he came to know the other junior officers better, he noticed that he kept running into one in particular: Casea Ferradi. He'd heard of Casea Ferradi back at the Academy, but she'd graduated before he started. He knew how rumors grow with time, and assumed that the stories of her beauty and her behavior were both inflated.

Barin first noticed Lieutenant Ferradi because of her hair—that uncommon golden blonde, like Brun's, but different. Brun's hair had a life of its own; it curled vigorously even when just groomed, and when she was upset or excited, and raked her fingers through the curls, it looked like an uncombed poodle. Lieutenant Ferradi's hair lay in a sleek wave beside her perfect cheekbones. Blondes were rare in Fleet. Perhaps that accounted for Lieutenant Ferradi's nickname, Goldie, which he heard in the junior wardroom the first night.

He noticed her next because she kept showing up where he was, and speaking to him. She was a jig on the watch rotation, so of course she would be where he was part of the time. But he began to realize that he saw her more than any other jig, even when she wasn't on shift watch.

He hadn't thought about her being in Esmay's class at the Academy until she brought it up.

"You know Lieutenant Suiza, don't you, Ensign?" That, while initialling the midwatch report.

"Yes, sir."

"I wonder if she's changed much," Ferradi said. "We were classmates, you know."

"No, sir, I didn't know that." He wondered if she might have some insight into Esmay's recent behavior, but felt reluctant to ask her.

"I mean," Ferradi went on, as she fiddled with the datawand, "she was such a stiff, formal person. Not really friendly. But from what everyone says, she's such a born leader—so I was wondering . . ."

Tiny alarm bells rang in his backbrain, but his forebrain was ahead of them. "She's fairly formal, yes . . . but I believe it has something to do with her background."

"Oh yes." Ferradi rolled her eyes. "Both of us were the colonial outcasts, you know. I'm Crescent Worlds—I think they expected me to insist on wearing one of those trailing silk things." Her hands fluttered and waved. Barin had no idea what she meant, and his expression must have showed it because she laughed. "Oh—I guess you haven't seen the bad storycubes about us. I think they got the costumes from back on

Old Earth, because of course no one actually wears them. Long flowing garments that cover young women from head to toe, but flutter fetchingly in the breeze."

Barin had no time to pick out what detail had set off the alarms again, because she'd gone on, her pleasant, slightly husky voice soft and amused.

"But Esmay—Lieutenant Suiza—she told me once her whole family was military. Very formal, very correct. Which is why I can understand her having a quarrel with the Speaker's daughter, but not how she could lead anyone anywhere."

Barin had his mouth open before caution stopped him; he had to say something. "I—didn't know the quarrel was common knowledge."

Ferradi laughed again. "I don't see how anyone could keep it quiet. It was on the newsflashes, after all. Screamed like a harpy, is what I heard, and told the Speaker's daughter she had no more morals than a tavern whore."

"It wasn't like that!" Barin said. He couldn't have said how it wasn't, since Esmay had been loud and insulting, but his instinct was to protect Esmay.

Ferradi looked at him with an indulgent smile that made him feel like a small child. "That's all right, Ensign; I'm not asking you to turn your back on a Fleet hero."

She made him feel uncomfortable. She was always looking at him . . . he would glance up and discover those clear violet eyes, and an amused quirk to her mouth. She seemed to impinge on his space in a way that Esmay never did. Brun, though she had been overtly interested in his body, had backed off without rancor when refused. But this . . .

He went into the gym convinced that whatever was going on was his fault. He had done something—what, he couldn't figure out—that aroused her interest. He climbed onto the exercise machine he'd reserved, and set the controls. Past the warmup phase, into the sweaty part of the workout, his mind drifted to Esmay. She was exec of a specialty ship now; he could imagine her in a rescue situation . . . she might do something spectacular, and get back in everyone's good graces.

"Hello, Ensign." The husky voice broke his concentration. There beside him, on the next machine, was Ferradi. Barin blinked, confused. She hadn't been signed up for that machine; he'd made sure of that. But now she was warming up, her body as sleek as her golden hair in a shiny exercise suit that outlined every curve. Barin, panting slightly, nodded a greeting.

"You're a hard worker," she said, starting her own machine. "I guess that goes with being a Serrano, eh?"

He had to say something; she was still looking at him and it would be rude to ignore her—possibly even insubordinate.

"It's . . . expected . . . sir," he said.

"No need for formality in the gym," she said. "I approve . . . of the attitude, and the results, Barin." Her look ranged over him, with particular attention he couldn't mistake.

Well, he would have to say something . . . but before he could, Major Oslon climbed onto the machine on Ferradi's other side.

"Hey, Casea . . . let Serrano finish his workout. He's too young for you anyway. I, on the other hand . . ."

She gave Barin a last lingering look before turning to Oslon. "Why, Major . . . you're incorrigible. Whatever makes you think I'm after Ensign Serrano?"

"Glad to know you're not. I must have been misled by the fit of that exercise suit."

"This old thing?" Barin had seen less obvious flirting from professionals at the trade, but Oslon didn't seem to mind. He and Casea bantered awhile, and when he invited her to a game of parpaun, she agreed—with a last lingering look at Barin that bothered him all over again.

A few days later, Barin was on his way through Troop Deck on a routine inspection of the traps in the heads—hairballs in the traps were a constant problem. A peculiar *crunch* caught his attention. He hesitated. Another, and then another. Which compartment was it in? He looked around, trying to locate the sound . . . slightly behind him, and to the right. A slither-and-bump, followed by the sounds of something heavy being dragged, came next, and pinpointed the source: D-82.

Barin looked in, to see Master Chief Zuckerman, face almost purple with rage and exertion, dragging someone by the heels.

"Chief—what's going on?"

"Outa my way!" Zuckerman said, breathing heavily. The Chief did not seem to recognize him; his eyes were dilated.

"Chief—" Barin could not see clearly past him, but the limpness of the legs Zuckerman held bothered him. He lifted his gaze a little . . . down the row of racks to one with a depression where someone had been sitting . . . a needler case on the pillow . . .

"Chief, put that down." Barin had no idea what had happened, but it was trouble all the same. He reached back for the alarm beside the hatch.

"Oh, no you don't, you *puppy!*" Zuckerman dropped the man's feet and charged. Barin ducked aside, and Zuckerman kept going, bouncing off the opposite bulkhead. By then Barin had slapped the alarm, cutting in local scan.

"Security, ASAP!" Barin said. "Man down, possible assault!"

Zuckerman turned, more slowly than he'd charged. "Not *possible*—the bastard attacked me. Me, a master chief with . . . with . . . twenty . . . twenty . . ." He shook his head. "He shouldn't have done that. Not right."

"Chief," Barin said, cautiously. "What happened?"

"None of your lip, boy," Zuckerman said. His eyes narrowed. "What the devil are you doing wearing officers' insignia? That's illegal. You want to get tossed out? You take those pings off your uniform this minute, Pivot."

"Master Chief Zuckerman," Barin said. "I asked you a question." For the first time in his life, he heard the Serrano bite in his own voice—the family pride that knew, bone-deep, what it was.

Zuckerman stared at him, his face blanking a moment. Then he looked confused. "Uh . . . Ensign . . . Serrano? What's . . . what's that you were asking me, sir?"

"Chief," Barin tried again, but cautiously. Where was Security? How long would it be? "I'm watch officer today. I heard something funny, and came to look. You were in 82, dragging someone, and there's a needler case on a rack." He paused. Zuckerman stepped forward, but Barin put up his hand. "No. Don't go in there. Security's on the way; I want nothing disturbed. Can you tell me what happened?"

"I—he—he was going to kill me." Zuckerman was sweating now, his face shiny with it. His hands opened and closed rhythmically. "He pulled a needler; he said he'd never be caught." He shook his head, then looked at Barin again. "Son of a bitch actually tried it—if I didn't have good reflexes, I'd be dead in there. So I—so I grabbed his hand, got the needler, and—and hit—" He turned pale and sagged against the bulkhead. "I hit him," he whispered. "I hit him . . . and then I hit him . . . and—"

"Chief. Stay where you are. Can you do that?"

Zuckerman nodded. "Yes, sir. But I—but I don't know—"

"Just *stay* there. I need to check the guy. What's his name?"

"Moredon. Corporal Moredon."

"All right. I'm going in; I want you to stay exactly where you are." Again, the Serrano tone—he could hear it himself; he could see its steadying effect on Zuckerman.

Moredon lay where Zuckerman had dropped him, unmoving. Barin stepped closer. Now he could see the bruises and blood on the man's head, and a long streak of blood on the deck where he'd been dragged. Was he breathing? Barin couldn't tell; he knelt beside the limp body. Yes. Through the open mouth he could just hear a low snore, and feel the moist breath against the back of his hand.

He stood up, and went back to the corridor. Zuckerman stood where he'd been told, and down the corridor came a Security team, with medical assist.

"Sir?" said the sergeant in charge of the Security team. His gaze flicked quickly from Barin to Zuckerman, down to Zuckerman's hands, back to his face, and Barin could see the puzzlement in his eyes.

"There's a man down in 82," Barin said crisply. "Head injuries, but he's breathing. You'll need to secure the area for forensic examination, and look for a loose needler."

"Yes, sir," the sergeant said. He waved the medical team forward, and gave the necessary orders to his team. Then he glanced at Barin again. "Did . . . uh . . . the man in there attack Chief Zuckerman, sir? Or you?"

"If you please, Sergeant, just see to it that the area is secured, and that the injured man is treated appropriately." Before the sergeant could comment, Barin turned to Zuckerman. "Chief, I need you to come with me to make a report. Can you do that?"

"Of course, sir." Zuckerman straightened up. "What's the problem?"

Barin wished he had an answer for that. "We'll let the Exec sort it out," he said. It occurred to him, as he led the way back up to command deck, that perhaps he should have brought along an escort. What if Zuckerman got violent again? Surely he wouldn't, but all the way up to command deck, his neck prickled at the thought of Zuckerman behind him.

He met Lieutenant Commander Dockery coming down the ladder from command deck, and came to attention.

"What is it, Ensign?"

"Sir, we have a real problem. Permission?"

"Go ahead . . . wait, who's that with you?"

"Chief Zuckerman, sir. There's been an incident—"

"I know you called for Security. At ease, both of you. Spit it out, then, Ensign."

Barin spit it out, aware all the time of Zuckerman—his age, his seniority, his record—standing there looking entirely too confused still.

Dockery glanced at Zuckerman. "Well, Chief?"

Zuckerman's voice trembled. "Commander, I . . . I don't quite know what happened . . ."

"Did this individual attack you?"

"I—I think so. Yes, sir, he did. It's—I can almost see it—"

Dockery gave Barin a look he could not interpret. "Did you . . . do anything with the Chief, Ensign?"

"No, sir."

"Was he sedated by security?"

"No, sir."

"You came up here with someone you're accusing of assault, without sedating him or putting him under guard?"

"Sir, he'd calmed down. He wasn't—"

Dockery touched one of the com panels on the bulkhead. "XO to med, stat response team to my location." He turned back to Barin. "Ensign, the Chief is clearly not himself. He needs medical evaluation prior to anything else."

"I feel fine, Commander," Zuckerman said. Indeed, he looked like the model of a master chief. "I'm sorry to have upset the ensign; I'm not sure why . . ."

"Just routine, Chief," Dockery said. "Just a checkup, make sure you aren't coming down with something."

A team of medics arrived, carrying crash kits. "Commander?"

"Chief Zuckerman's had a little spell of confusion this morning. Why don't you take him down to sickbay and check him out. He might need a little something to calm him."

"There's nothing wrong with me," Zuckerman protested. Barin noticed his neck flushing again. "I'm . . . sorry, Admiral!" He stared at Barin and saluted stiffly. Barin felt a coldness settle into his belly; he returned the salute, just to get Zuckerman to relax. "Whatever you say, Admiral," Zuckerman said, though no one had said anything in the surprise of seeing a master chief confuse a grass-green ensign with an admiral.

"Just a checkup," Barin said, afraid to let his gaze wander to see how Commander Dockery was taking this. Zuckerman was staring at him with an expression halfway between fear and awe. "It'll be fine, Chief," he said, putting what he could of the Serrano voice in it. Zuckerman relaxed again.

"By your leave, sir."

"Go along, then," Barin said. The medics led Zuckerman off, with the obvious care of professionals ready to leap to action.

"Well, Ensign," Commander Dockery said. "You've made a right mess of things, haven't you?"

Barin knew better than to protest that it wasn't his fault. "I know I did something wrong, Commander, but I'm not sure what I should have done."

"Come along, and I'll tell you as we go. Down on

Troop Deck, wasn't it?" Dockery strode off, leaving Barin to follow. Over his shoulder, he asked, "And just how much of Zuckerman's problem did you know about?"

"Me, sir? Not much . . . another NCO had said something, but he said it had been checked by another officer and nothing was found."

"Did you look for anything? Or did you just ignore it?"

"I looked, sir, but I didn't know what to look for. The times I talked to him, Chief Zuckerman seemed fine to me. Well, there was once . . . but it didn't seem that important."

"And you didn't see fit to pass on what this other NCO told you?"

Barin began to see the shape of his sin looming ahead. "Sir, I wanted to have something definite before bothering you."

Dockery grunted. "I'm just as unhappy to be bothered with trifles as anyone else, Ensign, but I'm even more unhappy to be bothered with a large problem that someone let get big because he didn't know what to do about it."

"I should have told you right away, sir."

"Yes. And if I'd chewed on you for bringing me vague unsubstantiated reports, well—that's what ensigns are for. To provide jaw exercise for grumpy executive officers. If you'd told me, or this other mysterious NCO had told me—and who was that, by the way?"

"Petty-light Harcourt, sir."

"I thought Harcourt had better sense. Who'd he tell before?"

"Uh . . . a Major Surtsey, who was transferred out. He said they'd done a med check, and found nothing."

"I remember . . . Pete told me about that before he left, but said he hadn't found anything definite. I said I'd keep an eye out . . . thinking my officers would have the good sense to pass on anything they heard . . ."

"Sorry, sir," Barin said.

"Well. All you youngsters make mistakes, but mistakes have consequences. In this case, if I'm not mistaken, the ruin of a good man's career."

They were on Troop Deck now, and Dockery led the way to the right passage and compartment as if he never needed to stop and think. Barin supposed he didn't.

The security team had cordoned off the passage, and as Dockery arrived so did a forensics team.

"Commander . . . all right to go on and start collecting evidence?"

"If it's been scanned. Come on, Ensign, I want to show you how to do this."

If Barin had not been so aware of his failings, it would have been a fascinating hour. But it was followed quickly by a less pleasant time in Dockery's office.

"Remember—the chewing out you get for bothering me with a nonproblem problem will never be as big as the one you get for not bothering me with a real problem."

"Yes, sir."

"Unless Zuckerman turns out to have an unsuspected medical problem—and anything big enough to excuse this would probably get him a medical out—he's in big trouble."

Something tickled a corner of Barin's mind. Medical problem? He cleared his throat. "Sir—?"

"Yes?"

"I—something I just remembered, sir, about another senior NCO back at Copper Mountain."

"Relevant to this?"

"It might be, sir. But it's not something I observed myself, it's just that when you said medical problem . . ."

"Go on, Ensign."

Barin related the story of the master chief whose crew was covering up for some strange memory lapses as succinctly as possible. "And, sir, back on *Koskiusko*, I remember being told that the master chief in inventory had had a breakdown after the battle . . . everyone was surprised, because he'd been in combat before, and he wasn't directly involved anyway."

"And . . . you're wondering what affected three master chiefs? Do you have any idea how many master chiefs there are in the whole Regular Space Service?"

"No, sir," Barin said miserably. So this one had been a stupid idea, too.

"Of course, by the time they're master chiefs, most of the problem cases have been eliminated," Dockery said. "But it is odd. I'll tell the medics and see if anyone has any ideas."

But his sins had earned him yet another chewing out, this time at the captain's hands.

"Ensign, Commander Dockery has had his chance at your backside—now it's my turn. But first, let's see if you understand what you did wrong—or rather, didn't do right."

"Yes, sir. I knew about a problem, and did not keep Commander Dockery or you advised."

"Because—?"

"Because I thought I should gather more data, keep a record of incidents, before bother—before telling anyone else."

"I see. Serrano, there are several possible motives for that action, and I want a straight answer out of you. Were you trying to protect Chief Zuckerman's reputation, or get yourself a bit of glory by bringing me a nice juicy bone?"

Barin hesitated before replying. "Sir, I think . . . I was confused at first. I was surprised when the other NCO told me about Zuckerman; my first thought was

that he had something personal against Zuckerman.
But when he said he'd reported it before and that
a major had taken it seriously . . . I thought it might
be a real problem. Except that medical hadn't found
anything. I didn't know why the NCO had confided
in me, in particular—it made me uncomfortable. So
I thought I'd keep an eye out, and document anything
I noticed—"

"And did you notice anything?"

"Not anything I could put a finger on, sir. There
was less respect for Chief Zuckerman than I would
expect to find among enlisted, but not enough to be
insubordination. I noticed that he was not interven-
ing in some situations where I'd have expected his
influence. But he'd made only two actual errors that
I'd documented—and even master chiefs are human.
I didn't want to go around asking questions—he
deserved better than that—"

"Wait there. You are telling me you made the
judgement—that you felt qualified to make the
judgement—that Zuckerman 'deserved better' than
your asking questions about him? Zuckerman liked
you, that much is clear. Were you swayed by his
favoritism to your family, or were you just out of your
depth completely?"

"Sir, I know now that I was out of my depth, but
I didn't recognize that at the time."

"I see. And you thought you'd keep a quiet eye
on him, document any problems, and bring your
report to—exactly whom did you expect to bring this
report to, assuming you came up with something?"

Under that cool gray gaze, Barin's mind kept trying
to blank out. But a lifetime's experience gave him the
right answer even in his panic. "To Chief Zuckerman's
commander in the chain, sir. Which would be Lieutenant Commander Orstein."

"That much is correct. And what did you expect
to happen when you presented such a report?"

"Sir, I thought Commander Orstein would review it, perhaps make his own investigation, and then take whatever action he felt necessary."

"And it would be out of your hands?"

"Yes, sir."

"And what did you think Orstein would do with you, the pup who dragged in this unsavory prize?"

"I . . . hadn't thought about that, sir."

"I find that hard to believe."

"Sir, no one could be happy to find a master chief losing his . . . losing effectiveness, sir. Master chiefs are . . . special." That wasn't the right word, but it was the only one he could think of.

"Yes, they are. So, if I read between the lines correctly, you figured Lieutenant Commander Orstein would chew you out and then—maybe—undertake his own investigation."

"Yes, sir."

"Tell me, Serrano, if you had found additional problems, are you certain you'd have risked that chewing out to report on Zuckerman?"

"Yes, sir!" Barin couldn't keep the surprise out of his voice.

"Well, that's something. Let me reiterate what I'm sure Dockery told you: it is annoying for a junior to show no initiative and bother a senior with minor problems, but it is dangerous and—in the long run— disloyal for a junior to conceal a serious problem from a senior. If you had reported this sooner, Chief Zuckerman's problems—whatever they are—could have been dealt with properly, in the chain of command, and I would not have been caught flat-footed and embarrassed. I presume you understand this, and I presume you won't do it again. If you do, the trouble you're in now will be as a spark compared to a nuclear explosion. Is that clear?"

"Yes, sir."

"Then get out of here and do better."

CHAPTER TEN

R.S.S. *Gyrfalcon*

Lieutenant Casea Ferradi knew she looked like a
recruiting poster. She intended to. Every hair on her
head lay exactly where it should, and under perfectly
arched brows her violet eyes sparkled with intelligence. Her features—strong cheekbones and clean-
cut jawline, short straight nose and firm but generous
lips—fit anyone's image of professional beauty.

It had been worth the risk of early biosculpt. All
she had ever wanted was to be a Fleet officer—no,
to be honest, a Fleet commander. She had first
imagined herself in command of a starship when only
a child, her parents had told her. Casea Ferradi was
born to be a hero, born to prove that a Crescent
Worlds woman could do anything.

Being a girl on the Crescent Worlds had been the
first handicap, and the second had been her face an
body—typical of her colony, but not like anythi
she'd seen in a Fleet uniform on the newsfeed
Delicate features, narrowing to a pointed chin, slo

183

wine-bottle shoulders, and generous hips—all prized in her culture—did not fit her dream.

Her parents had been shocked when she told them what she wanted—but at ten, even girls could speak to the sept as a whole, not just parents, about important decisions like marriage negotiations. She had taken her argument to the Aunts' Gossip, where her desire to go offworld was quickly approved—she was too intelligent by far to fare well in the local marriage market. Biosculpting, though—it wasn't until her father's mother approved that she knew she had a chance.

"They will not know she is from here, if she looks so different, so her unwomanly behavior will not disgrace us."

Three years of surgery—of the pain that strengthening her redesigned body caused her—and then she took the Fleet entrance exams, passed them, and left home forever.

Once at the Academy, Casea discovered that her new shape was not considered sexless and unfeminine by her peers. Her honey-blonde hair, falling sleekly to a razor-cut angle, was unique in her class. She had all the interest she could handle, and discovered that the behaviors she'd observed in her older sisters and cousins had quite an effect on the young men in her class.

Protected by the standard implant provided all Academy cadets, she moved from interest to experimentation, and from experimentation to enthusiastic activity. Lectures on the ethics of personal relationships rolled off her confidence without making any impact. If Fleet had been serious about it, she reasoned, the young men of renowned Fleet families wouldn't have been so eager to take her to bed, and the young women would not have received implants. And after all, the young men and women of the Chairholding Families made no secret of their sexual activity—Casea watched enough newsflash shorts to know that.

She was angered, rather than alarmed, to discover that some of her classmates were making snide remarks about her behavior.

"Casea—if it's alive, she'll take it to bed," one of the women drawled in the shower room one morning. That wasn't fair; she had no interest in the ugly or dull.

"She'll get herself in trouble someday," another one said, sounding worried.

"No—not the way she's going. Which of those guys is going to accuse her of seducing *him*?"

Others simply radiated quiet disapproval. Esmay Suiza, whom she had expected to be a natural ally—they were each the only cadet from their original worlds—turned out to be either a sanctimonious prig or a sexless lump. Casea wasn't sure which, but didn't care. After the first year, she gave up on Esmay: she hadn't the right qualities to be the plain friend of a popular beauty, and Casea could not tolerate the chilly, stiff earnestness of the girl.

But after graduation, she slowed down—sex itself was no longer as exciting—and began to consider her targets with more care. Her cultural background had taught her to look for more from a liaison than physical pleasure alone. Carefully, with an eye out for trouble, she explored the limits of Fleet's policy on what was delicately termed "personal relationships."

In her first assignment, she discovered that if she stayed away from men already considered "taken" by other women, she could hunt at will without arousing comment. So that had been it! She felt a happy glow of contempt for the idiot girls who hadn't simply told her which boys they fancied themselves. Testing this understanding, she turned her violet eyes on a lonely jig, who was quite happy to console himself with a lovely ensign.

But he wasn't enough. She wanted someone in command track. All the command track jigs aboard were paired already—she wrinkled her nose at the two who were wasted on each other, as she thought—and she was not attracted to the single male lieutenant. A major? Could she? She did not doubt her ability to get his interest, but—regulations were supposed to prevent him from dallying with junior officers in his chain of command.

Regulations, as everyone knew, could be bent into pretzels by those with the wit to do so. Still it might be better to look elsewhere . . . which led her to a major in another branch of technical track. It never hurt to have a friend in communications. On her next assignment, he was followed by a lieutenant in command track, and then—with some difficulty in detaching from the lieutenant—by another major. She learned something from each about the extent of her talent, and what advantages could come from such close associations.

Now, though, she was through with casual liaisons. She had found the right man. Against all expectations—she was sure that her grandmothers and aunts would be amazed—she had found a respectable, intelligent, charming young man whom even her father would consider eligible. That he was an ensign, and she a lieutenant, two ranks higher, meant nothing to her. He was mature for his age, and best of all . . . he was a Serrano. Family is everything, she had heard all her life. The one-eyed son of a chief is better than a robber's by-blow. And better family than Serrano— grandson of an admiral, with other admirals in the family tree—she could not hope to find.

The only snag was that rumor said he was, or had been, interested in Esmay Suiza. Casea discounted that. Esmay had been a nonentity, even aside from being a prig. Not pretty, with a haphazard set of features topped with fluffy, flyaway hair of nondescript brown. The boy had hero worship, that's all it was. Suiza had turned out to be a hero of sorts, but nothing could make her beautiful or charming. And now, if rumor were true, she was in trouble for being untactful—Casea could believe *that*, no question. If she ever had a lover, which didn't seem likely, it would be someone as unspectacular as herself, another nonentity, probably just as tactless and doomed to as inglorious a career.

Still, Esmay's present disgrace would make it easier for Casea to pursue Barin Serrano unhindered. And surely that Serrano grandmother wouldn't want him connected to someone like the bad Lieutenant Suiza. It would take very little, Casea thought, to make absolutely sure that no one ever admired Lieutenant Suiza again.

Elias Madero

It was getting harder to get up off the floor to use the toilet; Brun realized that in addition to the pregnancy she was getting weaker because she didn't exercise much. How could she? The compartment would have been small for one person; with an adult woman, a girl, and two small children, it was impossibly crowded. And at any time, one of the men might look in; she could imagine how they would react if they caught her doing real exercises. She tried to make herself pace back and forth, but she quickly ran out of breath, and leaned on the bulkhead panting. The girl watched her with a worried frown, but looked away when Brun tried to smile at her. As Brun had shared more of the work, the girl had accepted that help, but always with reserve.

That night when the lights dimmed, signalling a sleep period, the girl slept at her back, curled around her. Brun woke to a breath of air in her ear. She started to lift her head, and felt a gentle push downward. The girl?

"*Elias Madero*," came the words. "Merchanter."

Brun squirmed as if trying to find a comfortable position. Merchanter . . . the merchanter ship. This girl must be off that ship. Excitement coursed through her . . . she knew *something* now.

"'M Hazel," the girl breathed. Then she too squirmed, as if moving in her sleep, and rolled away.

The rush of joy from those five words burst through her. This must have been how Lady Cecelia felt, when she first made contact with the world again.

A wave of shame followed. Lady Cecelia had been locked in paralysis and apparent coma for months . . . and months more of painful rehab . . . and she had been old. Brun was young, healthy . . . *I am not defeated. I am only . . . detained on the way to victory.* So she might bear children for these animals . . . so she might be a prisoner for months, for years . . . but in the end, she was who she was, and that would not change.

She rolled over with difficulty, and looked through narrowed lids at the girl . . . at Hazel. She had been impressed before at the girl's patience, her consistent gentleness with the little girls, her endless invention of quiet little games and activities to amuse them. But she had given up hoping for any real contact, after the first long stretch of days . . . the girl was too scared. Now she appreciated the courage of this thin, over-worked, terrified girl . . . still a child herself . . . who cared for two younger children and Brun. Who dared, in the face of threats, to say a few words of comfort. She had lost everything too—parents, most likely. Were these children even her sisters? Maybe not, but no one could have done more for them.

She pushed herself up to use the toilet; on the way back she noticed that Hazel had rolled over again, as if offering Brun a niche convenient to her ear. Brun lay down, grunting, and pretended to sleep. Her arm slid sideways, touched Hazel's. She twisted—she was uncomfortable—and traced the letters of her name on Hazel's arm before moving her arm away.

Hazel turned, burying her face under her hair, and a soft murmur came to Brun's ear. "Brun?"

Brun nodded. A wave of excitement ran through her; the baby kicked vigorously as if aware of it. Someone besides the men knew who she was . . . an ally. She had made contact . . . it wasn't much, but it gave her hope, the first real hope she'd had.

The next day, she watched Hazel covertly. The girl seemed the same as always—busy, careful, quiet, patient, warm with the children and remote with Brun. When Brandy's restlessness grew toward a tantrum, Hazel intervened, steadied her . . . and Brun was reminded of an expert trainer with a fractious young horse. When she thought of it that way, she began to grasp how Hazel was using the children's need to steady herself. She could be calm, she could follow the senseless rules, because she had someone for whom she was responsible.

And who was Brun's responsibility? The words she had heard from Lieutenant Commander Uhlis came back to her. If she had been a Regular Space Service officer, her duty would have been clear—to escape, or if that was not possible, to live, gathering information, until she could escape. But she wasn't. And even if she had been—even if she pretended to be—was that duty enough to sustain a lifetime such as she faced? What if she never had a chance to escape?

The baby inside her moved, as if it were doing a tumbling act. Surely one baby couldn't make that much disturbance. Some people would say that it was her responsibility, but she did not feel that—it had been forced onto her, into her, and it was not hers at all. It was an abomination, as the men claimed she was.

Was she then her own responsibility? Her mouth soured. Not enough to make a lifetime as these men's slave tolerable, or even bearable. She had spent too many hours already planning how she could escape life, if not them, once they lowered their guard. Eventually they would.

But . . . what if there were a chance, however slim, to keep Hazel and the little girls from her own fate? Somewhere, she was sure, her father was searching. Fleet was searching. It might be years; it might be too many years . . . but it might not. Hazel was compliant not entirely from fear, but also from hope, the hope that some help might come—if she had not had some hope, she would never have dared share her name, and her ship's name, with Brun. So she, Charlotte Brunhilde Meager, could fix her mind on Hazel and the little girls—on saving them.

She did not let herself think again about how unlikely success was. Instead, she began thinking what information she needed, and how to get it. And she quit trying to catch Hazel's eye, quit trying to entice her into communication. The last thing she wanted now was trouble for Hazel.

Only a few days later, the men came for both of them, and the little ones. Brun almost panicked—had they realized Hazel had talked to her? That she had written her own name on Hazel's arm? But they were led along the corridors, farther than Brun had ever gone. Her bare feet were sore; her pregnancy made her awkward at the hatches. To her surprise, the men were patient, waiting while she lifted one leg then the other. They helped her down a slanting surface . . . to a space that opened out around her. She looked, her eyes unaccustomed to the distances after those months in the compartment. The docking bay of a space station, it looked like. All around were men, only men . . . she and Hazel and the two little girls were

the only females. The men guided her, gently enough,
to a hoverchair. With Hazel walking beside her, the
men pushed her chair a long distance. Chair and all,
she was moved through another docking bay into a
shuttle. Only five men now. At their command, Hazel
strapped the children into seats, and herself into
another. The men locked the hoverchair down.

When the shuttle hatch opened, Brun smelled
what could only be a planet. Fresh air . . . growing things . . . animals . . . hope rose in her again.
Planets were big; if she could once get loose, she
could find a way to hide, and then to escape. But
right now she could barely stand in this gravity, and
the heat almost took her breath away.

The men moved her hoverchair from the shuttle,
through a low-ceilinged boxlike building, and then into
a wheeled vehicle, also large and boxlike, where they
locked the chair down again. It had no windows in
back, but up front she could see out . . . until a par-
tition rose to cut off her vision. Panic choked her—
she was alone in that back compartment; Hazel—the
only person she knew—hadn't come with her. Hazel
wouldn't know where she was, no one would know,
she was going to be lost forever.

❖   ❖   ❖

Hazel watched under lowered lids as they took the
pregnant woman away in a groundcar. She still wasn't
sure of the woman's name, even though the woman
had traced it into her arm. Could "Brun" be right?
What kind of name was that? A nickname for something, most likely, but they had not dared talk enough
to make sure. Her yellow hair shone in the sun of
this planet, much longer than it had been when Hazel
had first seen her.

"I'm taking the children," one of the men with her
said. The others nodded, and moved away.

"Come along, Girlie," he said. Hazel followed him,
a little breathless with the unaccustomed exercise and

the oppressive heat, Brandy holding one hand and
Stassi the other. She wondered where the boys were—
she hadn't seen them for a long time. She wondered
even more about Stinky, and pushed that thought
aside too.

The man led them through a gate and across a
wide paved space so hot her feet burned. The little
girls began to whimper. The man turned. "Here," he
said. "I'll carry them." He scooped them up; they
stiffened, turning their faces to Hazel's, but they didn't
cry out. "Only a little farther," he said. Hazel stepped
as lightly as she could. He stopped at last, beside a
row of groundcars. A strip of something soft lay there.
"Stand on that," he told her. Hazel stepped onto it—
and it was cool beneath her feet. She let her breath
out in a sigh. He put the little girls down and they
each grabbed a hand.

He punched something on a control panel set on
a post, and one of the groundcars popped its doors.
The man got in, fiddled with the controls, then put
his head back out. "All of you, into the back," he
said. Hazel pushed the little girls into the back of
the groundcar—it was soft inside, with cool air coming out of vents. After she climbed in, the door
closed without her touching it. She noticed that
there were no door handles on the inside, either.

"I'm taking you home, for now," the man said. The
car moved off. Hazel looked out the windows . . .
but they were frosted, so she couldn't see. Between
the back seat and the front, a dark panel had risen
so that she couldn't see out the front, either. The car
moved smoothly, though, with no sudden jerks. After
some time, the car stopped, and the man opened the
door from the outside.

"Come along now," he said. "And be good."

They were on a wide paved street between stone
buildings perhaps two stories tall, with a park of some
kind just down the block. Hazel caught a glimpse of

bright flowers arranged in some sort of pattern, but dared not take a real look. Instead, she followed the man across a stone-flagged walk to the entrance of the nearest building, a heavy carved door opened by a shorter man wearing white trousers and overshirt.

Her escort led them into the house, down a hall, into a large room with big windows opening on a garden. "Wait here," he told Hazel, pointing to a place near the door. She stood, holding the little girls to her. He walked across the room, and sat in a chair that faced the door. A girl about Hazel's age, wearing a plain brown dress, scurried into the room, carrying a tray with a pitcher of some liquid and a tall mug. Hazel noticed that she kept her eyes lowered, moving with quick short steps that didn't stretch her ankle-length skirt. Hazel did not dare to watch her all the way to the man's chair, but she heard the gurgle of liquid, the tinkle of a spoon in a glass, stirring. The girl left, her busy feet slipping hurriedly past Hazel. Did she look at Hazel? The littles were looking at her; Hazel squeezed their shoulders in warning.

Across the silent room, she could hear the man swallow. Then more footsteps, from outside the room, hurrying. Short light steps, short heavier ones, and someone running . . . as those legs flashed past her, bare to the knee, in sandals, Hazel realized it must be a boy.

"Daddy!" The boy's voice was still a shrill piping, but full of joy. "Youah home!"

"Pard!" The man's voice, for the first time that Hazel had heard it, expressed something softer than command. "Were you good? Did you take care of your mothah?"

"Yes, *sir*."

"That's my boy."

The others were passing her now. She saw the small bare feet of three girls, the slim skirts that hobbled their ankles, and—so astonishing she almost forgot and lifted her eyes—a woman's feet angled up on high pointed heels, beneath full skirts that rustled when she walked.

The girls rushed forward; the woman strode, her heels clicking on the floor. Hazel peeked through lowered lids . . . to see a child hardly bigger than Brandy throw herself at her father's lap, giggling. "Daddy!" she said . . . but softly. A larger girl, head down, moved up to nestle against his side. One still larger moved to his other side.

The man kissed each girl, murmuring something in a voice that made Hazel want to cry. Her father had made that soft voice for her, when she sat leaning against him, her head resting on his shoulder. A sob rose in her throat; she choked it back, and stared at the floor again. She could feel the littles trembling; they wanted a cuddle too; they would break away any moment now. She clutched at them harder.

"I brought you something," the man said. "Looky there." Hazel could feel, as if it were sunlight, their gazes on her and the littles. "Found them on a merchanter we captured. The girlie's a bit old, but biddable. Been no trouble. The two little uns . . . well, one of 'em's too talkative. We'll just have to see." He swallowed again. "You take 'em on back and get 'em settled. Girlie's a virgin all right. Doc checked."

The woman's shoes clicked, closer and closer. Hazel saw the wide skirt . . . a wife's skirt? . . . and then a firm hand on her shoulder, pushing. She obeyed, walking ahead of the woman, bringing the littles with her. She had no idea what was coming, but . . .

"You kin look at me," the woman said. "In here." Hazel looked up. The woman had a broad, peaceful-looking face, with a crown of gray-brown hair in a braid above it. She had big broad hands, and a big broad body. "Let's see you, honey . . . that's the ugliest dress I ever did see."

Hazel said nothing. She wasn't about to get into trouble if she could help it.

"Didn't your folks teach you anything about sewing?" the woman asked.

Hazel shook her head.

"You kin talk, too," the woman said. "As long as you keep it low. No hollerin'."

"I . . . don't know how to sew," Hazel said softly. Her voice felt stiff, it had been so long since she said a whole sentence.

"Well, you'll just have to learn. You can't go around lookin' like that. Not in this family."

Hazel bobbed her head. Brandy tugged on her hand.

"Hungry," she said.

The woman looked down at the littles, her face creased with something Hazel could not read. "These littl'uns yours?" she asked. "Sisters?"

"No," Hazel said.

"No, *ma'am*," the woman said sharply. "Didn't your folks teach you any manners?"

"No . . . ma'am," Hazel said.

"Well, I sure will," the woman said. "Now let me think. You littl'uns will fit into Marylou and Sallyann's things, but you, Girlie . . . and we have to find a name for you, too."

"My name's Hazel," Hazel said.

"Not anymore," the woman said. "Your old life is gone, and your old name with it. You put off the works of the devil and the devil's name. You will put on a godly name. When we find the right one."

In the next weeks, Hazel settled into a life as unlike that she'd known as the raider's ship had been. She slept in a room with ten other girls, all near or just past puberty but unmarried: the virgins' bower. Their room opened onto a tiny courtyard separated from the main garden by a stone screen and walled off from anything but their room. The room's other entrance was to a long corridor that led back to the main house without passing any other door.

"So we're safe," one of the other girls had explained the first evening. She had helped Hazel unroll her bedding onto a wooden bunk, helped her straighten the cover properly. These were all, she discovered, daughters of the man who had brought her here . . . daughters of four wives, who had produced all the other children in the house. Only the children of his first wife were permitted in the great room . . . and only when he summoned them. The others, when he wanted to see them, went to the second parlor.

"Y'all are the first outlanders in our household," one of the other girls said.

"Can't no one have outlanders unless they've got enough children to dilute the influence of y'all's heathen ways," another girl said.

"So we can teach you right from wrong," yet another said.

In short order, Hazel was clad in the same snug long skirt and long-sleeved top as the others. She learned to shuffle in quick steps . . . she learned how to navigate the corridors and rooms of the big house, that seemed to sprawl on forever. She learned to stand aside respectfully when the boys ran down the hall, to duck her chin so that even the little boys, looking up, did not meet her gaze.

Once a day, she was allowed to sit with Brandy and Stassi, if all her work was done. At first they ran to her and clung, silent, crying into her shoulder. But as the days passed, they adjusted to whatever their life was like. She had asked, but they found it hard to tell her . . . and no wonder. They had been hardly able to talk clearly when the ship was taken, and too many things had happened. They had eaten honeycakes, or they had new dresses, was all they could say. At least they were being fed and cared for, and they had a little time each day to play in the garden. She saw them with the other small girls, tossing back and forth weighted streamers of bright colors.

Her work was hard—the other girls her age were accomplished seamstresses, able to produce long, smooth straight seams. They all knew how to cut cloth and shape garments . . . now they were learning embroidery, cutwork, lacework, and other fine needlework. Hazel had to master plain knitting, crochet, and spend hours hemming bedsheets and bath towels. Besides sewing, she was taught cooking—to the wives' horror, she did not even know how to peel potatoes or chop carrots.

"Imagine!" said Secunda, the master's second wife. "Letting a poor girl grow up knowing so little. What did they expect you to do, child? Marry a man so rich and dissolute he would expect your servants to do everything?"

"We had machines," Hazel said.

"Oh, *machines*," Prima said. She shook a finger at Hazel. "Best forget about machines, girl. The devil's ways, making idle hands and giving women ideas. No machines here, just honest women doing women's work the way it should be done."

"Prima, would you taste this sauce?" Tertia bowed as she offered it.

"Ah. A touch more potherb, m'dear, but otherwise quite satisfactory."

Hazel sniffed. She had to admit that the kitchen smelled better than any ship's galley she'd ever been in. Every day, fresh bread from the big brick ovens; every day, fresh food prepared from the produce of the garden. And she liked chopping carrots—even onions—better than those long, straight seams. The women even laughed—here, by themselves, and softly—but they laughed. Never at the men, though. None of the jokes she'd heard all her life, bantering between the men and women of the crew. She wanted to ask why; she had a thousand questions, a million.

But she'd already noticed that girls didn't ask questions except about their work—how to do this, when to do that—and even then were often told to pay better attention.

She did her best, struggling to earn her daily visit with Brandy and Stassi. The women were quick to correct her mistakes, but she sensed that they were not hostile. They liked her as well as they could have liked any stranger thrust into their closed society, and they were as kind as custom allowed.

❖   ❖   ❖

The closed car had gone an unknowable distance—far enough for Brun to feel mildly nauseated—when it stopped finally. Someone outside opened the door; a tall woman—the first woman she had seen on this world—reached in and grabbed her arm.

"Come on, you," she said. After so long in the ship, the accent was understandable, if still strange. "Get out of that."

Brun struggled up and out of the car with difficulty, not helped by the woman's hard grip. She looked around. The groundcar looked like an illustration out of one of her father's oldest books, high and boxy. The street on which it had driven was wide, brick-paved, and edged with low stone and brick buildings, none more than three stories tall. The woman yanked at her arm, and Brun nearly staggered.

"No time for lollygagging," the woman said. "You don't need to be sightseeing; get yourself inside the house like the decent woman you aren't." Brun could not move fast enough to satisfy the woman, even with one of the men helping—she was too big, too awkward, and the stones of the front walk hurt her feet. She glanced up at the building they were urging her towards and nearly fell up a stone step. But she had seen it—made of heavy stone blocks, it had no windows on this side, and beside the heavy door was a tall stout man who had the body language of every door guard Brun had ever seen. A prison?

It might as well have been, she found when she was inside and the matron was listing the rules in a harsh voice. Here she would stay until her baby was born, and a few weeks after, with the other sluts— unmarried pregnant women. She would cook, clean, and sew. She would be silent, like all the others; she was there to listen, not to talk. If the matron caught her whispering or lipspeaking with the other women, she'd be locked in her room for a day. With that, the matron pushed her into a narrow room with a bed and a small cabinet beside it, and shut the door on her.

Brun sagged onto the bed.

"And no sitting on the bed during work hours!" the matron said, flinging open the door with a bang. "We don't put up with laziness here. Get your sewing basket; you have plenty to do." She pointed at the cabinet. Brun heaved herself up and opened the door; inside was a round basket and a pile of folded cloth. "Decent clothes for yourself, first of all," the woman grumbled. "Now come along to the sewing room."

She led the way along a stone-floored corridor to a room that opened on an interior court; five pregnant women sat busy at their handwork. None of them looked up; Brun could not see their faces until she was sitting down herself. One had a wry face, pulled to the right by some damage; Brun could see no scar, and wondered what had caused it. But the warden tapped her head with a hard finger. "Get busy, you. Less lookin', more sewin'."

❖   ❖   ❖

"You did *what?*" Pete Robertson's voice rose sharply.

The Ranger Captain looked even more like a sick turkey gobbler, Mitch thought.

"We captured the trader without any trouble; the

crew and captain lied, and the females was all using abominations, so we killed 'em. There were five children aboard, though: three girls and two boys, and those we brought home. They're in my household now. We were still in the system, learning the big ship's control systems before taking it through jump, when this little yacht came in—"

"And you couldn't let it go—"

"Not after it slowed down and was sneakin' up on us, no. It would've got all our IDs. They might've traced back to where we got the ships from. So we grabbed it, and found a mighty important passenger, so she thought herself." Mitch grinned at the memory of that arrogant face.

"Abomination!" Sam Dubois hissed.

"She's a female, like any other," Mitch said. "I had her gagged, and muted her without letting her speak—she can't have contaminated any of us. Our medico said she was pure in blood, and after he took out her implants and made her a natural woman again—"

"She's one of them Registered Embryos," Sam said. "And you call *that* pure in blood?"

"Mixing genes from more'n one person—she might as well be a bastard—" Pete added. "You know what the parsons say about them."

"She's a strong, healthy young female who's now pregnant with twins," Mitch said firmly. "And she's mute, and she's safely in a muted maternity home. She's not going to cause any trouble. You better believe I was firm with her—she's quiet and obedient now."

"But why did you send the yacht back?" asked Pete.

If they were asking questions and not yelling at him, he was over the hump.

"Because it's about time we got a little respect, that's why. The talk on the docks is that we're just a bunch of pirates like any others. Common criminals. That's what the Guernesi are sayin' in their own papers; they're not tellin' the truth about us. So we make it clear we aren't goin' to put up with it—they can't just ignore us. God's plan isn't goin' to be held back by such as them. Besides that, once they started lookin' for that female—and they would look, considerin' who her father is—they could've found things we don't want them to know."

"And you bring the whole Familias down on us," Sam hissed. "Biggest power in this part of the galaxy and you have to make them mad—"

"I'm not afraid of anything but God Almighty," Mitch said. "That's what we all swear to, 'fore we're sworn in as Rangers. Fear God but fear no man— that's what we say. You goin' back on that, Sam?" He felt strong, exultant. New children in the home, shaping well. That yellow-haired slut carrying twins— God was on his side for sure.

"There's still no sense leadin' trouble home," Pete said.

"I didn't," Mitch said. "Sure, I claimed what we did for the whole Militia—but I didn't leave one scrap of evidence which *branch* it was. By the time they figure it out—if they figure it out, which I doubt— we'll be raisin' enough hell right there in Familias space that they won't have time to bother us. If they make one move against us, we blow a station or two— they'll back off. I told 'em that. Nobody goes to war for one female."

✧   ✧   ✧

Brun fretted in the confines of the maternity home. She was allowed to go into the walled courtyard, hobbling around the brick paths on her swollen, sore feet. In fact, she was required to walk five circuits each day. She was allowed to go from her dormitory to the kitchen, to the dining hall, to the bathing room or toilet, to the sewing room. But the only door out

was locked—and more than locked, guarded by a
stout man a head taller than she was. The other
occupants, all five of them, were as mute as she. The
woman in charge—Brun could not think of any word
that fit her position—was not mute, but all too verbal.
She ordered the pregnant women around as if she
were the warden in a prison. Perhaps she was; it felt
like a prison to Brun. She had to spend so much time
a day sewing: clothes for herself, clothes for the baby
to come, clothes for herself after the birth. She had
to help in the kitchen. She had to clean, struggling
to push a heavy wet mop across the floor, to scrub
out the toilets and sinks and shower stalls.

What kept her going was the thought of Hazel,
somewhere with those two small girls. What was
happening to Hazel? Nothing good. She promised
Hazel—she promised herself—that she would somehow get Hazel out of this.

She was examined every day . . . and as her time
came nearer, she found a whole new source of fear.
One of the other women, cutting carrots beside her
in the kitchen, suddenly bent and pressed a hand to
her side. Her mouth opened in a silent yell. Brun
could see the hardening under her maternity shift.

"Come along, you," the warden said. She glared at
Brun. "You help her, you." Brun took the woman's
other arm, and helped her stumble down the corridor,
into rooms Brun had not yet seen. Tiled floor . . .
narrow bed, too short to lie on . . . as the woman in
labor heaved herself onto it, she realized that this—
this utterly inadequate ramshackle arrangement—was
where women gave birth. Where she would give birth.
The woman writhed, and a gush of fluid wet the bed
and splashed onto the floor.

"Get basins, you!" the warden said to Brun, pointing. Brun brought them. When was the warden going
to call the doctor? The nurses?

There were no doctors, no nurses. The warden was

the only attendant, along with whatever women were in the house. The others edged in—some of them had done this before, clearly. Brun, forbidden to leave, stood against the wall, alternately faint and nauseated. When she sagged, one of the others slapped her face with a wet rag until she stood straight again.

She had known the facts of human reproduction since childhood. In books. In instructional cubes. And she knew—or she had known—that no one who had access to modern methods still gave birth in the old way. And certainly no one, no one in the whole civilized universe, gave birth like this, without medical care, without life support, without anything but a grim old woman and other pregnant women, in a room with unscreened windows, with the blood and fluids splashing onto the bare floor, splashing onto the women's bare feet. Her father's horses had better care; the hounds had cleaner kennels for whelping.

She tried not to look, but they grabbed her, forced her to look, to see the baby's head pushing, pushing . . . her body ached already in sympathy.

The baby's first cry expressed her own rage and fear exactly.

She could not do it. She would die.

She could not die; she had to live . . . for Hazel. To keep Hazel from this horror, she would live.

CHAPTER ELEVEN

Castle Rock

Lord Thornbuckle, Speaker of the Table of Ministers and the Grand Council of the Familias Regnant, successor to the abdicated king, had spent the morning working on the new Regular Space Service budget proposal with his friend—now the Grand Council's legal advisor—Kevil Starbridge Mahoney. All morning a succession of ministers and accountants had bombarded them with inconvenient facts that cluttered what should have been—Lord Thornbuckle thought—a fairly simple matter of financing replacements for the ships lost at Xavier. They had decided to lunch privately, in the small green dining room with its view of the circular pond in which long-finned fish swam lazily, in the hope that the peaceful spring garden would restore their equanimity. A spicy soup and slices of lemon-and-garlic roasted chicken had helped, and now they toyed with salad of mixed spring greens, putting off the inevitable return to columns of numbers.

"Heard from Brun lately?" Kevil asked, after reporting on his son George, now in law school.

"Not for several weeks," Thornbuckle said. "I expect she's in jumpspace somewhere; she wanted to visit Cecelia's stud before coming home for the hunt opening day."

"You don't worry?"

"Of course I worry. But what can I do about it? If she doesn't show up soon, I'll put someone on her tail—the problem is that as soon as I do, the newsflash shooters will know where to look, and the real sharks follow the bait."

Kevil nodded. They had both been targets of political and private violence, as well as intrusive newsflash stories. "You could always use Fleet resources," he suggested, not for the first time.

"I could—except that after Copper Mountain I'm not at all sure it's safe to do so. First she's nearly killed right on the base—they still haven't figured out who was shooting at her—and then the heroic Lieutenant Suiza takes it upon herself to question Brun's morality."

Kevil held his silence but one eyebrow went up. Thornbuckle glared at him.

"I know—you think she's—"

"I didn't say a word," Kevil said. "But there are two sides or more to any quarrel."

"It was unprofessional—"

"Yes. No doubt about that. But if Brun were not your daughter, I think you would find it more understandable."

Thornbuckle sighed. "Perhaps. She can be . . . provocative. But still—"

"But still you're annoyed because Lieutenant Suiza wasn't more tactful. I sympathize. In the meantime—"

The knock on the door interrupted him; he turned to look. Normally, no one disturbed a private meal here, and that knock had a tempo that alerted them both.

Poisson, the most senior of the private secretaries attached to Lord Thornbuckle's official position, followed on that knock without waiting. Unusual—and more unusual was his face, pale and set as if carved from stone.

"What is it?" asked Thornbuckle. His gaze fixed on the package Poisson carried, the yellow and green stripes familiar from the largest of the commercial express-mail companies, Hymail.

"Milord—milord—" Poisson was never at a loss for words; even when Kemtre abdicated, he had been suavely capable from the first moments. But now, the package he held out quivered from the tremor in his hands.

Thornbuckle felt an all-too-familiar chill as the food he had just eaten turned to a cold lump in his belly. In the months of his Speakership, he had faced crisis after crisis, but none of them had arrived in a Hymail Express package. Still, if Poisson was reacting like this, it must be serious. He reached out for the package, but had to almost pry it from Poisson's grip.

"You opened it," he said.

"With the others that came in, yes, milord. I had no idea—"

Thornbuckle reached into the package and pulled out a sheaf of flatpics; a data cube rolled out when he shook the package upside down. He glanced at the first of the flatpics and time stopped.

In a distant way, he was aware of the way the other flatpics slid out of his grasp, and fell slowly—so slowly—turning and wavering in the air on their way from his hand to the floor. He was aware of Poisson with his hand still extended, of Kevil across the table, of the beat of his own pulse, that had stumbled and then begun to race.

But all he could see, really see, was Brun's face staring into his with an expression of such terror and misery that he could not draw breath.

"Bunny . . . ?" That was Kevil.

Thornbuckle shook his head, clamping his jaw shut on the cry he wanted to give. He closed his eyes, trying to replace the pictured face with one of Brun happy, laughing, but—in his mind's eye, her haunted frightened gaze met his.

He didn't have to look at the rest. He knew what had happened, without going on.

He had to look. He had to know, and then act. Without a word, he passed the first flatpic to Kevil, and leaned over to pick up the rest. They had landed in a scattered heap, and before his hands—steady, he noted with surprise—could gather them together a half-dozen images had seared his eyes: Brun naked, bound to a bunk, a raw wound on her leg where her contraceptive implant had been. Brun in her custom protective suit, with a gag in her mouth, being held by gloved hands. Brun's face again, unconscious and slack, with some kind of instrument in her mouth. Brun . . . he put the stack down, and looked across at Kevil.

"My God, Bunny!" Kevil's face was as white as his own must be.

"Get us a cube reader," Thornbuckle said to Poisson, surprised that he could speak at all past the rapidly enlarging lump in his throat.

"Yes, milord. I'm—"

"Just do it," Thornbuckle said, cutting off whatever Poisson had been planning to say. "And get this cleared away." The very smell of the food on the table nauseated him. As Poisson left, he retrieved the flatpic Kevil had, and turned the whole stack carefully upside down. Two of the serving staff came and cleared the table, eyeing them worriedly but saying nothing. They had just gone out when Poisson returned with a cube reader and screen.

"Here it is, milord."

"Stay." Poisson paused on his way back out.

"Are you sure?" Kevil asked.

"The damage is done," Thornbuckle said. "We'll need at least one of the secretaries to handle communications. But first, we need to see what we're up against." He did not offer Kevil the other flatpics.

The image on the cube reader's screen wavered, as if it were a copy of a badly recorded original, but it was clear enough to see Brun, and the heavily accented voice on the audio—a man's voice—was just understandable. Thornbuckle tried to fix his mind on the words, but time and again he lost track of the man's speech, falling into his daughter's anguish.

When it was done, no one spoke. Thornbuckle struggled with tears; he could hear the other men breathing harshly as well. Finally—he could not have said how long after—he looked up to meet their gaze. For the first time in his experience, Kevil had nothing to say; he shook his head mutely. Poisson was the first to speak.

"Milord—will want to contact the Admiralty."

"Yes." A rough croak, all he could make. Brun, Brun . . . that golden loveliness, that quick intelligence, that laughter . . . reduced to the shambling, mute misery of that recording. It could not be . . . yet, though recordings could be faked, he knew in his heart that this one had not been. "The Admiralty, by all means. We must find her. I'll go—get transport." He knew as he said it how impossible that could be. In Familias space alone, there were hundreds of worlds, thousands perhaps—he had never actually counted—where someone might be lost forever. Poisson bowed and went out. He had not told the man to be discreet—but Poisson had been born discreet.

"We will find her," Kevil said, the rich trained voice loaded with the overtones that had moved courtrooms. "We must—"

"And if we don't?" Thornbuckle felt his control wavering, and pushed himself up out of the chair. If he stood, if he walked, if he acted, perhaps he would not collapse in an agony that could not help Brun. "What am I going to tell Miranda?"

"For now, nothing," Kevil said. "It might still be a fake—"

"You don't believe that."

"No. But I want someone expert with image enhancement to work on it before you tell her."

"Look at those," Thornbuckle said, gesturing at the pile of flatpics on the table. He stared out into the green and gold garden, the water dimpling as a breeze swept across it. Behind him, he heard Kevil's breath catch, and catch again. Then the chair moved, and he felt more than heard Kevil come up behind him.

"We will get her back," Kevil said, this time with no courtroom overtones. It was as if the rock itself had spoken. Not for the first time, Thornbuckle was aware of the depth of character that lay behind Kevil's easy, practiced manner. "Do you want me to concentrate on the search, or the administration?"

"I have to go," Thornbuckle said.

"Then I'll work with—whom do you want to act as Speaker while you're gone?"

"Could you?"

"I doubt it, not without starting a row. Your best bet would be a Cavendish, a de Marktos, or a Barraclough. I can certainly stay as legal advisor, and hold the carnage to a minimum. But you're the only one everyone trusts right now. Almost everyone."

"Your transportation is here, sir." Poisson again.

"I'll come with you this far," Kevil said. It was not a question.

"Thank you." Thornbuckle did not entirely trust his voice. "I'll . . . just wash up, I think." He gathered up the flatpics and the data cube, stuffing them back into the striped package. Kevil nodded and went on toward the side entrance.

Thornbuckle looked at his face in the mirror after splashing cold water on it. He looked . . . surprisingly normal. Pale, tired, angry . . . well, that he was. After the shock, the pain, came the anger . . . deep, and burning hotter every moment. Without his quite realizing how, it spread from the thugs who had perpetrated this most recent abomination to everyone who had contributed to it . . . the blaze spreading back down the trail Brun had taken, outlining in flame every person who had influenced her on that path.

When he left the dining room he was still in shock . . . by the time he arrived at the Admiralty, he was already beginning to think whom else to blame. Kevil, sitting beside him in the groundcar, said nothing to interfere with the inexorable progress of his rage.

At the Admiralty's planetside headquarters, a commander awaited him . . . someone he remembered from the briefings of the past week, when the replacement of ships from the Xavier action had been under discussion. He realized with a shock that Poisson had not told them what this was about—and then that Poisson had been right.

He nodded to the commander, and as soon as they were inside said, "This is not about the budget; I need to speak to the highest ranking officer present."

"Yes, sir; Admiral Glaslin is waiting. Secretary Poisson said it was confidential and urgent. But since I had met you before, he thought I should be your escort."

Admiral Glaslin—tall and angular, with a heronlike droop of neck—met him in the anteroom and led them into the inner office. "Lord Thornbuckle—how may we help you?"

Thornbuckle threw the package on the desk. "You can find these . . . persons . . . and my daughter."

"Sir?"

"Look inside," Kevil said quietly. "Lord Thornbuckle's daughter has been abducted and mutilated—"

The admiral's mouth opened, then he shut it firmly and emptied the contents of the package onto his desk. At the sight of the flatpics, his face paled from its normal bronze to an unattractive mud color. "When did you get this?"

"Just now," Thornbuckle said.

"It was delivered sixty-four minutes ago, at the palace, as part of the normal Hymail Express daily delivery; Secretary Poisson opened it because it was labelled *Personal*, and when he realized its nature, brought it immediately to Lord Thornbuckle." Kevil paused in his recitation until the admiral nodded. "We were eating lunch, at the time. We have also viewed the data cube."

"Same as the flatpics?"

"The data cube contains both a video record of the capture and an apparent surgical procedure, and audio threats against the government of the Familias Regnant."

"Lord Thornbuckle?" The admiral looked at him.

"I—didn't hear most of the words. Kevil will be correct, however. I want a copy, when you've made one—"

The admiral looked at Kevil. "Do you think that's wise—?"

"Dammit, man! I'm the Speaker; I know what I need!"

"Certainly. But I must tell you—this will have to go to the Grand Admiral—"

"Of course. The sooner the better. You have to find her—" Thornbuckle forced himself to stand, to shake the admiral's hand, to turn and walk out of the office, down the polished corridors, to the entrance where his car waited.

*   *   *

Twelve hours later, Thornbuckle woke from a fitful doze at the approach of the Grand Admiral's aide.

"They're here now, milord."

The conference room, as secure as any room could be, was crammed with officers. Thornbuckle reminded himself that the blue shoulder-flashes were Intelligence, and the green were Technical. At one end of the long black table, Grand Admiral Savanche leaned forward, and at the other was the only empty seat in the room, waiting for the government's senior civilian representative: himself.

He edged past the others to his place, and stood there facing Savanche.

"You've seen the recording," Lord Thornbuckle said. "What I want to know is, what kind of force are you committing to getting her back?"

"There's not a damn thing we can do," Grand Admiral Savanche said. After a brief pause, he appended, "Sir."

"There has to be." Thornbuckle's voice was flat, even, and unyielding.

"We can search," Savanche said. "Which we're doing. We have experts going through the intel database, trying to figure out who these people are, and thus where they might be."

"You have to—"

"My Lord Thornbuckle. Your daughter has not made any official checkpoint since Podj, sixty-two days ago. We have already begun running the traffic records and sightings from all stations—but there are thousands, tens of thousands, of stations, just in Familias space alone. You have three orbiting your own Sirialis. With the staff we can release for this, that's going to take weeks to months, just to sift the existing data."

"That's not good enough," Thornbuckle said.

"With all due respect, my lord, given the recent incursions by the Compassionate Hand and the

Bloodhorde, we dare not divert resources from our borders. They can certainly add surveillance for your daughter or her ship to their other duties; those orders have gone out. But it would be suicidal to put all Fleet on this single mission."

"Tell me what else you have done," Thornbuckle said.

"We know that she leased the yacht *Jester* from Allsystems; ten personnel identified as your personal militia boarded with her. Allsystems has provided us full identification profiles for that ship; if it shows up in Familias space, within range of any of our ships, we will know it. We know that she took it from Correlia to Podj without incident. Do you know where she was going next?"

"No." He hated admitting that. "She—she said she wanted to visit several friends, and check into some of her investments, before coming to Sirialis. She had no itinerary; she said if she made one, the newsflash shooters would find her. She said she'd be at Sirialis for the opening day of the hunt."

"So—you expected her to be out of contact."

"Yes. She had mentioned visiting Lady Cecelia de Marktos on Rotterdam, and perhaps even Xavier's system."

"I see. So when would you have considered her overdue?"

"I was beginning to worry—I expected her to call in more often—"

"You see, milord, it's a very large universe, and she is only one person. Our technicians are still working on the data cube and the flatpics, but so far nothing definite has shown up. The cube itself is one of the cheap brands sold in bulk through discount suppliers; the image has been through some sort of editing process which removed considerable data. The flatpics were taken with old technology, but the prints you have are simply copies of prints, not prints from negatives. That again reduced the data available for analysis." Savanche cleared his throat. "Right now, there is nothing whatever to give us any idea what we're dealing with, let alone where she is."

"But they said they were the Nutaxis something or other—"

"New Texas Godfearing Militia, yes. Something we never heard of before; it sounds utterly ridiculous to me. We are making discreet inquiries, but until something comes along—some confirmatory evidence—this might as well be the act of lunatics."

"And how long will that take?" Thornbuckle asked. "Don't you realize what's happening to her?"

Savanche sighed, the creases in his face deepening. "It will take as long as it takes . . . and yes, I understand your concern, and I can imagine—though I don't want to—what may be happening to her."

R.S.S. *Gyrfalcon*

"Ensign Serrano, report to the Captain's office. Ensign Serrano, report to the Captain's office." What had he done wrong this time? Lieutenant Garrick turned to look at him, and then jerked her thumb toward the hatch. Barin flicked the message-received button, and headed up to Command Deck.

When he knocked, Captain Escovar called him in at once. He was sitting behind his desk, holding what looked like a decoded hardcopy.

"Ensign, you knew the Speaker's daughter, didn't you?"

For an instant Barin could not think who this might be—what chairman, what daughter. Then he said, "Brun Meager, sir? Yes, sir, I did. I met her at Copper Mountain Schools, and we were in the escape and evasion course together."

"Bad news," Escovar said. "She was on her way back

to her family home when her ship was attacked by raiders."

Brun dead . . . Barin could not believe that vivid laughing girl was dead . . .

"She was *alone*?"

"Not quite. She'd chartered a small yacht, about like one of our couriers, and she had a small security detachment, her father's private militia." Escovar paused, as if to make sure that he was not interrupted again. Barin clamped his jaw. "The ship has not been found, but a message packet was sent to her father, via commercial postal service." Another pause. "The Speaker's daughter . . . was not killed. She was captured."

Barin felt his jaw dropping and bit down hard on everything he felt.

"The raiders . . . wanted her family to know that they had taken her, and what they had done." Escovar made a noise deep in his throat. "Barbarians, is what they are. Information has been forwarded to me; it should arrive shortly." He looked at Barin, over the top of the hardcopy. "I called you in because we have no adequate professional assessment of this young woman's temperament and abilities. I know she was referred to Copper Mountain by Admiral Vida Serrano, apparently on the advice of Commander Serrano. But her Schools files were wiped, when she left, as a security measure. If anything is to be done for her, we need to know what she herself is capable of, and what she is likely to do."

Barin's first impulse was to say that Brun would always come out on top—it was her nature to be lucky—but he had to base this on facts. He wasn't going to make rash assumptions this time about what he knew and what he merely surmised.

"She's very bright," he began. "Learns in a flash. Quick in everything . . . impulsive, but her impulses are often right."

"Often has a number attached?"

"No, sir . . . not without really thinking it over. In field problems, I'd say eighty percent right, but I don't know how much of that was impulse. They didn't let her do the big field exercise, for security reasons. She did have a problem . . ." How could he put this so that it wouldn't hurt her reputation? "She was used to getting what she wanted," he said finally. "With people—with relationships. She assumed it."

"Um. What did she try with you? And I'm sorry if this is a sore subject, but we need to know."

"Well . . . she found me attractive. Cute, I think was her word." Like a puppy, he had thought at the time; it had annoyed him slightly even as he was attracted to her energy and intelligence. "She wanted more. I . . . didn't."

"Aware of the social problems?"

"No, sir. Not exactly." How could he explain when he didn't understand it himself? "Mostly . . . I'm . . . I was . . . close to Lieutenant Suiza."

"Ah. I can see why. Exceptional officer by all accounts."

Then he hadn't heard. Barin felt a chill. He didn't want to be the one to tell the captain about Esmay's stupid explosion, or the quarrel they'd had.

"Brun is . . . like Esmay—Lieutenant Suiza—with the brakes off. They're both smart, both brave, both strong, but Brun . . . when the danger's over, she's put it completely aside. Lieutenant Suiza will still be thinking it over. And Brun would take chances, just for the thrill of it. She was lucky, but she *expected* to be lucky."

"Well, I know who I'd want on *my* ship," Escovar said. Then he touched a button on his desk. "Ensign, what I'm going to tell you now is highly sensitive. We have some information on the young woman's condition after capture, but that information must not— *must* not—spread. It will, I think, be obvious to you why, when I tell you about it. I am doing this because, in my judgement, you may be able to help us concoct a way to help her, if you have enough information. But I warn you—if I find out that you've slipped on this, I will personally remove your hide in strips, right before the court-martial. Is that clear?"

"Yes, sir." Barin swallowed.

"All right. The raiders left behind a vid they made of her after the capture. It's one of the ugliest things I've ever watched, and I've been in combat and seen good friends blown to bits. It is clear from this vid that the raiders intend to take her to one of their home planets and keep her there as breeding stock—"

"What!" That got out past his guard; he clamped his teeth together again. He'd thought of rape; he'd thought of ransom; he'd thought of political pressure, but certainly not that.

"Yes. And they've mutilated her: they've done surgery and destroyed her vocal cords." He paused; Barin said nothing, trying not to think of voluble Brun silent, unable to speak. Rage rose in him. "We do not at this time know where she is; we do not know if she is still alive or not—though we suspect she is. We do not know her physical condition at any time subsequent to the vid left by the raiders. It may be impossible to find her."

Barin wanted to argue, to insist that they must—but he knew better. One person—even Brun, even the Speaker's daughter—was not enough reason to start a war.

"I see no reason for you to view the vid," Escovar said. "It makes voyeurs of us, who would least want to participate in something like that. But this may be a requirement later, and you need to know that for calculated cruelty without much actual injury, this is the worst I've seen. The important thing is that what you know about her might make rescue possible. We don't want to shoot her by accident because we failed to understand her way of thinking."

"Yes, sir."

"I would like you to record every detail you can remember about her—anything, from the color of her underwear to every preference she ever expressed. We're trying to get more information from other people she knew, but you and Lieutenant Suiza have the advantage of understanding the military perspective, and having known her in a dangerous situation."

"Yes, sir."

"I put no deadline on this, but I do consider it urgent. The longer she is in their hands, the more likely that permanent damage will result, not to mention political chaos." Barin digested that in silence. He dared not ask how her father was taking it—the little bit that he knew.

"Is her voice—permanently gone?"

"No way to tell until she's retrieved. The surgeon who viewed this tape says it depends on the exact type of surgery they performed. But she could always be fitted with a vocal prosthesis. If the only damage is to the vocal cords, she can whisper—and a fairly simple prosthesis will amplify that. However, they may have done more damage that we don't know about, and since their intent is to silence her, they may punish any attempt to whisper."

"But how are we going to find her?"

"I don't know, Ensign. If you come up with any ideas, be sure to share them. We have been assigned to the task force charged with finding and rescuing her."

Only a day later, Escovar called him into the office again. "They found the yacht. It was dead in space, tethered to an unmanned navigation station; local traffic hadn't noticed it. It was found by the maintenance crew that went out to service the station.

Empty, and so far no idea where it came from.
Forensics will be all over it . . . there is evidence
of a struggle inside."

Barin's heart sank, if possible, even lower. A vid
of Brun was one thing, but her yacht, empty and
bearing signs of a fight, was not something likely to
have been faked.

"Did she say anything to you—anything at all—that
might give us a clue to where she could have been
when she was attacked?"

"No, sir. I brought the notes I've made—" Barin
handed them over. "Mostly we talked about the
courses, about the other students and instructors.
Quite a lot about Lieutenant Suiza, because Brun—
Sera Meager—asked about her."

Escovar flipped through the pages, reading rapidly.
"Here—she mentioned owning a lot of stock—did she
ever say in which companies?"

"Not that I remember," Barin said. "She may have,
but that didn't really interest me. She talked about
hunting—on horseback, that is—and bloodstock, and
something about pharmaceuticals, but I don't know
anything about that, so—"

R.S.S. *Shrike*

They had been in jump for eight standard days,
and Esmay had spent much of the last two shifts in
the SAR ready rooms, briefing the specialist teams
on the wonders of EVA during FTL traverses. Solis
had asked her to work up a training syllabus. She
would have expected this to take only an hour or so,
but the teams had ever more questions—good
questions. If it had been possible, they would have
gone EVA on *Shrike*; Esmay was glad to find that the
fail-safe of the airlocks worked here as well as on
Koskiusko, and no one could get out.

"We really should practice it, though," Kim Arek said. She had the single-minded intensity that Esmay recognized as her own past attitude. "Who knows when we might need it?"

"Someone should develop suit telemetry that works outside the jump-space shielding," someone else said. "The temporal distortion could kill you if you didn't know when your air was running out."

"What techniques do you use when your air is running out?" Esmay asked. "I know what the manuals say, but the only time I saw my gauge hitting the red zone, I found 'stay calm and breathe slowly' wasn't that easy."

"No kidding." Arais Demoy, one of the neuro-enhanced marines, grinned at her. "Imagine what it's like when you're not even on a ship, but knocked loose somehow. That happened to me one time, during a ship-to-ship. That's why we have suit beacons in the space armor. Try to go limp, if you can—muscle contraction uses up oxygen—and think peaceful thoughts."

The ship shuddered slightly, and everyone swallowed—the natural response to a downjump insertion; the insystem drive had been on standby for the past half hour, and now its steady hum went up a half tone.

"Prayer doesn't hurt," added Sirin. "If you're any sort of believer."

Esmay was about to inquire politely which sort she was, when the emergency bells rang.

"XO to the bridge; XO to the bridge—" She was moving before the repeat.

"Captain?"

Solis was glaring at her as if she had done something terrible, and she couldn't think of anything. She had been in his good graces; he seemed to have put aside his earlier animosity.

"We have received a flash alert, Lieutenant."

War? Esmay's stomach clenched.

"Lord Thornbuckle's daughter has been taken captive by an unknown force which threatens reprisals against Familias should any action be taken to rescue her. She has been mutilated—"

"Not . . . Brun!?" Esmay could feel the blood draining from her head; she put out a hand to the hatch coaming.

"Yes. There is, apparently, incontrovertible evidence of this capture. All ships are to report any trace of an Allsystems lease yacht *Jester* . . ." Solis shook his head, as if to clear it, and gave Esmay another long challenging look. "You don't seem pleased that your prophecy that Sera Meager would come to grief has been fulfilled—"

For a moment she could not believe what he said. "Of course not!" she said, then. "It has nothing to do with—I never wanted anything bad to happen—"

"You had best hope, then, that she is recovered quickly and in good health," Solis said. "Because otherwise, what everyone will remember—as I'm sure her father remembers—is that you bawled her out and she stormed away from Copper Mountain in a temper. You might as well realize, Lieutenant Suiza, that your future in the Regular Space Service depends on her future—which right this moment looks damned bleak."

She could not think about that; it was too dire a threat to think about. Instead, her mind leaped for any useful connection. "That trader," she said. Solis looked blank. "The little ship," Esmay said. "The one that trailed it in, the five bodies that weren't crew, but had been mutilated. That could have been Brun's ship."

Solis stared at her, then blinked. "You . . . may be right. It could be—could have been. And we sent the tissue for typing—"

"Sector HQ forensics—but they'll be coded as

related to the *Elias Madero*. And we don't have any beacon data on the little ship."

"No . . . but we have a mass estimate. All right, Suiza—and now, one more time, and I want the truth: is there even the slightest glimmer of satisfaction?"

"No, sir." She could say that with no hesitation. "I was wrong to lose my temper at the time—I know that, and I would've apologized if she'd still been there when we got back from the field exercise. And I would not wish captivity on anyone, any time, least of all someone like her . . ."

"Like her?"

"So . . . free. So happy."

"Umph. Well, I'm mostly convinced but I doubt anyone else will be. Better see you don't make any mistakes, Suiza. With the data we have aboard, we're sure to be called back to confer with the task force. You will be questioned about her, and one wrong word will ruin you."

Esmay put that out of her mind, and instead thought of Brun the laughing, Brun the golden. She had not thought of herself as religious—in her great-grandmother's sense—for years, but she found herself praying nonetheless.

Aragon Station, Sector VII HQ, Task Force Briefing

Barin found himself in the very uncomfortable position of being the youngest person at a very ticklish conference. He knew why he was there: he had trained with Brun on Copper Mountain; he and Esmay had saved her skin. He had known about her disappearance almost from its discovery for precisely that reason. But nothing in his training had prepared him to sit at a table with a Grand Admiral, his admiral grandmother, two other three-star admirals, a sprinkling of commanders—his cousin Heris among them—and the Speaker of the Council of Families of the Familias Regnant.

Nothing except growing up Serrano, which at the moment he felt was a distinctly overrated qualification.

Brun Meager's father, Lord Thornbuckle, was far beyond distraught . . . balanced on the thinnest knife-edge of stability Barin had ever seen in a previously functioning adult. In the harsh light that shone onto the polished table, Barin could see the fine tremor of the man's hands, the glitter of silver in his close-cropped blond hair as his head shifted in tense jerks from side to side, when someone spoke.

You've got to tell them everything. That's what his captain had said. Everything. But how could you tell a roomful of brass, in front of the woman's father, about her less admirable behavior? He sat very still and hoped against hope that something would interrupt this before he had to hurt a man already hurting so much.

"Grand Admiral Savanche, we have a flash-priority message—"

Savanche pushed himself back. "This had best be worth it." Barin knew that despite this almost-regulation growl, he was secretly glad to have something break the tension of the briefing. Savanche took the message cube, and put it in the player.

"It's from Captain Solis, aboard the search-and-rescue ship *Shrike* . . . they were pursuing leads in the disappearance of a Boros Consortium merchanter, and have been out of contact for weeks. He just heard about the yacht's disappearance, and—you'd better see this for yourself." He transferred output to the room's main screen.

Onto the screen came a section of star chart, with a corner window of Captain Solis.

"—trace of a very small craft in the system as well," he was saying. "We presumed at first that it was the raider's tail on the *Elias Madero*. When we located debris and bodies from the merchanter, amounting to the entire adult crew and one juvenile apprentice—but not the other apprentice, nor four small children—we also located five bodies which were not crew, and which we could not identify. My forensics team believes them to have been military, but they weren't Fleet, and the usual identification sites had been mutilated."

"There were ten . . ." breathed Lord Thornbuckle.

"We sent off a report on this to Sector, top priority, when we got back to Bezaire, but we had to use a commercial ansible. At that time we had not received word that the Speaker's daughter was missing. However, when we came out of jump at Sil Peak, we received that news and specifications of her ship. My Exec, Lieutenant Suiza, immediately thought of the other bodies we'd found. The ship trace we found is consistent with a yacht of the stated mass. We have the recovered bodies in storage; please advise next move."

"We own stock in Boros," Lord Thornbuckle said. "She was out there—she'd said she wanted to look into the olive orchards on . . . whichever one it is, I can't think. It has to be her . . . her yacht. Her guards . . ."

"Do you know anything about them, Lord Thornbuckle?"

"They're from my militia. Brun had . . . not gotten along with the Royal Space Service security personnel who had gone with her to Copper Mountain. There had been an incident—"

"And you say there were more than five—"

"Yes . . . there should have been ten." Lord Thornbuckle stared at the table between his hands. "She thought that was too many."

"Well, it's imperative that we get what evidence Solis has gathered as soon as possible." Savanche's eye swept the room and lighted on Barin. "Ensign—go find my signals chief and tell her I want a secure link to *Shrike*."

"Sir." Barin found the Grand Admiral's staff signals specialist hovering outside the room—someone had anticipated the need—and sent her in. He was glad to be out of there, and hoped he wouldn't be called back. *Shrike* . . . Esmay was on *Shrike*. He wondered how she was taking the news.

CHAPTER TWELVE

Shrike came into the system like an avenging angel, a high-vee insertion through a lane cleared for that purpose, and then shifted insystem in a series of microjumps . . . reducing a normal eight-day down transit to a mere eleven hours. Three tugs went out to meet her, and dragged her toward the station at a relative velocity that seemed reckless. Barin, aboard *Gyrfalcon*, lurked in scan and watched along with everyone else.

"Ensign—" He glanced back to find his captain beckoning, and followed him to his office.

"We've been getting realtime downloads from *Shrike* for the past hour," the captain said. "I want you to hand-carry this to the Grand Admiral's office—it's for his eyes only, and I want you to put it in his hands personally."

"Sir." Barin took the rack of four data cubes—a *lot* of data—and headed for the Grand Admiral's temporary suite of offices. He'd been couriering one thing and another since they'd arrived, so the

Admiral's staff listened when he said, "—in his hands personally."

"You'll have to wait, though. The Admiral's receiving a delegation from the Guernesi Republic."

"Fine." Barin found a spot out of the way of the traffic through the outer office, and let his mind wander to *Shrike*'s arrival . . . and her executive officer. Would he have a chance to see Esmay? Not likely; *Shrike*'s captain would certainly be the one coming to any briefings. Perhaps this new information would divert attention from his supposed expertise on Brun, which seemed more tawdry every time he thought of it. So she had wanted to bed him—so what? So she had been, in his mind, a difficult and headstrong individual . . . but whatever she had been, she didn't deserve what had happened to her. Once again he saw the video clip of the surgery and felt his own throat close; he swallowed with an effort.

"Hello, Ensign Serrano—"

His eyes snapped to the left, where Lieutenant Esmay Suiza stood with a challenging look . . . and a lockbag of data, no doubt.

"Lieutenant!"

"Wool-gathering?" she asked, in almost the tone of the old Esmay, the Esmay of the *Koskiusko*.

"Sir, my mind had wandered—"

"Just another minute, he said," the clerk at the desk interrupted. "If the lieutenant wouldn't mind going in with Ensign Serrano—"

"Not at all," said Esmay.

Barin tried not to stare, but—she looked so good. Nothing like Casea Ferradi; if she was priggish in some ways, she was at least clean.

The admiral's door opened, and a harried-looking commander waved them both in. "Come on Serrano, Suiza—he's waiting for both of you."

From within someone said "No!" very loudly. Barin

paused. "I won't have her—I don't want to see her." The commander holding the door closed it again. "—all her fault!" leaked out just before it snicked shut.

Thornbuckle. Still angry, still unreasonable . . . Barin gave Esmay a sidelong glance; she was staring straight ahead, almost expressionless. He wanted to say something—but what?—but the door opened again, this time to Grand Admiral Savanche.

"Lieutenant, I believe you have a hand-to-hand for me?"

"Yes, sir." Esmay's voice expressed no more than her face as she handed him the databag.

"Very well. Dismissed." He turned to Barin. "Come along in, Ensign." Barin tried to catch Esmay's eye, but she looked past him. He followed Savanche into the conference, his heart sinking rapidly past the deck toward the gravitational center of the universe.

"The tissue typing confirms that the unidentified bodies found at the site of the *Elias Madero* hijacking were those of five members of the ten from Lord Thornbuckle's personal militia: Savoy Ardenil, Basil Verenci, Klara Pronoth, Seren Verenci, and Kaspar Pronoth. This very strongly suggests that Sera Meager's ship was there at the time, and may have attempted to intervene."

Which meant that they knew, at last, where Brun's yacht had been when she was attacked. At last they could narrow the search to something other than all space everywhere. *Shrike*'s subsequent search for traces of the *Elias Madero* narrowed it further. Barin tried to fix his mind on the evidence and its logical consequences, but Esmay's set face kept intruding. She had been wrong, yes—but Lord Thornbuckle's outburst, his refusal to see her, was profoundly unjust. Brun's situation was not Esmay's fault.

"The Guernesi are working on data cubes recovered from the *Elias Madero*; they have already identified the organization—apparently it really is the New Texas Godfearing Militia, and they are attempting to find out which branch captured Sera Meager." The briefing officer, a commander Barin did not know, paused for questions. One only came, from Lord Thornbuckle.

"How long . . . ?"

When the conference was dismissed, Barin fully intended to go looking for Esmay. He wanted her to know that he, at least, was no longer angry with her. But the ubiquitous Lieutenant Ferradi caught him first. By the time he'd finished running the errands she assigned, he was due back aboard *Gyrfalcon* for his watch.

❖   ❖   ❖

Captain Solis met Esmay at the docking hatch for *Shrike*. "We need to talk," he said. He looked more tired than angry. "So far no one aboard knows about this—and I would prefer to keep it as quiet as possible."

"Sir." She hadn't done anything at all, but follow orders and take the data where she'd been told.

He sighed. "Near as I can tell—and I should be able to tell, or what am I doing with my rank?—your outburst back at Copper Mountain was just that, an outburst. You've done a good job for me; you're an effective leader. You fit your history, is what I'm saying. But acts have consequences, including mistakes, however rare."

Esmay thought about saying something, but decided there was no point.

"Lord Thornbuckle needs a villain," Solis said. "And since he can't get his hands on the real villains, he's picked you. He refuses to have you involved in planning the rescue; he doesn't even want you on the base. There's a very limited amount that we can do, given his position and his state of mind. However, I consider your knowledge of Sera Meager—and the investigation of the *Elias Madero* hijacking site—to be important resources. I've gone on record as saying so, and had my tail chewed by Admiral Hornan."

"Yes, sir," Esmay said, since the long pause suggested the need for some comment.

"You're going to have to stay out of everyone's way—I won't say I'm restricting you to *Shrike*, because that would be unfair, but until I can get you some kind of assignment that uses your talents, I strongly recommend that you consider spending most of your time there—and make sure you don't run afoul of Lord Thornbuckle or Admiral Hornan. The latter won't be easy—he's taking his position as Sector Commandant very seriously, and he would like to lead the task force when it acts. Since the Serranos are in Thornbuckle's bad graces, he may well get that assignment."

"Yes, sir." Why were the Serranos in trouble? That made no sense to Esmay, but clearly she should stay away from Barin until she got that figured out. The last thing she wanted was to get a Serrano in worse trouble.

"And if you do mingle, watch what you say—because someone else will be."

"Yes, sir."

"I'll do my best to keep you informed of the progress of the investigation and planning—now, get in there and keep my ship the way it should be."

"Yes, sir." Esmay saluted and went aboard, very little cheered by the knowledge that her captain no longer thought of her as a monster. Clearly, enough other people did.

❖   ❖   ❖

In the next few days, Barin did his best to search the station, but he did not see Esmay in any of the places where off-duty officers congregated. Her name was never down for a machine or swim lane at the gym; he could find no logon records at the library; she had no assigned quarters. Could she still be living aboard *Shrike*? He called up the ship's entry and found her listed as the XO—at least that was right—but no personal comcode number. He didn't want to call the ship's general number and have her paged; in the present climate, that might get them both in more trouble.

The next briefing began with a presentation by one of the Guernesi.

"Thanks to the data cubes recovered by *Shrike*, and skillfully enhanced by your technicians, we're able to identify the raiders as members of a religious-military organization which controls some six Earth-type planets in this area—" He pointed to a chart on display. "You'll notice that these are in the angle, as it were, between Guernesi and Familias space.

"Let me give you a little necessary background on the group that calls itself the New Texas Godfearing Milita, or the Nutex Militia, for short. Our historians have done extensive research on the fringe religions that formed colonies in the early days of expansion from Old Earth, because we've had unpleasant contact with many of them. This one claims to descend from founders in Texas—one of the United States, which was in North America, for those of you with an interest in Old Earth geography."

"I don't see the relevance," Lord Thornbuckle said. "We can learn the history later—"

"I believe you will, sir. Their present beliefs are relevant to your daughter's situation, and to any hope of intervention on her behalf. Their present beliefs grow out of their mythologized view of Texas history." He took a breath and went on. "Now, this state had at one time been—very briefly—an independent nation. As with other nations swallowed up by larger political units, a portion of its population clung to that memory and caused trouble. In the late twentieth, their reckoning, one of many militias and terrorist religious groups active in the United States was something called the Republic of Texas. At that time, it was not affiliated with a particular religious position, and did not have as rigid a view of gender roles as some others. But it existed in the same soup, as it were, and the flavors melded."

"Was it involved in terrorist acts at that time?" asked Admiral Serrano.

"We think originally not, except in collecting arms, evading taxes, and causing the local government as much administrative trouble as possible. However, in one recorded standoff with the authorities, its members did take hostages, and did announce an intent to form a separate government and bring down the existing one. It failed. But that failure led to an affiliation with the survivors of a failed religious fringe group. They explained the Republic of Texas failure as resulting from lack of faith, and explained their own as resulting from lack of military experience. That group bore the rather cumbersome name of the Republic of Godfearing Texans Against World Government. It quickly splintered, as such groups often do, into several, each of which had similar, but doctrinally distinct, beliefs. One of these called itself the New Texas Godfearing Militia. This particular branch believed that the decay of society which led to acceptance of tyranny was due to the influence of women, and that women had been allowed beyond the bounds set by God in Holy Scripture. Many other such groups existed at the time—universal education for women in North America was then fairly recent, and their entry into employment was blamed for male unemployment and discontent. Historians have found many texts advocating the return of women to 'traditional' roles, defined very narrowly.

"It is this branch of the original which made it to space, under a colonization contract which they promptly disavowed. They organized their own colonial government, based on a military unit found in the original state. Apparently, a mythology had arisen surrounding the Texas Rangers, so they denoted their elected officials 'rangers,' and appended the names of historical figures from the brief period of Texas nationality. That's important, because we have learned to track splits in the original group by their choice of names for their rangers. For instance, there's a branch that denominates their leaders Rangers McCullough, Davis, King, Austin, and Crockett. Another uses Crockett, Bowie, Houston, Travis, and Lamar. However, they all have in common a council of five rangers, headed by a captain. We've included a listing for each of the six known branches.

"Because this group formed by splintering, and considers individual liberty of utmost importance—individual liberty of males, that is—they are constantly breaking up and reforming alliances among themselves."

"Do they exchange prisoners?" asked another admiral.

"Almost never. We've retrieved a few men from them, by hefty threats. But never women. There's a double problem with their attitude towards women. They believe that allowing women in space, for instance, is a form of neglect—that men are bound by faith to protect women. So if they capture women, they consider that they are actually saving them from a worse fate."

"But they mutilated and killed those women—"

"That's the other problem. Their religious beliefs are, as with most such groups, extremely rigid on anything having to do with sex or reproduction. They believe women were created by God to serve men and bear children . . . and that they must be guided, if children, or forced, if adults, into the role divinely intended for them. They also believe that only male-female sexual activity is permissable; anything else is what they call abomination. So also is contraception and genetic engineering. So if they capture women who have contraceptive implants, evidence of genetic engineering, or who are, by virtue of their rank or behavior, 'usurping the authority of men,' they usually kill them."

"Brun's a Registered Embryo," Lord Thornbuckle said. "She's got the mark—what would they think of that?"

"Abomination, certainly. Interfering with God's plan for humans . . . and I assume like most unmarried young women, she also had a contraceptive implant?"

"Of course," Lord Thornbuckle said. "And beyond that, REs require a positive fertility induction. Brun wanted the implant mostly so she'd be like her friends, some of whom weren't Registered Embryos."

"It's surprising they didn't kill her," the Guernesi went on. "They must have considered her political importance worth taking the chance that God would punish them for allowing her to live. That's undoubtedly why they did such a thorough job with muting her, and proceeded immediately to induce fertility. In their own minds, they were reclaiming her for God's purposes, and sending a message to you and the rest of the Familias—"

"Then they're free-birthers—"

"Rabidly so; each adult male is entitled to as many wives as he can support, and free access to what they call 'whores of Satan.' All live-born children, however, are considered equally legitimate property of the acknowledged father—and if no father boasts of it, there are always people ready to adopt. If any of their own women rebel—and it does happen—they are muted and handed over to these breeding houses."

"How do you know so much?" Thornbuckle asked.

"Well, we share a border with two of the five systems they control, and they've come after our people repeatedly. Their beliefs name us as one of the abominations. If anyone is interested, we can provide copies of what they consider to be divinely inspired prophecy and law. They also trade with us, in very limited ways—in spite of our being, in their view, perverts and abominations, they have need of our skills sometimes. In order to protect our people, we've had to find out more about them. In fact, I'm afraid we may be indirectly responsible for this incursion into Familias space."

"What!"

"They had attacked one of our passenger ships, the third time in only a few months. It got away, but we felt they were becoming too bold. So, we smacked them, hard—went in and blew some of their fixed defense platforms, and told 'em God was punishing 'em for their errors. They know most of our people are what they call 'spiritual'—though of course, not the same faith. Anyway, my guess is that they reacted to this by looking for some way to regain their prestige. Stayed away from us—and the Emerald States, on their other side, had whacked 'em before they bounced off us—so they went after you. I should warn you—they probably have agents somewhere in your commercial networks, because every time *we've* caught them trying to hijack a big cargo ship, it's had illegal arms shipments on it."

"There was nothing like that on the *Elias Madero* manifest . . ."

"No. There wouldn't be. The way they operated in our space was they'd get something on a shipping agent, get the access to a hold—sometimes only one, sometimes several—then they'd have it stuffed with anything they could buy on the gray market." He tipped his head. "Lot of it came from the Familias, you know. You folks have a thriving arms industry."

"We're not alone in that," Lord Thornbuckle muttered.

"No. But of the stuff we've confiscated when we've caught them, around seventy-three percent comes from Familias sources, eleven percent from ours, and the rest from the Emerald Worlds." He paused; no one said anything. "I'd recommend a very thorough look at the Boros Consortium shipping agents, especially the one upstream of where the attack occurred. They don't usually wait long to grab after they've coerced someone into loading. Patience is not their strong point. You might also want to check your official military inventories; in both the Emerald Worlds and the Guerni Republic, they've attempted to gain converts within the military. Their emphasis on male supremacy and personal honor does find welcome in some cultures, and you're a multicultural entity."

A chill fell on the room; Barin recognized both fear and denial in the silence. As if they did not already have concerns about loyalty, after Lepescu and Garrivay. But before any of the military spoke, Thornbuckle did.

"So now you've narrowed it to—what—five planets? Six? But she could be anywhere."

"In theory, yes. But here's what else we've got . . ." A still shot of enhanced vid went up. "Thanks to *Shrike*'s extensive scavenging of the hijacking site, and the quick thinking of someone in the *Elias Madero* crew, we have video data of the hijackers themselves. "You can see that enhancement gives us the engraving on the leader's insignia . . . here . . . you can just make out BOWIE. So we know that this raid was led by a Ranger Bowie, and we know from other sources that only two of the settlements, Our Texas and Texas True, now title one of their rangers 'Bowie.' Knowing that, we'll need to get visual confirmation of *which* Bowie we're dealing with—and that may take some time."

"She doesn't *have* time," Thornbuckle said. "We have to find her . . ."

Barin saw the sidelong glances; he had heard the rumors, too. They had worse problems than a missing woman and threats against the government. Something would have to be done.

"We have field agents working on it," Grand Admiral Savanche said. "Since the Guernesi told us to expect terrorist attacks from these people, we've put out specific warnings to law enforcement on all orbital stations, shipyards, and in the larger cities."

Zenebra, Main Station

Goonar Terakian had come into the Rusty Rocket for a quiet conversation with his cousin Basil Terakian-Junos, out of the hearing of their other relatives and shipmates. They had business no one else needed to hear. Midweek, mid-second shift, they might have been lucky enough to find the bar empty except for Sandor the bartender and possibly Genevieve. Genevieve, Sandor said, was off somewhere shopping. But the bar wasn't empty. Propped against the bar was a young man whose shipsuit bore an unfamiliar patch, but his condition was all too familiar.

"You don't have a clue what's coming to you," the young man said. He was very young, and very drunk. Terakian ignored him, and ordered for himself and Basil. Perhaps the young fool would go back to talking to himself.

But he didn't. When Terakian moved to the far end of the bar with Basil, the young man followed.

"The blow is about to fall," the young man said. He had an accent you could slice for baklava. "And yet you walk in darkness, unaware."

"Go away," Basil said.

"You will not give the orders then," the young man said. "It will be too late for you, then."

Terakian looked past him at Sandor, who rolled his

eyes but said nothing. Drunks are drunks, an occupational hazard. But the Terakians were old customers, so he approached the young man. "Are you drinking or talking?" he asked.

"Gimme another," the young man said. He swayed slightly but he wasn't out yet, and Terakian figured he wouldn't remember anything anyway.

"About the Vortenya contract," he said to Basil, turning his back on the drunk. "What I heard from Gabe on the *Serenity Gradient* is that they're planning—"

The drunk tapped his shoulder, and Terakian turned angrily. The drunk shook a finger in his face. "You don't know what's coming to you," he said again.

"What are you talking about?" Terakian said, more than a little annoyed. "All I know that's coming to me is a half share in the ship when my uncle dies." He grinned at his cousin, who grinned back.

"Issa secret," the young man said. "But you'll know. You'll *all* know."

"Sounds like a threat," Basil said. "Oooh . . . I'm so scared . . ."

"You better be," the young man said. His bleary gaze focussed again. "All you . . . abominations."

"Egglayer!" Terakian's cousin said. He had a temper, and the scars to prove it.

But the young drunk didn't rise to that insult. He smiled an ugly smile. "You'll be sorry. When the stations blow, and the wrath of God smites—"

"Here now," Sandor said. "No god-talk in this bar. If you want to fight over religion, do it somewhere else."

The young man pushed himself back from the bar, took a few unlevel steps, then folded over and vomited copiously.

"I hate righteous drinkers," Sandor said, reaching for the vacuum nozzle racked behind the bar. "They can't hold their liquor." He looked at Terakian and his cousin. "You ever seen him before?"

"No," Terakian said. "But there's been a few of those patches around the last day or so, over in D-dock."

"Well, stick your head out and see if you spot any station security while I clean up. Don't want any trouble with the law for having served to a minor or something." Sandor yanked on the vacuum hose, and hauled it around the end of the bar toward the mess.

Terakian, who came through this station every two months, regular as clockwork, knew most of the station employees. He glanced down toward Friendly Mac's Exchange & Financing, and saw Jilly Merovic on her beat. He waved; Jilly waved back, and crossed the corridor, moving at her usual quick walk.

"Jilly's coming," he told the bartender.

"Good." Sandor had already sucked up most of the vomit, but the young man was sprawled unconscious. "Help me turn him over, will you?"

"Leave 'em face down, our ship medic says," Basil said.

"Well, then, pick up his head so I can suck up the rest of the puddle." Basil grimaced, but pulled the young man's head up by the hair as Sandor passed the vacuum intake under his face.

"What's going on?" Jilly asked from the doorway.

"New customer—he drank too much, threw up, and passed out on me."

"Um. You get his ID?"

"It *said* he was twenty-seven."

"All right, Sandor, I'm not accusing you of selling to minors. I just wanted to know if he had any medicals."

"Nothing stamped."

Jilly squatted beside the sprawled figure, then glanced up at Terakian and his cousin. "Either of you know him? Did he seem distressed?"

"No, we didn't know him, and he seemed drunk," Basil said. Terakian gave him a warning look; Basil was the kind to resent the interference of fate. They could always do their business later, if he didn't cause enough trouble to get them noticed.

"He was making threats," Terakian said. "Called us abominations, and said we'd get what was coming to us."

Jilly had opened the man's ID packet but she looked up at that. "Abominations? Are you sure that's what he said?"

"Yeah. And something about stations blowing up. Typical mean drunk, is what I thought. Probably his captain told him off, or his station molly took up with someone else."

"Ever hear of a ship called the *Mockingbird Hill*?" Jilly asked.

Terakian shook his head. "No . . . what is it?"

"An unaffiliated trader. This is Spacer First Class Todd Grew." She scanned the ship patch on the man's arm, then looked at the readout on her handcomp. "*Mockingbird Hill* all right, and she's berthed in D-dock. Paid up a thirty-day docking fee, and her cargo is listed as light manufactory."

"Aren't you going to call his ship for transport back?"

Jilly gave Basil a look that chilled Terakian to the bone, though he got only the edge of it. "No. Ser Grew deserves only the best medical treatment. You two keep watch on the door—if you see anyone looking for Mr. Grew, go cause trouble. Whatever you do, don't let them in here." Then, to the bartender. "I'll need your comjack."

"But you have your—"

"Now," Jilly said, with sufficient force that the bartender stepped back. Terakian was glad to see another man react the way he felt. He nodded at Basil and they went to the door as Jilly had ordered. He couldn't hear what she said . . . but a long life in Familias spaceways left him no doubt as to the identity of the men in unremarkable clothes who came through the bar's back door and bundled Todd Grew into a gurney before he woke up. Even as they were taking him out the back, one of them approached Terakian.

"May I see your ID please?" It was not really a request. Terakian pulled out his folder; the man glanced at it, and without looking up said, "Officer Merovic says she knows you—has for years."

"That's right," Terakian said. Cold sweat trickled down his back, and he hadn't even done anything wrong. That he knew of. "Off the *Terakian Blessing*, Terakian and Sons, Limited."

"And you?" the man said, looking at Basil.

"Basil Terakian-Junos. Off the *Terakian Bounty*."

"Cousins," the man said. "You're the brawler, aren't you?"

"I can fight," Basil said.

"Basil—"

"It doesn't bother me," the man said. "Just wanted to be sure I had the right Terakian cousins. Now let me give you some advice." Orders, he meant. "This never happened, right?"

"What?" asked Basil.

Terakian elbowed Basil. "We just came in here for a little family chat—"

"Right. And you saw Officer Merovic and bought her a drink."

"Yessir. And nobody saw anything?"

"That's it. I know how you people are with your families, but I'm telling you, this is not a story to tell, and there's no profit to be made off it."

Terakian doubted that—anything Fleet security cared about this much usually involved plenty of profit—but he was willing to concede that he couldn't make anything off it.

"And how long should our family conference continue?" he asked.

"Another fifteen minutes should about do it," the man said pleasantly.

Fifteen minutes. They still had time to deal with the Vortenya contract negotiations, if Jilly didn't insist on sitting with them for her drink.

Aragon Station, Sector VII HQ

"Thanks to an alert security force on Zenebra, we now have both proof of planned terrorist attacks, and some more specific information about Sera Meager's most probable location."

"And that is?"

"An unaffiliated trader, *Mockingbird Hill*, bought used from Allsystems Salvage four years ago . . . showed up at Zenebra Main Station, and paid thirty days' docking fee upfront. That in itself was a bit surprising, but the stationmaster just listed it in the log, and didn't specifically alert Fleet; we hadn't given out a list of warning signs, because we didn't want to cause widespread panic. One of the crew, however, got drunk in a spacer bar, spewed his guts out, and had said something to the locals which alerted security. They called Fleet, and when we interrogated him, we found he was one of that cult, and the trader was stuffed with explosive, designed to blow any station they chose. They hadn't intended to blow Zenebra, particularly, but they were sited there in case called on to act somewhere in that sector."

"And Sera Meager?"

"According to one of the others, the Ranger Bowie on the vid from *Elias Madero* is from the branch known as Our Texas; this group was from Native Texas, who are apparently allied with them at present."

"And the Guernesi have agents in place on . . . let's see here. Home Texas, Texas True, and . . . what do you know? Our Texas."

"Yes . . . and that agent should be able to confirm whether they still have a Ranger Bowie, and whether we've got the right man—and planet."

Caradin University, Department of Antique Studies

Waltraude Meyerson, peering through the eyepiece of the low-power microscope at an exceedingly rare photograph which might—if she was lucky—finally answer the question of whether a certain Old Earth politician was male or female, ignored the comunit's chime until it racked up into an angry buzz. She reached out blindly, and felt around on her desk until she found the button and pushed it.

"Yes!"

"It's Dean Marondin . . . we have an urgent request for a specialty consult in your field."

"Nothing in my field is urgent," Waltraude said. "It's all been dead for centuries." Nonetheless she sat back and flicked off the microscope's light.

"It's a request from the highest authorities . . ."

"About ancient history? Is it another antiquities scam?"

"No . . . I'm not even sure why, but they want to know about Old Earth politics, North American . . . so of course I thought of you."

Of course. She was the only North Americanist on the faculty, but chances were that some idiot bureaucrat wanted to know the exchange rate of Quebeçois francs to Mexican pesos in a decade she knew nothing about . . .

"So what's the question?"

"They want to talk to you."

Interruptions, always interruptions. She had taken the term off, no classes, so she could finally put together the book she had been working on for the past eight years, and now she had to answer silly questions. "Fine," she said. "I'll give them fifteen minutes."

"I think they need longer," the dean said. "They're on their way."

Great. Waltraude stood up and stretched, working out the kinks that hours over the microscope had put in her back, and looked vaguely around her office. "They" implied more than one—they would want to sit down, and both chairs were piled with papers. Some people thought it was old-fashioned to have so much paper around, but she was—as she insisted—old-fashioned herself. That's why she'd gone into antique studies in the first place. She had just picked up one stack, and was looking for a place to put it, when the knock came at her door. "Come in," she said, and turned to find herself facing two men and two women who scared her into immobility. They looked as if they should all be in uniform, though they weren't.

"I'm sorry if we startled you," said one of the women. "But—do you know anything about Texas?"

Three hours later she was still talking, and they were still recording it and asking more questions. She was no longer scared, but still confused about why they'd come.

"But you really should ask Professor Lemon about that," she said finally. "He's the one who's done the most work on North American gender relations in that period."

"Professor Lemon died last week in a traffic accident," the woman said. "You're the next best."

"Oh. Well—" Waltraude fixed the other woman with a gaze that usually got the truth from undergraduates. "When are you planning to tell me what's going on?"

"When we get you to Sector VII Headquarters," the woman said with a smile that was not at all reassuring. "You're now our best expert on Texas history, and we want to keep you alive."

"My sources—" Waltraude said, waving at the chaos of her office. "My book—"

"We'll bring everything," the woman promised. "And you'll have access to Professor Lemon's as well."

Lemon had refused for years to share his copy of a Molly Ivins book Waltraude had never been able to track down through Library Services. He had even reneged on a promise to do so, in exchange for her data cube of thirty years of a rural county newspaper from Oklahoma. Access to Lemon's material?

"When do we leave?" asked Waltraude.

CHAPTER THIRTEEN

Sector VII HQ

"The admiral wants you," the jig said. Esmay looked up from her lists. What now? She hadn't done anything bad again, surely.

"On my way," she said, forcing cheerfulness into her voice. Whatever it was would be made no better by a long face.

In Admiral Hornan's outer office, the clerk nodded at her soberly, and touched a button on the desk. "Go right in, Lieutenant Suiza."

So it was serious, and she still had no idea what was going on. They had chewed all the flavor out of her sins so far; what else was there to attack?

"Lieutenant Suiza reporting, sir." She met Admiral Hornan's eyes squarely.

"At ease, Lieutenant. I'm sorry to say I have sad news for you. We have received a request relayed by ansible from your father for you to take emergency leave . . . your great-grandmother has died."

Esmay felt her knees give a little. The old lady's blessing—had she known? Tears stung her eyes.

"Sit down, Lieutenant." She sat where she was bidden, her mind whirling. "Would you like tea? Coffee?"

"No . . . thank you, sir. It's—I'll be fine in a moment." She was already fine; a translucent shield protected her from the universe.

"Your father indicates that you and your great-grandmother were close—"

"Yes, sir."

"And says that your presence is urgently needed for both legal and family matters, if you can possibly be spared." The admiral's head tilted. "Under the circumstances, I think you can well be spared. Your presence here is hardly essential." He might as well have said it was grossly unwelcome; Esmay registered that but felt none of the pain she would have felt before. Great-grandmother dead? She had been a constant, even in self-exile, all Esmay's life, all her father's life.

"I—thank you, sir." Her hand crept up to touch the amulet through her uniform.

"I'm curious to know, if you would not mind telling me, what legalities might require a great-grandchild's presence at such a time."

Esmay dragged her mind back to the present conversation; she felt she was wading through glue. "I'm not entirely sure, sir," she began. "Unless I am my great-grandmother's nearest female relative in the female line . . . and I'd have thought it was my aunt Sanibel."

"I don't follow."

Esmay tried to remember birth years—surely it had to be Sanni, and not herself. But Sanni was younger than her father. "It's the land, sir. The estancia. Land passes in the female line."

"Land . . . how much land?"

How much land? Esmay waved her hands vaguely. "Sir, I'm sorry but I don't know. A lot."

"Ten hectares? A hundred?"

"Oh no—much more than that. The headquarters buildings occupy twenty hectares, and the polo fields are—" She tried to think without counting on her fingers. "Probably a hundred hectares there. Most of the small paddocks up by the house are fifty hectares . . ."

The admiral stared; Esmay did not understand the intensity of that stare. "A small paddock—just part of this land—is fifty hectares?"

"Yes . . . and the large pastures, for the cattle, are anywhere from one to three thousand hectares."

He shook his head. "All right. A lot of land. Lieutenant—does anyone in Fleet know you are that rich?"

"Rich?" She wasn't rich. She had never been rich. Her father, Papa Stefan, her great-grandmother . . . the family as a whole, but not her attenuated twig on the end of the branch.

"You don't consider thousands of hectares a sign of wealth?"

Esmay paused. "I never really thought of it, sir. It's not mine—I mean, it never was, and I'm reasonably sure it's not now. It's the family's."

"My retirement estate," the admiral said, "Is ten hectares."

Esmay could think of nothing to say but "Sorry," and she knew that was wrong.

"So might I conclude," the admiral went on, in a tone of voice that set Esmay's teeth on edge, "that if you were to . . . choose to pursue family responsibilities, rather than a career in Fleet, you would not be starving in the street somewhere?"

"Sir."

"Not that I'm advising you to do so; I merely find it . . . interesting . . . that the young officer who was capable of telling the Speaker's daughter she was a spoiled rich girl is herself . . . a rich . . . girl. A very rich girl. Perhaps—for all the reasons you elucidated for Sera Meager's benefit—rich girls are not suited to military careers."

It was as close to an instruction to resign as anyone could come, without saying the words. Esmay met his eyes, bleak misery in her heart. What chance did she have, if senior officers felt this way about her? She wanted to argue, to point out that she had proven her loyalty, her honor—not once, but again and again. But she knew it would do no good.

The admiral looked down at his desk. "Your leave and travel orders have been cut, Lieuteant Suiza. Be sure to take all the time you need."

"Thank you, sir." She would be polite, no matter what. Rudeness had gotten her nowhere, honesty had come to grief, and so she would be polite to the end.

"Dismissed," he said, without looking up.

The clerk looked up as she came out.

"Bad news, sir?"

"My . . . great-grandmother died. Head of our family." Her throat closed on more, but the clerk's sympathetic expression looked genuine.

"I'm sorry, sir. I have the leave and travel orders the admiral told me to prepare . . ." The clerk paused, but Esmay offered no explanation. "You've got a level two priority, and I took the liberty of putting your name on a berth for the fastest transit I could find."

"Thank you," Esmay said. "That's very kind—"

"You're quite welcome, sir; just sorry it's for a sad occasion. I notice your end-of-leave is given as indeterminate—I'm assuming you'll notify the nearest sector HQ when you know how long you'll need?"

"That's right," Esmay said. The familiar routine, the familiar phrases eased the numbing chill of the admiral's attitude.

"That would be Sector Nine, and I'll just add the recognition codes you'll need—and here you are, sir."

"Thank you again," Esmay said, managing a

genuine smile for the clerk. He, at least, treated her as if she were a normal person worth respect.

Her transport would undock in six hours; she hurried back to her quarters to pack.

❖   ❖   ❖

Marta Katerina Saenz, Chairholder in her own right, and voter of two other Chairs in the Family sept, had been expecting the summons for weeks before it came. Bunny's wild daughter had at last fallen into more trouble than youth and dash could get her out of, though the news media had been fairly vague about what it was, having had her listed first as "missing" and then as "presumed captured by pirates." She suspected it might be worse than that; pirates normally killed any captives or ransomed them quickly. Bunny, who had succeeded Kemtre as the chief executive of the Familias Grand Council, had actually done quite well in the various crises that had followed the king's abdication—the Morellines and the Consellines had not in fact pulled out; the Crescent Worlds hadn't caused trouble; the Benignity's attempt at invasion in the Xavier system had been quickly scotched. But rumor had it that his daughter's disappearance had sent him into a state close to unreason. Rumor was usually wrong in details, Marta had found, but right in essence.

She herself was the logical person to call in for advice and help. Family connections and cross-connections, for one thing, and—paradoxically—her reputation for avoiding the hurly-burly of political life. Her axes had all been ground long since, and stored in the closet for future need. Several of the Families had already contacted her, asking her to make discreet inquiries. Moreover, she had helped Bunny in the Patchcock affair, and she knew the redoubtable Admiral Serrano. In addition, whatever trouble Brun had gotten herself into involved this side of Familias space—that was clear from the number of increased Fleet patrols, and the way her own carriers were being

stopped for inspection. So it was natural that someone would think of asking her to—what was the
phrase?—"assist in the investigations."

She did not resent the call as much as she might
have a decade or so earlier. That affair on Patchcock
had been much more fun than she'd expected, and
the aftermath—when she'd tackled Raffaele's difficult
mother about the girl's marriage—even more so.
Perhaps she'd had enough, for a while, of secluded
mountain estates and laboratory research. Perhaps it
was time for another fling.

Though by all accounts this would be no fling.
When she boarded the R.S.S. *Gazehound*, which had
been sent to fetch her, she was given a data cube
which made that clear. Marta had met Brun more
than once, in her wildest stages, and the vid of Brun
helpless and mute was worse than shocking. She put
it out of her mind, and concentrated instead on testing
her powers with the crew of the R.S.S. *Gazehound*.

Captain Bonnirs had welcomed her aboard with the
grave deference due her age and rank; Marta had
managed not to chuckle aloud at that point, but it
wasn't easy. He seemed so young, and his crew were
mere children . . . but of course they weren't. Still,
they responded to her as her many nieces and
nephews had, treating her as an honorary grandmother. For the price of listening to the same old
stories of love, betrayal, and reconciliation, she could
acquire vast amounts of information the youngsters
never knew they were giving.

Pivot-major Gleason, for instance, while apparently
unaware of any conflict between his loyalty to the
Regular Space Service and that to his family, was
carrying undeclared packages from his brother to his
sister-in-law's family: packages that, under the scrutiny
now given such mail, would have been opened and
inspected by postal authorities. He didn't see anything
wrong with this; Marta hoped very much he was

merely hauling stolen jewels or something equally innocuous and not explosives.

Ensign Currany, in the midst of asking advice on handling unwanted advances from a senior officer, revealed that she had a startling misconception of the nature of Registered Embryos which suggested a political orientation quite different from that she overtly claimed. Normally this wouldn't have mattered, but now Marta had to wonder just why Currany had joined Fleet—and when.

She discovered that an environmental tech had a hopeless crush on the senior navigator, who was happily married, and that the curious smell in the enlisted crew quarters emanated from an illicit pet citra, kept in a secret compartment in the bulkhead behind a bunk. It was brought out to show her, and she enchanted its owners by letting it run up her arm and curl its furry tail around her neck. She overheard part of a furious argument between two pivot-majors about Esmay Suiza—one, having served aboard *Despite*, insisted she was loyal and talented; the other, who had never met her, insisted she was a secret traitor who had wanted Brun to be captured and had probably told the pirates where to find her. She would like to have heard more of that, but the argument ended the moment they realized she was lurking in the corridor, and neither would talk more about it.

By the end of the twenty-one day voyage, she was remembering exactly why she normally lived in isolation: people told her things, they always had, and after just a few weeks of it, she felt stuffed with the innumerable details of their lives and feelings. Therapist had never been her favorite self-definition.

Marta prepared herself for her first meeting with Bunny; she knew, from the tension all around her, that whether she liked it or not, she was everyone's favorite candidate for therapist where Bunny was concerned. She swept into the room with her usual flair, hoping it would have its usual effect on him.

This time it did not. Lord Thornbuckle looked up at her with the expression of a man very near the edge of sanity. Desperate, exhausted . . . not the expression one wanted to see on the chief executive of the Familias Regnant, someone on whose judgement the security of the entire empire depended.

Marta moderated her instinctive verve, and instead walked quietly across the room to take the hand he held out to her.

"Bunny, I'm so sorry."

He stared at her silently.

"But I know Brun, and if she's alive, we can and will help her."

"You don't know"—he swallowed—"what they did to her. To my *daughter*—"

She did know, but clearly he needed to tell her. "Tell me," she said, and held his hand through the recitation of all the horrors he knew Brun had endured, and the ones that might have followed. She interrupted this latter list.

"You can't know that—you can't know, and until we know for certain, you must not waste your strength worrying about it."

"Easy for you to say—"

"It was my niece you sent off to rescue Ronnie and George," Marta said crisply. "It is not easy to say, or to do, but people of our rank have responsibilities. Yours is heavy, but not beyond your strength, if you will quit adding to the load by imagining even more horrors."

"But Brun—"

"What you are doing by tearing yourself up does not help her."

"I don't know what to do . . ."

"Where's Miranda?" Bunny's exquisitely beautiful wife was, under her beauty, a woman of spun-steel endurance, capable of enforcing sense on her husband—one of the few who could.

"She's . . . back on Castle Rock. I didn't want her out here."

"Then, in her place, I will tell you what to do. Eat a hot meal. Sleep at least nine hours. Eat another hot meal. Don't talk to anyone about anything important until you have done so. You will be even more miserable if your bad judgement, born of hunger and exhaustion, harms Brun's chances."

"But I can't just sleep—"

"Then get medication." Marta paused a moment for that to take effect, and went on. "Bunny, I'm terribly, terribly sorry that this has happened . . . but you simply must not go into this as you are."

"Who called you here?" he asked, at last reacting to her immediate presence.

"It doesn't matter. I'm here; I belong here, because those people are only a jump point away from my home; and I'm taking charge of you, at this moment, because I'm older, meaner, and you daren't hit me."

With that, she punched in a call to the infirmary and the kitchen, and stood over Bunny until he had downed a bowl of soup and a plate of chicken and rice. Then she insisted that he take the medication provided, and nodded to his valet. "Don't let him up until morning, or he's slept ten hours, whichever comes latest. Then make him eat again."

From the startled, but relieved, expressions of those around her, Marta judged that no one else had been able to make the Speaker see reason. He was, after all, the Speaker of the Grand Council. She felt her lip curling. That was exactly why she let someone else vote her Seat most of the time, all this ridiculous social etiquette getting in the way of common sense.

Her next stop was a brief call on Admiral Serrano, who was said to be in line to command the task force.

On her way through the interminable layers of military bureaucracy between the outer and inner office, she heard a sleek blonde female officer murmur to another woman, "Well, it was Suiza, after all." Both shook their heads.

Marta decided she didn't like the sleek blonde, on no more evidence than the unlikely perfection of her bone structure and perfect grooming. She said nothing, but filed the comment away.

Vida Serrano looked almost as harried and exhausted as Thornbuckle had. Marta blinked; she had not expected this.

"What happened to you?"

"Lord Thornbuckle," Vida said. "He's furious with the Serrano family in general, and me in particular."

"Why?"

"Because he thinks it was his daughter's attachment to my niece Heris which led her into what he calls 'dangerous interests.' Of course, there was that regrettable incident at Xavier, but it certainly wasn't Heris's fault. Then I recommended that she go to the Fleet training facility at Copper Mountain to get some practical knowledge—and I had hoped, some discipline as well—but that blew up in our faces when she was shot at, then quarrelled with Lieutenant Suiza and stormed off on her own. Still, it was my recommendation, so it's my fault." She heaved a sigh and managed a weary smile. "I really had thought she was ready for something like Copper Mountain. Lord Thornbuckle himself introduced his daughter to Lieutenant Suiza, but apparently that young woman is not at all what she seemed."

"I'm confused," Marta said, sitting down firmly. "I thought young Brun had managed to get herself captured by pirates and hauled off somewhere. I saw the vid of her mutilation, that's all. But I've heard nasty comments about Lieutenant Suiza from more than one person, and this is the first I've heard of

Brun taking any military training. And 'shot at'—was that part of a course, or something else?"

"One thing at a time," Vida said, suddenly looking more like the admiral she was. "Brun was accepted as a civilian trainee—she signed up for courses in search and rescue, and similar adventurous things. I was hoping, frankly, that she'd realize how well her talents suited us and join Fleet formally."

"Brun?" Marta snorted. "You could no more make that girl into an officer than a mountain cat into a sheepdog."

"So it seems. Perhaps she was on her best behavior with me. At any rate, while she was there, she was the target of at least two assassination attempts—one nearly fatal, in part because she insisted on doing what everyone else did, and eluding her assigned security detail. Her father wanted her to leave, and she refused. He recognized Lieutenant Suiza from all the publicity, and tried to enlist her help in making his daughter cooperate with her security detail. Apparently his daughter did agree, and things went along fairly well for a few weeks. Witnesses say that she kept trying to make friends with Suiza, who wasn't willing."

"Why?" Marta asked.

Vida shrugged. "Who can know? She was taking extra courses herself, doubling up, but all we know for sure is that she and Brun quarrelled the night before the field exercise in escape and evasion. Lieutenant Suiza was extremely rude and abusive—I've heard the tapes myself—and according to some sources, she had been previously heard to make disparaging remarks about the senior Families and the Grand Council. Highly unprofessional."

"Why didn't this come out at the time of the courts-martial?" Marta asked. "Surely if she'd had a bad reputation, it would have been a matter of some interest during the investigation of the mutiny."

Vida threw out her hands. "I don't know. I wasn't involved in that investigation, except in the most preliminary stages; all the background work was done at headquarters. Frankly, I had trouble believing that of her—I'd met her several times, you know—but the scan record is undeniable. Moreover, she admits she said those things to Sera Meager."

"Odd," Marta said. She filed that away in the same mental cubbyhole as the sleek blonde's remark. "So—what happened to Brun, then?"

Vida related what was known. "We're keeping it as quiet as we can, which isn't very. The newsfeeds have agreed, for now, but who knows when they'll change their mind? Clearly these people want it known: they keep leaking vid and other material—everything except location—to the newsfeeds. Worse, we still do not know where she was taken—and until we know that, we can hardly formulate a plan to get her out. The Guernesi are cooperating in every way, but so far we are still sifting through a very large sandpile looking for one very small diamond."

"Well." Marta gazed past Vida at the wall screen— a pattern of slowly shifting bands of color—for a long moment. "I'll tell you what I've accomplished. I put Bunny to bed with his stomach full of decent food, and I think I've terrorized the medical staff into keeping him down for at least ten hours."

"I am impressed."

"You should be. I presume you wanted me for my knowledge of the region?"

"Your ships travel it regularly—we wondered if there was anything in any of the logs that might reveal a trace of the ship or ships that Brun was on."

"What are we looking for?"

"A Boros Consortium container ship—a heavy— called the *Elias Madero*, perhaps traveling in association with one or more ships of about patrol-class."

"I presume you want this information extracted without informing my entire staff?"

"If possible, yes."

"I'll do the datasuck myself." Marta stood up. "Now you, m'dear, need to take my advice to Bunny. A hot meal, a long sleep. For a woman your age, you look like hell."

Vida laughed. "Yes, Marta. Are we convening the aunt's coven again?"

"No . . . Cecelia would be no help on this, and her feelings for Brun would be almost as obstructive as Bunny's. You and I should be able to handle it."

"If your esteemed friend will quit putting obstacles in my path," Vida said, shaking her head. "He's so convinced there's a conspiracy of Serranos, I'm lucky to be still on the task force."

"Um. I'll see what I can do, when he's had some sleep. I should at least be able to insist on his eating and sleeping on a sane schedule. Now, what can you give me for doing the suck on my own database?"

"Well . . . we've gathered the best we've got. Take your pick—here's my private list." Vida handed over a data cube. "You might want to work through Heris; she's got the really good techs with her at the moment."

"Fine. Now what's our conference schedule?"

Between meetings and a long and abortive attempt to extract data about the Boros ship from her own databases (no one had reported anything like it), Marta pottered about, as she thought of it, listening and learning how Fleet fit together. Much like any large organization, including her own pharmaceutical firms, but subtly different. Yet it was made up of people, and people were people the universe over.

Take this matter of Esmay Suiza. She had heard of Suiza—everyone with a newsfeed had heard of Suiza, first for the Battle of Xavier, and then for the *Koskiusko* affair. A rising young hero, a tactical genius, a charismatic leader. And she was here, executive officer of a ship in the task force . . . but she was *not* here . . . nowhere in the lists of officers tasked with this or that planning, was Esmay Suiza listed. Her captain sat in on some meetings . . . she never had, it seemed.

It seemed stupid. Suiza was the obvious source of recent, detailed knowledge of Brun's performance and attitudes. Surely Bunny's irrational dislike wasn't affecting everyone's judgement. Was she on some secret assignment? When she turned out to be on leave, that seemed the most likely explanation. But according to gossip, she was in disgrace, and had been sent away.

A cover story, of course. Marta wondered what kind of cover story they'd concocted. She knew what she would have done. She managed to be in one of the rec rooms one evening, looking by design as close to a potty old woman as she could manage, and kept her ears open.

Of course, they all knew who she was, in a way. Ordinary old civilian women weren't hanging out in the junior officers' recreation room. But they all had grandmothers, and she had perfected an earthy chuckle in the years of having nieces and nephews and cousins visiting. Soon she had a circle around her, bringing her drinks and snacks, and chatting happily.

She didn't even have to drop the topic herself. A female ensign nudged another. "Look—there's Barin now."

They both looked, and Marta looked too. A darkly handsome, compact young man with a worried expression made his way across the room to the drinks dispenser; that same sleek blonde followed him.

"With Casea on his heels," the other ensign said.

"Lieutenant Ferradi to you, Merce—she is senior." That was a male jig, whom Marta had already pegged as stuffy and overly precise.

"She is what she is," the ensign said. Her eyes slid to Marta, encountered the unexpected, and she blushed.

That confirmed what Marta had already expected. These young people—so transparent.

"It's too bad," the first ensign said. "I'd like to get to know him, but I can't—"

"Well," said the jig, "she may be . . . whatever . . . but she's better than Suiza, and that's who he was supposed to like before."

Marta gave him a smile for doing her work for her, and cocked her head. "Suiza? That girl who's the hero?"

Nervous glances, eyes shifting from side to side. No one spoke for a moment, then the first ensign said quietly, "She's—not such a hero right now, Sera."

"Why?" asked Marta, ignoring the signals that this was a ticklish subject. Directness often worked, and besides, it was more fun. But this produced more sidelong looks, more shifting about. Finally, the same ensign answered.

"She—said bad things about the Speaker's daughter. Said she didn't deserve to be rescued."

Marta blinked. That was not the kind of cover story she would have invented, and it wasn't something Admiral Serrano had told her. She had mentioned a row at Copper Mountain, but nothing since. That kind of rumor could hang around and damage someone's career years later. "Are you sure?" she asked.

Nods, some reluctant. "It started before, is what I heard," the jig said.

"It's all rot!" another jig said. "I don't believe it—someone made it up—"

"No, it's true. They have a tape. I heard Major Crissan talking to Commander Dodd, and he said he heard it himself. She quarrelled with Sera Meager at Training Command, something about a course they were both in, and they nearly asked for her commission."

"I don't see what you could say bad enough for that."

"Well . . . it had something to do with her loyalty, or something."

Something something something. A clear sign of uncontrolled rumor, Marta thought. She prodded a bit.

"Well, but—she is a hero, isn't she? I mean, she brought her ship back and saved Xavier . . ."

"Yes, but why? That's what they're asking now. People I know who knew her in the Academy say she wasn't that talented then. She wasn't even command track. How could she get that good without anyone knowing, unless she had help? And not wanting to rescue Sera Meager—"

"I'm sure she does," said Suiza's defender, getting red in the face. "But nobody listens—"

"Just because you have a bad case of hero worship, you can't ignore the facts. Sera Meager is a Chairholder; we exist to protect Chairholders, and—"

"What class was she in?" Marta said, before that turned ugly.

That led to an explanation she did not want about the way the Academy named its classes, on a rotation having nothing to do with the standard calendar. "So anyway," that informant finished up, when Marta felt her eyes about to glaze over, "she's in Vaillant class, six years ago." Marta converted that quickly to standard dates, but reminded herself that she'd probably have to ask for classmates by the Fleet's peculiar reckoning. But her informant went on, clearly in earnest to be complete. "Her classmates will be jigs—that's lieutenant, junior grade, sera—and lieutenants. Everyone who doesn't mess up badly is promoted from ensign to jig at the same time, but there's a selection board for lieutenant, with a 12-month range. Lieutenant Suiza was promoted in the first selection; some of her classmates will be promoted in the next few days."

So, to find Esmay's classmates, she could confine herself to lieutenants, for the most part. And some of them promoted behind her might have reason to wish her ill. Casually, without apparent intent, Marta began trolling through the assortment of lieutenants. Most were, she found, either classmates or within one year of Esmay Suiza's class. Some had hardly noticed her at the Academy; others claimed to have known her well. And a few had more immediate information to share.

"I just can't believe it," said the redhaired lieutenant with the mustache. Vericour, his name was. "I mean— Esmay! Yes, she got angry, and yes, she said things she shouldn't have—but she'd been working twice as hard as anyone else. They should have cut her some slack. You'd have thought she murdered the girl."

"You're a friend of hers?"

"Yes . . . at least, we were together at Training Command; we studied together sometimes. Brilliant tactician—and a nice person, too. I don't think she ever said half of what people say—"

"Perhaps not," Marta said.

"But Admiral Hornan says I should stay away from her—she's poison. And Casea Ferradi claims she was saying all sorts of things in the Academy . . . but why they listen to Casea, I can't figure out."

"Casea?"

"Classmate of ours. She's from a colonial world too—one of the Crescent Worlds group, can't remember which. Tell you the truth, before I met her, I had heard the women there are . . . well . . . shy. Casea was an education in that respect."

"Oh?" Marta gave him a grandmotherly smile, and he blushed.

"Well . . . junior year . . . I mean I'd heard about her, and she . . . she said she liked me. I suppose she did, as long as it lasted."

"She likes men . . ." Marta said, trailing it out.

"She likes sex," Vericour said. "Sorry, sera, but it's the truth. She went through our class like—like—"

"Fire through wheat?" suggested Marta. "And now she's always with that Ensign Serrano, isn't she?"

"Poor kid won't know what hit him," Vericour said, nodding. "I'd heard she was after bigger game, working her way up—but maybe she thinks the Serrano name's better than rank alone. And right now, when they're under a cloud, what with Lord Thornbuckle being so angry with them, she probably thinks she has a better chance."

"She is attractive," Marta said. "And I suppose she's efficient in her work?"

"I suppose," Vericour said, without any enthusiasm. "I was never on the same ship."

"I wonder if Ensign Serrano is actually taken with her."

"It wouldn't matter," Vericour said gloomily. "She has her ways, has Casea."

A few days downside, working through the civilian databases and ansible, gave her even more insight into the Suiza controversy. She had identified five classmates, including the sleek blonde Ferradi, who were actively spreading, if not inventing, wicked-Suiza stories. All five were at least one promotion group behind Suiza. If that wasn't the green-eyed monster, she didn't know what was. Suiza's former co-workers and commanding officers, on the other hand, seemed incredulous that anyone would believe such stories. One and all, they insisted that if she had had an argument with Brun Meager, and if she had been insulting, then Brun must have deserved it.

Marta wasn't sure about that—couldn't be, until she

met Esmay Suiza in person—but she was willing to swear that whatever the nature of the original offense, malice and envy and spite had blown it out of all proportion.

The nature of the original offense still eluded her. Unless Suiza had snapped under the pressure of work—which didn't seem likely given her history—Brun had precipitated the fight. How? Given Brun's past history, the most likely cause was that she'd come between Suiza and a lover, but gossip didn't credit Suiza with any lovers. Indeed, gossip went the other direction. Block of ice, cold fish, frozen clod. Barin Serrano was supposed to have liked her, when he was on *Koskiusko*, but that could be mere hero worship, and Vericour had said Suiza was cool to him at Copper Mountain.

What could Brun have done? Marta was careful not to ask this question of the youngsters. Most of them, it was clear, thought that being the victim of piracy turned Brun into a shining martyr figure, untainted by any human error other than getting caught. Marta knew better. Brun was, by observation and Raffaele's report, intelligent, quick-witted, brave, and full of mischief as a basket of kittens. If she had wanted some reaction from Suiza she did not get, she might well have put all her inventive genius to work making trouble. That still led back to interference with a man Suiza wanted—but the problem was that Suiza supposedly had no preferences. Unless it was Barin, but for that she had no evidence.

CHAPTER FOURTEEN

The pains started at night. Brun woke up, to find herself knotted around her hardened belly. It eased, but she knew at once it was not a cramp from supper. It was . . . what she most feared. She lay back, stretching a little. She was just dozing off when another pain curled her forward again.

She had no watch, no clock. She had no way to tell how the pains quickened. She had to use the toilet suddenly. Levering herself out of bed, she went into the corridor. Down the length of it, she saw the glint from the door-guard's eyes watching her. Damn him. She struggled toward the toilets, but another pain caught her, doubling her up against the wall. Through a haze of pain, she saw the guard stand up, move toward her. The pain eased; she leaned on the wall but went on. Into the toilet room . . . at least they had toilets, she thought muzzily. She was hardly a meter from it when fluid gushed down her legs, hot and shocking.

"You!" It was the warden; the guard must have wakened her. "Come on!" The woman grabbed her arm, pulled. Yelled at the others to wake up. Brun doubled up again; the woman tugged at her arm. But it hurt too much; she was too weak. She sagged to her knees, gasping. It was unfair that she couldn't scream, unfair that this pain could not be met as it should be, with the protest it deserved.

Now the other women were around her, tugging and pushing, but she huddled there on her knees, unwilling to rise. Why should she? Suddenly the warden stuck something under her nose, an acrid smell that made her throw her head up to escape it. With a grin of triumph, the woman yanked on her arms again. With the others' help, she got Brun up, and together they half-dragged, half-carried her down the corridor and into the birthing room. By then the pain had eased, and Brun clambered onto the birth-bed herself. She might as well.

To her surprise, the rest of the birthing went faster than the one she had watched. Weren't first births supposed to be slower? She couldn't remember; she couldn't think. One pain after another flowed down her body, pushing, pushing . . . the other women wiped her face with damp cloths, stroked her arms. The warden alone scolded her, telling her to breathe or push, waiting with a folded towel for the baby that was—surely—just about to come.

And then it did—with a last wrenching pain, she felt the pressure ease suddenly; a thin cry rose from nowhere. The women all gasped together; the warden scowled.

"Too little. You have puny babies."

But then another pain struck, and Brun curled into it.

"Ah—" The warden handed off the first baby to one of the other women. "Two babies! Good!"

The second was born crying lustily. The warden put them on Brun's chest. "Give suck," she said. Brun had no idea how, until the warden turned the babies and pressed Brun's nipples into the little mouths.

"Help her," she ordered one of the other women. She herself washed Brun, while the others cleaned the room.

By afternoon, Brun was back in her own room, lying exhausted on her bed, with a baby on either side. She felt nothing for them. They were no more her babies than . . . than any stranger's baby. Less. They had been forced on her; strangers had made use of her body to produce them.

Two babies. Brun slid into darkness on that thought.

"No breeding for half a year," the warden told her the next day. "You feed your babies; you help with work here one month, then you go to the nursery. Nursery for five months—maybe with twins, six months. Then to breeding house."

Half a year . . . she had half a year to get strong, to escape, to find a way to contact someone who would let her father know where she was.

But in the days after the birth, Brun began to despair again. How could she help Hazel if she couldn't find her? How could she find her when she couldn't ask questions? She lay motionless unless the warden prodded her to get up . . . she fed the babies only when ordered, ate only when ordered. Feeding the babies hurt; she had not imagined that babies would suck harder than her lovers had. But she was too weak, too miserable, to do more than hiss in pain each time someone put them to her breasts. She didn't notice when someone took the babies away, bringing them to her only for nursing. Someone had to put them to her breasts; someone had to clean them—and her—when they soiled her.

Then one day a cooler wind blew through the doors and windows, carrying with it a scent of harvest fields. And something—something familiar. Brun shifted in her chair; the babies shifted. One of them lost its hold on her nipple, and whimpered. Without noticing, she moved it back. Something—what was it? She dozed again, but woke at the next cool gust. Oak leaves, stubble fields. Hunting, if she were home. All at once the full memory hit her: Opening Day, with all three hunts gathered before the big house, the clop of the horses' feet, the panting and whining of hounds, the clink of glasses, the voices . . . but even in imagination, she saw herself silent, unable to reply to the greetings. She saw the faces of friends staring at her, shocked, disapproving . . . and she was standing barefoot on the sharp gravel, all the others on tall horses, hard-hooved horses stamping near her bare feet . . .

She would never be home. Her thoughts slid down the same spiral of depression . . . but this time stopped short of darkness. No. She was young, she had a long life to live. Lady Cecelia had survived without a voice, and she had been blind and paralyzed as well. Help had finally come; she, Brun, had been part of that help. Somewhere, people were trying to plan help for her. She had to trust that, believe that her family and friends would not leave her here forever, alone. She had survived so far; she had borne twins with no medical care worth mentioning, and lived . . . she would live to hunt again. She would ride; she would speak, and those who had silenced her would listen. Her head came up.

"This is good," the warden said, coming out to pat her on the shoulder. "Many mothers feel sad after babies, especially twins. But now you're better. Now you will be all right."

She was not all right, but she could be . . . perhaps. Brun fought the darkness back, made herself begin to live again. The next day, she reached out for the babies as they were brought to her. She didn't even know what they were . . . not only whose, who was the father, but whether they were boys or girls. She looked. Boys. Both boys . . . one with pale orange hair, one with darker, thinner hair. She could see nothing of herself in either one, and she knew that one of the men had had red hair and a shaggy red beard.

She still felt nothing for them, not even the mild flicker of interest she used to feel for other women's babies. She had thought babies amusing at times, when they were older than this and had learned to smile. She had felt the odd pang of tenderness . . . but not now. These were just . . . little animals who had lived in her flesh, and now fed at her expense. At least the nursing was less painful—even a relief, when her breasts were swollen with milk.

She watched the other women with their babies. Muted though they were, they clearly loved the babies, cuddling them, stroking them, laughing soundlessly when one of the infants did something amusing. They spoke to them in hissing whispers and little clicks whenever the warden was far enough away. They peered at each other's babies, smiling and nodding over them—and the same with her twins. She could not reciprocate.

Now that she could force herself to her feet again, she was expected to help with the work. But she had never cared for an infant, let alone in these primitive circumstances. The wrapping of diapers baffled her completely.

"It's as if she never did anything until now—can you believe a grown woman not knowing how to peel vegetables? To put a child to breast?" The warden complained to the other women, who nodded and hissed in response.

Brun seethed. She could have told them why she didn't have their backwards, primitive skills. She had not been trained to make beds and clean toilets and chop vegetables and wipe the bottoms of dirty little brats. She held pilots' licenses on half a dozen worlds;

she could ride to hounds with the Greens; she could take down and reassemble the scan systems of a medium cruiser as fast as any technicians . . .

And here her skills were worth nothing. They thought she was stupid or crazy, because she couldn't do what they did so easily.

"She's an abomination. Of course the heathen don't teach their daughters properly." That was the warden's explanation for everything she did wrong.

She was not a heathen, nor an abomination, but surrounded by those who thought she was, she found it harder and harder to remember her real self. It was easier to scrub the floor the way the warden insisted on, even if it would have been more efficient the other way. Easier to change the babies the way she was told, to cut vegetables the way she was told.

If only she had been really stupid . . . but her intelligence, recovering from the birth, awoke again. Recipes were boring, perhaps, but she remembered them just the same, automatically assigning them to categories. Sewing was even more boring than recipes, poking a needle in and out of cloth over and over. Why did they have to do everything the hard way? Not everything, she reminded herself . . . just the work assigned to women. Electricity for light, running water . . . but only men had access to computers and all that computers stood for.

Scraps of history she had hardly listened to in class floated up from a retentive memory. There had been other societies which resisted making life easier for women, because then they might turn away from the traditional role of wife and mother. Way back on Old Earth, cultures which didn't let women drive groundcars or fly or learn to use weapons—others which forbade women to teach in mixed classes, to become doctors. But that was long ago and very far away . . . and this was here and now.

*　　*　　*

In the quick glimpse she caught of the street when she and the babies were transferred to the nursery, she could not distinguish any landmarks. It was a chill, raw day; she shivered in the wind that whipped down the street. She was put in the back of the same kind of closed groundcar, where she could see nothing of her route, and driven some incalculable distance with four definite turns.

The front of the nursery looked slightly more welcoming, with shuttered windows instead of blank stone overlooking the street. A distant roar—Brun looked up to see the obvious plume of a shuttle launch in the distance.

"Eyes down!" said the driver, slapping at her head. But she exulted . . . she knew now where the space-port was, or at least what direction.

Inside, the matron greeted her less harshly than the warden at the maternity house, and she could hear women's voices in the distance. Women's voices? The matron led her to a room large enough for a bed, two cribs, and a low wide chair with a leg rest that was obviously intended for nursing. She had a small closet, a chest, and the inevitable sewing basket was on a bedside table.

The matron helped her settle the babies in their cribs, helped her make the bed, and then led Brun off to show her the house. In the upstairs rooms, the more privileged women could look out through slatted shutters to the streets below—but Brun had only a glimpse before the matron pulled her away. An upstairs sewing room had rear-facing windows that looked out on a long, walled garden full of fruit trees; a few apples hung from some of them. Beyond the wall—Brun tried not to stare, told herself she would have time to look later—beyond the wall she could see a street, and the buildings across it . . . and beyond more buildings, open land, rough fields and distant hills.

*   *   *

The women in the nursery had slightly more freedom. They were supposedly regaining their strength for another pregnancy; they were encouraged to walk out in the orchard, as well as do the housework and cooking. Not all the women were muted, either. They had come, Brun learned, from other maternity homes or from private homes . . . servant women whose children would be reared elsewhere when they returned to their duties. The women who supervised them inspected the babies and mothers daily for cleanliness and any sign of illness, and supervised the preparation of household chores and cooking, but otherwise treated their charges with pleasant firmness. The muted women had perhaps less pleasantness and more firmness, but no active unkindness.

They continued to teach Brun the skills they thought all women should have. Brun had not known that such things were possible, but she watched the other women produce socks and gloves and mittens from several wooden sticks and balls of fuzzy yarn. She was handed a pair of sticks, and shown—over and over—how to cast on, how to knit a plain stitch. It was the most boring thing she'd ever done, the same little movement of the hand over and over and over, even worse than sewing seams. Then they handed her another stick, and taught her to knit a tube. Something clicked in her mind—this sort of thing, done with finer yarn and on a machine, made some of the things she'd worn. Sweaters, for instance: three tubes sewn together. Stockings . . . leggings . . . tubular knits. It was interesting in an intellectual way, one of the few things that was.

It got colder, and Brun shivered. The other women, warm in their knitted shawls and sweaters, shook their heads at her.

"You must work faster," one of them told her. "You will be cold if you have no winter clothes." In winter, they explained, they wore long knitted stockings under their skirts, held up with a peculiar arrangement of straps and buttons. The stockinged feet did not break the rules against shoes, because they were not hard-bottomed. In households, some women even wore backless clogs in wet or snowy weather, if they needed to go to market, but here they would not.

Here also Brun was formally introduced to the beliefs of her captors. They assumed that outlanders had no morals, and no beliefs worth mentioning. So they began with the basics, as Brun assumed children were taught. God, a supernatural being who had created the universe. Man, the glory of creation. Woman, created to be Man's comfort and help. Evil powers, rebellious against God, who tempted Woman to usurp Man's position.

For once muteness had its utility; Brun could not be made to recite the Rules and Rituals, as the other women did. And since women did not "discourse"—a word which they interpreted to mean speaking or writing about Godly matters—she was not asked to write answers to the questions asked ritually of others. Women were not encouraged to read or write anyway—although recipes and compendia of other household knowledge were permissable. But they clearly feared contamination by anything a heathen abomination such as a Registered Embryo might commit to paper, or do to a book she read from. She was not allowed to read or write anything at all. They could not test her memory, or her understanding.

But she had an excellent memory. She could not hear the same words over and over without storing them away. The words of the prophets . . . the word of God Almighty. The rules and their corollaries . . . quite reasonable, if you accepted the premises, which Brun did not. If in fact you believed that women had been created as men's servants and comfort, then . . . anything women did which was not serving men would clearly be wrong. And this was not something women could determine. Only God could make the rules, and only men could interpret them.

It all made sense, except that it was ridiculous, like the ridiculous logic of paranoia. The notion that she was not as much a person as, say, her brothers . . . or, to go one step away, that Esmay Suiza was less a person than Barin Serrano . . . was absurd. She knew that. She knew how to demonstrate that, if only she could have explained; she was sure that every woman in the nursery would understand, if only . . .

But she was mute, all her knowledge and intelligence locked away. In her world, in the world she knew, the individual's voice was honored; parents and teachers and therapists like those who had worked with Lady Cecelia tried to ensure that each person had every opportunity to communicate. She remembered Cecelia's struggles, and the many who had helped her. Here, no one thought an abomination had anything useful to say. As long as she could understand and obey, that was enough.

She ached, burned, to free this world's women . . . to show them that they were as human as men. In her mind, in the dark hours, she made all the speeches, wrote all the lectures, proved over and over and over again to an audience of shadows what she could never say.

In the daytime, Brun forced herself to walk on the gritty paths, toughening her feet as well as her legs, whenever exercise was permitted. She walked in all weathers, even when frost and snow numbed her to the knees before she was halfway to the first trees. The twins weighed her down—but she thought of them like the heavy packs in training. Additional strength would come from lugging them around . . . she would be stronger sooner, and more able to escape. Twice a day she walked the length of the orchard and back . . . soon she could walk farther, in the lengthening days that must mean a warmer season was coming. She even welcomed the hard work of mopping and cleaning, as she felt herself growing stronger. In the evenings, in her room, she attempted the exercises that had once come so easily. At first she worried that they would notice, and forbid them, but no one commented. Other women too, she discovered, did exercises to tighten their slack bellies, to recover flexibility.

In the darkest times, she practiced the swift movements of unarmed combat . . . only two or three strokes each time, in case of observation, but a little every day. She matched hands and feet against each other, the quietest way she could think to achieve the hardening she needed for a killing stroke.

The showings, where proven breeders were displayed for men who might choose them next time, were less humiliation than she'd expected, and more worrying. In the showings, she did her best to look exhausted, weak, helpless, broken. It wasn't hard to look tired . . . she pushed herself to shaky exhaustion every day. But she could feel the muscle building on her legs again, in her arms, in her abdomen. Would they believe that came from carrying the babies? From walking in the orchard? From the simple exercises the others did?

But they could not expect what she intended to do with the muscles she built with such effort. Eyes squeezed shut, she reminded herself which basic moves would build the strength and speed she needed for killing.

The other women did not so much avoid her as ignore her. When the babies were wriggling happily on quilts on the floor, they exclaimed over the strength and vigor of her boys as they did over the qualities of their own. The staff gave her directions— which chores to do—in much the same tone as anyone else. The speaking women naturally talked most to each other; the muted women had a private language of gesture, and a public one of broader gestures and elaborate lipspeaking and hisses. The speaking women would include the mutes if one of the muted women made the effort to get their attention. Some even befriended one—for cooperative baby care made friendships useful for both. But Brun could not enter into the lipspeaking of the other muted women. Occasionally, if she were alone with another woman, and faced her directly, she could make herself understood with a combination of gesture and mouthing— if the topic was something obvious. *Where is the sewing basket?* or *What is that?* They were willing to show her where things were, or how to do a chore. But she had no topics in common with them, except babies, and she did not care that much about the babies, any of them. They were all—hers and the others'—proof of what she hated. And she knew they saw her as a dangerous person . . . tamed by muting, but potentially a source of soul-killing deviancy. Her lack of interest in the babies was another proof, to them, of her unnatural, immoral upbringing.

The babies were moving from creeping to rocking on their hands and knees when a new mother arrived at the nursery. She was very young, and had a slightly dazed expression. The other women spoke to her in short, simple sentences, a little louder than usual. Brun wondered if she'd been drugged, though she had seen no evidence that women were given drugs. On the third day, she approached Brun. "You're the yellow-hair from the stars?" She had the usual soft voice, but a little hesitancy in it.

Brun nodded. Up close, she decided that it wasn't drugs, but some innate problem, that gave the girl that odd expression and halting speech . . . and the social unawareness that let her approach the unapproachable.

"You traveled with another girl—more my size—and two brats?"

Brun nodded again.

"She said you was nice. She liked you. She said."

Brun looked hard at the girl. She had to be talking about Hazel. Where had she seen Hazel?

"She's doin' fine. I just thought you'd like to know." The girl smiled past Brun's shoulder, and wandered off, leaving Brun tethered to the twins.

Hazel was all right. A surge of relief swept through her. When that girl had left wherever Hazel was, to go to maternity—or was Hazel in maternity? Brun shook her head; she could not keep track of time. It was hot, or it was cold, daylight or dark; that was all she knew. But Hazel was all right, less time ago than Brun knew for sure. If only she knew *where*.

Several days passed before the girl sat down beside her again to nurse her baby.

"They call her Patience now," the girl said. "It's a good name for her 'cause she never makes trouble. She's real quiet and works hard. Prima says they'll be able to marry her as a third wife for sure, maybe even a second, even though she can't sew good. They been trainin' her for market girl, and she goes there by herself now." A wistful note in that soft voice—had this girl wanted to go to market? By now Brun was sure the girl was retarded; no one would let her go out alone for other reasons than the restrictions on women. "But she doesn't have your yellow hair," the girl said, staring at it with frank admiration. "And she won't talk about the stars, 'cause Prima said not to."

Brun could have strangled her, for having a voice and not saying what Brun really needed to know. She picked up a twin and removed from his mouth the pebble he'd put there. She could not feel any affection for them, but she wasn't about to let a child—any child—choke to death.

"She don't look big enough to have babies, though," the girl said, petting her own child. "And her blood's not regular yet. The master says—"

"Hush, you!" One of the women in charge came by and tapped the girl on the head. "You're not here to gossip about what your master says. You want your tongue pulled?"

The girl's mouth snapped shut, and she clambered out of the chair, holding her baby to her.

The woman shook her head at Brun. "She's simple, she is. Can't remember from day to day what the rules are, poor thing. We have to keep an eye on her, so's she doesn't get herself in trouble. If she gets in the habit of talking about her master here, even to you, she might do it back at her house and then they'd have to punish her. Best nip it in the bud." She patted Brun's head, almost affectionately. "That is pretty hair, though. Might win you a chance at wifing, when you've borne your three. Just you give me a nod, if the girl starts talking about men's doings again, like a good girl, eh?" Brun nodded. As long as they'd let the girl talk to her.

The girl avoided Brun for days. But late one evening, she slipped into Brun's room.

"She don't scare me," she said, clearly untruthfully. "I'm from Ranger Bowie's house; he's the only one can mute me. They can't. And he wouldn't, long as I don't argue or nothing. Telling you about Patience isn't arguing. It's explaining. Explaining is fine as long as it's not men."

Brun smiled, a smile that seemed to crack her face. How long had it been since she last smiled?

"I wish they hadn't muted you," the girl said. "I'd sure like to know what it's like out there . . . Patience, she won't tell me about it." She stopped, listening, then crept closer. "I wisht I had your hair," she said, and put out a hand to stroke it. Then she turned and vanished into the dark corridor.

Brun traced what she'd heard on the wall, fixing it in her mind, as she once would have repeated it aloud. Ranger Bowie. What an odd name. She didn't remember the men using any name like that on the ship . . . had they even called each other by name?

❖   ❖   ❖

The nondescript man in the checked shirt bellied up to the bar and ordered. Beside him, two men were talking about the Captain's choice of policy.

"Well, we're free men but I don't see any call to stomp in an ant bed. It's my right, but I'm not stupid enough—"

"You're calling the Captain stupid?"

"I'm saying that taking outlander women for our own needs is one thing, but taking that one—and then bragging about it—is just asking for trouble."

"It proves we're strong." That speaker turned to the man in the checked shirt. "And what's your opinion, brother?"

He smiled. "I heard she had yellow hair."

The first speaker snorted. "Everbody knows that. They're hoping she'll put her hair on her babes."

Someone down the bar leaned forward. "You talkin' about that gal from space? The yellow-haired slut? She had twins, did you hear? One redhead, one dark. Odds on, they're double-fathered."

"No!" The man in the checked shirt widened his eyes, the perfect picture of a country bumpkin in for one of the festivals.

"I'd bet on it. She won't be out for another two months, though. They say the twins need her milk longer, being smaller."

"Ah. I'd hoped."

The other men looked at each other, sly grins twitching their mouths. This one probably had only one wife, and her homely as a tree.

"Well, who wouldn't? Don't get that many blondes,

do we? Put your name on the list, is all I can say. They're showing her now, if you want to see if it's worth the tax."

"Before I put down on the list, believe I will."

"Crockett Street Nursery, then."

He was not the only one who wanted to see the outworlder blonde mute, who had birthed twins. They'd been confirmed fraternal and double-fathered, which meant she might throw twins again. A woman who could drop two eggs at a time was even more desirable. He took his number, and when it was called pushed into the room with the others in that group.

At first he wasn't sure. He had been shown pictures—moving and still—of Brun in childhood, adolescence, and adulthood. Closeups, distance shots, everything. He had thought nothing could disguise her. But the yellow-haired woman before him was not the same Brun—if it was Brun at all. Her slender strength was reshaped now—her body blurred and broadened with the children she'd carried, her breasts heavy with milk. She stood heavily, arms hanging by her sides. Her yellow hair was long, lank, nothing like the lively tousled curls in the pictures. Her blue eyes were duller, almost gray. But his practiced eye noted what was not concealed . . . the bone structure of her face, her shoulders, the exact shape of her fingers and toes. This had to be the woman he sought. He looked for the RE tattoo, but the short wrap such women were allowed during a showing covered the area where it might have been.

Two guards stood with her, their staves held to prevent the men from touching her.

"Devil's own," one of the men near him muttered.

"Satan's snare," said another. "Good thing they muted her."

"Yup. But the babies look strong." The babies were

on display as well, naked cherubs in a playpen. They grinned toothlessly at the watching men.

"Not worth it to me," said a black-haired man, and spat on the floor. "I'm not risking my soul for that." He pushed past the others and walked out.

Another laughed. "There speaks a man without the tax. She was just as wicked afore he looked at her."

"And it's our duty to convert the heathen," said another. "I reckon another couple of birthings'll convert her."

"What—you'll bid for her wifing?"

"Might do. Might do worse."

"Might do better . . ." They chatted on. Brun stared past them. Why didn't she lower her gaze, he wondered, the way the other women did. Then he knew why . . . she was neither virgin nor wife, and the worst had happened already. What could they do to her now? He shivered, and the man next to him glanced over.

"What is it, brother?"

"Nothing."

❖   ❖   ❖

Hazel's duties as a servant required her to go into the street each day with the garbage. When she had demonstrated that she would perform this task exactly as directed, looking neither to right nor left, even when unaccompanied, Prima decided to try her out as a market girl. She was still clumsy in her sewing; she would be more marketable for other skills. As near as she could tell, from what she dared let the girl tell her about the abominable behavior of those outworld heathens, the girl had been among merchants and traders all her life.

So, first in the company of Mellowtongue, Hazel went to the market to carry home those items which the garden did not produce. She was required to look at the ground two paces before her, and carry the basket at waist height, and speak to no one, not even if spoken to. Mellowtongue answered those inquiries which must be answered. Hazel performed exactly as ordered, on that and all the trips that followed.

The first time she was sent out alone, for just one item, she was watched, from a distance, by one of the other servant women, one too senior to be a market girl, but reliable in her gossip. She went directly to the correct stall, waited with head down until the stallkeeper called her house name, and held out the basket and payment without looking up. She was sent again, and then again, and then—in company with the head cook—learned to haggle respectfully with the stallkeepers.

She took nothing on herself; she pilfered no treats; she was submissive even to the unfair scolding of the cook on the matter of some wilted greens.

So, in a few months, she was sent regularly to market on market days. And there, by keeping her ears stretched to the fullest, she heard gossip about the yellow-haired outlander, the heathen woman who was in the maternity house . . . and then had birthed twins . . . and then nearly died of the birth sadness . . . and then moved to the nursery. Days later she heard which nursery. Days after that, one detail after another trickled into street talk. She said nothing; she asked no questions, and told no tales. When market girls from other houses tried to make friends, with quick murmurs, she ignored them.

She kept her eye on Brandy—now Prudence—and Stassi—now Serenity. Day by day, the little girls seemed to forget their former life. Quick, bouncy, darting Brandy was still more active—but she had transferred her passion for blocks and construction toys to sewing and weaving. Already she had made a stuffed doll for Stassi, and then a dress to put on it. She seemed to grasp easily the way that cloth could be shaped to fit bodies. She was fascinated by the movement of the great looms in the weaving shed, and had explained to Hazel (who could not figure out how they worked) how the rise and fall of rows of little rings would produce different patterns in the cloth. Both girls had friends their own age, and seemed far more attached to the women who cared for them than to Hazel.

Reluctantly, Hazel gave up the idea of including the littles in an escape. They were too small; they could not run and climb and fight. They would be obvious—no way to conceal the fact that they were children, and they had had no training in the boys' world, so they could not pass as boys. Most of all—she could see that they were happy and secure, and that the women of the household liked them. Even Prima, inclined to be stiff with the other women's children, had smiled at Brandy-Prudence, and stroked her dark curls. If she could get away—if she could get Brun away—the littles would not suffer for it. No one here blamed children for things like that. They would be cared for better than she could care for them—better, she suspected, than the Distressed Spacers' Home would care for them if she did get them back to Familias space safely. And . . . they were happy. They had lost one family, one world—she could not tear them away from another.

So she waited her chance. She could live here the rest of her life . . . she had the knack of fitting in, she always had . . . but she didn't want to. She had to admit she liked the food, the beautiful garden, the sense of security, the luxury of what seemed infinite space in which to move—she had never realized just how *much* space a person on a planet might have available, how big "outdoors" actually was. But she remembered too well the comfort of her old clothes, the freedom of movement, the friendships not bound by gender or race or beliefs. Here she would always be an outsider; she wanted to feel part of a family again. She missed the technology, the sense she'd had, in *Elias Madero*, of being part of a greater civilization spread across the universe.

Besides, there was the blonde lady. They had exchanged names. On the whole world, only she knew who Hazel really was, where she was from—and on the whole world, only she knew that the blonde lady's name was Brun. She, Hazel, could survive here, but that lady had no chance.

Brun. She rehearsed the name, keeping it alive. Even at the time, even frightened as she had been, and determined to protect the littles, she had felt a stubborn flare of rage at what the men had done to the other woman. Muting Brun had been wrong, even more wrong than muting a woman brought up in their world. Nothing anyone did—nothing, not ever— deserved that punishment. And Brun had done nothing, any more than Hazel had. They had been wrong; they had stolen her, and then they had stolen her voice.

Hazel knew Brun would want to escape. Any woman would, who had lived in freedom. And Brun . . . even at the worst, Hazel sensed a burning determination to do more than survive. But voiceless, locked up as she was, with twin babies, she could not possibly do it alone. Hazel would have to figure out a way. It wasn't going to be easy, not with babies . . .

To herself, in the night, she rehearsed—but only in her head, never aloud—the things she knew to be really true. She was Hazel Takeris; her father had been Rodrick Takeris, on the engineering staff of the *Elias Madero*, commanded by Captain Lund. She had passed her G-levels and qualified for junior apprentice in a competitive exam; her pay scale had been upgraded once on the voyage.

Brandy and Stassi had been Ghirian and Vorda's daughters, but Ghirian and Vorda were dead. The blonde woman was Brun, and her father was named something like "rabbit." Out there among the stars was a universe where girls could wear whatever they chose, look men in the eye, choose their own careers and partners. Someday . . . someday she would find it again.

CHAPTER FIFTEEN

All the way to Sector IX HQ, where she switched to civilian transport, Esmay felt she had a fiery brand on her forehead and back, defining what most Fleet personnel thought of her. She kept to herself as much as possible, trying to think how to explain to her father her precarious state in Fleet. Perhaps the funeral and its aftermath would distract him. For it seemed she was in fact her great-grandmother's heir.

Her previous visit to Altiplano had begun with pomp and ceremony; this time she had the ceremony, but no pomp, and no newshounds. Her father met her in the inbound reception lounge; she almost did not recognize him in the formal mourning garments of black, with elaborate curlicues of black braid on breast and sleeves of the tight short jacket with its black-beaded collar, the full black pants tucked into low black boots with turned-up toes, and the flat black cap with the shoulder-length tassel hanging past his left ear. Left ear, heart ear, direct line of descent . . . that came back to her at once.

He had brought one of the estancia maids to help her into the clothes she must wear. In the ladies' retiring room, she changed from Fleet uniform to the layers of white: long pantaloons under a petticoat, a short white chemise. The outer layers were all black, like her father's. Wide-sleeved black blouse finely tucked down the front, full black skirt, black brocade short vest heavily overbeaded in jet, a wide black waistcloth in a diamond-patterned weave, black-on-black. Women's boots, with the top rolled down to reveal the black silk lining. On her head, a stiff black cap sitting squarely across her brow, with a rolled knob at either side. Esmay had seen this at other Landbride ceremonies; she had never expected to wear it, and she had never witnessed the whole ceremony—outsiders never did.

The weight of the clothes burdened her almost as much as the secrets she carried.

Slowly, in a cadence old as the mountains, they walked from the reception area to the shuttle bay. She was used to being a half step behind him, if not more; but now, slow as she walked, he would walk slower.

It was real. She was the Landbride. For no one else would her father slow his steps.

On the shuttle down, he spoke briefly of the arrangements, then left her with a sheaf of old-fashioned paper . . . the family copy of the old rites in which her great-grandmother had lived her long life. Esmay read carefully. She could have a coach— she *would* have a coach—but the more she could do by herself, the better. She had never witnessed the ceremony of Landbride's Gifting, though she had heard others talk of it. At the shuttlefield, it was just past sunset, with a fiery glow behind the mountains. By the time they were out of the city, night closed around them; Esmay switched on the light in the passenger compartment and kept reading. Then her father touched her arm, and pointed ahead. Esmay switched the light off and peered into the darkness.

On either side of the road, flickering lights resolved into rows of black-clothed figures holding candles . . . the car slowed and stopped. Her father handed her out. Esmay this time was first in lighting the candles at the shrine . . . remembered without prompting the words, the gestures, the entire ritual. Behind her, she heard the respectful murmurs.

They walked from there, slowly, up to the great entrance and up the long drive, and the others closed in behind them. The house loomed, darker than the darkness around it. Then candlelight appeared from inside—the family, each carrying a candle. Esmay entered a chill dark space where normally light and warmth held sway. No fires would be kindled until after the ceremony; luckily the new rules had allowed fire and light during her travels, until she arrived onplanet.

She walked through the house, and lit one of the tiny candles in each room—a promise of the Landbride's coming. Then through, and out to the Landbride's Gift, the heart of the holding, and the place where the first Landbride in her heartline had made claim long, long ago.

There the priest waited for her, with the basket that held the braided coil of her great-grandmother's hair. Esmay shivered suddenly, her imagination caught on the possibility—no, the certainty—that someday her own unruly hair would be coiled in such a basket, its strands, however short or meagre, braided formally and tied off with silk cord.

Her great grandmother's body had long been buried, of course, and the new pale gravestone set above it. But her hair awaited this final ceremonial dance. No musicians played. In the dark night, by flickering candlelight, Esmay led the women of the estancia in slow procession around each Landbride's gravestone, starting with the oldest, and ending with the latest. The men, standing around the margin of the space, stamped a slow rhythm, but did not follow.

When the dance was done, Esmay took the silvery braid from its basket and held it high, turning to show it to everyone.

"The Landbride . . ." came the hushed whisper from many throats. "The Landbride has died . . ."

"She who was Landbride is no more," Esmay said.

"She has gone into darkness," the people said.

"She has returned to the land," the priest said. "And her spirit to the heavens."

"Her power is released," Esmay said. She untied the silk cord, and untwisted the strands of the braid. The night wind sighed down off the mountains, cold around her legs even through the layers of clothes. Candle flames streamed sideways; a few went out.

"Into the heavens . . ." the people said.

Esmay untied the second cord, at the top of the braid, and held the loosened braid high in her open hands. A gust of wind picked up one strand, then another. She heard the next gust coming, shaking the trees around the glade. When she felt it, she leaped up, tossing the hair free . . . and landed in darkness, all the candles blown out.

"Now is the death; now is the sorrow born!" In darkness and windy cold, the people cried out, and burst into the formal wails of mourning. One voice, quavering, old, sang the story of her great-grandmother's life, a counterpoint to the mourning cries. It had been a long life; it was a long dirge, and it ended only when the darkness crept back under the trees with approaching dawn. Light strengthened moment by moment; one by one the mourners fell silent, until at last there was no sound nor movement. Far off, it seemed, a rooster crowed, and another answered.

The priest with his tall black hat had turned his back, to face the sunrise. The women helped Esmay back through the crowd, into the curtained tent she had not seen for the darkness. Quickly they stripped off the black vest, waistcloth, skirt, blouse, boots. Over the pure white underclothes, they helped her into the Landbride's traditional outfit: white blouse, with wide pleated sleeves ending in a hand's width of frothy lace; white skirt pinstriped in green; white doeskin vest embroidered and beaded in brilliant color with flowers and vines and fruit . . . and to top it all, the hat with its two blunt points, from each of which a gold tassel fell past her ear to her shoulder. Around her waist, the scarlet and purple striped waistcloth, folded and tied precisely. In its folds, a narrow belt to which was hung on her right hip a sickle's curved blade, its metal varicolored with age, but its edge still gleaming. On her left side, slung from a shoulder strap, she had a pouch of seed. Soft green boots, lined in yellow silk, would come later—for the first, she would go barefoot.

Back outside, the risen sun streamed through the trees in long red-gold shafts, but the dew beneath her feet felt icy cold. Someone behind her struck a bell, and at its lingering mellow tone, the priest turned to face her. He raised on outstretched hands a long sharpened stick. The men moved to stand behind him.

"From night comes day," the priest said. "By the grace of God. And from the death of one comes the life of another, as the seed in the ground dies to live as the grain that blows in the sun."

Esmay lifted her arms in the ritual gestures.

"Does any here challenge the Landbride's lineage?" the priest asked. "Or is there cause she should not be wed?"

Silence from the people, and the nervous chattering of a treehopper, who cared nothing for ceremony. The priest waited out a full count of a hundred—Esmay counted it out in her own mind—then nodded.

"So it shall be . . . this bride to this land, to the end of her life, or her willing gift to her heir." He held out the digging stick.

The next part had seemed ridiculous and more theatrical than archaic when Esmay read it, but wearing the old costume in the early morning light, with the digging stick in her hand (far heavier than she expected), and the sickle and seeds . . . it felt right in a way she had not imagined.

She strode out into the little circle of grainland kept for this purpose, and planted carefully each year. Though the season was wrong, and what she planted would not grow, it still felt connected to some larger ritual which would work, which would bind the land to her, and her to the land. She was not sure she wanted that, but she was sure what she had to do.

With the digging stick, she pried up the three holes at the corners of an equilateral triangle, pushing through the earth until they were big enough. Old stains on the tip of the digging stick made clear how deep was the right depth. Her helpers picked up the loosened clods and put them in a copper bowl. Then, taking the old sickle blade which would have no handle until this was over, she laid the edge of the blade to the palm of her left hand. It hardly hurt at first, and the blood ran redder than her sash into the bowl, into the clods of earth, darkening them. When it was enough, the women nodded, and she held out her hand for someone to bind in the kerchief that would henceforth be laid under the kitchen hearthstone.

Her hand was beginning to throb. Esmay ignored it, and hung the sickle back on her belt. Then she spat into the bowl, onto each clod. The women nodded again, and she stepped back. They poured a few drops of water from a jug of springwater and, using paddles carved of wood from orchard trees, kneaded the earth and blood and water into a ball.

Esmay took five seeds from the sack and dropped them carefully into the first hole—and the women laid a small lump of the mixture in the bowl on top of it. Again . . . and again. Then the women set the bowl on the ground in the triangle, and divided the remaining lump into five smaller ones, each carefully shaped into a loaf, and laid a tripod of sticks over them, with a tuft of dry bristlegrass atop. The priest approached, and took from around his neck the crystal that formed the center of his scapular, the symbol of the star. But so early in the morning, it could not focus enough sunlight . . . no. For one of his assistants brought forward a pot, in which was a coal from the fire on the hearth, kept live since that fire had been quenched.

The fire, fed carefully, baked the earthen loaves hard and dry. While it baked, the musicians began to play, wild heartrending dances. When it was baked, the Five Riders came forward. Esmay broke the lump apart, and each took a section, mounted, and rode away. They would place the loaves in the boundary shrines, where the earth from her planting, her blood, and her spit, would declare the land hers. It would be days before the last one, far to the south, was set in its little stone house.

By now, the smells of food had wafted across from the kitchens; with the Landbride's dawn, fires could be lit, and cookstoves heated. Fresh hot bread, roast meat . . . Esmay sat on a throne piled with late flowers as the feast was carried out to her guests.

When the crowd around her thinned, her cousin Luci came up. "I have your accounting," she said. "The herd has done well."

"Good," Esmay said. She sipped from the mug someone had handed her, and felt dizzy from the fumes alone. "Could you get me some water? This is too strong."

Luci laughed. "They want to follow the old ways into the bedding of the Landbride, do they? I'll bring you water." She darted off, and was back soon, this time with a handsome young man at her heels.

"Thanks," Esmay said, taking the jug of cool water.

When the long ceremony was over, Esmay's step-mother led her to the suite her great-grandmother had occupied. "I hope you will stay awhile," she said. "This is your home . . . we can redecorate the rooms—"

"But my room's upstairs," Esmay said.

"Not unless you wish it. Of course, if you insist . . . but this has always been . . . it's the oldest part of the house . . ."

She was trying to be tactful, and helpful; Esmay knew that, just as she knew that she was too tired, after all this, to discuss anything calmly. What did it matter, after all, where she slept?

"I think I'll lie down awhile," she said instead.

"Of course," her stepmother said. "Let me help you with these things."

Her stepmother had hardly touched her, as near as she could remember—it felt strange indeed to have help from her. Would she have helped, years ago, if Esmay had let her? A disturbing question, which she might reconsider after a long nap. She was in fact a deft maid, quick with the fastenings, and she knew exactly when to turn away, the outer garments folded carefully in her arms, and leave Esmay alone.

Esmay woke in late afternoon to the chill light of an overcast sky—clouds had moved in. Nothing looked right . . . and then she remembered. She was not upstairs, not in her own bed, but in great-grand-mother's. Except it was her own now, in a way that the bed upstairs had not been . . . hers not by cus-tom, or assignment, but by tradition and law. Every-thing was hers now . . . this bed, the embroidered panel on the wall with THE EYES OF GOD ARE ALWAYS

OPEN on it (her great-grandmother had done the needlework herself, as a young girl), the chairs . . . and the walls around them, and the fields around the walls, from the distant marshy seacoast to the mountain forests. Fruit trees, olive trees, nut trees, gardens and ploughland, every flower in the field, every wild creature in the woods. Only the livestock might belong to others—but it was she who would grant grazing rights, or refuse them, which land could be put to plough, and what would be pasture.

She pushed the covers aside, and sat up. Her stepmother—or someone—had laid out more normal clothes. Not anything she'd brought, but new— soft black wool trousers, and a multicolored pullover top. Esmay found the adjoining bath unit, and took a shower, then dressed in the new clothes.

In the hall, Luci was talking quietly to Sanni and Berthold. Sanni looked at her, a long considering look. "You slept well?" she asked. Esmay had the feeling that the question meant more than it said.

"Yes," she said. "And now I'm hungry again."

"A few minutes only," Sanni said, and turned toward the kitchen.

"Welcome home," Berthold said. He looked slightly wary.

"Thank you," Esmay said. She was trying to remember if her new status changed anything but the land titles . . . was she supposed to change the terms of address for Berthold and Sanni, for instance?

Her father came out of the library wing. "Ah— Esmay. I hope you're rested now. I don't know how long you can stay, but there's a great deal to be done."

"Not until after eating," Sanni said, reappearing. "We're ready now." Esmay realized they had been waiting for her.

The meal made clearer than any explanations how her status had changed. She sat at the head of the table, where her great-grandmother had sat on the rare occasions she joined the family at table . . . which deposed Papa Stefan from his position as her representative. She had not imagined he could look so small, hunched over his plate halfway down the table. She ate slowly, watching and listening, trying to feel out the hidden currents of emotion.

Her stepmother and her aunt Sanni, for instance, were eyeing each other like two cats over a plate of fish. In what way were they rivals? Her father and Berthold, though studiously polite, seemed both particularly tense. Of the youngsters, only Luci was at the table—the young ones, she supposed, had been fed informally earlier.

"Have you decided whom to name as your heir?" her stepmother asked. Sanni shot her a look that should have had gray goosefeather fletching, it was so sharp.

"Not now," her father said.

"No," Esmay said. "I haven't—it's all too new. I will need to consider carefully." She would need to look at the family tree; she had no idea who might be eligible. It might even be Luci. That wouldn't be so bad.

"The paperwork starts tomorrow," her father said. "All the judicial red tape."

"How long does that last?" Esmay asked.

He shrugged. "Who knows? It's not something we've done for a long time, and since then some of the laws have changed. It's no longer enough for the family to swear agreement to the whole change; it has to be done piece by piece."

It sounded far worse than Administrative Procedures. If the whole family had to pledge peaceful acquiescence to the change in ownership of each field, each woodland patch . . .

"At least, much of it can be done by proxy, now. My guess is that it will take hours, if not days—and all to do over again when you abdicate." He sounded more tired than resentful; Esmay considered that he had probably taken on most of the family responsibility on her behalf since her great-grand-mother died.

"If she abdicates," Papa Stefan put in. "She should stay, marry well, and be the Landbride we need. She's been a hero to the world—she has proved herself—but they cannot need one young hero as badly as we need her here. She could retire now."

Her father gave her a look, and a tiny lift of the shoulders. He knew what her career meant to her, as he knew what his meant to him—but there was much he didn't know, as well, and at the moment, Esmay could almost see the wisdom of leaving Fleet before they forced her out.

"It may not be me that you need, Papa Stefan, but someone who has lived here all along, who knows more—"

"You can learn," he said, his spirits rising as he had someone to argue with. "You were never stupid, just stubborn. And why should you serve the Familias Regnant? We have not even a Seat in their Grand Council. They do not respect us. They will use you up, and discard you at the end, whenever you dis-please them, or they tire of you."

That was too near the mark; Esmay wondered if some word of her disgrace had leaked through the newsnets. But Berthold jumped in.

"Nonsense, Papa. Young officers of her quality are rarer than diamonds at the seashore. They won't let her go easily. Look what she's already done."

"Finished eating, is what she's done," her step-mother said. "Dessert, anyone?"

Esmay was glad enough to have the subject turned, and accepted a bowl of spiced custard gratefully.

Next morning, the legal formalities began. Her

father had brought an entire court to the house: judge, advocates, recording clerks and all. First, although Esmay had openly accepted her heritage in the ceremony, she must now swear that she had done so and sign the Roll, her signature beneath her great-grandmother's, where anyone could compare its slightly awkward simplicity to the lovely old-fashioned elegance of her great-grandmother's writing. But three lines above, someone had signed in awkward childish letters that looked even worse.

Once she was sworn in as heir, the true Landbride, the real work began. Every Landsteward, including Papa Stefan and her father, had to submit an accounting of the management of each division of the Landbride's Gift. Esmay learned things about the family estancia she had never known, because in her great-grandmother's long tenure as Landbride, changes had been made before Esmay was born which had now to be explained. From the trivial (the decision to move the chicken yard from one place to another, to accommodate a covered passage to the laundry) to the major (the sale of almost a third of the cattle lands to finance artillery and ammunition for her father's brigade in the Uprising, and its eventual repurchase), the last 70 years of history were laid out in detail.

Esmay would have stipulated that the accounts were correct, if she could, but the judge would have none of it. "You were away, Sera. You cannot know, and although these are your family, and you are naturally reluctant to consider them capable of the least infidelity or dishonesty, it is my duty to protect both you and the Landbride Gift itself. These accounts must be scrutinized carefully; that is why we brought along the accountants from the Registry."

And how long would that take? She did not want to spend days sitting here watching accountants pore over old records.

"Meanwhile, Sera, as long as a representative of your family is here to answer any questions, we need not detain you."

That was a relief. Esmay escaped, only to be captured by Luci, who had in mind a lengthy discussion of the herd she managed for Esmay. From one accountant to another—but Luci was so eager to explain what she'd been doing, that Esmay did not resist as she was led through the kitchens, out the back of the house, and into the stable offices.

"You hadn't said what direction you wanted to take," Luci said. "So I decided to sell the bottom ten percent at the regional sales, not under your name. Your reproductive rates are above the family average, but not much—"

"I didn't know they could be improved at all . . ."

"Oh yes." Luci looked smug. "I started reading offworld equine reproductive journals—couldn't afford a lot of what they talked about, but I made some changes in management, and everyone smirked at me until the first foal crop. Then they said it was normal statistical variation—but your second foal crop hit the ground this year, and it was a point ahead of last year's."

Esmay had never had any interest in equine reproduction, but she knew natural enthusiasm when she saw it. She had definitely picked the right manager for her herd . . . and maybe more than that.

"What did they say about selling off the bottom end without the family name? They were branded, weren't they?"

"No . . . I decided to defer branding until after the cull period. Papa Stefan was angry with me, but it was your herd, so he couldn't stop me."

"Mmm. And what criteria are you using for culling?"

"Several things." Luci ticked them off on her fingers. "Gestational length—early or late is one cull point. That could be the mare, but there's evidence it may be the foal, too. Time to stand and suck, and vigor of suckling; if they're outside a standard deviation on time to standing, or if they don't have a strong suck, that's another cull point. You already have good performance mares in that herd—but you'll benefit by having additional survival vigor."

Esmay was impressed. "I assume you'll cull mares later?"

"With your permission, yes. And while they're young enough to sell on . . . according to the articles I read, after three foals you should know if length of gestation, foaling problems, foal vigor, and milk production are due to the mare. I can show you the references—"

"No, that's all right. You've done very well. Tell me what you think we should do with this herd."

"Produce exportable genestock," Luci said promptly. "We have the perfect outcross genome for at least five other major horse-breeding worlds. All our horses have been performing—we've culled for soundness, speed, and endurance. I entered a query in one database, to see if anyone knew of, or would be interested in, what we've got, and the response was promising. Here on Altiplano, with the reputation our family has, we can sell live animals, but the export costs are far too high to export anything but genestock . . . so I would concentrate on the most salable genestock."

"Sounds good to me," Esmay said. "When do you think we might see a profit on it?"

Luci looked thoughtful. "Not immediately. Since we usually do live breeding, and have never exported genestock, we'd need an investment in equipment. I put the income from the cull sales into a fund for that, pending your approval."

"Would genestock from the rest of the family holdings, or from Altiplano in general, be salable?"

"I would think so. Possibly even other livestock, like our cattle . . ."

"Then I'll see if it's possible to make an investment from family funds, and then you could rent the facilities."

"Would you really?"

"If it's possible, yes. Why not? It would benefit not only our family, but all Altiplano."

Luci nodded, looking satisfied. She made a notation in one of her books, then gave Esmay a challenging stare. "You look worse than you did when you left," Luci said.

"You have less tact," Esmay said, nettled.

"Was it the fighting?" Luci asked. "They say the Bloodhorde is terrible."

"No." Esmay turned over a leaf in the studbook. "I don't really want to talk about it."

Luci cocked her head. "You weren't this grumpy before, either. You looked horrible for a day or so, then better—and you were helpful to me. Something's wrong."

The girl was persistent as a horsefly, with the same ability to go straight to the blood of it. It crossed Esmay's mind that tactical ability could be shown in more than one way.

"I have had some problems. There's nothing you could do."

"Well, I can wish the best for you." Luci moved restlessly from door to window and back. "If you were my age—" A long pause, which grew uncomfortable.

"What?" Esmay said finally.

"I'd say you were lovesick," Luci said. "You have all the signs."

"Lovesick!"

"That's just the way Elise said it, when she thought no one knew. But they did. Is it lovesickness, or something else?"

"Luci." There was no way to explain. She tried

another approach. "There are things I can't tell you about. Fleet things. Sometimes bad things happen."

"Esmay, for pity's sake—I grew up in a military household. I can tell worry about a war from a personal worry, and you needn't try to pretend that's what's going on."

"Well, it is, Persistence. Great-grandmother died; I've had to take on the whole estate; there's a lot to worry about."

Luci turned the conversation back to the horses, and for an hour they spoke only of this line or that, this outcross line or another. They walked up to the house together, still deep in the intricacies of fourth-generation distribution of recessives. At the door Luci said, with the most spurious wide-eyed innocence Esmay had seen, "Are you going to marry and settle down here, cousin, the way Papa Stefan wants?"

In the hearing of half the kitchen staff and Berthold, who had wandered into the kitchen before the meal as usual. Silence fell, until one helper dropped her knife.

"I'm a Fleet officer," Esmay said. "You know I told everyone I would have to appoint a trustee, and an heir."

"Yes," Luci said. "I know that. But you hadn't spent even a week on Altiplano yet. You could change your mind, especially if things aren't going well in your Fleet."

Berthold snorted. Esmay could have done without that; Berthold's humor was uncomfortable at best.

"You see what she's like," he said, around a couple of olives he'd filched.

"I'm ready for lunch," Esmay said. "And those had better not be the export-quality olives . . ." Her warning glance took in the cooks and Berthold. He wagged a finger at her.

"You sound exactly like Grandmother. She could squeeze oil out of the very smell of olive."

"Lunch," Esmay said, leading the way. "A morning spent with lawyers and accountants, then Luci, has starved my brain."

Darien Prime Station

Pradish Lorany turned the pamphlet over and over in his hands. He wasn't sure about this. Yes, it was totally unfair that Mirlin had taken the children and moved away—that Sophia Antera had been promoted over his head—that over half the seats on the station citizens' council were held by women. He loathed the very thought of artificial births and manipulation of the human genome—if that wasn't interfering with God's plan, he couldn't think of anything that was. But while he agreed in principle that society was corrupt and degraded, and that it all began with the failure to understand the roles God had ordained for men and women, he could not quite convince himself that therefore it naturally followed that blowing up people was a Godly act. Especially since Mirlin and the children would die, too. He wanted respect from women, and leadership by men, and an end to tampering with human reproduction, but . . . was this the way to do it?

He thought not. He made up his mind. He would continue to support the Gender Defense League; he would continue to argue with his former wife that she was misunderstanding his reasons for disciplining the children by traditional methods . . . but he would not attend the next meeting with the representative of the Godfearing Militia who had attempted to recruit him to help place explosive charges.

In a spasm of disgust, he threw the pamphlet toward the orifice of the station's recycling system, but he turned away before it slid into the chute . . . and did not see it miss, to land right in front of the PLEASE ENSURE TRASH ENTERS HOPPER sign.

Nor did he see the prune-faced old woman who glared at his retreating back as she stooped to pick up the crumpled pages and put them in carefully— but who stopped, her attention arrested by the glaring grammatical error in the first sentence. Sera Alicia Spielmann, as ardent a grammarian as she was a supporter of public neatness, took the pamphlet home to use as a bad example in her next complaint to the local school trustees . . . but when she read it, she called her friend whose grandson was a member of station security, instead.

She did not connect the "lazy litter-bum" or her own actions with the discovery, two days later, of the corpse of one Pradish Lorany who had been brutally attacked in his own apartment. Others made that connection.

CHAPTER SIXTEEN

Altiplano, Estancia Suiza

After lunch, Luci followed Esmay into the Landbride's quarters with obvious intent. Esmay, who'd been hoping for a time alone to think things over, decided she would have more peace if she let Luci talk herself out. "So what is it now?" she asked, half laughing. "Do you have five other schemes for the estancia, or are you planning to take over the government?"

Luci, it seemed, loved a boy—young man, actually—in a neighboring household. "Your father is set against it—I don't know why," she said. "It's a good family—"

"Who is it?" asked Esmay, who had a suspicion. At the name, she nodded. "I know why, but I think he's wrong."

"Is this another of those things you can't tell me about?" Luci asked with a pettish note in her voice. "Because if it is, I think it's mean to let me know you know . . ."

"Come all the way in, and sit down," Esmay said,

shutting the door carefully. No one would disturb them now. She gestured to one of the comfortable chintz-covered chairs, and sat in another one herself. "I'll tell you, but it's not a pleasant tale. You know I was miserable the last time I was here, and I suppose no one told you why . . ."

"No one knew," Luci said. "Except that you had some kind of fight with your father."

"Yes. Well . . . there are too many secrets going around, and now that I'm Landbride, I'm going to do things differently. Back before you were born, when I was a small child, and my mother had died, I ran away."

"You!"

"Yes. I wanted to find my father, who was off at war. I didn't understand about war . . . it had been safe, here. Anyway, I ended up in a very dangerous—" Her throat closed, and she cleared it. "A village right in the middle of the war. Soldiers came."

"Oh—Esmay—"

"I was . . . assaulted. Raped. Then one of my father's troops found me—but I was very sick . . ."

"Esmay, I never heard of this—"

"No, you wouldn't have. They hushed it up. Because the soldier that did it was in my father's brigade."

"No—!" Luci's face was white to the lips.

"Yes. He was killed—old Seb Coron killed him, in fact. But they told me it was all a bad dream—that I'd caught my mother's fever, which I may have, and anything else was a fever dream. All those nightmares I had—they made me think I was crazy."

"And you found out, finally—?"

"Seb Coron told me, because he thought I knew already—that Fleet's psych exams would have found it and cured me." She took a deep breath and let it out slowly. "So . . . I confronted Father, and when I identified the face in the regimental rolls, he admitted it. That it had happened, that I remembered correctly."

From white, Luci went rage-red. "That's—hideous! Lying to you like that! I would've—"

"And the thing is," Esmay went on, remotely cheered by Luci's response. "The thing is, the person who did it was of that family. The man you love is his nephew, his older brother's son—"

Luci's face whitened again. "Arlen? You can't mean Arlen. But he was killed in action—they have a shrine to him in the front hall."

"I know. He *was* killed in action—by Seb Coron for assaulting a child—me."

"Oh . . . my." Luci sat back. "And his father was commanding something—so your father didn't tell him—? Or did he?"

"I don't know if his family knows anything at all, but even if they do it was all kept quiet. He got his medals; he got his shrine in the front hall." She could not quite keep the bitterness out of her voice.

"And your father doesn't want anything to do with their family . . . I understand . . ."

"No . . . they stayed friends, or at least close professionally. I think my father considered it an aberration, nothing to do with his family. I danced with his younger brother when I was fourteen, and he said nothing. He'd have been delighted if I'd married Carl. But he's worried now, because he knows I know, and he isn't sure what I'll do."

"I'll—I'll break it off, Esmay." Luci's eyes glittered with unshed tears.

"Don't be ridiculous!" Esmay leaned forward. "If you love him, there's no reason to break it off on my account."

"You wouldn't mind?"

"I . . . don't know how I'd react, if he looks much like Arlen did. But that shouldn't matter, to you or the family, if he's suitable otherwise. Is he a good man?"

"I think so," Luci said, "but girls in love are supposed to be bad judges of character." That with a hint of mischief.

"Seriously . . ."

"Seriously . . . he makes my knees weak, my heart pound, and I've seen him at work—he wants to be a doctor, and he helps out in the estancia clinic. He's gentle."

"Well, then," Esmay said, "for what good it will do, I'm on your side."

"What good it will do? Don't be silly—you're the Landbride. If you approve a match, no one's going to argue with you."

That had not occurred to her, having never contemplated a match herself. "Are you sure?"

"Of course I am!" Luci grinned. "Didn't you realize? What happened when you—" She sobered suddenly. "Oh. Did it—what happened—make you not want to marry?"

"It may have," Esmay said, ever more uncomfortable with where this was heading, onto turf that Luci clearly knew well. "I didn't think of it at the time—I just wanted off-planet. Away from it all."

"But surely you've met someone, sometime, who made your knees weak?"

Before she could say anything, she felt the telltale heat rushing to her face. Luci nodded.

"You did . . . and you don't want anyone to know . . . Is it something . . . outworldly?"

"Outworldly?" Barin was an outworlder, but she wasn't sure that's what Luci had meant.

Now it was Luci blushing. "You know—those things people do that—we don't do here. Or at least, not officially."

Esmay laughed, surprising both of them. "No, it's nothing like that. I've met people like that, of course—they don't think anything of it, and they're quite ordinary."

Luci had turned brick red by now. "I always wondered," she muttered. "How . . ."

"We had that in the Academy prep school," Esmay said, grinning as she remembered her own paralyzing embarrassment. "It was part of the classes on health maintenance and I nearly crawled under the desk."

"Don't tell me; you can show me the data cube," Luci said, looking away. Then she looked back. "But I do want to know about him—whoever it was—is?"

"Was," Esmay said firmly, though pain stabbed her. "Another Fleet officer. Good family."

"Did he not love you?" Luci asked. She went on without waiting for an answer. "That happened to me—the second time I fell in love, he didn't care a fig about me. Told me so quite frankly. I thought I'd die . . . I used to ride out in the woods and cry."

"No, he—he liked me." Esmay swallowed and went on. "I think—I think he liked me a lot, actually, and I—"

"Well, what happened, then," Luci said.

"We . . . quarrelled."

Luci rolled her eyes. "Quarrel! What's a quarrel? Surely you didn't let one quarrel end it!"

"He's . . . angry," Esmay said.

Luci looked puzzled. "Is he violent when he's angry? You still love him—that's obvious. So why—?"

"It's—mixed up with Fleet business," Esmay said. "That's why I can't explain—"

"You can't stop now," Luci said. "And I'll bet most of it's about you and him anyway, and nothing to do with any universe-shattering secrets. You trust me with your horses and your money; you ought to trust me to keep a few stupid secrets about Fleet."

The logic made no sense, but Esmay was past caring; she'd held it in as long as she could; she had to talk to somebody. As simply as she could—which turned out to be not very simply at all—she explained about Barin, about her transfer to command track, and her arrival at Copper Mountain. And Brun. When she first mentioned Brun, Luci stopped her.

"So—*that's* the rat in the grain bin."

"She's not a rat . . . she's a talented, bright, attractive—"

"Rat. She went after your man, didn't she? I can see it from here. Used to getting what she wants, probably started falling in love at twelve—"

Esmay had to smile at Luci's tone. "It's not that simple, though. I mean, that's what I thought—that's what other people said, with all the time she spent with Barin—"

"And why weren't you spending time with him?"

"I was taking double courses, that's why. They both had more time off—everyone had more time off than I had. And then she talked to me . . . she said she wanted to be friends, but she was always telling me how to dress, how to do my hair—"

Luci pursed her lips. "You could use some advice there—"

"It's *my* hair!" Esmay heard her own voice rise, and brought it down with an effort. "Sorry. She wanted to talk about Altiplano, and about our customs, and it sounded so . . . so condescending, and one day she was talking about Barin, and I just . . . blew up."

"Told her to keep her sticky fingers off your man, did you?"

"Well . . . not exactly. I told her—" She didn't want to repeat those angry phrases, which echoed in her head sounding far worse than they had at the time. "I called her names, Luci, and told her she had no morals worth mentioning, and should go away and quit corrupting people."

"Oof. I can see I don't ever want you mad at me."

"And then I had to leave for the field exercise in Escape and Evasion—no, I'll tell you about that later—and when I came back she'd left Copper Mountain, and my commander was furious with me for what I'd said to her. She was under surveillance, being the Speaker's daughter, so they had it all recorded, and somehow the news vids had got hold of it. Barin—I thought he'd slept with her, and then he was mad at me for thinking he would. And as if that weren't bad enough, she was later captured by pirates, and they tortured her and took her away— and everyone's blaming me."

Luci gave her a long, cool look and shook her head slowly. "Landbride you may be, and Fleet officer, and decorated hero, but you've been acting like a school-girl with her first crush. Your brains have all gone to mush."

"What!?" After the previous conversation, she had expected some form of sympathy, not this.

"Yes," Luci said, nodding. "I guess I can see why— no background at all. But still—what a wet ninny you've been! Let me tell you something, cousin, if you don't get yourself back to wherever Barin is and tell him all about it—why you blew up at Brun, and that you love him—you will be confirmed as a total complete idiot."

Esmay could say nothing for the shock; she was aware that Luci was thoroughly enjoying what must be her first chance to lecture an elder.

"All right, this was your first love affair. But you've made every mistake there is."

"Like what?" Esmay said.

"Like not telling him. Not telling this Brun person. She may be the sort who snatches other peoples' lovers for the fun of it, but if you didn't even *tell* her—"

"How could I? We hadn't—and anyway there are the regulations—" Quickly she outlined the relevant portions of the code of conduct.

"Poppycock," Luci said confidently. On a roll, ready to lecture, apparently for hours—Esmay wondered if she had been like this with Brun. No wonder Brun had flounced away; if she'd known how to flounce, she'd have done it herself. "You weren't exploiting Barin; emotionally you're younger than I am. You could be reasonably careful and professional without turning into an icicle."

"I don't know . . ."

"I do. You are a fool if you sit here playing about at being Landbride, when you don't really care about this land at all—"

"I do so care about the land!"

"In the abstract, yes. And you'd like it to be here, unchanged, when you visit. But you can't convince me that you feel really passionate about whether coastal pastures are crossfenced to allow HILF grazing or left open and grazed in alternate years."

"Er . . . no." Esmay scrabbled at her memory, trying to think what "HILF grazing" was.

"Or whether we quit buying cattelope breeding stock from Garranos and develop our own breed, and if so, on what criteria."

"Not really . . ." She hadn't known they had been buying cattelope from the Garranos.

"Or whether to bring in new rootstock for the nut trees, or top-graft with the latest varieties onto the old."

"I suppose not." Rootstock? Top-graft? She had not suspected her great-grandmother of knowing anything about any of this.

"Well, then. You have always wanted a wider world, and you made your way into it. You found love there—that *proves* it was the right choice for you." That was a line of reasoning Esmay had never heard, let alone thought of, before. "Don't let anyone take it away from you," Luci finished, triumphantly.

"They can," Esmay said bleakly. "They can ask me to resign my commission—"

"Have they?"

"No, not yet. But Admiral Hornan hinted at it."

"There's more than one admiral, surely. Esmaya— you are older than I am, and you are the head of my family now, but you cannot be a good Landbride if your heart is somewhere else. You want a career in Fleet, you want this man Barin—*go get them*. No one in our family has ever been shy about going after what he or she wanted. Don't break with tradition." Luci sat back, arms crossed, and gave Esmay a challenging stare.

The tumult inside subsided gradually. It seemed so simple to Luci, and it wasn't simple . . . and yet it was. If she had a goal—and she did—then why wasn't she pursuing it? Why had she been side-tracked? And, more importantly, what could she do about it?

"They're organizing an attempt to free Brun," Esmay said. She could talk calmly now. "The ship I was on is part of it. I should be part of it, but Lord Thornbuckle is blaming me for the whole thing—he insists that he doesn't want me to have anything to do with it. And someone I knew in the Academy is sticking to Barin like dried egg to a plate—"

"He's the sort of man other women want," Luci said, with no heat. "You said that—"

"Yes . . . but she's a bad one, really."

"So what would it take to get you back in Barin's good graces, so you can find out if he still loves you, and back in your admiral's good graces?"

"I don't know . . ." She paused. "I don't know if Barin will ever forgive me . . ."

"He might not," Luci said frankly, "But you won't know that until you see him again. And the admiral?"

"I suppose—if I could convince them somehow that I don't hate Brun, and I didn't ever say that she deserved what she got—"

"They think you said that?"

"Casea—the woman who's after Barin—says I did. Says she knew me at the Academy and I was always

saying things about the senior Families. Of course I
didn't . . ."

"Muerto de Dios," Luci said. "I would have a knife
for that one if I saw her. But if she's having to lie
about you to keep Barin away from you, then he's
not that eager for her. Go back, Esmay. Go back and
make them know how good you are."

"And you, cousin?"

"And I will breed horses, and—with your consent
and support—marry the man I love and have babies."

"And be Landbride someday?" Esmay asked, after
a decent interval.

"That is entirely up to you," Luci said. "I don't
want that job too soon, I can tell you. At least let
me prove my abilities with your herd before I take
on another."

Esmay sat alone as the light dimmed, thinking over
what Luci had said. She knew what she wanted—she
was supposed to be a tactical genius—so it should be
possible to figure out what she could do to get herself out of the mess she was in. If she could retrieve
her intelligence from the mush her emotions had
made . . .

And yet, what she wanted had more to do with
emotions than brains: what she wanted was love, and
respect, and honor, and the sense that she was serving
something worth serving.

She could do nothing about it here. With every
passing minute, she realized that no matter how hard
she worked, or how pleasant a life she could contrive
here, as one of the wealthiest women on the planet,
she would never satisfy her own desires, her own
needs, by being a Landbride, even the best Landbride
she could be. She would always know she had run
away from trouble. She would always know she had
failed. In her mind's eye, she could see herself—her
civilian self—meeting an older Barin far in the future.

They would be polite. He would admire, politely, her empire. And then he would go away, and she . . . she blinked back tears, and pushed herself up from the chair.

The judge and the advocates and auditors were annoyed when she walked in on them, and insisted that she must soon return to Fleet.

"We understood you had indefinite leave."

"My pardons, sirs, but there are events afoot which I cannot discuss, but which make it very desirable that I return as soon as I can. I must know how long this will take."

"We could, if we hurried, have the transfers ready within five days . . ."

Esmay had already looked up the commercial passenger schedules. "Sirs, the next ship leaves in five days, but the one after is another twenty days. I'm sure you can have all ready in four days, with all the cooperation and resources of this house."

"It will hardly be possible," said one of the advocates, but the judge waved him to silence.

"You have honored Altiplano already by your deeds, Sera; for you, this is possible. Not easy, but possible."

"My thanks are eternal, and I will place the household at your service."

On the last of the four days, having signed the last paper, Esmay asked her father to come to the library, scene of that earlier confrontation. This time, however, she put that aside, and asked his advice. With the same precision and organization that she might have briefed someone on a military problem, she told him what she faced. "So you see, far from being a credit to our house, I am in disgrace," she said. "But I cannot change that here—and if I stay here—"

"I see," he said. He nodded, sharply. "You are a credit to this house, Esmaya, and to Altiplano; you will never be a disgrace in my sight. But I agree: for your own sake, you must clear your name. If you cannot, you are always welcome to return, and you must not give up your Landbride Gift until this is over. Stand or fall, it will be as the Landbride Suiza."

She had been more than half afraid he would demand that she give it up; her eyes filled.

"As for the matter of the Speaker's daughter—you were wrong, there, and you know it. Her rudeness does not excuse yours. But your reasons for not claiming the man's affection makes sense to me, though perhaps not to those with different ways. Still—they will not hold it against you, if you can prove that you wish her no harm, and can convince her, when and if she is rescued. As for the man— even I have heard of Serranos. A remarkable family, and well suited to this house. You must have made friends, Esmaya, and this is the time to call on them."

"Approach them?"

"Yes. When under attack, seek allies—you cannot fight all Fleet alone, and when people are lying about you, you need those who will not. If you say nothing, if you avoid them, they can more easily believe the lies are true." His voice grew husky. "Thank you, daughter, for your great courtesy in confiding this to me . . . I always did care for you."

"I know." She did know, and she also knew it had not been enough—but it was all he had to give. Bitterness rolled over her one last time, and then washed away.

With her family's advice in her ears, and more resources than she had ever had at her disposal, Esmay chose to take the fastest transport she could find. Civilian fast-transit passenger ships were almost as fast as Fleet, and more reliable in schedule—she would not risk being told there was no more room when she held first-class tickets. She had never traveled this way before. In her stateroom, with access to the first-class exercise and entertainment facilities, she thought of Brun, who had grown up thinking this was normal.

If captivity and brutality were bad for an ordinary person, how must they be for a girl who had experienced luxury, with every whim indulged? How could she withstand the shock? She had taken the E&E course, yes, but Esmay doubted she had taken the lectures about nonresistance, passive resistance, seriously. Brun had no habit of passive survival. She had no experience of being silenced, of having no one listen to her. She would fret, rebel, bring on herself more punishment and abuse. Only if she had a possibility on which to focus her mind and effort—only if she could imagine herself into a different future—would Brun be able to concentrate her resistance into that hope, and not waste herself on futility.

So far as Esmay knew, from the little she'd been allowed to know after being banished in disgrace, the planning had concentrated on a covert operation to extract Brun, with no consideration of her own need for activity. They were clinging to the hope that she had survived, but they didn't consider finding a way to include her help in her own rescue. They were thinking of her as a passive object, something to be snatched from a thief—just as her captors had thought of her as a passive object, some valuable to be stolen and appropriated for their own use.

Just as she herself had been only an object to the man who raped her in childhood—and had himself been only a disgusting object to the sergeant who killed him—and she again had been only an object when her family ignored her memory of the rape and made her into the outcast with nightmares who lived at the far end of the house. She wondered suddenly if Brun's family had ever seen her as a person, not a decorative object . . . if all her wild behavior had been as much a cry for recognition as Esmay's dreams.

And she, too, had treated Brun as a silly piece of

decorative statuary—she had not seen the person behind the pretty face, the lovely hair, the exuberance. Familiar guilt rolled over her, and she pushed it away. Guilt would not help. Remorse would not help. Brun the person was in trouble, and Esmay the person would have to figure out how to help her—and not by ignoring the person she was.

She put her mind back on the problem, as she spent an hour in the ship's countercurrent swim salon.

Brun was, or had been, pregnant. Would pregnancy give her a reason to stay alive, or not? Would babies? She had told Esmay, the day of the disasterous argument, that she didn't want children . . . but that didn't mean she hated them.

That stuffed toy. Esmay stopped swimming, and the pool's current pushed her back to the edge. That stuffed toy from the *Elias Madero* . . . there had been children aboard, and no children's bodies had been found. If—perhaps—the Militia had kept the children, if Brun had been with them, would that give her a focus? Something to live for? Some reason to be patient, in a way that nothing in her past had made her be patient?

It might. Esmay climbed out of the pool, dried off, and went back to her stateroom hardly noticing those who spoke to her. She spent the last days of the transit putting together everything she remembered about the debris from the trader, and Brun, and trying out one scenario after another. If she had fixed on the children as a means of staying sane, she would want to bring them out too. How could that be done? Esmay didn't let herself think it might be impossible.

❖   ❖   ❖

Sector VII HQ

Casea Ferradi was having more luck with blackening Esmay Suiza's name than with capturing Barin

Serrano. She had managed to get herself assigned to Admiral Hornan's personal staff with only the slightest, insigificant pressure on the major—now lieutenant commander—she'd known so well on her first ship. Everyone knew she'd been Suiza's classmate, so her opinion had been asked more than once—she hadn't had to create opportunities to talk about Esmay. With Suiza off on leave to her home planet, Casea didn't even have to worry about contradiction.

"And she really said she thought the Great Families were a ridiculous institution?"

Casea didn't answer directly; she stared thoughtfully into the distance in a way that suggested noble reticence. "I think it's because Altiplano has no Chair in Council," she said, after a long pause. Neither did the Crescent Worlds, but that didn't matter. "There's no tradition of respect, you see."

"I'm surprised they didn't notice anything when she was in the Academy," Master Chief Pell said. He was, though enlisted, senior enough to have access to files in which Casea had particular interest.

"She kept a low profile," Casea said. "Actually, so did I—we were both outsiders in a way, you know. That's why we were together so much, and why I didn't realize that what she said was important." She shook her head, regretting her own innocence. "Then I got absorbed into things, you see, and just . . . didn't notice."

"It's not *your* fault," Pell said, just as she had meant him to say.

"Perhaps not," Casea said. "But I still feel bad about it. If I'd only known, maybe all this could've been prevented."

Pell looked confused. "I don't see how—"

She should have picked a brighter one. "I mean," Casea said, edging nearer to her intended message, "if I'd realized how bitter she was toward the

Families, perhaps she would never have had any
influence on Sera Meager."

Pell blinked. "You can't mean—she actually had
something to do with the capture itself? I thought
that was accidental; she just happened to enter the
same system where they were plundering that
merchanter . . ."

"A very handy coincidence, don't you think? And
Sera Meager had traveled widely . . . I find myself
wondering why she happened to take that particular
shortcut at that particular time."

"And you think Lieutenant Suiza told her about
that? Or told them—"

"I don't suppose we'll ever know," Casea said. The
chances of this rescue succeeding were, in her
unspoken opinion, so close to zero as made no
difference.

"But—but does the Admiral know about this? That
would be treason . . ."

"I'm sure someone else has thought of it," Casea said.
"I'm only a lieutenant, and it occurred to me . . ."

"But you knew her before," he said. "Those more
senior might not know what she said at the Academy."

"Well . . ." Casea feigned reluctance, though it was
getting harder. She had trailed this particular theory
across several potential helpers, and so far had no
takers. Even Sesenta Veron, who had been telling his
own wicked-Suiza stories, thought it was impossible.

"I think you ought to tell the Admiral," Pell said.
Then, with returning caution, "It would help if you
had any documentation."

"I'm afraid not," Casea said. "The only files which
might contain useful references are all well out of my
clearance."

The following silence lasted so long she almost gave
up, but at last Pell's sluggish processors put two and
two together. "Oh! You need access. Er . . . what files
did you have in mind?"

"I did just wonder if anything had come up during the investigation of that mutiny."

"But surely you don't think—I mean, she was *decorated* for that action—"

"I think they might have been asking questions they didn't ask before," Casea said. "Even if they didn't look too carefully at the answers."

Pell shook his head. "It won't be easy, Lieutenant, but I'll see what I can do. I'll have to see who I can talk to over in legal . . . but I'll let you know."

"Thanks," Casea said, giving him the full benefit of her violet gaze and her smile. "I just want to help."

✧   ✧   ✧

Barin Serrano was used to Fleet politics; he had grown up in that dangerous sea. He navigated the tricky currents of influence at the task force headquarters with care, noticing which competing Fleet families were taking advantage of Lord Thornbuckle's present annoyance with the Serrano name. The Livadhis were split, as usual: some were proclaiming their friendship and loyalty to various Serrano seniors like his grandmother, while others were passing snide remarks in the junior officers' recreation areas. Barin ignored the insults, but kept track. Someone in the family would need to know this, when he had enough data.

In another compartment of his busy brain, he began looking for signs of trouble in other master chief petty officers. Once is accident, twice is coincidence . . . he was willing to admit that Zuckerman could be an accident, and the others he'd heard of only as rumors, but if they were true . . . something was going on. His captain would've reported it, but in the present crisis, would anyone listen?

His duties consisted mostly of hand-carrying data cubes back and forth; he spent plenty of time kicking his heels in someone's front office, and thus had plenty of time to chat with people with lots of time-in-grade.

" . . . Like you take Chief Pell," an impossibly perky female pivot-major was saying. "I don't know if it's the strain of all this, or what, but he's not the man he was last Fleet Birthday."

"Really?" Barin's mental ears rose.

"No. Why, the other day I had to look up access codes for legal investigations for him—I'm not even supposed to know the lockout sequences, but he started asking me to keep track of that six months ago—and he couldn't remember *any* of them."

"My, my," Barin said, his mind flickering over the reasons why Admiral Hornan's chief administrative NCO would be poking into legal investigations now, when supposedly the admiral was after Barin's grandmother's job as task force commander. Was he trying to get something on Heris Serrano, who had been through a sticky legal process? "I don't suppose you'd know whose files he was sucking . . . ?"

"That awful Esmay Suiza," the pivot-major said, with a toss of her head. "The one that practically *sold* poor Lord Thornbuckle's daughter to the pirates."

Barin managed not to leap over the desk and snap the girl's neck, but it was an effort.

"Whatever gave you that idea?" he murmured.

"Well, everybody knows she hated her. And I heard Lieutenant Ferradi say that if everyone had known what *she* knew about Lieutenant Suiza, she'd never have been allowed *near* Sera Meager."

Barin mentally moved a marker in his head to change Casea Ferradi's label from "nuisance" to "enemy."

"She's so beautiful, isn't she?" cooed the pivot-major.

"Mmm?"

"Lieutenant Ferradi. You're lucky she likes you; she could have any man on the base."

"She probably has," Barin said without thinking; he looked up to find her outraged, glaring at him.

"—Them all thinking about her," he amended quickly. She held the glare long enough to let him know she wasn't convinced, then relaxed.

"She's a fine officer, and Chief Pell thinks so too. So does the admiral."

Did he . . . did he indeed. Barin went out thinking hard in several directions, and nearly ran over the fine, beautiful Lieutenant Ferradi.

"Oh—Ensign—"

"Yes, sir?" He managed to smile at her.

"Have you heard anything from Lieutenant Suiza?"

"No, sir. I believe the lieutenant is on leave, isn't she?"

"Yes, but—actually I wanted to talk to you about her."

Now it was coming. He gripped his temper firmly by the collar, and waited.

"I know you . . . used to be friends."

"We served together on *Koskiusko*," Barin said.

"I know. And I heard you were friends. And I'm sorry, but—I think you should know that continuing that friendship would not be in your best professional interest."

As if Ferradi cared about his professional standing, other than to take advantage of his family name.

"I have not had any contact with Lieutenant Suiza since Copper Mountain," Barin said.

"Very wise," she said, approving.

Barin headed back to *Gyrfalcon*'s berth, hoping that Captain Escovar was aboard. This time he knew when to call for help.

CHAPTER SEVENTEEN

Escovar was not aboard; he was at another meeting.

"Is there something I could answer?" asked Lieutenant Commander Dockery. Barin hesitated only a moment.

"Yes, sir, quite possibly, but it would be better somewhere else."

"Trouble?"

"Perhaps."

"Sten, you have the bridge," Dockery said. And to Barin, "Come on, then—we'll use the captain's office."

Barin had just time to realize that he might be scuttling several careers, not just his own, when Dockery turned to him.

"Out with it, then. Found another problem with master chiefs?"

Barin's jaw almost dropped. "As a matter of fact, sir, possibly yes. But that's not my main concern."

"Which is?"

Best get it out quickly, before he was tempted to soften it. "Sir, an officer from this ship has accessed records which she has no legitimate interest in, and may have given false information about someone else."

"Hmm . . . that's a serious charge about an indefinite—I presume you have a name for each of these?"

"Yes, sir." Barin took a deep breath. "Lieutenant Ferradi talked a master chief named Pell—who incidentally is known to his juniors to be forgetting things this past year—into accessing Lieutenant Suiza's legal records from the court-martial."

"It didn't occur to you that she might have had orders to do so? She is on Admiral Hornan's staff for the present . . ."

"No, sir. If she'd had orders, she'd have gone through channels, not Chief Pell."

"And you also accuse her of giving false information about Lieutenant Suiza? What kind of false information?"

"She's said a lot of things about what Es—what Lieutenant Suiza was like in the Academy. Now I was too far behind to have witnessed any of this directly, but other people who were there don't have the same account at all."

Dockery pursed his lips. "I know that Lieutenant Ferradi's been interested in you, Ensign—it's been fairly obvious. Scuttlebutt had it that you were . . . 'falling under her spell,' I believe, is the term I heard used most. Are you sure this isn't just a lovers' quarrel you're trying to make official business? Because if so, you're about to be in more trouble than you were in over Zuckerman."

"No, sir, it is not a lover's quarrel. I have no interest in Lieutenant Ferradi and never did."

"Mm. The other rumor was that you had been in love with Esmay Suiza—" Barin felt his face getting hot; the exec nodded. "And so the other possibility I see is that you're accusing Lieutenant Ferradi of unprofessional behavior toward another officer because you're still besotted with Suiza and can't stand to hear her criticized."

"Sir, I became . . . very fond of Lieutenant Suiza when we were both on *Koskiusko*. I think she's a fine officer. We quarrelled at Copper Mountain, over what she'd said to Brun Meager"—and to him, though he wasn't going to mention that at the moment—"and I haven't seen her since. Whether I have a bad case of hero worship, which is what Lieutenant Ferradi's told me, or a friendship, or—or something else, doesn't really matter. What does, is whether the stories Ferradi's spreading about her are true."

"If they were true, what would you think?"

Barin felt a pain in his chest squeezing out hope. "Then, sir—I would have to change my opinion."

"Barin, I'm going to tell you something, in confidence, because right now you need to know it. Casea Ferradi has been trouble for every commander she's had—it's why she's at the back of her class's promotion list—but she's never quite managed to get herself thrown out. If Lieutenant Suiza hadn't had that quarrel with Sera Meager, if Lord Thornbuckle hadn't fastened on her as the scapegoat in this mess, no one would be paying the slightest attention to Ferradi's accusations. Now they are—and if she's so far overreached herself as to break regulations concerning legal paperwork, we've got her at last. Tell me, do you know if Koutsoudas is still running scan on your cousin's ship?"

"I think so, sir." Where was this leading?

"Good. We're going to need really good scan to catch her in the act, because she's no dummy. And by the way, good job on finding Pell. We've found two others here . . . though we haven't figured out what the problem is yet."

A half hour later, Barin was on his way to the berth of the *Navarino*, his cousin Heris's ship. Heris was at home to family members—he had the distinct feeling that if he'd been an ensign named, perhaps, Livadhi or Hornan, he might have cooled his heels for an hour before getting in to see her.

"You want my scan techs sucking for you? What's wrong with yours? Escovar's always been able to pick good people."

Dockery had left it to him how much to tell, but this was family. Barin made it as short as he could, emphasizing that he had thought at first it was Heris's record Ferradi was after, in order to help Hornan wrest command of the task force from Admiral Serrano.

"Are you *involved*?" The emphasis clearly meant culpable as well.

"No, and yes," Barin said. "Lieutenant Ferradi also happens to see me as her ticket to the Serrano dynasty."

"Does she now?" Heris looked suddenly very dangerous indeed, as if a sleeping falcon had waked, and aimed its deadly gaze at a target. "And what do you think she's done, that you need Koutsoudas to discover?"

"Gone hunting in supposedly secure legal files, and possibly altered data, sir." That last was his own guess; Dockery hadn't been impressed by it, but he was sure that if Ferradi would lie verbally, she would not be above fudging the records. Why else risk tinkering with those files at all?

"Ah. Well . . . tell you what. You can have a couple of hours of Koutsoudas' time—but I get the whole story afterwards."

"Yes, sir."

"And your captain owes me dinner."

Now how was he going to explain *that* one? He returned thoughtfully to *Gyrfalcon*'s berth, and reported his success to Dockery. "Koutsoudas will be along after lunch, sir," he said at last.

"Good. In the meantime, I want you to go destroy property and get yourself chewed out."

"Sir?"

"Go find Lieutenant Ferradi—which shouldn't be hard, as you say she's been adherent—and figure out some way to damage her datawand. I want her to have to initialize another. I don't care how you do it, as long as you don't damage the lieutenant—but I will mention that just dropping one in an alcoholic beverage is not sufficient. On the other hand, the application of sufficient point pressure is."

Barin set out on this mission with the uneasy feeling that Dockery's past might be more interesting than he had thought. When—and why—had Dockery discovered that dropping a datawand in alcohol wouldn't damage it?

Ferradi found him just as he was turning into the junior officers' mess and recreation area. "Lunch, Ensign?" she asked brightly.

"Oh—yes. Excuse me, Lieutenant—" He made a show of patting his pockets. "Drat!"

"What?"

"I was supposed to check on something for Commander Dockery, and then Major Carmody asked me something else, and—I forgot my datawand. It's back aboard. I'll have to go back—unless I could borrow yours, sir?"

"You should carry it with you all the time," Ferradi said, pulling out hers. "What did Dockery want?"

"Spares delivery schedule," Barin said promptly. "He says they've shorted on pre-dets the last four times. You probably know all about it."

"Oh—yeah. Everyone's complaining." She handed over the wand, and Barin looked around. The nearest high-speed dataport was out in the corridor.

"I'll just be moment," he said. "I heard they have Lassaferan snailfish chowder today—" Sure enough, she went on to the serving tables. Snailfish chowder was a rare treat.

Barin found the high-speed port and jammed the

datawand in. Nothing happened; it lit up normally. He pulled it back out, looked around, and shoved it in as hard as he could. Its telltales came up normal again. He pulled it out and looked at the tip. Someone had designed it to withstand normal carelessness . . . and he realized that a high-speed dataport probably had internal cushions to protect the port side of the contact as well. Fine. Now what? She'd be looking for him any moment.

A thought occurred. He went back into the lounge, waved to Lieutenant Ferradi, who had found a seat at a small table facing the entrance, and pointed at the head, then strode quickly in that direction, as if in urgent need.

Heads were full of hard surfaces; Barin tried one after another, between flushes, until he'd produced a crumple at the datawand's tip by catching it between the door and its jamb, and then squashing it with the door as a lever. He'd had no idea datawands were that tough.

"Sorry, sir," he said to Lieutenant Ferradi, as he seated himself and handed her the wand. "Some kind of bug, I expect."

She had tucked it away without looking at it. "So— you're not having chowder?"

"No, sir. In fact, I think I'll just sit here, if that's all right."

"Of course." She gave him one of her looks from under long eyelashes. Despite his opinion of her, he felt a stir . . . and she knew it. He could have strangled her for that alone. He hoped very much he'd done enough damage to that datawand.

❖　　❖　　❖

Esmay changed into her uniform aboard the ship that had brought her, and took the tram over to the Fleet side.

"Lieutenant Suiza," she said to the security posted at the entrance to the Fleet side of the station.

"Welcome home, Lieutenant." The greeting was merely ritual, but she felt welcomed nonetheless. Beyond the checkpoint, the corridors were busy. No one seemed to notice her—and no reason why they should.

She paused to check the status boards. The task force was still here; her ship was still docked at the station. She entered her name and codes, and found that she was still on the crewlist, though coded for "leave status: away." All other leaves had been cancelled.

"Well, if it isn't Lieutenant Suiza," came a voice from behind her. She turned, to find herself face to face with Admiral Hornan. He was looking at her with considerably less than pleasure. "I thought you had indefinite leave."

"I did, sir," she said. "But we got everything taken care of back home, and I came back at once."

"Couldn't leave it alone, could you? Think you'll have a chance to gloat over the Speaker's daughter, if we get her out?"

"No, sir." Esmay managed to keep her voice level. "Gloating was never my intention."

"You did *not* think she richly deserved what she got? That's not what I heard."

"Sir, I neither said, nor thought, that Brun deserved being kidnapped and raped."

"I see. You did, however, say that she wasn't worth going to war over."

"Sir, I said that no one makes war over one person, not that she wasn't worth it. That is what others have said, as well."

The admiral made a noise somewhere between a grunt and a growl. "That may be, Lieutenant, but the fact remains that what is on the record is your statement that she wasn't worth a war."

Before she could answer—if she could have thought of an answer—the admiral turned away. So much for making allies. She couldn't think of anything she might have said to change his mind.

Esmay had never really thought about the people who might be annoyed, or envious, because of her success. That first triumph had felt so fragile: she had not planned to be the senior survivor of a mutiny, and her struggle to bring her ship back to Xavier, and help Commander Serrano, had been a desperate struggle, one she did not expect—even at the last moment—to win. How could anyone resent it when it was clearly more luck than skill? As for the *Koskiusko* affair . . . again, it was pure luck that she had been there, that she had not been snatched, like Barin, by the Bloodhorde intruders.

But now, thinking about it, she realized that her peers were used to thinking of her as a nonentity, no threat to their own career plans. They had kept a closer eye on more credible rivals. The very suddenness of her success must have made her seem even more dangerous—to those inclined to think that way—than she really was. They would doubt her real ability, or fear it.

So she had . . . enemies, perhaps . . . in Fleet. Competitors, anyway. Some would want to frustrate her goals; others would want to ride her coattails to their own.

Once she'd thought of it, she felt stupid for not thinking of it before. Just as people had interacted with her without knowing what her internal thoughts and feelings were—seeing only the Lieutenant Suiza who was quiet, formal, unambitious—so she had interacted with the others without knowing, or caring much, what their internal motivations and goals were. She had been concerned what those senior to her thought of her performance, of course . . . she paused to consider that "of course," then set that aside for later. The problem was, until recently she had been just existing alongside others, unaware of them except where interaction was required. So she had no idea which of them thought of her as a rival, and which as a potential friend. Except for Barin.

She arrived at her assigned quarters still thinking this over. She had unpacked her duffel and was looking up references on the cube reader when the doorchime sounded. When she opened the door, she was facing an elderly woman she had never seen before in her life, a civilian woman who carried herself with the confidence of an admiral—or a very rich and powerful person.

"You don't look like a desperate schemer," the old woman said. Her night-black hair was streaked with silver, bushing out into a stormy mass, and with her brilliantly colored flowing clothes, she looked like a figure out of legend. Granna Owl, or the Moonborn Mage or something like that. "I'm Marta Katerina Saenz, by the way. My niece Raffaele went to school with Brun Meager. May I come in?"

"Of course." Esmay backed up a step, and the woman came in.

"You are, I presume, Lieutenant Esmay Suiza, just returned from leave on Altiplano?"

"Yes . . . Sera."

Marta Saenz looked her up and down, very much as her own great-grandmother had done. "You also don't look like a fool."

Esmay said nothing as the old woman stalked about the room, her full sleeves fluttering slightly. She came to rest with her back to the door, and cocked her head at Esmay.

"No answer? Indirect questions don't work? Then I'll ask outright—*are* you a heartless schemer, glad to make profit out of another woman's shame and misery?"

"No," Esmay said, with as little heat as she could manage. Then, belatedly, "No, Sera."

"You aren't glad the Speaker's daughter was captured?"

"Of course not," Esmay said. "I know that's what people think, but it's not true—"

The old woman had dark eyes, wise eyes. "When you have called someone—what was it? oh, yes—a 'stupid, selfish, sex-crazed hedonist with no more morals than a mare in heat,' people are going to get the idea you don't like her."

"I didn't *like* her," Esmay said. "But I didn't want this to happen to her." She wanted to say *What kind of person do you think I am?* but people had been thinking she was bad for so long she didn't dare.

"Ah. And did you think she was morally lacking?"

"Yes . . . though that still doesn't mean—"

"I honor your clear vision, young woman, which can so easily find where others are lacking. I wonder, have you ever turned that clear vision on yourself?"

Esmay took a deep breath. "I am stubborn, priggish, rigid, and about as tactful as a rock to the head."

"Um. So you're not casting yourself as the faultless saint in this drama?"

"Saint? No! Of course not!"

"Ah. So when you decided she was lacking in moral fiber, you were comparing her to an objective standard—?"

"Yes," Esmay said, more slowly. She wasn't even sure why she was answering this person. She had been over this so often, without convincing anyone.

The old woman nodded, as if to some unheard comment. "If I were simply going by Brun's past behavior, I'd say there's a man at the bottom of this."

Esmay felt her face heating. Was she really that transparent? The old woman nodded again.

"I thought as much. And who, pray tell, is the young man on whom Brun set her sights, and whom you think you love?"

"I do love—" got out before Esmay could stop it. She felt her face getting hotter. "Barin Serrano," she said, aware of being outmaneuvered, outgunned, and in all ways outclassed.

"Oh, my." That was all the old lady said, though she blinked and pursed her lips. Then she smiled. "I have known Brun since she was a cute spoiled toddler they called Bubbles—"

"Bubbles?" Esmay could not put that name with what she knew of Brun. "Her?"

"Stupid nickname—gave the girl a lot of trouble, because she thought she had to live up to it. But anyway, I've known her that long, and you are right that she was as badly spoiled as it's possible for a person of her abilities to be. My niece Raffaele was one of her close friends—and Raffa, like you, was one for getting other people out of scrapes. She got Brun out of a lot of them."

Where was this leading? Esmay wasn't sure she was following whatever chain of logic the old woman was forging; she was still too shaken at having admitted—to a stranger—that she loved Barin Serrano. She was hardly aware that the emotional atmosphere had changed, that the old woman wasn't as hostile as she had been.

"Tell me that Brun Meager has *no* morals, and I find myself defending her. But tell me that she cast covetous eyes on your young man, and I am not only willing to believe it, but not even mildly surprised. She's been that way since she first discovered boys."

Was that supposed to excuse her? Esmay felt the familiar stubborn resentment. The old woman paused; Esmay said nothing.

"If you're thinking that making a habit of stealing other women's men is even worse than happening to fall in love with one of them, which is what your face looks like, that's true. She collects them like charms on a bracelet, with reprehensible lack of concern for anyone's feelings. Or she did. Raffa said she'd been more . . . er . . . discreet in the past few years. Apparently someone she took a fancy to refused to have a fling with her."

"Barin . . . didn't," Esmay said. Then, realizing how many ways that could be taken wrong, she tried to explain. "I mean, he wasn't the one, but he also didn't. He said . . ." Her voice failed her. After a miserable pause, during which she wished she could evaporate, the old lady continued.

"But what you should know is that while Brun's moral qualities are certainly immature, the girl had the right instincts about many things. She's been wild, heedless, rebellious—but she's not wittingly cruel."

"She said things to me, too." That sounded almost childish, and again Esmay wished she could just not be there.

"In the heat of an argument, yes. She would. Both of you sound rather like fishwives in the tape." The old lady picked up and put down a datawand and a memo pad. "Suppose you tell me how you met her, and what happened then?"

Esmay could see no reason for doing so, but she felt too exhausted to protest. Dully, she recounted the story of her first sight of Brun arguing with her father, and what followed, up to the point where Barin arrived.

"Let me see if I have this right. Brun admired you, wanted to be your friend, but you found her pushy and uncomfortable."

"Sort of. I'd seen her throw that tantrum with her father—"

"That sounds like her—and like her father, for that matter. Stubborn as granite, all that family. Back when her father was a boy, he had almost that same argument with *his* father. But since he was only ten years old, it was easier to deal with. So, from the first,

Brun impressed you as spoiled and difficult, and you wanted no part of her."

"Not exactly," Esmay said. "If I hadn't been so busy, taking double courses, I might've had time to talk to her. She kept wanting to go off somewhere and have a party, when I had to study. But that doesn't mean I wanted her to get hurt."

"And knowing Brun, she would've counted on her charm—she probably couldn't figure out why you weren't being friendlier. A natural ally, she would have thought—ran away from a repressive home and made a career for herself, and *her* family isn't interfering."

"I suppose . . ." Esmay said. Had that been what Brun was thinking? It had not occurred to her that Brun could ever think of them as having much in common.

"And then, on top of that, she made a play for your man. I wonder if she was serious about that, or if she just thought he could help her get to you?"

"She asked him to sleep with her," Esmay said, angry again.

"Ah. Unwise of her, at best. And you suddenly thought of her as a rival, a sneak, and a slut, did you?"

"Mmm . . . yes." Put like that, it made her seem even more naive than she was. If that were possible.

"And you got mad and reamed her out for it. But, my dear, had you ever bothered to tell her you were in love with the man?"

"Of course not! We hadn't made any promises . . . I mean . . ."

"Have you told *anyone*?"

"Well . . . only when I went home for Great-grandmother's funeral, I told my cousin Luci."

"Who is how old? And what did she say?"

"She's eighteen . . . and she said I was an idiot." Esmay blinked back sudden tears. "But she—she's had those years at home, and her mother—and no one ever told me—"

The old lady snorted. "No, I don't suppose how to conduct a love affair is one of the courses taught at the Academy or the prep school."

"What they said was not to become involved with people above or below in the same chain of command, and avoid all situations of undue influence."

"That sounds like a recipe for confusion," Marta commented.

"In the professional ethics segment at Copper Mountain," Esmay said, "there was more about that— and I started worrying about what I might do to Barin—"

"Professionally, you mean?"

"Yes—I'm two ranks senior, he's just an ensign. It seemed natural at first—and we weren't in the same chain of command—but maybe I shouldn't, anyway. I told myself that," Esmay said, aware of the misery in her voice. "I tried to think how to talk to him about it, but—but *she* was always there, and I didn't have time—"

"Oh . . . my. Yes, I see. She had the experience, and you didn't. She had the time, and you didn't. And you would not see her being concerned about her effect on his career, either, I daresay."

"No. It was always 'Barin, since Esmay's being no fun, let's go into Q-town for a drink or something.'"

"I've met the young Serrano," Marta said. Her finger traced a line on the built-in desk. "Handsome boy—seems very bright. His grandmother thinks rather well of him, and tries not to show it."

"How is he?" asked Esmay, her whole heart waiting for the answer.

"Thriving, I would say, except for the woman he's got on his trail. One Lieutenant Ferradi, as slickly designed a piece of seduction as I've ever seen. I wonder who did her biosculpt. He's at that age, Lieutenant Suiza, where young men of quality are full of animal magnetism and some women behave like iron filings. Tell me, if you will, who noticed whom first between the two of you?"

"He—came to me," Esmay said, feeling the heat in her face.

"Ah. No iron filing tendencies in you, then. Typical—the magnets prefer to join other magnets: like to like."

"But I'm not—"

"A magnet? I think you misjudge yourself; people often do. The most distressing bores are most sure they fascinate; the least perceptive will tell you at great length how they understand your feelings; every hero I ever knew was at least half-convinced of his or her own cowardice. If you were not a magnet, so many people could not be so angry with you."

Esmay had never looked at character that way, and wasn't sure she agreed. But Marta went on.

"You're a born leader; that's clear from your record. That, too, is a magnet quality. You repel or you attract . . . you are not, as it were, inert. Brun's the same—and when magnets aren't attracted, they're often repellent to one another. You got, as it were, your like poles too close together."

"I suppose . . ."

"Tell me, if you hadn't been working so hard, and if Barin hadn't been there, do you think you'd have found anything to like in Brun?"

"Yes," Esmay said after a moment. "She could be fun—the few times we had a few minutes together, I enjoyed it . . . I could see why people liked her so much. She lights up a room, she's bright—we were on the same team for the E&E class exercises, you know. She learned fast; she had good ideas."

"Good enough to get herself out of her present predicament?"

"I . . . don't know. They wouldn't let her take the field exercise—that's one thing she blamed me for, and I had nothing to do with it. But against a whole planet—I don't think that would've helped. What worries me is that they aren't paying attention to her character in the planning—"

"I thought you said she had none—"

Esmay waved that away. If this woman, even this one woman, would listen to what she'd worked out, maybe it would help Brun. "I don't mean sexual morality. I mean her personality, her way of doing things. They're talking—they were talking—as if she were just a game piece. Unless she's dead, she's planning and doing *something*—and if we don't know what, we're going to find our plans crossing hers."

"But the Guernesi said there's no way to communicate with her—that pregnant and nursing women are sequestered, and besides, she can't talk." Still, Marta's eyes challenged Esmay to keep going.

"She needs to know she's not forgotten," Esmay said. "She needs to know someone thinks she's competent—"

"You sound as if you thought you understood her," Marta said.

"They silenced her," Esmay said, ignoring that invitation. "That doesn't mean she can't think and act. And—did they tell you about the children on that merchant ship?"

Marta frowned. "I . . . don't know. I don't think so. What does that have to do with Brun?"

Quickly Esmay outlined her new theory. "If they didn't kill those children, if they were taking them, they'd have put Brun in with them. That might be enough to keep her alive—if she thought she had a responsibility to the children. And she'd be planning some rescue for them, I would bet on it."

"I suppose it's possible . . ."

"And besides, for her to come out of this in the end, even if she is rescued, she needs to feel that she had some effect. It's one of the things they taught us, and Barin knows from experience . . .

a captive who is just rescued like a . . . a piece of jewelry or something . . . has a much harder time regaining a normal life. She was not just captured; she was muted, and then raped—made pregnant. All her options closed. They should be thinking beyond getting her out, to getting her out with some self-respect left."

Marta looked at her with a completely changed expression. "You're serious . . . you couldn't have come up with that if you didn't really care. That's good thinking, Lieutenant—excellent thinking. And I can tell you that you're right—the planning group is not considering any of those things."

"Can you get it across to them?"

"Me? It's your idea."

"But I don't know how to get anyone to listen to me. They're so convinced I wanted something bad to happen to her, none of them will let me near the planning sessions, let alone speak. If you tell them, maybe they'll consider it."

"You're not asking for credit—"

Esmay shook her head. "No. Brun's the one in critical danger. Of course, I'd like to be the one to come up with the best solution . . . but it's better that someone comes up with it, than have it ignored."

"I'll . . . see what I can do," Marta said. "In that and other situations."

❖   ❖   ❖

Admiral Serrano frowned as the door opened, but her expression eased as Marta Saenz swept through. "Marta! I heard you were back from downside. We missed you the past few sessions. Lord Thornbuckle was actually making sense when you left, but he's foaming at the mouth again."

"I was prowling amongst the troops, as you'd put it. And I just had a little conversation with your Lieutenant Suiza," Marta said.

"Her." The admiral frowned again. "A very

disappointing decision, encouraging her switch to command track. She's not working out at all."

"You've got the bull by the wrong leg," Marta said. "Did you know the girl was besotted with your grandson?"

"I know they formed an attachment on *Koskiusko*, which I'm glad to see is no longer important."

"Oh, but it is," Marta said. "The silly child fell madly in love for the first time in her life, and nothing in her background told her what to do when a rich, beautiful, charismatic blonde moved in on her love life."

"But she's—what?—almost thirty."

"She's also Altiplanan, lost her mother when she was five, and apparently no one told her about anything to do with love. So when she finally fell, she fell like the side of a mountain. Something she heard in a class on professional ethics started her worrying about whether she should have—as if rules ever affected gravity or love—and while she was fumbling around trying to put her emotional affairs in order, Brun started playing come-hither with your grandson. Who resisted, by the way, but Esmay didn't know that when she blew up."

"I can hardly believe—"

"Oh, it's true. And your grandson is equally besotted with her, though he's tried to fight it. He was angry and hurt that Esmay didn't trust him, and— since he wasn't the one feeling unsure and jealous— he was appalled at her attack on Brun."

"Where did you get all this . . . inside knowledge of my grandson's head?"

"His heart, not his head. By poking around being a nosy old woman and then a more . . . er . . . traditional grandmother than you are. He could hardly confide his guilty passion to you, now could he? Not when his lady love was in your black book and he knew your position was shaky, with dear Admiral Hornan doing his best to grab your command."

Admiral Serrano looked thoughtful. "They both still think they're in love, do they?"

Marta chuckled. "All the symptoms. They blush, they tremble, they look shy—it's rather sweet, actually, as well as unmistakeable. I admit my fondness for young love, messy though it often is. It's why I helped Raffa and Ronnie get free of their appallingly stiff-necked parents. So you can quit looking for hidden political motives in Lieutenant Suiza's behavior—this is the oldest story in the book."

"That may be, but it doesn't excuse—"

"What she said? No. But if her commander had known from day one that this was a squabble over a man, would he have handled it the way he did?"

Admiral Serrano pursed her lips. "Well . . . probably not. We do get late bloomers from time to time, and they do usually make a mess of things at least once." The admiral sounded thoughtful, less harsh.

"Making a mess of love is part of growing up," Marta said, nodding. "Making a mess of someone's career, however, requires the connivance of others."

"I don't follow you." But the dark eyes were alert, watchful.

"Well . . . as the resident sweet old lady in this facility—" The admiral snorted, and Marta flashed a quick grin but went on. "The youngsters tell me things. They always have. It's why I was Raffa's favorite aunt. I'd already begun to wonder how so shining a young hero could become everyone's favorite wicked woman quite so fast. I suspected that someone else's interest lay in making Lieutenant Suiza look as bad as possible, and I found that the tainted effluent, as it were, led to a few sources quite remote from Copper Mountain. That's why I went planetside, so I could do a little discreet database poking from a civilian facility."

"And you found—?"

Marta held up her hand and ticked off points on her fingers. "I found Academy classmates of Esmay's who were jealous of her success—who resented her honors—who would be quite happy to see her back in tech track, or out of Fleet, because she can fight rings around them. Much that's been attributed to her has come from these sources, and they've put the worst possible interpretation on what she *did* say. The people who've actually served with her are confused and upset right now, but find it hard to believe she could be the way she's now being painted. I found others who want to get influence with your grandson because he's a Serrano . . . who are very glad to put a barrier between him and Lieutenant Suiza."

"All very interesting—but are you sure you're hearing the truth?"

"Vida—remember Patchcock? My nose for this kind of nastiness—"

"Yes . . . all right . . . but that doesn't get Lieutenant Suiza off the hook for what she actually said and did. And there's a witness to her saying that Brun wasn't worth starting a war over."

"So did I, m'dear. So did you. So did the Guernesi ambassador, more than once. We wrapped it in platitudes, but you know and I know that no one— not even the Speaker, and certainly not his daughter— is worth starting a war for. Taken in context, what she actually said cannot be construed to mean that she thought all those things attributed to her."

The admiral spread her hands. "So—what do you propose to do about this? Since you came here, I presume you have a plan in mind."

"Well . . . having played fairy godmother to at least three other romances recently—you know about Raffa and Ronnie, but you don't know about the others— I feel I'm on a roll where love is concerned. If Esmay and Barin can work out their problems—"

"You mean you aren't planning to do it for them?" That with a challenging grin.

"Of course not." Marta made a prim face. "Children learn by doing. But if they can work it out—and since they're both still smitten, I expect they can—that will take the teeth out of some of the other criticisms. After all, if a Serrano is her lover—"

"Ah—so *that's* why you tackled me first. So I wouldn't tell young Barin to avoid her?"

"Got it in one. Incidentally, if you thought Suiza was bad, you ought to see what's working on him now. One of Esmay's classmates, and a very sleek piece of work she is, too. Knows everything Esmay doesn't know about men, and since she's also a colonial, from one of the Crescent Worlds, you have to wonder where she got that kind of skill. Rumor has it, from seducing her senior officers."

"Pull in your claws, Marta—I won't do anything to warn Barin off. And I already know about Lieutenant Ferradi—she may have done even worse than you know, according to Heris. If so, her doom is about to be upon her: Heris lent Koutsoudas to the cause."

"You're going to tell me, I trust? No? Wicked woman—but then you are an admiral." Marta's chuckle ended. "There's another thing, though. Lieutenant Suiza, when I talked to her, had what I think are some very good insights into Brun's situation and some concerns about the planning. She is convinced that no one will listen to her, and asked me to pass these ideas on, as my own. I'd much rather get her involved in the planning herself—"

"Can't be done," Admiral Serrano said crisply. "Lord Thornbuckle's adamant. Apparently he had liked her when he met her at Copper Mountain, and feels that this proves she is . . . treacherous, was his word. He will not have her involved at all. And I doubt you can change his mind. Not in the time we have left."

She glanced at the wall calendar and Marta

followed that glance. A red rectangle covered the most probable dates for the end of Brun's pregnancy; a green one covered the time the Militia were known to allow before rebreeding a captive. That was their target; somewhere in that period they had to extract her—or face even more difficult problems.

"All right. One war at a time. I'll present Esmay's ideas; they certainly make sense in terms of my knowledge of Brun's character."

CHAPTER EIGHTEEN

Marta found Esmay at work in a cubicle, paging through a report, looking thoughtful.

"I've just talked to Admiral Serrano," Marta said. Esmay flushed a little, the reaction Marta had hoped for. "I told her I thought the reports of your hardheartedness and political ambitions were exaggerated . . . and why." The flush deepened, but Esmay said nothing. "You will find that she creates no barrier to your relationship with Barin . . ."

"If I ever have one," Esmay said. She looked up, tears standing in her eyes. "What if he won't speak to me?"

"Well, then, you have to see that he does."

"But Casea's always around—"

Marta sat very straight. "You are not going to make that mistake again! Think, child! What do you know about that young woman? Does she have a good reputation?

"No . . ." Esmay's voice trembled slightly.

"Do you really think Barin is the kind of man who prefers that kind of woman?"

"No . . ." Her voice failed completely.

"Then quit being a wet lump, and give him some help in getting free of her. Be someone he can prefer, with some reason." Marta cocked her head. "Personally, I'd recommend a good haircut, to start with. And a really well-cut exercise suit."

Esmay flushed again. "I—I couldn't."

"What—you can't show what you've got, because she's displaying herself like a fruit basket? What kind of nonsense is that? Come along—" Marta stood up, and watched Esmay rise slowly. "I know perfectly well you're just moving things around in here trying to look busy. Your commander's angry with you, nobody has any real work for you—so I'm demanding your services as an escort."

"But you—"

"My dear, before you embarrass yourself again, I'm not just Raffaele's aunt . . . I hold my own Seat in Council, though I usually let Ansel vote it for me, and if I wanted to grab any officer up to and including Admiral Serrano for an escort, no one, least of all Vida, would stand in my way. Bunny himself is putty in my hands when I'm in this mood. And you are, after all, the Landbride Suiza. Now come along and quit making difficulties."

Marta was glad to see the salutary lift of spine which that produced, and thoroughly enjoyed her sweep through the corridors of the HQ complex, with Esmay Suiza a silent shadow at her side. She could almost see the shock, and imagined it trickling icewater-like down certain spines. The particular blonde spine she most wanted to discomfit didn't appear—well, that would come later.

❖   ❖   ❖

Esmay hung back as Marta led her toward the doors of the most fashionable salon in the city. She had heard of Afino's—including from Brun, who had recommended it heartily.

"No one's ever been able to do anything with my hair," she said miserably, as she had more than once on the way downside. "It's too fine, and thin, and it frizzes—"

"And probably all you do is wash it, brush it, and cut it off when it gets too long," Marta said. "Listen— you are not your hair. You have choices. You want Barin, and you want to regain your professional reputation. This will help."

It still seemed more than a little immoral. Her hair had always been her downfall, in the style sense, and she could think of nothing that would improve it but yanking it out and starting over from the genome. The serious noises the head of the salon made when he looked at her scalp made her want to sink through the floor.

"You have the fine hair," he said. "Perhaps your parents also, or perhaps you have had a high fever when you were young?"

"Yes, I did," Esmay said.

"That may be it. But it is very healthy; you have not been doing anything stupid, as some women do. And you are a Fleet officer—you want something practical, easy to keep, but looking more . . . more . . ."

"More like it's intended to be something," Marta put in. "Less like dryer fluff."

"Ah. A more permanent solution would be the genetic one, but you said the matter was urgent."

"Yes. Although in the long run, Esmay, he's right— it's expensive, but you can have your hair genetically reprogrammed."

So—even a salon like this thought that replacing it from the roots out was the best approach. But she hadn't actually thought it was possible.

"It would change your genetic ID slightly," the man said. "You would have to report it to your commander, and they would have to approve, and then change your records. But it has been done. On the other hand, there's nothing wrong with your hair as it is, once we determine the best way of cutting it."

With scissors, Esmay thought but did not say.

Three hours later, she stared at her reflected image with astonishment. It was the same hair, but somehow it had consented to take a shape that suggested both competence and charm. Smooth there, a bit of curl here. Fluff was perhaps the wrong word . . . but she couldn't think of another. She looked like herself, but . . . more so. And under the tutelage of the salon's staff, she had learned to do it herself, from sopping wet to final combing.

After that, Marta dragged her off to the neighboring dress shop. "You need off-duty clothes. I've seen you in those exercise suits."

"I sweat," Esmay said, but with less strength in the protest.

"Yes, but you don't have to sweat while eating dinner." Marta prowled, sending Esmay into the changing room again and again until she was happy with the result—by which time Esmay was finally beginning to understand what the fuss was about. The blue and silver exercise suit was as comfortable as the ones she usually wore, but looked—she had to admit—stunning. And the others . . .

"The people you think were born looking good were born looking red and wrinkly just like everyone else," Marta said. "Yes, there are faces more beautiful than others, bodies more easily draped than others. But at least half the people you admire aren't, on form alone, beautiful. They make the effect they have. Now some people don't care about effect, and don't need effect, and nobody needs it all the time. At home, when I'm out in the garden, I look like any plump old woman in dirty garden clothes. I don't care, and neither does anyone else. But when I'm being Marta Katerina Saenz, with a Chair in Council, I dress for effect. Right now you need all the effect you can manage: it will do no good, and much harm, for you to skulk around headquarters looking ashamed of yourself. It helps people think you're guilty."

Hair, clothes, even a session in a day spa, from which she emerged feeling utterly relaxed. Two days after they'd left, when her new clothes were stowed in her compartment, Marta led her back to the lieutenant commander in charge of Esmay's section.

"Here she is—you can have her back for a while, but I may need her again. Thank you, Lieutenant Suiza; you've been most helpful."

Lieutenant Commander Moslin looked from one to the other. "You're . . . satisfied, Sera Saenz?"

"With Lieutenant Suiza? Of course. Best personal assistant I ever had. Excuse me; I mustn't be late to meet Admiral Serrano." With a wave, Marta departed, leaving Esmay under the lieutenant commander's mistrustful gaze.

"Well . . . I thought she was Lord Thornbuckle's friend, and here she's sticking up for you . . ."

"I think," Esmay said, following Marta's briefing, "I remind her of a niece or something. But of course I did my best."

"Yes. Well. I suppose you can get back to that report you were working on . . ."

Esmay could feel his gaze on her as she walked off. She knew he had sensed some difference, but couldn't pinpoint it. She could . . . and was amazed that she had never bothered to learn such simple things before. She saw Casea Ferradi coming toward her, and assumed the expression Marta had recommended. Sure enough, Casea almost stumbled.

"Lieutenant Suiza—"

"Hello, Casea," Esmay said, inwardly amazed and delighted.

"You're—I thought you were on leave."

"I'm back," Esmay said. "But busy—see you later." It could be fun. It could actually be fun. Buoyed up by that thought, she smiled serenely at Admiral Hornan around the next corner.

Barin came to attention. "Ensign Serrano reporting, sir."

His grandmother looked up. "At ease, Ensign. Have a seat. We have family business to discuss."

Family business did not put him at ease, but he sat and waited. His grandmother sighed.

"Marta Saenz tells me that you and Lieutenant Suiza had a row over Brun Meager."

Barin almost let his jaw drop, but tightened it in time. "That's . . . not exactly how it happened, sir."

"Mmm. Well, however it happened, and whatever the current status of your feeling for Lieutenant Suiza may be, I wanted you to know that from my perspective, as your grandmother, I have no advice to give. About her, at least. About someone else you've been seen with, I have the advice you can probably guess. As an admiral, I would like to see Lieutenant Suiza perform at her best—she has a strikingly good best—and would like whatever circumstances might contribute to that end, to happen. So if you feel you can do her some good, go ahead."

"She's—not speaking to me."

"Are you sure? Perhaps she thinks you're not speaking to her. Especially since there are others who might have an interest in keeping you two apart."

"Lieutenant Ferradi—" Barin said, through clenched teeth.

His grandmother looked at him as if he were a toddler; he knew that look. "Among others. Barin, you're old enough to know how our family name attracts envy as well as admiration. Lieutenant Suiza's rapid rise to fame and promotion has had a similar effect. It has come to my attention that there are people who feel it in their interests to have you and Lieutenant Suiza at cross purposes. If you did not care for her, it would be one thing, but since you do, it seems to me that it is a matter of family honor not to let them succeed. Subject, of course, to your own feelings."

"Ah . . . yes, sir—Grandmother."

She gave him a frank grin. "Sir Grandmother must be an unusual title, but I'll take it. Seriously, Barin—do you love this woman?"

"I thought I did, but—"

"Well, think again. Think, but also feel. It is not for me to play Cupid; if you two are meant for each other, you shouldn't need a Cupid. But take nothing for granted. Clear?"

"Yes . . . Grandmother."

"Good. If there's fallout, I'll deal with it. I trust your judgement, Barin—just be sure you have enough data to base it on." She paused, but he said nothing. What was there to say? With a crisp nod, she reverted from grandmother to admiral. "Now—how's that investigation of Lieutenant Ferradi coming?"

"I don't know," Barin said. "Both my captain and my exec told me to keep my nose somewhere else, so I have."

"Amazing," his grandmother murmured, in a tone that made his ears heat up. "Well, we're closing in on our active dates—it would be a help to me to know what's going on. I'd like you to go mention that to Heris, and let her murmur it to your captain's ear—or whatever it takes. Klaus still wants my job, and since he hasn't commanded anything but a desk for the past nineteen years, I'm unwilling to let him make a hash of it. Your ostensible message to Heris is that we're having a family celebration since the Fleet Birthday festivities will be very restrained this year. This is what you can—and should—tell anyone. But carry this—" she handed over a data strip. "For her hand only, and use the family handshake."

"Yes, sir."

"Dismissed."

✧　　✧　　✧

"She's a natural-born weasel," Koutsoudas said, pointing out the graphic he had made of Lieutenant Ferradi's illicit activities in the legal database. "If we hadn't had that primed datawand, she might've got away with it, even with me on scan."

"Well, what has she done?" asked Captain Escovar.

"She used Pell's access codes into the first level, and then someone else's—would you believe Admiral Hornan's?"

"How'd she get those?"

"I have no idea, sir." Koutsoudas was watching the vid screen now, on which Lieutenant Ferradi's neat blonde head was bent studiously over a console. "Possibly from Pell . . . and while it's none of my business, you should probably know there's rumors that Pell's been called in for an off-cycle physical."

"So he has," Escovar said.

"And three other master chiefs here as well . . . it's making some of us nervous, tell you the truth."

"In what way?"

"Beyond my area of expertise, sir." Koutsoudas had the expression of a man not in the mood to trust anyone.

"Mm. Concerns have been expressed at higher levels than mine, as well."

"Just as well, sir. Ah—there she goes." Onscreen, Ferradi inserted her datawand into a port in the console. "Bet she inputs a file this time—look at her left hand. Yeah—there it is." On Koutsoudas' graphic, an orange line snaked along a tangle of other lines, and made its way into a blue box, where it flashed steadily. "Altering data, sir: that's one hundred percent clear."

"Do we know what the data were prior to alteration?"

"I don't, no sir. But I do know there was a secure

backup made last night, blind copy to a storage unit she'll never find. And the trace on her wand will prove she altered something, and where in the file it is."

✧　　✧　　✧

"These are very serious charges, Commander Escovar," Admiral Hornan said. "I've found Lieutenant Ferradi to be a most efficient officer . . ." His glance at Barin mixed suspicion and resentment in equal portions. Barin reminded himself that this man was his grandmother's rival.

"The admiral is right—these are serious charges. That is why I brought them to you rather than calling Lieutenant Ferradi in myself. Under the circumstances—political as well as military—it seemed preferable to have you in on this from the beginning—"

"Not the beginning, if you've already done the investigation—"

"Only enough to be sure the original allegation was founded on fact, admiral. There's more to do—"

"Well, let's just hear her side of it—" Hornan touched his comunit. "Lieutenant Ferradi, would you come in, please?"

"Right away, Admiral." The slightest pause, then, "Should I bring the latest information from that database search the admiral asked about?"

"Uh—not right now, Lieutenant." A flush crept up Hornan's neck. Barin dared a sidelong glance at Escovar and saw that he had not missed it. So . . . just how deep into this was Hornan?

In only a few moments, Casea Ferradi came into the admiral's office, wide-eyed and smiling, a smile that widened into a quick grin meant to be complicit when she saw Barin, and sobered when no one smiled back.

"Admiral?"

"Casea—Lieutenant—these officers have made

some serious charges against you. I want to know what you have to say."

"Against me?" For just an instant, in profile, Barin saw a flicker that might have been panic, but her calm returned. "Why—what am I supposed to have done?" She looked at Barin. "Did I bother poor Ensign Serrano? I didn't mean to . . ."

Hornan cleared his throat. "No . . . Lieutenant, I must ask: have you accessed any Fleet records which you are not cleared to access?"

"Of course not," Ferradi said. "Not without specific orders to do so."

"Which would give you authorization, yes. Are you sure of that?"

"Yes, Admiral," Ferradi said. Barin watched the pulse in her neck beat a little faster.

"Have you altered any data in any records whatsoever?"

"You mean like—watch records or something? No, sir."

"Or in a database? Have you ever intruded into a database and altered records?"

"Not without specific orders to do so, no, Admiral." But that telltale pulse was faster now.

"Then if I told you that you were alleged to have intruded into the records of the investigations surrounding the mutiny on *Despite*, and alleged to have changed certain files containing interview data on Lieutenant Esmay Suiza, you would deny it."

"I would, Admiral." Ferradi flushed suddenly. "I deny it absolutely, and moreover I would consider the source." She rounded on Barin. "Ensign Serrano, Admiral, has a grudge against me . . . he thought his family position gave him a right to . . . to take liberties beyond his rank. I had to be quite firm with him and he knows I could have reported him for harrassment. He probably made up this nonsense just to get back at me—"

Barin felt the blood rushing to his head, but a stern look from Escovar kept him silent. Admiral Hornan gave a short nod in Barin's direction, and cocked his head at Escovar.

"Well, Commander? I find the foolish behavior of a hot-blooded young man of a high-status family more likely than illegal acts by someone like Lieutenant Ferradi . . ."

"Admiral, with all due respect, that won't do. Lieutenant Ferradi was pursuing Ensign Serrano, not the other way around. I knew it, and so did everyone else on the ship. You will find references to Lieutenant Ferradi's behavior in her previous fitness reports; her present position in the last promotion cohort of her class reflects that behavior."

"That's not true!" Ferradi said. Her high color was patchy now, flushing and fading on those perfect cheekbones.

"And while her sexual proclivities would not, in themselves, be cause for disciplinary action as long as she did not interfere with anyone's fitness for duty, her intrusion into secured databases, her altering of the data, and her lies about other officers—including Ensign Serrano—would be."

"And you think you have proof of this?" Hornan asked. Barin watched Ferradi pale, as the change in his tone and expression got through to her. He could almost feel sympathy, because in that moment Hornan was changing sides, preparing to divest himself of an embarrassment.

"Yes. We have the records of such intrusion, from a datawand initialized for Lieutenant Ferradi, along with vid records of her using it that are contemporaneous with the intrusion and alteration."

"I didn't . . ." Ferradi breathed. But the admiral did not look at her now.

"How detailed are these records?"

"Extremely, Admiral. They include all the

authorization codes she used to complete her intrusion, and to fake—I presume—the orders for the alterations."

Now the admiral did look at Ferradi, and Barin hoped very much no such look would ever be turned on him. "I would have to see such proof," he said slowly, with almost no expression. "But if you have it—"

"We do, Admiral."

"Then Lieutenant Ferradi is, as you say, facing serious charges. Lieutenant, your datawand, if you please."

Ferradi pulled it out slowly, and laid it on the admiral's desk.

"And that report you were working on is—where, Lieutenant?"

"On my desk, Admiral. But the admiral knows who—"

"You will consider yourself confined to quarters, Lieutenant. You will speak to no one except the investigating officer, when such has been appointed."

"But Admiral—it's a plot—it's—"

"Dismissed, Lieutenant."

Barin shivered as she turned and passed him. He had disliked her; he had come to despise her; for what she had almost done to Esmay, he could have hated her. But he would have wished on no one the devastation he saw deep in those violet eyes.

When the door had closed, Escovar said, "Admiral—she used your access codes. I'm afraid there's no way to keep that out of the records."

"Well—she would, wouldn't she, if she wanted to alter data? She'd have to have someone with enough authority."

"Did you give her those codes?"

Hornan pulled himself up. "Commander, I may have been an idiot, but you are not the person who will handle the investigation of this matter. It goes to internal security, as you very well know. And I will answer their questions, to the best of my ability, but not yours." He paused, then went on. "I suppose you're going to tell me I now have to revise my opinion of Lieutenant Suiza?"

"No, Admiral, I'm not. What the admiral thinks of Lieutenant Suiza is the admiral's business; she's not my officer. But if the data are tainted—"

"Oh yes, oh yes." Hornan waved a hand. "First things first. We have to inform internal security, and then Grand Admiral Savanche. He's going to be so pleased about this! Just what he needs, something else to worry about—" He hit the com-unit control so hard it double-buzzed. "Get me internal security—"

"Admiral Serrano's going to have a clear run with the task force," Escovar commented on the way back to *Gyrfalcon*.

"Why, sir?"

"Because Hornan's not going to risk what you might say if he tries for it. Don't play stupid, Ensign—you know as well as I do that he must have been involved at some level. For one thing Ferradi isn't smart enough to get his codes without his help. And Pell couldn't help her—he couldn't remember his own codes, let alone the admiral's. Now if that civilian— Lady Marta whatshername—can put a collar on Lord Thornbuckle, we might finally get this rescue attempt off the ground."

"Sir."

"It's been a mess," Escovar went on, lengthening his stride. "It wouldn't have been easy anyway, but Thornbuckle's been more hindrance than help, and Hornan has kept putting obstacles in the way—and I would never have suspected that nailing Ferradi would get rid of the other problems, too."

Such as what to do about Esmay Suiza. Barin

waited for his captain's dismissal, then made his way to the first public com booth he could find, and looked up Esmay's comcode. She had one now, he was glad to see.

Her voice answered, crisp and professional.

"Lieutenant—it's Ensign Serrano. I—" How was he going to say this? "I'd like—I need—to talk to you."

A long pause, during which he felt himself turning hot, then cold, then hot again.

"In the office, or—I mean—" Her voice had softened, and sounded almost as tentative as his.

"Anywhere. There's something you need to know, and besides—" *Besides, I love you madly* was not something he could say over a public line.

"How about the base library. Ten minutes? Fifteen?"

"Fifteen; I'm just outside *Gyrfalcon*."

He made it in ten, nonetheless, not realizing until he almost overran a pair of commanders strolling ahead of him just how fast he was going. Patience. Calmness. He paused in the library entrance, and didn't see her coming in either direction. Ducked inside, and—there she was.

"Lieutenant . . ."

"Ensign." But her eyes glowed; her whole being glowed. And there were people who had thought he might be attracted to Casea Ferradi!

"I'm so sorry—" he said, and found that his words had tangled with hers. The same words. Silently, he looked at her, and she looked back.

❖   ❖   ❖

Waltraude Meyerson had been watching the young female officer's lame attempt to pretend an interest in the online catalog. She was waiting for someone; it was not the first time Waltraude had seen a student hanging around waiting for another; she could not mistake it. Sure enough, a few minutes later a young male officer arrived. They spoke; they paused; they blushed and stammered. It was all very

normal, but also very distracting when she was trying
to correlate Professor Lemon's data with her own
for the impeccably organized report she would
present in a few hours.

The librarian was, of course, nowhere to be
seen; he never was at this time of day. That didn't
bother Waltraude ordinarily, since she didn't need
his help to navigate her own and Professor Lemon's
databases, but he was responsible for keeping order.
Without his direction, and left to their own devices,
these two would murmur sweet nothings for
hours . . . she knew their type. Waltraude rose to
her full height and cleared her throat. The two
looked at her with the guilty expression typical of
young love.

"This is a library, not a trysting place," Waltraude
said firmly. "Kindly go pursue your passion elsewhere."
Shock blanked their expressions for a moment, then
they turned and left quickly. Better. Perhaps now she
could find a way to convince these military people
that the key to extracting people from a hostile society
would come from better thinking, not more guns.

❖   ❖   ❖

"I love you madly," Barin said, the moment they
got out the door.

"Me, too," said Esmay, and blinked back tears.
Then she giggled. "Wasn't she *awful*?"

"Yes—oh, Esmay, let's not ever *ever* fight again."

"My cousin Luci says people in love can fight and
get over it."

"And her background is—?"

"More experience than I've got. She said I was an
idiot."

"Maybe," Barin said, daring to close in, after a
quick look up and down the corridor, and smell her
hair. "But you're *my* idiot." He looked her up and
down. "Dear idiot. Lieutenant, sir." He felt like
dancing down the corridor, or walking on his hands,

or something equally ridiculous. "Oh, and by the way—Lieutenant Ferradi is confined to quarters and will be facing charges."

"What!?"

"I can't tell you all of it—I mean, I'd better not, at least not out here, but that's why I had to avoid you after you got back—I was supposed to pretend to go along with her."

"I think she lied about me," Esmay said.

"She did more than that—she was trying to insert incriminating stuff in your old personnel and legal files. But we really shouldn't discuss that right now."

"Fine. Let's discuss—"

"Us," Barin said. "Maybe with something to eat?"

❖   ❖   ❖

"So—now that your agent has confirmed that she's there, and knows where she is—we get to the specifics." The speaker, a commander with the shoulder flashes of headquarters staff, put up a chart. "It's not unheard of for men to sneak over the back wall of the nursery compound for a quick poke at some woman they particularly want. He can grab her, bundle her into his groundcar, and be out of the city in twenty minutes."

It sounded like a ridiculous plan to Marta, but she had given up trying to convince them that they had to cooperate with Brun, not treat her like lost luggage. She glanced across the room at Professor Meyerson, who had come with her usual stack of books, papers, and data cubes. Meyerson had footnotes and bibliography to back up her views—which were similar to Marta's—but that hadn't worked either.

"What if she resists?" asked a female commander across the room. "How will she know this man is our agent?"

"He can tell her," the first commander said.

And she's supposed to believe that, Marta thought,

after almost two years of captivity? It might work, or Brun—being Brun—might clobber the fellow and take the car herself. And then where would they be? She would have no idea where to go, and they would have no idea what had happened.

"He tells us that for enough money he can get her passage offworld in a small atmospheric shuttle. He will take her out of the city, provide a disguise, and then send her to this other person. Our present plan is to insert an SAR—which can approach quite close in microjumps—to pick her up, with the rest of the task force standing by at a distance in case of trouble."

Someone else asked the question Marta wanted to ask, about system defenses, and she listened to the answer with half her mind, the other half wondering what Brun was doing. Not sitting still waiting to be rescued, that much she was sure of.

✧   ✧   ✧

Brun picked up the paring knife, and slid it into her sleeve. The matron was supposed to count the knives each day, but she didn't. She liked to doze in her own room, after swigging from an earthenware jar, and a good half the time left the kitchen unlocked. Brun had checked that repeatedly, making sure that her theft had a reasonable chance of going unnoticed.

The knife's pressure against her arm, under the bands she'd tied to hold it, gave her courage again. She had waited as long as she could; she dared not wait longer for rescue. Neither she nor her babies had to live in this place . . . but when she laid the blade to the moist soft neck of the sleeping redhead (she was sure which *his* father was), she knew she could not do it. She didn't love the babies, not as mothers were reputed to do, the way the other mothers here seemed to love theirs, but she didn't hate them, either. It was not their fault; they had not engendered themselves on her unwilling body.

She could not take them with her when she

escaped, though. She was going to have to disguise herself as a man, somehow . . . and men did not carry babies around the streets, even if two squirming and all-too-vocal babies would not have slowed her down too much. If she left them behind, they would be squalling for their next meal in just an hour or so . . . yet she could not face killing them, just to give herself a longer start.

Another idea occurred to her. Though the nursery had no drugs that she knew—and she knew nothing about which, if any, of the herbs in the pantry might put the babies to sleep, there was a simple soporific available to anyone with access to fruit and water and a little time.

In late afternoon she walked as usual in the orchard, carrying one baby on her back and the other in front. Her feet had toughened; the gravel paths no longer hurt her. Beneath the long skirt, her legs had developed ropes of hard muscle from the exercises she'd sweated on. Without the babies, she would be able to move fast and far; she would be able to fight, if she was not taken off-guard. She did not intend to be off-guard again. If only she knew *where* . . . where to find Hazel and the little girls, where to find open country in which—she was sure— she could hide.

Out of sight of the house, she slid the knife into her hand, and then laid it in the crotch of an apple tree. She checked to be sure that the blade would not glint in the light and catch someone's eye. She stuffed some of last year's fallen leaves around it, and strolled on, coming back to the house with a spray of wildflowers in her hand.

Two days later, she pilfered a jug from the kitchen. She carried it into the orchard, concealed in the sling she now used to carry the babies. It was the wrong season for ripe fruit, but she had dried fruit, always available to the women, honey, and water.

The mix fermented in only a few days of warm sunshine. It smelled odd, but definitely alcoholic. She tasted it cautiously. It had a kick . . . enough, she hoped, to put the babies heavily to sleep.

Sector VII HQ

As the task force planning crept onward, Marta kept a weather eye on Bunny. He had not softened his opposition to Esmay Suiza, even when it became obvious that much of the evidence against her had been lies and more lies. Why not? She had known him most of his life; he was neither stupid nor vicious. His reputation for staying calm in a crisis, and being fair to all parties, had made him the one person the Grand Council would trust after Kemtre's abdication. So why was he, at this late date, trying to make sure Suiza didn't go with the task force?

She was tempted to contact Miranda, conspicuously absent, but refrained. Never get between man and wife, her grandmother had taught her, and in her life she'd seen nothing but grief come of it when someone tried. So, five days before the task force was due to depart, she tackled him privately.

"Don't start," Bunny said, before she even opened her mouth. "You're going to tell me Suiza isn't that bad, that she's earned her slot as exec on *Shrike*, that it's not fair to pull her off—"

"No," Marta said. "I'm going to ask you why you blame Suiza for Brun's behavior."

"She drove her into a frenzy—" Bunny began. Marta interrupted.

"Bunny—who chose Brun's genome pattern?"

"We did, of course—"

"Including her personality profile?"

"Well . . . yes, but—"

"You told me before, you deliberately chose a

risk-taking profile. You chose outgoing, quick-reacting, risk-taking, a girl who would always find the glass half-full, and think a roomful of manure meant a cute pony around the corner."

"Yes . . ."

"And you got a charming, lovable scapegrace, full of mischief as a basket of kittens, and you enjoyed it for years, didn't you?"

"Yes, but—"

"You spoiled her, Bunny." He stared at her, his ears reddening. "You chose for her a personality profile, a physical type, and a level of intelligence which would *predictably* make her likely to get into certain kinds of trouble . . . and what did you do, in her young days, to provide the counterbalance she needed, of judgement and self-control?"

"We'd had other children, Marta. We were experienced parents—"

"Yes, for the bright conformists you designed first. And they turned out well—you had given them what they needed." Marta calculated the pause, then went on. "Did you give Brun what she needed?"

"We gave her everything—" But his gaze wavered.

"Bunny, I know this sounds like condemnation, but it's not. Brun is a very unusual young woman, and she would have needed a very unusual childhood to bring her to her present age able to handle her talents safely. It's no wonder you and Miranda, enchanted just like everyone else with that explosion of joy, didn't provide the kind of background that would do her good." She paused again; Bunny almost nodded—she could see the softening of the muscles in his neck. "But it's my opinion that your real objection to Esmay Suiza—perhaps unknown to you—is that she's like Brun with a throttle, with controls. And her father, whatever he's like, did a better job for his daughter than you did for yours."

Bunny reddened again. "She's not anything—"

"Oh yes, she is. Have you read the combat reports on her? I have. Intelligent, very. Charismatic—yes, especially in a crisis. Risk-taker—she came back to Xavier and saved the planet—and incidentally, Brun. Brun thought they had a lot in common; that's why she was dogging Suiza like a little girl tagging a big sister."

"I . . . can't believe that."

"I can't believe you're still not seeing your own part in this. That's why you didn't want Miranda out here, isn't it? She'd admit it, and she'd argue with you."

"I . . . I . . . can't . . ."

"Bunny, it's still not your fault. I think you made mistakes, but so does every parent—your father certainly did with you. But it's also not Lieutenant Suiza's fault. She didn't drive Brun into a mindless frenzy that lasted thirty-odd days. She had a quarrel which would've been over with the next day if they'd had a chance to make up—and in your heart you know that. Channel your rage where it should go, to those thugs who took her, and quit trying to lay your guilt on Suiza."

He was looking away from her; she waited until the muscle in his jaw quit twitching.

"We need everyone's best, to get her out," Marta said, more gently. "Lieutenant Suiza's best is very good—and it could save Brun's life."

"All right." He had not moved, but the tension had gone out of him. "As far as I'm concerned, she can go. But . . . but if she does *anything* to harm Brun's chances—"

"I will personally take her hide off in strips," Marta said. "Nice narrow ones, very slowly. With Miranda on the other side, and Vida Serrano in the middle. And you can have her kidneys on toast, for all I care."

That got a laugh, though a choked one. "It's so small a chance," Bunny said, after a pause. Marta could hear the tears close to the surface. "So small . . ."

"You just increased it," Marta said. "Now—shall I tell the admiral, or will you?"

CHAPTER NINETEEN

The man in the checked shirt, true to his persona as country bumpkin in the city, had wandered up and down the various streets, visiting the breeding houses once or twice, and coming again to look at the showing of the yellow-haired infidel from space. He had told several men at the bar he frequented that he was afraid she wouldn't be released for breeding before he had to go back "up the hills." Finally one of the men made the suggestion he'd been waiting for . . . go around to the back of the orchard, and wait for her. No harm done if she was bred a few weeks early, and likely no one would ever know. Watch a day or so, see when she went out, and who went with her.

He was watching when she went to the last-but-one apple tree and put something in its crotch. Well. That was interesting. She looked a lot more like what he'd expected out here, in the orchard, than during the showings. But would she cooperate, when the time came? If she wouldn't, he'd have to drug her—and she would be difficult to lug over the wall, big as she was. And it looked like she might have plans of her own . . . he hoped they wouldn't trip him up.

He walked on, and made his arrangements. He needed a groundcar; he walked across the city to rent it for cash from the spaceport vendor.

✧   ✧   ✧

Simplicity—an apt name, Brun thought—had told her about all sorts of things the other women mentioned only in passing. She realized that they could not imagine not knowing, while Simplicity was fascinated anew with every detail of her life. Unlike Brun, she kept track of time, and in her artless chatter had revealed the clues that let Brun begin tracking market days even while confined to the nursery. She had not previously paid attention to what the staff carried in their hands when they went out . . . but now noticed the size and shape of the baskets and bags, and their contents when they returned. From that, she thought she had a schedule figured out. Someone went out every day to get small amounts of fresh greens. Three times a week, several of the staff women went out and returned with a wide variety of supplies, not merely food but also needles, pins, thread, yarn, scrub brushes, hairbrushes, soap . . . whatever was needed for daily work which the women could not supply for themselves.

Starting with their holy day, they had market day, then skip two, then market day, then skip one, then market day, then holy day. The week's rhythm revolved around the holy day, rising in tension toward it . . . so Brun decided that the first market day would be the best for her purposes. Several of the staff women would be gone, and everyone would be more relaxed after the rigors of the holy day . . . ready to do the least in daily chores, to relax with the babies in the garden enclosures in the soft spring air. None of them walked as much in the orchard as she did, unless the staff directed, which they did only around harvest time.

The hard thing would be to find the house where

Hazel stayed, since she could not ask questions—and to conceal her muteness. She did not know if men were ever muted—probably not, since their beliefs required them to recite from the sacred texts daily—or whether some men might be mute from birth or accident, but she suspected that a mute man might be subject to investigation. Still, she knew it was a large household near a market.

Simplicity had described the house at length: its gardens, its weaving shed, its woolhouse, its several kitchens, the quarters for children, for wives, for the master—she had once been allowed to sweep there, but she had knocked over a little table. They had not punished her, but she had been banished to parts of the house with fewer breakables . . . which had been a relief, Simplicity had said, smiling, because she didn't have to worry so much. What she could not describe— what it never occurred to her to describe—was its location. Brun realized the girl had hardly ever been out of it, and thus had no way to describe where it was in relation to anything else.

On the midweek market day before she planned to go, Brun decided to test her plans. She would nurse the babes to fullness, mingling a little of the home brew into her milk . . . they were greedy feeders, and she had discovered that if she dripped sugared fruit juice down her breast, they'd take it along with her milk. Then she'd see how long they slept . . . which would give her some idea how long she had to find Hazel.

She finished her chores, and noticed that all but two of the staff had left to go to market. She picked up the babies, and caught the attention of one of the remaining staff women. She nodded toward the orchard.

"Go ahead, then. A good day for a walk," the woman said. Brun mimed eating. "Oh—you want to take your lunch out there? Fine. I'll ring the bell for you to come back, in case you fall asleep."

Brun took a small loaf of bread, fresh-baked that morning, and sliced off a hunk of cheese, laying the knife neatly back in its place. The woman had poured her a jug of fruit juice and water—and on this day, Brun noticed that this was an unnecessary courtesy. She smiled; she could not help it. The woman smiled back, clearly pleased.

She could not afford this . . . offer of friendship, if that's what it was. She took the jug and her lunch, tucked them into the sling where the redhead lay content, shifted the back sling until the other baby was balanced better, and moved out onto the paved terrace between the nursery buildings and the orchard.

She strolled, in her usual way, along the right-hand path, pausing now and then to look up into the trees at the hard green fruit that would be ripe in a few months. This was not the day; this was merely practice. Why, then, was her heart beating so wildly that she felt it must be drumming loud enough to hear? Why was her breath coming short? She tried to relax, reaching out to stroke a branch heavy with fruit. But the babies caught her tension and began to squirm and whimper. The one in back flailed at her head with his arms.

That, oddly enough, steadied her. She moved on, more quickly now—though today there was no hurry—to her favorite spot near the far end of the orchard. When she'd first made it this far, up the little rise, she'd been able to see the building through bare branches, but now the orchard trees were in full leaf, and she knew they could no more see her, than she could see them.

She laid the babies down on the little quilts folded into the slings, and put her lunch down as well. The babies rolled and played, cooing, making wide-handed swipes at each other. She bit off a hunk of bread as she watched, thinking over her plan again, trying to improve it. But it was such a tissue of improbables . . . if she made it twice as good, she would still have less than one chance in a hundred of success.

The darker one found a leaf to explore, and managed, with great effort, to pick it up. The redhead noticed his brother was no longer paying attention, and put his own foot in his mouth instead. Brun finished eating, and by then they were getting fussy, looking at her. In her mind, she heard a voice somewhere between her own and Esmay's: *All right then. Let's do it.*

Nursing both at once was harder now that they were bigger, but she was used to it. She leaned back against the tree, and let her mind drift . . . one way or another, in less than seven days, she would be somewhere else. Maybe dead . . . she wasn't going to be taken alive, not again. But maybe . . . somewhere . . . she couldn't picture it, quite. Her mind threw up pictures from her past life—hills, valleys, forests, fields, island beaches, rocky ledges. The shuttlefield on Rotterdam, then the shuttle, rumbling down the runway, taking off, the sky darkening, darkening, the stars . . .

She shook her head abruptly. The twins had taken most of her milk; it was time to try out her brew. She added a little honey, to make it sweeter, and dribbled it into their mouths as they sucked. Redhead made a face, and snorted before going on, but the dark-haired one didn't pause in his rhythm.

She had no idea how much to use. Not as much today; she didn't want anyone to notice, and worry about them. Did babies go to sleep with a spoonful or a cup? She had no idea. Their sucking slowed, finally, and their mouths fell away . . . they gained a kilo whenever they fell asleep, she thought. Carefully, she laid them on the little quilts. Asleep like this . . .

she could almost . . . but no. Not now. She told herself firmly what she already knew: they would be loved, cherished, given every opportunity this world held, because they were boys. That their mother had been an outlander heathen abomination would not affect the care given them.

They would look this way—this vulnerable, this beautiful—when she left them on the market day after the holy day. She stared at them, eyes narrowed. She could leave them—she *had* to leave them—and she would leave them.

She levered herself up and stood, fastening her dress and then stretching. She found the knife she had hidden, and turned it in her hands. She could go now . . . no. Better stick to her plan, such as it was. But one thing she could do, with a knife in hand. She might die—it was likely. Her family might not know where she was. But she could leave a record that would not be found until fall, if they noticed it then.

With the sharp tip of the paring knife she marked the tree under which the babies lay, thin scorings that would scar into visible marks later. Maybe. Her name, every syllable of it.

She wanted to write more. She wanted to scribble with that knife blade on every tree, saying what had been smothered all this time . . . but she stopped herself. No more indulgence. She had to try the wall today, to measure her strength against its height. She tied a length of yarn around the knife and hung it around her neck, then took the cloth strips she'd made and bound them tight around her breasts. When it was time to go, really time, she would bind her breasts before she fastened her dress . . . but this was only practice.

With a last glance at the sleeping babies, she turned and walked over to the wall. A last glance back, to make sure she could not been seen through the thick leaves . . . no. She turned to the wall again, steeling herself. It was the quiet time of day, after lunch. Chances were there was no one on the other side right now. If there were . . . if they saw her . . . she hesitated. Today was not *the* day. She didn't have to jump the wall today, and it would be disasterous if she were caught unprepared.

She looked back at the babies. Still sleeping. When she turned again to the wall, a man was looking over it. Brun stood frozen, immobilized with shock.

The man stared at her. "Brun?" he said softly.

Her heart lurched, then pounded. Someone who knew her name—who *used* her name. It must be a rescue. She nodded, giddy with relief.

"Can you climb over?"

She nodded again, and a wad of brown cloth flew toward her. She dropped back, furious. But his voice came over the wall, urgent and barely loud enough to hear. "Put that on. Cover your dress, and your hair. Not many have such light hair. Then wait for me to call—I'm watching for groundcars. Don't bring the babies; they'll be cared for."

The babies. She had given them only a few drops each—would they sleep long enough? She yanked her long skirt up around her waist and ran to them, fumbled at the jug, and poured more of the honeyed brew onto her hand. Would they suck? Could they swallow? Their mouths caught at her finger, sucking, and she dribbled more brew into each mouth. Then she dragged the garment on—a hooded cloaklike thing, too warm for the day—and ran back to the wall. Even in those few moments, she was aware how *good* it felt to have her legs free, not bound by the narrow skirt. While she waited, she thought how to make him understand that they had to find Hazel and the little girls. She could not go without them; if she could not save her babies from this world's horrors, she must save them.

"Now," he said. She stood up; the wall was not as

tall as she was, and she made it easily. It was wide
enough to lie on; she rolled the cloak around her and
then dropped off, to be steadied by his waiting arm.
"Are the babies inside?" he asked. "When will they
cry?"

How did he think she could answer that? She
mimed drinking, then sleeping, and he nodded.

"Come along," he said. "We have to get to the car."
He took her arm. "Look down," he reminded her.
Fuming, Brun looked down at the rough pavement
and went where he directed. She didn't want to argue
with him in the street, where anyone might see, but
she had to convince him about Hazel.

He stopped beside a groundcar parked in a row.
He opened the driver's door, and then the back doors
popped open. "Get in," he said. She looked him full
in the face, and mouthed *Hazel*. He paled. "Look
down! Get *in*," he said. "Before someone notices."

She slipped into the back seat, and leaned forward,
waiting for him. As soon as he closed his own door,
she tapped his shoulder. He glanced back.

Hazel.

"I can't understand you. What's wrong?"

Damn the idiot fool. How had Lady Cecelia kept
from bursting? There on the seat beside him were
a map and notebook, with a pen. She reached over
and snatched at it, wrote GET HAZEL in large
letters, and then RANGER BOWIE HOUSE. He
read, then paled even more.

"We can't do that! No one can get in there!
Dammit, woman, you want off this planet or not?"

She tapped GET HAZEL again, glaring into his
face, trying to give him a mind-to-mind transfusion
of her determination.

"Who the hell is Hazel, anyway?"

She wrote again: GIRL ON SHIP. GET HER
AWAY TOO.

"Can't do it," he said, starting the groundcar.

"Now you sit back, and I'll take you where it's arranged—" The barrier between them started to rise; Brun lunged forward, putting her weight on it, and the barrier stopped, its mechanism whining loudly. "Get *back*, you fool." The mechanism that moved the barrier gave a grinding noise and died; the barrier slid back the small distance it had risen. She paid no attention, wriggling over the barrier into the front passenger seat. Up here the windows weren't frosted. The man jerked the groundcar out of its parking space and accelerated. "Gods, woman, if they see you up here—"

She held the paper out: GET HAZEL.

"I can't, I tell you! The five Rangers are the most powerful men in town. Ever since Mitch Pardue got elected Ranger Bowie, he's been angling for the Captaincy. I can't barge in there and get some fool girl. I got you; that's what I contracted to do."

Brun glanced at the groundcar controls, at his movements as he turned, slowed, sped up again, made another turn. Simple enough. After the next turn, she grabbed the wheel and yanked it hard. He yanked back, and stared at her long enough to almost hit another groundcar. "Dammit! Woman! It's no wonder they muted you—Heaven knows what you'd say if you could talk!"

She scribbled rapidly on the notebook. GET HAZEL. IT'S MARKET DAY—SHE GOES OUT. MARKET NEAR RANGER BOWIE HOUSE. She pushed that in front of his face; the groundcar swerved again; she lowered it slightly, so he could read and see over it.

"Can't do it. Too dangerous. I have it all planned out—"

She poked a finger into his ear, hard, and laid the pruning knife on his thigh, pointed where he could not ignore it. The groundcar swerved wildly, then he got it back on his side of the street. "You're crazy, you are. All right, we'll drive past Ranger Bowie house. And the damn market. But you've got to get in the back. If anyone sees—" He glanced at her, and she bared her teeth. "All right, I said. I'll do it; we'll go past. But you're going to get us killed—"

With some care, Brun reversed herself into the back seat, making sure that she had enough weight on the barrier to prevent its coming back up, if the controls weren't actually broken. She laid the knife at the back of his neck . . . it would do no good there, unless it was strong enough to slide between the vertebrae, but she judged it too obvious to hold it to his throat.

"They told me you were wild, but they didn't tell me you were crazy," the man grumbled. Brun grinned. They hadn't known what had been done to her, or they'd have known how crazy she was.

"That's Ranger Bowie's house," the man said finally. Brun stared, uncertain. It was one of five huge houses arranged around the sides of a plaza . . . in the center was a huge five-pointed star outlined in flowers and grass. Pretty, really, if you weren't trying to escape the place. "Ranger Houston, Ranger Crockett, Ranger Travis, and Ranger Lamar. Ranger Travis is Captain right now. The nearest market to Ranger Bowie's house is down this street . . . the women's service door is right down there, see?"

Brun saw a shadowed gap in the long stucco wall. As they drove past, she could see the door set back from the sidewalk, and the little alcove for the gate guard. They went past one cross street, then another. Ahead, down this street, a rope blocked off traffic beyond the next cross street.

"That's the market—groundcars can't go there. Nor you. Now you've seen there's nothing we can do, we can—"

Brun pressed the tip of the knife just below his ear. With her other hand she scrabbled for the pen and notebooks, and printed, GO AROUND, KEEP LOOKING.

On the third circuit, Brun spotted a woman walking toward Ranger Bowie House, baskets in each hand, still some blocks from it. Something about the quick, short shuffle caught her eye. She tapped the driver's shoulder.

"That her?" He eased the car closer.

It was hard to tell . . . the dark head bent forward, the slim body gliding along with those short, quick steps enforced by her dress. But as the car slid past, Brun caught a glimpse of the serious face, that tucked-in lower lip. She tapped the man's arm again, hard.

"I'm gonna regret this, I know I am." But he pulled the car to the curb and got out.

"You. Girlie." Hazel stopped, eyes on the ground. "You from Ranger Bowie House?" She nodded. "I got business there. Get in back." He popped the rear doors. Brun could *feel* Hazel's confusion, her uncertainty, her near-panic. "Hurry up now," he said. "I don't want to have to tell Mitch you're lazy." She ducked into the car, then, eyes still down. Then she saw Brun, and her eyes widened. Brun grinned. The driver got back in, grumbling, and tried to raise the shield, but the mechanism made only a faint noise and the barrier didn't go up. "Sit low," the driver said, and drove off quickly.

"Brun . . . what . . . where . . . ?" Hazel's voice was soft as mothwings.

Brun mouthed *escape*, but Hazel shook her head. So Brun made a rocket of one hand, and jerked it upward. Hazel stared, then grinned.

"Really?" Hazel almost bounced on the seat with excitement, but her voice was soft. "I was trying to figure a way—I'd found out where you were, an' all, an' I told Simplicity as much as I could without getting in trouble, hoping she'd see you—"

Brun nodded. She mimed the groundcar taking

them to the rocket. She didn't know if that was the plan—she still didn't know what the plan was—but surely that was the gist of it. Then she showed Hazel the notebook and wrote: LITTLE GIRLS.

"We can't take them," Hazel said.

YES.

"No—we can't—I already decided that, months ago. They're happy, they're safe, and they wouldn't make it anyway."

Brun stared at Hazel. This . . . *child* had decided? But Hazel's expression didn't waver. She was not just a child.

"We have to," Hazel said. "Leastways—" Brun winced at the local expression. "At least," Hazel corrected, "we have to try. You, for sure. And your babies?"

Brun shrugged, and wrote: CAN'T TAKE THEM. TOO RISKY. TOO LITTLE.

"See? Same with Brandy and Stassi. We can't do it."

The driver spoke up. "Glad one of you's got sense. All right now . . . we got us a little problem. I'd planned to pass Brun off as a man—brought along men's clothes for her; they're under the seat there—but I don't know what to do about . . . Hazel."

Brun mimed a purchase to Hazel, and nodded to the driver. *Tell him.* Hazel looked scared, her mouth pinched tight. Then, in a high thin voice she said, "Brun says buy some."

"Buy some! Buy some, she says. And just how am I supposed to stop and buy some?"

But he pulled over a few streets further on, and made his way to a sidewalk vendor. Brun, peeking over the barrier, saw him choose blue pants, a brown shirt, and high-topped boots like most of the men wore, and a hat. He was back in just a few minutes, and when he started the car again, he threw the clothes over the barrier.

"You change now, both of you. Put your dresses

under the seat. I'll get rid of 'em later. You'll have to cut your hair, but not here—mustn't leave hair in the car. I've got knives for both of you."

As the car sped on, over the streets and then into the countryside on a roughly paved road, Brun and Hazel struggled with the confined space in the back seat, each other, and the clothes they had to get off and put on. Brun, having more to take off, went first; Hazel helped her bind her breasts as flat as she could. Then Hazel, and Brun tore a strip off the bottom of her dress to flatten Hazel as well. Getting into the long pants while trying to stay low, out of sight of passing groundcars, meant lying across the seat—and each other. Hardest to put on were the boots—stiff leather on feet that had been bare for more than a year. It would all have been funny if they hadn't been so afraid of being caught, and they actually did giggle when they finally stuffed the hated dresses under the seat. Brun felt it had been worth it already—she had not laughed, really laughed, since her capture, and even though she could make no sound, the laughter eased her. Hazel tucked her hair up, and jammed the hat on her head; Brun pushed her hat down on top of her head.

Hazel, Brun thought, looked like a real person again. She sat leaning forward now, eyes sparkling with excitement, her face no longer obscured by hair. Her clothes fit a little loose and the sleeves of her shirt were up the wrist a little, as if she had almost grown out of them. Hazel looked at her, smiling, and then lifted Brun's hat to push her hair more firmly under it. Brun felt that her own pants were bulky and too loose—but anything was better than that clinging skirt.

Their driver glanced back. "Not likely to be seen, out here," he said. "You do look different, I'll say that. You aren't embarrassed to wear men's clothes?"

Brun shook her head.

"Well, that's good, because they're gonna be looking

for two women in dresses, not two men. Remember now, you have to walk like men—big steps—and look other men straight in the eye. We—they—don't like shifty folk. Now I'm gonna let you off up here in about a mile—" Whatever distance that was . . . Brun still hadn't figured out feet and inches and ells. "And then you'll have to hike over them hills—" He pointed at a line of hills ahead. "Soon's you're out of sight, you got to cut your hair *real* short, like no woman would. So you can take your hat off without bein' spotted as women. You take your hat off to womenfolk, even though they aren't supposed to look at you—it's polite. And men'll see you."

The map he gave them, along with a canteen and a packet of food, was supposed to guide them on the next stage. Brun looked at it and grinned in relief. Someone had marked it in standard measurements, not this planet's idiot miles. Someone had also printed, in a hand she thought she knew, *Brun—we're here*.

From the pulloff, a trail led up into the hills. A signpost had a string of names on it; Brun ignored them. After a few wavery strides, her legs remembered how to stretch, and she found her balance in the ridiculous boots. Hazel staggered once, grimaced, but moved up beside her.

They were out of sight of the road in less than a hundred meters, and into thick scrub. Brun made scissor movements next to her head, and Hazel nodded. They slipped off the trail and into the head-high bushes, to do some barbering.

Brun made it clear, with gestures, that they must catch the hairs they cut off. She had no idea what to do with them, but they weren't going to leave them around as obvious trail markers. As her hair came off, as the wind reached her scalp, she felt her brain cooling, felt the lessons she'd been taught in the Fleet escape and evasion course coming back to her. She twisted the cut hanks of her own hair into a roll of the appropriate size, put it in one of the spare socks, and stuffed it down the front of her pants. Hazel goggled, then choked back a laugh that was half shock. Brun shrugged, and swaggered a few steps. *We're men; we need men things.* Hazel had less hair for hers, but she was younger anyway. And it did make her look more like a boy.

She struggled up the trail in those ridiculous boots . . . she'd have been more comfortable barefoot but men didn't go barefoot. Stupid people, she thought. Only really stupid people would assign footgear on the basis of gender rather than use, and choose these blistering boots for walking somewhere.

Hazel would have talked, but Brun waved her to silence. Voices carried, in the open, and Hazel's soft voice wasn't very boylike. Brun didn't know if she could do a boy's voice, and didn't want to find out she couldn't.

So when they heard the men talking, she had a few seconds warning. She caught Hazel's eye, jerked her chin up, and walked on. Around the next curve in the path came a pair of men, dressed much as she and Hazel were, though one of them had a bundle on his back. Brun stared straight at the first man, then the second, and tightened her lips. They gave her a short nod, and strode by in silence. Brun felt herself start to shake and lengthened her stride. Hazel grabbed her arm and squeezed, hard. Brun nodded. Neither looked behind as they struggled on up the hill.

They had made it over the first ridge, and halfway up the second, when Brun's breasts began to throb. She glanced at the sky. Drat. The twins would be waking now, beginning to whimper, even if no one had found them before.

"What?" asked Hazel softly. Brun put her hands to her breasts and winced. Hazel said "Swelling?" Brun nodded. Minute by minute, they throbbed more,

until she felt she could not stand it . . . but her feet
hurt almost as much.

Take your pick, she thought. At least you're out
here. And she took as deep a breath as she could of
the fresh hill air. She would walk her feet to bloody
stubs, and let her breasts explode before she would
go back to that miserable nursery.

"You miss your babies?" Hazel asked.

Brun shook her head violently. Hazel looked
shocked; Brun regretted her vehemence, but . . . she
felt what she felt. If they had been someone else's
babies, she might have felt a pang of softness for
them, she had liked babies, when someone else took
care of them—but not these. She set her face reso-
lutely to the trail and struggled on.

Near sundown they came to the clearing marked on
Brun's map. Here they were supposed to be met . . .
or she was; whoever it was wouldn't expect Hazel.

The man who stepped out of the shadow of the
trees not only didn't expect Hazel, he didn't want her.
"I didn't get paid for two," he said roughly. "What
are you trying to pull, missy?" Brun glared at him.
Then she took the notebook from Hazel and wrote:
SHE GOES TOO.

"I wasn't paid . . ." the man began. Brun made
the universal signal for money—and saw it recognized,
proving once again that humans had a common origin, something she'd been willing to doubt this past
year and more. She pointed to the sky, then rubbed
her fingers again. Money there, if you get us there.
The man spat.

"All right. But I don't want to hear any complaints
when it's crowded in the shuttle."

Brun stared around. Shuttle here? This was no
shuttlefield. But the man was walking quickly along
the shadowed edge of the clearing, and she
followed.

"We got us a ways to go, and I guess it's lucky

I brung a extra. Hope you can ride." With that, he ducked into the trees and Brun smelled . . . horses.

This was not how she'd planned to ride again. She had imagined herself on one of her father's hunters, galloping over the fields of home. Instead, Brun had to stretch her sore legs on the wide barrel of a brown horse with all the character of a sofa, because Hazel, who had never been on a horse before, had to have a saddle. The man swore he couldn't ride bareback—and if he was used to that armchair for a saddle, no wonder. At least her body had not forgotten that balance.

"By God, you *can* ride," the man said, as she moved up beside him. Brun smiled, thinking non-smiling thoughts, and he looked over at Hazel. "That's it," he said. Brun glanced over; Hazel looked terrified. She was clutching the knob that stuck up from the front of the saddle as if it could anchor her, and trying to strangle the horse with her legs. Brun caught her eye, and gestured down her own body: *Sit straight, head up, relax your legs.* Hazel straightened.

They rode through the night, meeting no one at all on the trail. Brun shifted as one spot after another wore raw. She had wanted to wear pants again; she had wanted to ride again, but this—she thought of the old saw about being careful what you asked for. The man spoke occasionally: "That way's Lem's cabin." "Over there's the pass to Smoky's place."

When first light began to give shape to the treetops on the slopes above them, their guide slowed. "It's only a tad more," he said. "Just down this slope." At the foot of the slope, they came out of trees and brush to find a long grassy field ending in a steep hill. Brun could not see anything resembling a shuttle. Was this a trap after all? But the man led the way along the edge of the field, and she realized it might be a grass runway. It was longer than it looked; when she glanced back along it, the far end was hidden in ground fog. The hill, as they neared it, revealed a hangar door set into it. That was promising. Set back under the trees was a log cabin with a peaked roof; beyond it was a larger log building, a barn, and in between was an enclosure of peeled poles where two more horses and a cow munched hay.

The man led them up to a gate set into the enclosure, and swung off his horse as if he'd only ridden an hour or so, not all night. Neither Brun nor Hazel could dismount alone. The man had to help them, pushing and tugging. He swore at them. Brun wished for the ability to swear back. She had not been on a horse in years, and in between she'd borne twins—what did he expect after riding all night bareback? She was sure she'd worn all the skin off her thighs and buttocks. As for Hazel, she'd never ridden before; she'd be lucky if she could walk at all in a few hours.

In the cabin, a stocky woman prepared breakfast for all of them. She never looked at them, never spoke, but set plates in front of them and kept them full. Brun raged inwardly, but they could not take all the women on this planet. *I will come back,* she vowed silently. *Somehow . . .*

After breakfast, Brun managed to stand up; she gave Hazel a hand. Outside, the man was opening the hangar door, and at last Brun could see what was waiting for them. Her grin broadened. It was a little mixed-purpose shuttle, the same kind she'd been in when Cecelia had sent her back to Rockhouse. She could fly it herself if she had to. She thought briefly of knocking the man on the head and doing just that, but she had no idea how he planned to evade Traffic Control—if this place even had Traffic Control. It did have warplanes, though, and she had no desire to meet them.

With considerable difficulty, Brun helped Hazel up the narrow ladder into the shuttle. The man was already busy at the controls; he glowered when Brun made her way forward and settled herself in the other control seat. "Don't touch anything!" he said sharply. Brun watched. Everything looked much the same as on Corey's ship. Although the names of the measures were strange, she could identify most of the instruments. The man ran down the same sort of checklist.

The little craft bumped its way down the field, engines screaming, gaining speed with every meter. But could it possibly be enough? The trees at the far end approached too rapidly—Brun could remember going much faster than this at Rotterdam. Suddenly, the shuttle rose into the air as if hoisted on a crane . . .

"Short field ability," the man said, grinning. "Surprised you, didn't I? She needs a third less runway, and she can clear a hundred feet when she goes up."

Sun streamed in the cockpit windows; Brun stared avidly at the control panel. Her mind had been so hungry, all this time, for something real, something to do. She glanced back at Hazel; the girl grinned, pointing to the gauges. Yes—a spacer girl, she would have had the same hunger. But now Hazel was looking out and down, at the shadowy folds of hills and valleys receding as they rose. Was this, perhaps, her first planet? Brun had never thought of that. Higher . . . there was a river, winding between hills, with a roll of ground fog like wool resting on the hill to windward. The craft climbed steeply, and the view widened every minute. Over there should be the city they came from, with its spaceport . . . yes. Small— smaller than she expected, though the spaceport had landing space enough for a dozen shuttles.

The radio crackled; their pilot spoke into his headset, but it was so noisy Brun couldn't hear what he said. Higher . . . higher . . . the morning sky that had been a soft bright blue darkened again. The gauge that must be an altimeter had reeled off thousands and ten thousands, but Brun didn't know what the unit of measure was. It neared sixty thousand somethings, and passed it. Then the pilot pulled the nose up even higher, and pushed a button on the left side of the cockpit. Acceleration slammed her back in her seat as a penetrating roar came from behind. The sky darkened quickly to black; stars appeared.

She noticed a streak of sunlit vapor climbing below them; their pilot yelled something into his headset. The vapor trail turned away. The pilot pointed through the front window. Brun peered back and forth, not seeing what he meant, until Hazel tapped her arm. "Ten o'clock, negative thirty . . . their space station." Then she could see it, as its shape passed over a sparkling expanse of white cloud on the bulging planet below. She had been there, on the inside, unable to see . . . and now she was here. Free. Or almost free.

The man handed Brun a headset; she put it on. Now she could hear him. "Changing from lift engines to insystem—we're supposed to rendezvous with something out here. Dunno if it's military or civilian or what. They gave me code words to use."

The craft lurched as he switched from one drive to another, then the artificial gravity kicked in, and she might as well have been sitting in a model shuttle on some planet's surface. Quiet, too, just as it should have been, with only the faint crisp rustle of the ventilation system. She glanced back at Hazel, who was grinning ear to ear. It felt right to her as well, then. She peered out at the stars, burning steadily . . . but she could not recognize any of the geometry. What system was this?

"Might's well take a nap, now she's on auto," the man said. He switched off the banks of instruments useless with this drive, yawned, and hung his headset on a hook. "I'm going to." He closed his eyes and slumped in his seat.

Brun slid her headset down around her neck, but did not follow his example. Too much was at stake. "I'm really tired," Hazel whispered. "And my legs . . ."

Brun mimed *sleep* at her, and watched as Hazel dozed off. The man was snoring now, snores of such complexity that she was sure he couldn't have faked them. She put out her hand to the controls, and he didn't stir.

So here she was, on her way . . . she touched her knives, reminding herself that she was not going to be recaptured, if anything went wrong. And out there somewhere, Fleet waited. She was sure it would be Fleet; her father would not have risked anything less in taking on a whole planet. She hoped it wasn't far out, and she hoped very much that whatever ships were there did not include one Lieutenant Esmay Suiza. She was not ready to face that, on top of everything else.

An hour passed, and another, and another. Despite herself, she yawned. She would have taken a stimulant if she'd had one; she scolded herself for eating such a big breakfast. Another yawn . . . Her eyes sagged shut, and she struggled to open them, only to yawn again. She looked at her shipmates. The man was snoring in a different pattern now, but just as loudly. Hazel slept neatly as a cat, curled into herself on the bench seat. Brun tried pinching herself, changing position, taking deep breaths . . . but in that steady, warm stillness, she slept in spite of herself.

CHAPTER TWENTY

Brun woke abruptly with the feeling that something was very wrong. They were in free fall . . . but they had been on insystem drive, with the artificial gravity on. The pilot was awake, and changing switch positions on the main board. Brun looked at Hazel, who was also awake, hanging upside down above the bench where she'd slept. She reached back, tapped her arm, and nodded toward the pilot.

"What are we doing?" Hazel asked. Her voice was high with tension.

"End of the line, girlies. I been talking to them over there—" He gestured, and Brun looked out to see a dark shape against the starfield. What it really was, or how far away, she couldn't tell, but she could see the ovoid shape of a warship. Fleet? "I get more from them, for turning you in, than from you, for taking you on. An abomination was one thing—I didn't bargain on a runaway from Ranger Bowie's house."

Not Fleet. Brun's stomach tightened. The pilot smirked at them, and opened his mouth to speak into the headset. Brun uncoiled from her seat, twisting in

393

midair, and slammed both booted feet into the side of his head. Hazel squeaked—no other word for that short alarmed sound, but then pushed off the overhead to get her forearm around the man's neck and hold it against the tall seatback while Brun untangled herself from the cords and wires her attack had landed her in.

"What do I do if he—" Hazel began, when the man jerked against her arm, and then grabbed at her arm and tried to free himself. But he was strapped in, and Brun already had her knife out, and a firm hold on the back of his seat for leverage; she jammed the knife under his ribs and up, just as she had been told. He twisted, struggling, for a moment longer, then slumped . . . that long elephant-skinning knife had the length to reach his heart. Brun stared at Hazel, who was white with shock.

But they had no time for shock. Catching her feet under the copilot's seat, she unhooked the pilot's harness, and started pulling his body out of the seat, pushing it to the back. Drops of blood followed it, floating, dispersing.

"Can you . . . pilot?" Hazel asked. Brun grinned at her and nodded, then clambered into the seat. Hazel climbed over the pilot, still snorting a little but beyond help, and made it into the copilot's seat, strapping herself in quickly.

Insystem drive . . . where was insystem drive again? And she didn't want to run them right into that warship . . . she gestured to Hazel: rotate us, point us that way. Parallel to the warship's axis, toward what she hoped was its stern. Hazel touched the controls, and the stars wheeled crazily. Brun ignored that, and her ears, and found the inset black square that should be the insystem drive startup. She pushed it. Nothing happened. What else . . . oh. Yes. Safety release . . . she tried again, in sequence. Release, startup, drive on . . . and the sudden apparent lurch of the dust in the cockpit told her they were under drive again. Now for the AG . . . down there. One tenth . . . and the dust settled, leaving the cockpit clearer. Behind her, the pilot's body thumped to the deck. A little red globule slid past her gaze and attached itself to her shirt . . . blood. The pilot's blood.

And she'd never thought about what would happen if she'd cut his throat in zero-G. They could be drowning in the stuff, unable to see any of the controls . . .

Maybe her luck was back. But she wouldn't count on it. She notched up the insystem drive. If she had the pilot figured right, he was a smuggler or something and his personal shuttle would be overpowered, up to and maybe beyond the structural limits of the craft. She found the accelerometer, and the V-scale, but the blasted thing was in mph, whatever that was, rather than meters per second. Still—it was fast, and going faster.

Hazel touched her arm. She had found the scan controls. Two screens came up: systemwide and local. Local was the problem, Brun thought. The warship behind them was lighted up like a Christmas tree with active weapons scans. But according to Esmay, anything as small as a shuttle was hard to hit . . . if it was far enough away. Well, the answer to that was to get far enough away—and that meant speed. She notched the drive up again. The little craft still felt stable as rock. Corey's had gone faster—she notched it up again, and again.

Hazel tapped her arm. On the system scan, several ships were flagged with weapons markers. And behind, the warship had swapped ends and was in pursuit.

It had always been a small chance. She'd known that. Better to die out here, than back there. She hoped Hazel felt that way—she cocked her head at the girl.

"It'll be close," Hazel said. "But I like it."

Well . . . close or not, that was the right attitude. Brun pointed at the drive controls, and mimed shoving it to the line. Hazel looked at the scan, and nodded. What the hell, Brun thought. It can't be worse. She rammed the control all the way to the end of the slot. The drive rose from a deep whine to a high one, and the shuttle vibrated down its length.

And behind them, on the scan, an explosion marred the pattern. If she had not accelerated—

"We could jump, couldn't we?" Hazel asked. "These shuttles are jump-capable."

They could jump, but where? Supposedly, there was a Fleet ship insystem, waiting to pick them up. If only she could find that—

Another explosion; the little ship shivered as fragments impacted its minimal shields.

"Another one!" Hazel said, pointing. Brun glanced at the scan—and saw another weapons-lighted warship. They weren't going to make it through this—she might as well jump, and sort it out later, if she could. She found the jump controls, and started the checklist . . . never leave out the checks, Oblo had told her, because you can get killed just as dead by a malfunction as by an enemy.

Navigation computer on; target jump point selected; insertion velocity—not good, but she dared not slow. Her hands raced over the controls, but she left nothing out. When she was ready, she tapped Hazel on the shoulder, and pointed to the jump-initiation control. Hazel nodded, and Brun pushed it.

Nothing happened. Brun pushed it again—some of these controls stiffened if not used regularly.

"It's asking for a validation code," Hazel said, nudging Brun and pointing. On a side panel, a small display had lit, with the words VOICE RECOGNITION VALIDATION REQUIRED PRIOR TO JUMP INSERTION.

Brun hissed. The one thing they couldn't do was

produce an approximation of the pilot's voice, and whatever code words he'd used. She slammed her fist once more against the useless button, and turned her attention to what they *could* do.

This system was woefully short of useful pieces of rock, at least near the planet. No moons to land on— she would have given a lot for a moonlet with caves to hide in. So—make use of the terrain you've got, her instructors had said. No terrain in space, though. If she could get back to the planet, they could hide out in the wilderness . . . or they could be recaptured as they tried to land. That was worse than death; she'd dive this thing into the ground before she let that happen. She glanced at Hazel. The girl was pale-faced, but calm, waiting for Brun to do something.

Terrain. It all came back to escape and evasion, and in space that meant outrun or hide out. They couldn't outrun the warships, and there wasn't any place to hide. Except—what if they went straight for the *Elias Madero*, docked at the space station? Could they get in it from outside? Hide in it? It would take a long time to find them, time in which Fleet might be coming. Or might not.

She looked around the cockpit. Somewhere, the pilot must have had local space charts—they had not run into any of the things which must be up here, the various satellites and stations. She didn't spot charts, but she did spot a noteboard. She scribbled *Local charts* on it and handed it to Hazel. Hazel said, "We're not going back, are we?"

Not exactly, Brun thought, and mouthed. *Hide*. Hazel seemed to understand the mouthed words, and nodded.

Backed off from its maximum velocity, the little ship could maneuver surprisingly well. Brun kept an eye on the scans as she jinked back and forth, counting to herself in a random sequence she'd once memorized for the pleasure of it. Her other eye was on the fuel gauge—rapid maneuvering ate up fuel at an alarming rate.

"Local nav charts up on the screen," Hazel said. Brun spared a glance. Little satellites, big satellites, space stations—she hadn't realized this place had more than one station—and a large number of uncategorized items. Most were drifting in a more-or-less equatorial orbit, though a few were in polar orbits. In size, these ranged from bits as small as pencils to stations a kilometer across. She needed something big enough—an orbital station would be perfect, but of course there wouldn't be one.

Hazel leaned past her and tapped something. Brun glanced again. Something long and skinny, much bigger than the shuttle, and marked on the chart with a large red X. The shuttle shivered, as a near miss tore at its shields. Whatever it was would have to do. She nodded at Hazel and pointed to the nav computer. She couldn't figure a course to it in her head, not and dodge hostile fire. In a moment or two, the course came up on the nav screen, along with an estimate of fuel consumption. Very close . . . they'd have to spend fuel to dump vee, and spiral around the planet on a much longer approach than Brun really wanted, with ships shooting at her.

And if she was really lucky, maybe the two enemy ships would run into each other, and remove that problem.

Minute by minute, as the shuttle curved back toward the planet, Brun expected the bright flash that would be the last thing she ever saw. Behind—to either side—but none of them as close as they had been. The boost out had taken hours . . . how long would it take to get back using all the power she dared? How much of the outbound trip had been unpowered? How long had she slept before waking to zero G? She didn't know; she didn't have time to think about it, only time to watch the scans, and the nav screen, and do what she could to conserve their fuel.

"One's out," Hazel said suddenly. Brun nodded. One of their pursuers had miscalculated a boost, and was now out of sight behind the planet. The other, farther away, was probably out of missile range— at least, nothing had blown up anywhere near them for some time. The other red-marked icons she could see now were farther away, and didn't appear to be chasing her. Yet. She could have used Koutsoudas' enhanced scan; she didn't even know what size those things were. Even ordinary Fleet scan would have told her that, and located any Fleet ships insystem as well.

They might actually make it. She glanced at the fuel gauge again. Enough to decelerate to match their target . . . and that small margin over which would give her a chance to try a last wild gamble. She linked the autopilot to the nav computer for the approach, trusting the universe enough to take this moment to stretch before trying to dock to an uninhabited derelict.

The little shuttle lay snugged to the station, hidden from several directions by the sheltering wing of the station. Brun hoped its thermal signature would be hidden as well, but she didn't trust it. They might be detected from the ground as well as space. She looked around. The dead pilot nuzzled the stained plastic of the bulkhead, held there by one of the ventilation drafts.

They needed pressure suits. While she wasn't actually naked, she felt the hungry vacuum outside . . . her clothes were no protection. They needed to get off the shuttle, and onto something bigger, with more air.

They needed a miracle.

Make your own miracles, Oblo had said. The

escape-and-evasion instructors had said the same thing.

Brun spotted what might be a p-suit locker, and aimed Hazel at it. Sure enough, inside was a smudged yellow p-suit easily large enough for either of them. One p-suit, not two. Hazel clearly knew how to check out a suit; she was running the little nozzle of the tester down each seam. Brun waited until Hazel had checked it all, including the air tanks.

"It's fine," Hazel said. "Both tanks full—that's six hours, if I understand their notation."

Six hours for one person. Could Fleet get from where it was to here in six hours? Not likely. The shuttle's air supply was much bigger—they would have air for four or five days—but if the warships found the shuttle, they would be dead before then.

Priority one: find another p-suit.

Priority two: find air.

"Weapons would be nice," Hazel said, surprising Brun again. The girl seemed so docile, so sweet . . . was she really thinking . . . ? From her face, she was.

With the helmet on, Hazel tested her com circuit. She would use it, they'd decided, only to tell Brun she was on the way back . . . no need to let everyone on the planet know where they were, if they hadn't been spotted.

With Hazel gone, Brun took the opportunity to search the dead pilot. Like all the men, he had packed a small arsenal: a knife at his belt, another in his boot, and a third up his sleeve, as well as a slug-thrower capable of putting a hole in the hull— what did he want with that aboard a ship?—a needler in the other boot, and two small beamers, one up the other sleeve, and one tucked into the back of his belt.

Hazel's voice over the com: "Bringing suits." Suits? Why suits plural? Brun hissed the two-syllable signal they'd devised for acknowledgement. "Problems . . ."

Damn the girl, why couldn't she say more . . . or nothing?

Soon enough—sooner than Brun expected—she heard the warning bleat of the airlock's release sequence, and then muffled bumps and bangs as Hazel cycled through. An empty p-suit came out first, scattering glittering dust from its turquoise skin. Turquoise? Brun rolled it over, and there on the back was a label—BlueSky Biodesigns—and a code number whose meaning she could not guess. Hazel next, in the pilot's dirty yellow p-suit, towing another turquoise model. Then two spare breathing tanks, lashed to the second p-suit. When they cleared the hatch, Brun reached behind her to dog the inner lock seal, as Hazel popped her helmet seal.

"Brun—it's really strange in there. I found a suit locker right away, but the tank locker beside it was empty. So I had to hunt around. And I've never seen a station like it—"

Brun tapped her shoulder, and Hazel stopped. Brun wrote: LABORATORY. GENETIC ENGINEERING.

"Oh. That might explain the broken stuff, then. But listen, Brun, the oddest thing . . . remember how this p-suit's fitted for males? All the suits in the station lockers—the ones I looked in, anyway—are fitted for females. That's why I brought two. It's a lot more comfortable . . . and near's I can tell these suits have all the functions we need. And I found women's clothes scattered around, soft shipsuits. Better'n these rough things, if your legs are as sore as mine."

Brun hated it when haste blurred Hazel's accent into conformity with that of the locals. But she was right. Already Hazel was unsuiting, packing the pilot's p-suit away with practiced skill as she came out of it, hardly swaying as she steadied herself with first one hand then another. Brun opened the first turquoise suit and found the clothes. Soft fleecy pants and tops, in colors she hadn't seen for far too long: bright, clear, artificial colors. Hazel had brought an assortment, bless her, different sizes and colors.

"You're so much taller," Hazel said, "I hope what I got is big enough . . ."

Brun nodded. She watched Hazel try to wriggle out of her clothes, wincing, and struggle into the softer ones. She chose dark green; the top had an embroidered design of flowers and swirls. Brun had found a pair of black pants that seemed longer than the rest, and a cream-colored shirt that was bigger around—even bound, her milk-swollen breasts had added to her size.

"Should we use the shuttle's wastecan before we suit up?" Hazel asked.

Brun shook her head. They would need every recycled bit of air and water. She started trying to shuck her own pants and realized that she was simply too stiff; it hurt too much. Hazel moved to help her; Brun held one of the grabons, and gritted her teeth as Hazel started to pull the stiff pants down.

"Is this the pilot's blood, or yours?" Hazel asked.

Brun shook her head, shrugged, and then nodded. It made no difference—the pants had to come off. Hazel worked them free, muttering.

"You're raw . . . from the riding, I hope. I didn't know it was so much worse without a saddle, or I'd have switched off with you—" She couldn't have done it, but Brun appreciated the offer, even as the breath hissed between her teeth.

"We have to put something on this," Hazel said finally. The chill air bit into the raw places and Brun shuddered at the thought of anything touching her. "I'll look." Moments of silence; Brun kept her eyes shut and tried to steady her breathing. It wasn't as bad as being raped; it wasn't as bad as being pregnant; it wasn't nearly as bad as childbirth. She had survived all that; this was just . . . an inconvenience. She opened her eyes and smiled at Hazel, who was watching her with a worried look. "I found a medkit, and put it in the other p-suit," Hazel said. "One of those emergency kits they always put near suit lockers." Brun nodded, and freed a hand to wave a go-ahead signal.

The bite of the painkilling spray would have gotten a yelp from her if she'd had the voice to yelp with, but the almost-instant cessation of pain was amazing. She'd forgotten how fast good meds worked. Hazel followed that with a spray of antibiotic and skin sealant. Brun unpeeled her hands from the grabon, and was able to snag the soft black pants she'd chosen and put them on herself.

Then into the p-suits, where the plumbing fixtures connected as they ought, and all the gauges and readouts worked. Brun sniffed the air coming from the nose filters—nothing she could smell, and the ship's suit-check said it was safe. They filled the suits' water tanks from the shuttle tanks. Brun folded an extra set of shipsuits into padding for the back of her p-suit, and Hazel followed her example. They packed up all the food they could find in the shuttle, and stuffed the p-suits' external storage.

All this had taken longer than Brun hoped, but according to the shuttle's scans, no active scan had pinged them yet. Now, she finished setting up the autopilot for what she hoped would be an effective screening action. Ideally, they would have been able to tie into the shuttle's scans from within the space station, and send it off under remote control. But Brun had long since given up waiting for ideal conditions. She would send it off on a time delay, giving them time to get well into the station. Hazel had left the outer lock open, with an air tank lashed in the gap just in case some officious bit of old programming was still operating and tried to shut it . . . so they didn't have to worry about entrance.

With the little fuel left aboard, she couldn't set up a very complicated course, and she had to assume that ground-based radars had plotted their whereabouts anyway. Probably one of the warships was even now maneuvering in for an attempt to recapture them. For maximum acceleration, Brun decided to run the takeoff and insystem drives together . . . something no experienced pilot would do, but it was the only way to get the ship well away in a hurry.

When she was done, she nodded at Hazel, and they both sealed up. They had made their plans; they had said all they had to say, until they were in the station. They crammed into the tiny airlock, and cycled out.

Outside was a confusion of highlight and black shadow; Brun followed Hazel along the length of the shuttle's hull to the station's wing. From here, she could see that there was a shuttle docking bay—if she'd known that, they could have been safe inside hours ago, because it looked as if it had passenger tubes still deployed. No time for that now. Hazel led her from one grabon to another toward the emergency lock portal.

They were almost to the portal when the grabon she held bounced in her hand, then vibrated strongly. Brun looked back. The shuttle's dual drive had come alive, and the little ship slid away from the station, its takeoff reaction engine exhaust glowing against the dark. It moved faster—faster—out into the sunlight, where it glittered like a bright needle.

Would their pursuers believe it? The course she'd plotted would have been hazardous for an experienced pilot, requiring extreme maneuvers to reverse-burn and survive atmospheric reentry, but it was the most direct way to the ground—if you didn't mind burning up along the way. They had no women pilots; even with what they knew of her background, they might think—she hoped they would think—that she was a panicky female who didn't understand orbital mechanics, who was running directly for cover.

She hadn't grown up hunting foxes for nothing.

She looked around again, trying to spot any of the warships. There, possibly—a dark shape blotting out part of the starfield. And there, below them, the more pointed shape of another shuttle, against the cloudfield on the planet below.

She felt her lips stretching in a grin that had no humor in it. Coming to catch her, were they? They'd get a surprise . . .

R.S.S. *Shrike*

Sneaking a task force into a system with a single mapped jump point had taken considerable tricky navigation, especially since they knew few details of the defensive layout. Esmay, as *Shrike*'s executive officer, had checked and double-checked every one of the short FTL hops that had brought them into the system via the jump point in another, nearby— nearby in stellar terms. But it had been a difficult period; some of the jumps had required flux levels well above those recommended. Once in the system, microjumps with low relative-vee insertion had hopped them in, apparently without detection, until they were positioned to observe the escape.

For days now they had hung unnoticed, well above the ecliptic, monitoring all transmissions from the planet. Far out, the rest of the task force waited in case of need, trading hours of scan lag for obscurity. *Shrike* had acquired several specialist crew who— according to Admiral Serrano—would enhance their chances if anything went wrong. This included Koutsoudas at scan, and Warrant Officers Oblo Vissisuan and Methlin Meharry, all three of whom had worked with Brun before. Esmay, watching Koutsoudas' enhanced scan at work, helped map everything it picked up.

At present, the enemy warships insystem included four lightweights in classic tetragonal array around the planet about half a light-second out, and another lightweight docked at the orbital station. Of the lightweights, three were escort-size, and two patrol-size. Three light-minutes out, something that massed like a half-sized cruiser seemed to represent the enemy's idea of a forward defensive force. All these had their weapons systems live, a careless convenience that made it easy for Koutsoudas to analyze them.

Word on the extrication had been mixed. The Guernesi agent in place had sent off a signal at the agreed frequency, but with "cows" instead of "cow" and mention of a price increase. The plan had not included bringing the babies . . . what could the plural mean? Had there been another woman with Brun? That could be disastrous; pursuit might follow more quickly or the other woman might resist. Esmay wondered if the second person could be the older girl from the merchanter.

Koutsoudas, listening in on transmissions, picked up something about "Ranger Bowie's patience" having disappeared, and more about a search under way for "the abomination."

"They know she's gone—I hope she got clean away."

"That's probably why Ranger Bowie's patience is gone—he captured her."

"Maybe."

When Koutsoudas acquired the shuttle's signal hours later, the tension increased again. Esmay felt she could hardly breathe. Now on the scan screens, the bright dot moved out, and out, coming ever nearer. If the plan worked perfectly, in a day or so they would rendezvous with the little craft, take Brun aboard, and jump outsystem before the enemy realized they had been there. Then—with Brun safe— the rest of the task force would have time to blockade the planet and start negotiating the return of the other prisoners. If the plan didn't work . . . a cascade of contingency plans devolved from any point of discovery.

"Go get some food, people," Captain Solis said. "It's going to be a long wait. Suiza, that means you, too— go eat, then sleep; be back in four hours."

Esmay tore herself away from the screens, and found she could actually down a full meal—she had skipped a couple without even noticing. She knew she should sleep, but she lay on her bunk not sleeping, thinking of Barin over on *Gyrfalcon*, of Lord Thorn- buckle back at Sector, of the remarkable Professor Meyerson . . . the alarm woke her, and she rolled off her bunk, smoothed her hair—much easier, these days—and headed for the bridge.

There she found a grim mood unlike that earlier.

"That sonuvabitch has sold them out," Koutsoudas said. He bent over the scan. "He's cut out the insystem drive, put 'em on a zero-G ballistic for that Militia ship—" The enemy ships were still holding their tetragonal formation.

"What're our options?"

"We can microjump between them and the warship, but the backwash might get 'em. Stuff I'm getting is a minute old; we aren't sure where they are."

"It's worth a try."

"Wait!" Koutsoudas held up a hand. "Hot *damn* . . . she wasn't fooled—"

"What's—?"

"There—I can't get focus on the cabin good enough, but there's something going on . . . what— there's *three* people in there, not two!"

"Rotation!" called another scan tech. Koutsoudas glanced at his screen.

"You're right, Atten. Let's see . . ." But they all saw that the shuttle's icon had come alight with the cone that meant acceleration. The cone lengthened, then lengthened again. Vectoring away from the planet, past the warship . . .

"Gotta be Brun," Koutsoudas said. "She's remembered to run past him. Come on, girl, knock it to the wall."

Moment by moment the cone lengthened, an arrow angled away from the planet, toward the distant freedom of deep space. But the little ship was deep in the gravity well, and the warship had the high ground.

"Weapons discharge!" yelled the other scan tech. They groaned; the shuttle was still in easy missile range of the warship. But just before the plotted course intersected, the cone lengthened again.

"That girl's born to win," Koutsoudas said. "She sucked that out of 'em like a pro. 'Course, their systems are optimized to hit big slow things—notice it didn't blow where it should have. They didn't change the arming options. Hope she figures that out. They'd have to be lucky—"

"Another enemy ship on the chase!" said the other tech. "Intersecting—more weapons discharges." The second ship, one of the patrol class, had left its station on the tetragonal array, and boosted to intercept.

Koutsoudas grunted. "Come on, girl—do something—" The cone shifted shape, its tip changing direction, the colors fragmenting and reforming. "Dammit, not that!"

"She's trying to dodge—she can't make it that way. It gives 'em time to get in position."

"It might work—if they don't think to reset their targeting options—if they don't get a lucky hit. But she'd do better to run this way. If she knew we were here . . ."

Esmay watched the displays, her heart pounding.

She could imagine herself in Brun's place—every move Brun made was one she would have made, again and again.

"She's heading back—" the scan tech said. "Is she going to try to land on the planet?"

"No," Esmay heard herself saying. "She's heading for the orbital stuff."

"You think so?" Koutsoudas asked, without looking up. "And what makes you think that, Lieutenant?"

"It's her style. She'd have tried to jump, and something prevented her—that ship should have jump engines, but maybe they're not working. Failing that, a straight run would make her an easy target . . . so she dodged about, but that uses fuel. So she's looking for cover."

"That's a lot of thinking for someone just hauled out of prison," someone said.

"She wouldn't panic," Esmay said. "She's smart, brave, and a risk-taker."

"That's the truth." Koutsoudas flashed a quick grin. Then he sobered. "But she's in real trouble here—unless she's planning to toss herself out the door in a p-suit and hope they shoot the shuttle down. And—there's still two live ones in the shuttle. She brought someone with her."

"If they have multiple p-suits," Esmay said, "she'll probably try that. But given what we know about these people, I doubt there were p-suits for all of them aboard. We should microjump in closer."

"And tell their system we're here? Before the rest of the task force comes in? I thought you were the one who said one woman wasn't worth a war."

Would they always misinterpret that? Anger put an edge to her voice that even she could hear. "When there was a chance to get her out without one, no. In present circumstances, when a covert extrication has gone sour, it's the only way to get close enough to do her any good."

Captain Solis gave her a long look. "You would risk the entire operation—?"

"Microjump to within fifteen seconds scan delay, yes, sir, I would. Give 'em something else to think about. They know she was intended to meet something; they don't know what."

"They don't know for sure it was in this system—"

"If the pilot turned, he'd have told them everything up to the recognition codes. They know someone's waiting for her. We might as well show something—any delay can help her, and we can maneuver sufficiently for the integrity of this ship."

"Suiza, that sounds a lot more like the hero of Xavier." He turned to the communications officer. "Give me a tightbeam, and load a compressed summary of scan; we'll also drop a beacon. Thirty seconds to jump, people."

Shrike popped out of its microjump at low relative system velocity, and the scans cleared.

"Total blackout 2 minutes 45 seconds," Koutsoudas said. Scan lit with the shuttle's beacon and the others—three escort-size warships, two patrol-size, something that massed like a half-size cruiser, and a clutter of small craft. All blazed with live-weapons warning icons. "They'll acquire us in a second or so—and we should be picking up active scan signals shortly—there . . ." The warships icons all showed acceleration cones; those already under boost had the skewed cones of ships changing direction. "Looks like we're sucking 'em off the shuttle." The skewed cones lengthened as those ships pulled away from their pursuit, to redirect their attention to the newcomer.

The shuttle's position had moved; it was clear now that it was running back toward the planet, with rapid changes of acceleration to make it a difficult target. The screens blinked as the SAR kinked in a tiny microjump, then cleared again. The enemy icons responded more slowly this time. Good. Anything to confuse them, distract them. Another jink, to within a half-second, and then another. A distant explosion, where one of the enemy had released a missile at more than maximum range, to detonate uselessly. It was low enough now to be in the orbital trash. It disappeared around the far side of the planet from them. Long minutes passed, while they waited, jinking in random sequence microjumps to keep the enemy guessing. If Brun had slowed enough, it would be another hour and a half before the icon reappeared.

Too soon, they saw it again, now moving rapidly in a suicidal dive for the surface.

"They'll burn up on the first pass, going like that," Koutsoudas said. "What the hell is that girl thinking of? Did she lose control of the ship?"

"Maybe she doesn't have enough fuel for a proper descent," someone else said. "Maybe she'd rather burn—"

"She's not in the ship," Esmay said. She could feel her heart pounding; she knew without question what Brun had done.

"What, you think it's flying itself? You're the one said they probably didn't have p-suits; they couldn't have spaced themselves."

"Unless they found something with p-suits, or an air supply," Esmay said. "If they did . . . I can see Brun sending the shuttle off as a decoy."

"The only active station—the only thing up there with air and p-suits—is the main station, where *Elias Madero* is docked," Koutsoudas said. "I can guarantee they didn't dock there—leaving aside the fact that if they did, they'd have been captured, because it's occupied."

"Uh-oh."

They turned. The Militia ships had not waited to see if the shuttle would burn. From safely outside the danger zone, they'd sent missiles in pursuit, and a dying flare of the screen showed that they'd hit it.

"Well," Captain Solis said. "That's that. Barring Lieutenant Suiza's unlikely suggestion that there are two p-suits now floating somewhere in orbit, they're dead. No one survives a direct hit on a shuttle."

Esmay had been flipping through Koutsoudas's scan catalog of the orbiting trash. "Here's something—and it's consistent with the origin of that burn."

"It's derelict," Koutsoudas said after a quick glance. "There's an old reactor at the core, but the rest of it's at ambient temp."

"It's big enough," Esmay said. "The shuttle course tracks back—"

Koutsoudas sighed, and pulled up an enlarged version of the thumbnail in the catalog. "Look—it's big, but it's a wreck. Even from here you can see that whole sections are open to vacuum . . ."

Esmay blinked. Open to vacuum they were, but— she remembered the Special Materials Fabrication Unit, open just like this. "Could it have been a vacuum processing or manufacturing facility?"

"They don't have anything like that," Captain Solis said. "They buy or steal their space-made products."

"They do now," Esmay said. "Didn't the Guernesi ambassador mention a facility that used to be here— from before the Militia took over this planet?"

"The operative word is derelict, Lieutenant. Even if Brun and her companion made it there, it won't do them any good. No air, no food, no effective shields, no weapons."

"It might've had p-suits, sir. Even if it was ransacked by the Militia, they might not have taken everything. I think she's there, and I think we should go get her."

"I think you're trying to redeem your career, Lieutenant, at the cost of other people's lives." Solis glared at her.

Silence descended on the bridge; Esmay could hear every breath anyone took. Then she heard her own. "Sir, the captain has a right to whatever opinion of me the captain holds. But that woman—those women—have one chance only for survival, and that's someone on our side getting to them with air and protection before either their air runs out or the bad guys figure out that the shuttle was a decoy. If the captain thinks I'm a conniving glory-hound, there are others on this ship who can do the rescue. But it needs to be done."

Solis gave her a long look, which she met squarely. "You would volunteer for such a mission?"

Of course leaped into her mouth, and she bit it back. "Yes, sir."

"Mmm. Who should go, do you think?"

"A full SAR team, sir. Even though we know of only two personnel who may have medical problems, we should anticipate that the Militia may send a boarding party . . . having figured Brun's thinking just as I have. We may be fighting; we will, at the very least, be doing a rescue under hostile conditions."

Solis looked around the bridge, and his gaze came to rest on Koutsoudas. "You've worked with Brun Meager—"

"Yes, sir."

"What do you think?"

"Sir, I think Lieutenant Suiza's right about how Brun thinks—she's very quick, very ingenious, and willing to take risks. If she did dock to any of the junk we've found orbiting this planet, that derelict station is the obvious place. If she's not dead, then that's where she'll be. Suiza's also right that if she did dock there, it would've been detected by any decent ground-based sensing system. We can't assume they don't have one. If I were the Militia, I'd have shuttles on the way—and in fact, we've spotted shuttle take-offs, three altogether."

Solis looked past Esmay. "Meharry—you're also specially assigned to this mission—what's your assessment?"

"The lieutenant's on target, Captain. And the longer we sit around here jawing about it, the worse off Brun's going to be."

"Would you trust Lieutenant Suiza on a mission like this? Or is she grandstanding?"

Esmay was aware of Meharry's unquiet presence behind her. Rumor had spread many stories of Meharry, most of them unpleasantly concentrating on her lethal talents. "With me along, sure, Captain. Personally, I think she's straight, but if I'm there she won't have a chance to screw up."

"Lord Thornbuckle has insisted all along that Sera Meager would not want to see Lieutenant Suiza," Solis said, his tone still cool.

"I think Brun would be glad to see anyone on our side," Meharry said. "And from what I saw at Xavier, and heard from people on *Kos*, the lieutenant is ideally suited to this sort of thing." That could be taken more than one way, but Esmay wasn't feeling picky.

"Very well. Lieutenant, you'll take Team One, and Warrant Officers Meharry and Vissisuan." Esmay did not need to be told that they would be watching her, as much as helping Brun.

Freed at last to do what she knew she was best at, Esmay felt her spirits rising. Their mission was beyond difficult—but so had others been. Brun might not be on the derelict, or if she was, she might already have died from any of a thousand things. If they found her, they might find a corpse, or they might all be blown up by a Militia missile, aimed or stray.

None of that mattered now. Clear in her mind was the plan, as if someone had drawn it in scarlet ink on white paper . . . she heard herself explaining it in crisp phrases to the others. And they responded to her confidence, her enthusiasm.

By the time she was in the pinnace, her p-suit on but not sealed, and the gloves flipped back, the first flurry of action had settled to a purposeful, organized bustle.

The captain's voice in her ear caught her attention. "Lieutenant—you were right about two things. Koutsoudas says he's picked up a single signal from the derelict, something he believes only Sera Meager would send. Fleet frequencies, Fleet codes, and a message that the fox has gone to ground. And there's at least one shuttle headed for the derelict. We can't get you there before it arrives; our jump limit will leave you at least five minutes behind them."

"Yes, sir."

"The rest of the wave's insystem, and I've been in contact with the admiral. I'm sending both SAR teams, and the other pinnace will have all the supplies we can stuff into it. You have discretion to use whatever force is necessary to protect Sera Meager and her companion. We will be sending reinforcements when we've dealt with the other ships, but that may be some hours. Is that clear?"

"Yes, sir." Hours . . . it might be days before they were reinforced. And they would have no heavy weapons. The sonic riot-control generators used in aired-up stations wouldn't work on a derelict open to vacuum . . . what could she use? "Meharry—"

"Yes, sir." Meharry's eyes had a feral glitter reflecting Esmay's own enthusiasm.

"Captain tells me we're going to be docking five minutes behind a hostile shuttle. The station's supposedly not aired up—at least, some of it isn't aired up. We'll need more than small arms."

"On it." Meharry ducked out, leaving Esmay staring at blank air. Well, she'd been with Heris Serrano

for years . . . and this was how it was supposed to
work . . . tell the good ones what to accomplish and
then get out of their way. But she hadn't expected
to feel quite this . . .

"Lieutenant—" It was a squad of the neuro-
enhanced troops, heavily laden with weapons segments; their sergeant handed her a screenful of official
numbers and letters for her signature—if they came
back without all eight CFK-201.33-rs, it would be her
job to explain where they had gone . . . and she
hadn't a clue what they *were*, or any of the long list
of components below them. She ran her command
wand aross the bottom of the list, and handed it back.

"We'll be first out as usual . . ." the sergeant said,
with not quite a question mark.

"Right," Esmay said, dragging her mind back from
Meharry's disappearance and the mysteries of Fleet
inventory control to the immediate tactical problem.
"And with hostiles ahead of us, and no idea whether
our rescue targets have pressure suits."

"Piece of cake," the sergeant said. "None of the
hostiles are going to be female, from what I hear, and
our targets are. So we just shoot the bad boys, and
leave the girls alone."

CHAPTER TWENTY-ONE

"What now?" asked Hazel. Brun shrugged. She needed to think. She was hungry, thirsty—she sipped at the helmet tube—and very, very sleepy. And her legs hurt; the anesthetic spray was wearing off.

What could they do, with the few weapons they had? She could almost hear Commander Uhlis's voice yelling at her in the class: your best weapon is between your ears. Yes, and she'd like to keep it there, preferably in one piece.

"If we could get the artificial gravity on," Hazel said, "then we could turn it off."

Brun supposed she meant in order to confuse their enemies—but it would gain them only minutes, if that. It would certainly reveal their presence—the gravity generator wouldn't be on if no one was here. A vague plan began to form in her brain, shapeless as rising mist.

Exploring the controls while in a p-suit was a lot safer than playing around with them otherwise; Brun grinned as she remembered Oblo's cautionary tales. She prodded one after another, seeing what worked.

"Lights!" Hazel said. That was obvious. But was

it lights in this room or overall? Brun waved a wide-armed gesture; Hazel nodded and pushed off to explore. Brun peered at the panel. If she could figure out how to bring up station scan, there should be an idiot display somewhere on the main board that would tell her what she needed to know, in several languages and nonverbal symbols. Since the controls worked at all, she ought to be able to bring up station scan.

The rocker switch, when she found it, was located underneath a foldout panel. Brun pushed it with a silent prayer for luck . . . and the displays came up, flickering badly at first but steadying. How long had they been off? And what was powering them now? She looked for the idiot display.

There. As she'd expected, one of the languages on the display was her own . . . another was Guerni. She couldn't read the third at all, but that didn't matter now. She flicked through the opening menu: station layout, environmental system controls, life support, emergency procedures (which included a section on biohazard containment), power system, communications.

Station layout made clear what the place had been—a biological laboratory of some kind; probably—Brun thought—one of those fairly common at colony startup, which tailored biologicals for the specific conditions found downside. Many colonies had them . . . but why, then, was this one derelict?

The station had been clearly divided into living space for the workers, and eight labs separated by locks and seals—three on one arm, and five on the other. The big open gap was, Brun saw, out near the end of one arm; they had docked under a solar-collecting panel halfway down the other.

❖   ❖   ❖

Deep in the station's core, the system's expert slept, as it had slept for decades of local time. All peripherals were offline; all sensors shut down. Its last instruction set lay uppermost, ready to execute if anyone turned on the power, but hard vacuum and random radiation had changed a few bits here and there. Normally that would have been no problem; its self-repair mechanisms were necessarily robust, designed for industrial use in space. But they were not designed for decades on a derelict that had been vandalized in a hurry, its expert laid to rest in half the time required.

When the lights came on, a trickle of power ran through its connections, shunted there by the designers who intended the expert to be functioning whenever the station was occupied. Slowly— slowly for its design—the expert woke, layer by layer. Power in the lines meant someone had returned; that gave permission for it to draw power on its own and engage the self-check and self-repair routines. The topmost instruction set began executing, inhibiting return of some active functions. Those who inhabited the station now might be either legitimate employees or intruders . . . if they were intruders, the expert was not to reveal itself by independent action, but instead isolate them and transmit a call for help.

Passive scan devices collected information. Two humans, female by all parameters, wearing female-design employee p-suits whose code numbers were in the directory: emergency evacuation suits from Laboratory Two. The expert engaged suit telemetry cautiously; the suits' inhabitants didn't notice. Neither human fit a known profile, but a quick check of the decay data from the reactor indicated that it had been decades since the expert was put to sleep. Therefore it was unlikely that these employees would be known to it.

One, in the control room, was following a rational restart procedure on station control functions. The expert did not interfere, but observed. She seemed to know what she was doing. The other was exploring the corridor leading to the second arm. The expert turned its attention to the outside world.

❖   ❖   ❖

Hazel came back to the control room. "Lights are on all down that corridor. I couldn't see into all the compartments, though. The ones I could, some were dark and some weren't. You must've hit a main switch."

Brun nodded, and pointed to the panel that controlled lighting. It indicated power to the lights throughout, with a summary of lights switched off, and lights not functioning even though switched on. She pointed at other panels; Hazel leaned closer. She had found the power reports for both the internal reactor—now nearly depleted, and producing less than 40% of its former power—and the solar panels, also below nominal. With the damage they'd seen on the outside, she could believe that. Still, the station had been designed to support research and manufacturing; the power still available would easily restore life support throughout, if they could find the air for it.

The air for the central core she had already found—the heat generated by the reactor had nurtured the base beds of the environmental system all these years, and the slowly accumulating air had been stored under pressure. But should they air up? External air would free them from the need to carry tanks around, and extend the effective life of the ones they had. Yet airing up the station would prove someone was aboard—it would be easily detectable from the outside. Moreover, if intruders blew the station, and they didn't have their suits on, they'd die.

Brun was still mulling this over when Hazel brought her a handcomp with voice output . . . Brun grinned, and grabbed it. It had the standard plug connections, so Brun jacked it into the suit intercom connection on the outside, and tapped some of the preset message keys. She had a choice of three languages, and twenty preset messages. "All correct," said a tinny male voice with a strong accent. She looked at Hazel and cocked her head.

"I didn't hear it," Hazel said. "Maybe you have to hit the transmit key inside the helmet to transmit to other suits."

A nuisance. Brun fumbled with the comp and bumped the helmet transmit button with her chin as she keyed the preset message. "All correct."

"Got it!" Hazel said. "Now maybe we can find one with more capability."

"All correct," Brun tapped again. Then she hit each key once, to be sure what the messages were, and again to practice how to say "Help!" and "Danger!" and "Shift report." One of the keys transmitted no voice signal, but an electronic bleep that was probably, Brun thought, some kind of ID code for a central computer. She hit that one only once.

Besides the preset messages, the handcomp had key input for other data. Brun tried tapping out "Does this work?" but Hazel shook her head.

❖   ❖   ❖

The expert system awaited whatever instruction would follow the authorization signal. "Does this work?" fit no protocol, but its natural-language processing was up to the task of interpreting it. It must mean "Did the expert system receive that authorization and can it receive keyboard input?"

"At your service," it transmitted through the correct frequencies. Both humans stopped in the way that humans did when presented with novel or unexpected data.

"What was that?" asked the one who had not transmitted the authorization code. The expert waited for the other to reassure her, meanwhile retrieving a complete suit readout indicating fatigue toxins and mild hypothermia and analyzing the vocal patterns to conclude that this individual was a pubertal human female, a native speaker of Gaesh with the accent common to the nearby merchanters of the Familias Regnant rather than that of the Guerni Republic. It instructed the suit to warm up a bit, and increase oxygen flow.

Meanwhile, the other, without speaking, was tapping rapidly on the keyboard of her handcomp. The expert was able to interpret, despite errors in input, that she knew she was communicating with an expert system.

"The system will take over vocal communication," the expert said to the other one.

"All correct," Brun transmitted, hoping Hazel would understand that the expert was going to relay from her own keyed input.

"There are vocal synthesizers of more power and suitability in laboratory 1-21," the expert said. "Although major equipment was destroyed, my optical sensors report that some of the small synthesizers seem to be unbroken."

"Can you guide us there?" Brun asked, aware that the expert was echoing her input as a voice to Hazel.

"Easily, but I have instead empowered a mobile unit to fetch them. Spacecraft approach; my analysis suggests that they are upcoming from the surface."

"Plan?" Brun asked.

"Data," the expert replied. "Non-enemy spacecraft in system . . . too far away."

Non-enemy . . . Fleet?

"Can you contact them?"

"Transmitters nonfunctional. Estimated time to restore transmission capability . . . 243 standard seconds. What are the parameters?"

Hazel, who had said nothing for several exchanges, said, "How could we know Fleet frequencies and codes?"

Brun smiled to herself. She knew. One after another,

she entered the figures, carefully defining each: frequencies, frequency changes with intervals, identification codes, including the one she had been given once as her personal ID. Then, with great care, she entered the message she wanted to send. Her eyes kept blurring, but she blinked the tears back fiercely. Time enough to cry if she got Hazel to safety.

And the little children. But she could not think of that now. One thing at a time.

"These frequencies and codes are not those in my library for the Regular Space Service of the Familias Regnant," the expert said. It was capable of expression, and it sounded fussy.

"Check date," Brun keyed in. "Codes change."

A long pause ensued. "It has been a very long time," the expert said finally. "I assumed the date was an error resulting from damage done when the station was overrun. . . ."

"Time to intruder arrival?" keyed Brun. Some expert systems were complex enough to lose themselves in endless recursive self-examination. "And transmitter function?"

"Ninety-seven seconds until transmitters functional; I will send your message as soon as confirmed. There is a high probability that nontarget vessels may be able to intercept the message; you have provided no cipher."

"They already suspect we're here," Hazel said, voicing Brun's thought. "And if the Militia know we're here, it's better that Fleet knows it too. I suppose, Brun, it's because of your father—"

"All correct," Brun keyed. She really did want a better voice synthesizer; her fingers were already tired, and she had a lot more to say.

"ETA of intruder shuttles from the planet now ranges from one hour ten minutes, to three hours one minute," the expert said. "Unless they change course, which they have the capacity to do . . . now, three shuttles apparently approaching from the planet."

Three shuttles . . . why did they think they needed four shuttles to capture two women? Or were they coming out to fight Fleet with shuttles? Surely they weren't that stupid.

"Weapons discharge," the expert system said. "Nearby ship, identifying itself as Militia cruiser *Yellow Rose*, launched missiles at Fleet vessel of unknown type."

✧   ✧   ✧

The enemy shuttle had been run right into the gaping hole in one arm of the station. No doubt the Militia knew what was open and what wasn't— assuming they were the ones who'd made it a derelict. If they'd been in a regular warship, Esmay would have lobbed a missile into that bay, and blown the shuttle first off. But an SAR shuttle did not normally venture into hostile territory; it mounted no external weapons, and they had had no time to improvise. With that in mind, Esmay kept the length of the station between her shuttle and the enemy's, and snugged in under one of the power panels at the far end. Again, mission constraints changed the usual procedures. They dared not blow a hole in the derelict's hull, lest Brun and her companion be hiding behind just that piece of hull. They shouldn't be, but no one knew what conditions were like inside. Moreover, it would take at least four hours to rig one of the portable airlocks and carefully incise a new hole in the station hull. So the teams would have to insert through a known entrance, which all concerned knew was the best way to make a target of themselves.

The best they could hope for was that the Militia intruders weren't already in place. The neuro-enhanced squad didn't seem too worried. Esmay, waiting near the tail of the line, saw the bulky figures pause at the emergency lock, and then move in, far faster than she had expected. Perhaps this meant the station had no air pressure.

"Lieutenant, the artificial gravity's on."

That shouldn't be . . . the station was a derelict. But she could feel through her own body the tug of a gravity generator. Which meant a sizeable power source, more than could be accounted for by the tattered, misaligned power panels. Would there be air? Had Brun turned things on? Esmay shook those questions off. What mattered now was getting in. If there was gravity, then the fighting would not favor the zero-G trained.

Inside, they were met with the chaotic remnant of systematic vandalism, all visible under ordinary ceiling panel lights. P-suits cluttered the corridor, all turquoise with a BlueSky logo and code number on the back. Someone had drawn five pointed stars and other curious symbols on the corridor bulkhead in brown pigment—or blood. The tank locker beside the suit locker was empty of breathing tanks. Air pressure was as near vacuum as made no difference . . . but why was there any pressure at all? Why were the lights on?

Esmay tried a cautious hail on the frequency Koutsoudas had given as that of Brun's transmission . . . no reply.

❖   ❖   ❖

Nothing damaged a man's reputation more than unruly women. Mitch Pardue knew even before he launched that he could kiss the Captain's position goodbye for at least ten years. He might even be voted out as Ranger Bowie. Even if he got them back, those fool women had cost him something he'd worked for twenty years and more.

The abomination he could understand. She was crazy, even without a voice. But the girl's defection hurt. Prima had been so fond of her, and the other wives as well. She'd worked hard, and they'd treated her like one of the family. Maybe that was the problem. Maybe they'd been too lenient. Well, he wouldn't make that mistake with the little girls. That bossy one, already showing off in the weaving shed—he'd see that she didn't stay bossy. As for Patience . . . he'd already half-promised her as a third wife to a friend of his, but now that wouldn't do.

Why couldn't the girl have realized how much better off she was in his household? Why were women so perverse, anyway?

He almost let himself think God had erred in creating women at all, but pulled back from that heresy. That's what happened if you started thinking about women—they led the mind astray.

If they were on the derelict station—and he was certainly sure they were—he would capture them and make an example of them. The yellow-haired abomination they would have to execute; he hated killing women, but if she escaped once, she might again. The girl . . . he would decide that later, after he learned exactly what had happened. When they'd finally found a witness, it seemed that a man had told her to get in the car. If so, she might not be guilty of anything but stupidly following a man's orders, which was all you could expect of a woman. He hoped that was it.

"Ranger Bowie!" That was his pilot. He leaned into the cockpit.

"What, Jase?"

"There's a weird ship out there, scan says."

Weird ship. It must be a ship the women had planned to meet.

"What's our defense say?"

"Says it's weird, Ranger. Not anything they know, a lot smaller than a cruiser. But it can do those little short jumps like the Familias fleet—"

"It's looking for them," he said. "It's not a warship, or it'd have shot up our ships first thing, same as we would. A little transport of some kind." The worst of it was that it meant the Familias now knew where they were—and more ships might follow. Sufficient unto the day is the evil thereof, he told himself. First things first. Get these women under control, or all hell would break loose.

Though if he'd known, he might've asked for a shuttle of space-armored troops from the *Yellow Rose*. Their p-suits were hardened, but not against the kind of weaponry a Fleet vessel would have. Still, they'd probably hold their fire if they thought the Speaker's daughter was in the midst of it.

His uncle had been one of those who trashed this godless excrescence in the first place; he'd grown up on the stories. They'd talked about blowing it up time and again, but always decided it might be useful someday. Useful! Just showed what happened when you compromised on a moral duty. He watched as the pilot brought them in to the old shuttle bay. When he felt the solid clunk of the shuttle's grapples on the decking, he stood and pushed his way back to the hatch.

"Now y'all listen here," he said. "We're goin' in to look for those women. Not to play around gapin' at stuff, or even takin' the time to trash it. There's warships insystem; we need to get this done and get back where we can do some good. Understand?"

They nodded, but he had his doubts.

"All the weapons they can have is what that guy had in his shuttle. Maybe a couple of knives, a .45 or two. And they're women, and not used to zero-G or vacuum. They'll have p-suits on, probably ones that don't fit good. So we don't have anything to worry about if we use sense. Just don't go wanderin' off where one of 'em can blow you away too easy. And be sure your personnel scans are set on high power."

He pulled his helmet shield down, locked it, and checked the suit seals of the man in front of him; the man checked his. Terry Vanderson—good man, reliable. Then he turned and led the way out of the shuttle's airlock.

The regular airlock from the shuttle dock to the station corridor operated normally, but there was no air inside. He'd expected that. The women would've taken a tank or so from the shuttle when they left it, and they'd be low on air by now.

Inside the airlock, they stood in a short corridor that ended in a T-intersection. He'd looked at his uncle's old notes, and knew that each arm of the station was a warren of laboratories and storage rooms—they would have to clear each of these. He looked at his scanner. Nobody near—but they would check, then close and secure each compartment.

"Don't forget the overheads," he reminded his men. Not that they needed it; they'd been on more than one hostile boarding.

Lewis and Terry peeled off to check the outer end of the arm. It seemed to take forever, but it probably wasn't more than five minutes before they were back. Now they moved along the corridor toward the station hub.

❖　　❖　　❖

"I can't believe this," Oblo muttered. "They're just walking along like they're on a picnic." On scan, the twenty suited figures moved in a clump, checking compartments and doors, but without any real caution. Nobody on point, nobody watching their backs. "And they're not in space armor, just p-suits. Brun could just about take them herself, if she had any kind of weapon."

"They think they're up against two unarmed women," Esmay said. "Once someone calls to tell them we're here—"

"Someone should have, by now," Oblo said. "Unless they're not listening."

That led to questions Esmay had no time to

answer. Was there someone else in the Militia eager
to have this mission fail? And why?

The assault troops moved forward, secure in the
knowledge that their armor would foil scan not
specifically designed to penetrate it. Esmay felt the
familiar surge of excitement; she wanted to be up with
them, but more important was finding Brun and the
girl. Scan showed a pair of p-suited life signals on
this side of the core, in a compartment off a side
corridor. The problem would be letting them know
she and the others were friendly—the armor, designed
for combat effectiveness, did not have insignia in the
visible spectrum.

✧   ✧   ✧

All the compartments in that wing had been
checked and secured, and Mitch Pardue felt pretty
good as he led his men into the central core. Careful
scanning had shown nothing there—the women, if
they were alive, would be huddling somewhere in the
far wing, close to the hotspot where they'd had the
shuttle. He felt a pleasant tension as he thought of
them—of the fear they would be feeling, the help-
lessness . . .

"Let's go, boys," he said, and stepped out into the
wider space of the core corridor.

They passed what had been a lounge area, the
chairs now in a random tumble on the deck, and
came to the control area. Here, Ranger Bowie paused.
It had been a little surprising to find the artificial
gravity still on—he clearly remembered his uncle
talking about how they had pushed the bodies down
the corridors in zero-G—and he wondered if perhaps
the women had knocked the controls about by
accident.

"Wait a minute," he said to the others. "I wanta
check on somethin'." They drifted across the space
with him, as interested in the old station as he was.
He leaned over the control panel, trying to read the

labels . . . not in decent Tex, but in scripts he recognized as those used in the Familias Regnant, the Guerni Republic, and the Baltic Confederation. Heathens, all of them. Sure enough, the dust had been messed around; he could see what might be the marks of suit gloves here and there. He saw the gravity control panel, and was reaching for it when his vision blanked and he was pulled violently backwards.

"Lambs to the slaughter," Esmay heard through her comunit. "We should space 'em now, or you want prisoners?"

"Can you get any ID?"

"Well, one of 'em's got that star thing on his p-suit, and he looks like the leader of the bunch that took the *Elias Madero*."

"Yes, we want prisoners," Esmay said firmly. "Especially that one." She wanted to hear how it went, but finding Brun was still a priority, and the scan traces kept moving—as if Brun were deliberately evading them. Perhaps she was.

"Team Blue!" That was from outside, from the other team's scan specialist.

"Lieutenant Suiza here."

"Two shuttles approaching, with unshielded transmissions. They're planning to go in and kill everyone they find."

That made no sense—and then it did. If these people were as given to factionalism as reported, then this would be an excellent chance for one faction to rid itself of the leaders of another.

"They know we're here, right?"

"Yeah—but they think they can take us. I estimate twenty per shuttle—total of forty, say again four-zero armed personnel. No heavy weaponry."

That was lucky. If they'd had heavy weapons, or ship weapons, they might have decided to blow the station.

"Have they indicated where they're going to land?"

"One of them coming into the same shuttle bay as the first. They want to get in behind the others—the one's going to come in on the end of this wing."

"Ah . . . the old pincers movement."

"Yes, sir."

"Mr. Vissisuan," Esmay said. "Expect forty intruders, in two shuttle loads, small arms only. According to backscan, they know we're here, but think we'll be easy to subdue. They've divided their force, and expect to catch us between them."

"Sir. Plan?"

"Until we have Brun and the girl safely away, that has to be our first priority. Right now it looks like Brun is between us and the incoming shuttle. So we'd better move fast. Beyond that, secure the prisoners we have, and take prisoners if possible." If they could pick off some high-ranking Militia, perhaps they could avoid a battle and get the children out safely.

❖   ❖   ❖

Brun hoped the expert system knew what it was doing. It kept shifting them from one compartment to another, supposedly far from the Militia's personnel scans. It said it was still trying to retrieve a better vocal synthethizer, too, and had dispatched another two mobile units. She wanted to ask if it had received any answer from Fleet—surely they'd be doing *something*—but she simply could not get her fingers to work on the keyboard, and Hazel could not understand her gestures. She was so tired . . . she hoped it was only exhaustion and not hypoxia.

"Brun—wake up!" That was Hazel's voice; she sounded on the edge of panic. "I feel things in the decking—vibrations—"

It must remind her of her own capture. Hiding in these vandalized rooms, waiting for someone to come, not knowing who—it must bring back all her nightmares. Brun tapped her arm, and grinned. Hazel grinned back, but there was no mirth in it.

She could feel the knocks and vibrations herself. Someone closer, and more than one. She tried again with the compad keyboard, and keyed "Fleet assistance?"

"I'm not sure," the expert system said in her ear. "There have been two landings, another two are imminent. Multiple intruders aboard, hostile to one another." Then some of them must be friendly, Brun thought. But she wasn't sure. "Not all the same shapes of shuttles, but no recognizable ID codes from the ones that appeared nearby."

Appeared? Launched from a larger ship that had microjumped nearby?

"Try Fleet codes on com channels," Brun keyed.

"I cannot access any transmissions from one set of intruders," the expert said. "I don't know what frequencies to use."

Shielded suit communications. That sounded more and more like Fleet, but how could she contact them? Someone should be listening in for unshielded transmissions— "All bands," Brun said. "Use the codes I gave you."

The deck bucked, and Brun and Hazel lost contact in the low gravity, bouncing into one of the bulkheads. Brun's compad flew another way, its jack yanked from her suit connection. Hazel scrambled after it, as another series of vibrations and blows shook them. Something must have rammed the station, something with a lot more mass than a single person. Brun could see into the next compartment, where the bulkhead had torn loose at the corner, leaving a triangular hole. The station could be coming apart around them; they might be flung loose into space, tiny seeds from a puffball head.

Brun fought down the panic. Right now, right this instant, they still had air, they still had intact p-suits, and they weren't freezing or full of holes. Hazel edged back to her and held out the compad and connector.

❖   ❖   ❖

The scan tech watching the incoming Militia shuttles reported that one was likely to impact rather than dock. "He's coming in with way too much relative vee; gonna knock this station sideways— counting down . . . seven, six, five, four, three, two, one—" The deck bucked; in the minimal artificial gravity, a cloud of dust rose and hung like a tattered curtain. "They've made a mess out of the end of that arm, but don't seem to have damaged themselves much, worse luck."

"Keep us informed," Esmay said. She had Meharry and five others with her as she tried to follow Brun's scan signal through the maze of passages.

"Lieutenant!" That was the backdoor scan again. "I've got transmissions in Fleet code from the station itself—identifies itself as the station expert system."

"What's it want?"

"Says two employees told it to contact us and gave it the codes. Says it's trying to protect them, and can we prove we're friendly?"

"The only person here who might know any Fleet access codes was Brun—but she was supposedly unable to talk."

"But it can't contact this individual now—says a communications device failed."

Great. "Can it direct us to her?"

"It says yes, but it won't until we can prove that we have a legal right to be here, and that she knows us."

Worse and worse. Expert systems had a reputation for rigid interpretation of rules.

"Tell it to confirm to her that we respond to Fleet codes, and ask her to sign a yes or no acceptance of our ID."

"Yes, sir." A pause followed, then, "It's trying, sir." After another pause, "It says she wants to know who it is. A name."

Esmay thought a moment. According to her father, Esmay was the last person Brun would want to see, or should see. But that was a name she'd know.

"She knows us, Lieutenant," Meharry said. "Methlin and Oblo—she'll recognize that."

"Go ahead," Esmay said. "Tell it that."

Another brief pause, and then, "It's agreed. It's going to mark the way, and tell Sera Meager someone's coming."

"Tell it to give her a description of our suits, so she'll know us from the others," Esmay said.

Now her helmet display lit with the icons of the intruders: twenty red dots displayed on a graphic of the station wing. Esmay followed the expert system's directions with her team; the others moved down the main corridor to intercept those landing.

Here in the secondary corridor, occasional turqoise p-suits lay like dead bodies. Every one gave Esmay a chill, but the expert urged them on, via the relay through the scan tech. At last, a compartment door slid open ahead of them. Cautiously, Esmay edged forward . . . and there they were. Brun, recognizable through the facemask of the p-suit, and a scared-looking young girl. Meharry moved past Esmay and cleared her helmet faceshield so Brun could see her. Brun staggered forward, moving as if she had serious damage, and fell into Meharry's grip.

"Medical team," Esmay said. They came at the double, and unfolded the vacuum gurneys that allowed life-support access to a p-suited patient outside pressure. Only then did she think of asking scan for the frequency that the expert and Brun's suit must be using. She glanced around the compartment, to see an obvious gap where bulkhead sections had warped apart. Was that from the recent impact of the

Militia shuttle, or old damage? She couldn't tell; it didn't matter.

Brun struggled to free herself from Meharry's grip, and gestured at the girl. The medics unfolded another of the gurneys, and unzipped it. They rolled each woman into her own, then zipped and sealed, and popped the tanks. The transparent tents inflated, leaving sleeved access ports for treatment.

The girl started talking right away. "Please—she can't talk—she needs a way to communicate—"

"Sure, hon . . . what's your name, now?"

"Hazel—Hazel Takeris. And she's Brun—she was using a compad with voice output, but the plug broke."

Esmay found the compad, and slid it into the transfer portal of Brun's gurney. She could see Brun cycle it through, then hold it without using it. Plug broken? It must mean that she had needed to plug it into her p-suit. Brun made the universal sign for *Air up?* and Esmay responded. Brun popped an arm seal on her suit, just as their safety instructor had taught them: never trust anyone's word on air pressure. Then she peeled back one glove, and tapped one of the compad's keys.

"All correct," announced the audio pickup from inside the gurney.

"Sera Meager?"

"All correct."

"Can you describe your current status?"

"No." That, as Esmay could see, was another button. The thing must have had preprogrammed messages. What was the keyboard for, then?

"Can you type complete answers?"

"No."

Esmay turned away to consider their overall position. The Militia that had crunched into this wing were about halfway to their part of the wing, though coming down the main corridor.

"Trouble . . ." scan said. "Big trouble."

"Bad guys on the other end are carrying explosives. Can't see if the ones on this end are, but they could be."

❖   ❖   ❖

The mobile units available to the expert system were secondary models which had survived the initial vandalization by looking like simple boxes. It had taken longer than the expert expected to recharge one of them, get its tracks moving, and send it off to Laboratory 1-21 to look for voice synthesizers. But now it was on its way. The expert kept an area of higher artificial gravity moving along with it, to keep its tracks in firm contact with the deck plating. The expert prided itself on carrying out all orders, no matter how complex, simultaneously. It dispatched another, and then another, in case the first should be disabled somehow. Clearly it was important to get a communications device to the taller human.

The first unit reached the lab, and extended a pincer-arm to pick up one of the synthesizers, just as an impact rocked the station. The unit flipped off the deck, and out of the area of higher gravity; it flew across the lab, into the corridor, and impacted the opposite bulkhead just behind the group of neuro-enhanced marines that had stalked past. The rear marine slagged it before it had time to fall to the floor, yelling "Hostile!"

"What is it?" Kim Arek asked. She was surprised and delighted to find that her voice didn't crack.

"This thing just flew out the hatch at me—"

"Something bounced loose by the hit?"

"Looked like one of those robot bomb-crawlers, what I saw of it."

"Well . . . keep an eye out for others."

❖   ❖   ❖

Pete Robertson, Ranger Travis and Captain of Rangers, had plenty of time to think on the way up from the surface. It was all Mitch's fault, and God's judgement on Mitch's hasty ways and unhealthy attachment to outlander technology was about to land on all of them. He made up his mind, and called the others—they would make sure no one used that heathen station for anything ever again, and that Mitch paid the price for his unbelief.

He had no real hope that they'd get out of this in good shape—not with the appearance of enemy ships in the system—but at least they'd take care of their own dirty laundry first. And Mitch would never be Ranger Captain: he would see to that himself.

The two enemy shuttles that had docked to the derelict would present no problem if they simply blew the derelict up—and he'd toyed with the idea of having *Yellow Rose* and *Heart of Texas* do that before they went out to fight the invaders, but he'd rather do it himself. It felt right.

So, huffing a little in his hardened p-suit, he shuffled carefully off the shuttle with the rest of the Travis crew, and led the way down the corridor that lay open before him. Sam Dubois, Ranger Austin, had landed at the far end of the long structure—both groups would set explosive charges as they converged on the enemy, and then retreat—and blow the station. The odd thing was, his personnel scanners detected only a small cluster of life forms way up ahead, in the central core, and two off to the right somewhere. Hadn't Mitch caught the women yet? He smiled to himself, forgetting for the moment the missing enemy from the shuttles.

When the little tracked crawler trundled out of a side corridor, he spun and with practiced ease drew and fired. Bullets ricocheted off the thing's hard shell and holed the bulkhead in a scattered pattern. The machine came on, a jointed arm holding some device . . . behind it was another one, just coming into view around a corner.

"Git those!" he said, and drew again. Behind him, the Travis crew clumped up, and someone's shot shattered the device the thing was holding. But the crawlers came on, more slowly. "They can't catch us," he said. "Come on—" and turned back to move on the way they'd been going.

Which was now blocked by huge figures in black armor, holding weapons he'd never seen.

"Get'm boys!" he yelled, and fired.

Then the strange weapons belched streams of something gray that shoved him back into his men, and glued them all into one immobile mass. When the next explosion came, from the far end, he had a sudden stark fear that it would ignite the charges his crew had left behind, and blow them all. He was not, he discovered, nearly as ready to meet his Maker as he'd always claimed.

❖   ❖   ❖

"Dumber than dirt," Jig Arek said, with some satisfaction. "You'd think they never heard of riot control."

"We still have one bunch loose," Oblo said.

"Belay that," Meharry said, in what for Meharry was a tense voice. "We've got worse problems. Brun and Suiza fell off the station."

CHAPTER TWENTY-TWO

One moment, Esmay had been checking where everyone was; the next, with no warning, the gurney tent ruptured; air puffed out. Live fire, it had to be. Esmay threw herself on the gurney, covering Brun's body, and slammed Brun's faceshield shut. Even through her armor, she could feel Brun breathing; she could see Brun's face, rigid with fury or terror—she couldn't tell which—but the mask was clear, which meant that air and filters were both working. She pushed herself up a little and locked the elbow position so her armor wouldn't crush Brun if something hit her hard. Something thumped into her armor once, and again; someone fell over her; excited voices yelled in her suit com. She ignored them; she and her armor were between Brun and whatever was going on, and someone else could handle that.

Then the deck bucked hard, buckled, and the damaged bulkhead peeled away. She caught a glimpse of other suited figures tumbling—someone grabbing for the other gurney—and some blow thrust her toward the opening, out into the brilliant sunlight.

By the time she realized she was tumbling

outside the station, she knew she was still clinging to Brun, the armor's power-assisted gloves
clamped to the frame of the gurney. The view
beyond shifted crazily: light/dark, starfield/planet/
station. She tried to focus on the helmet readouts,
and finally found the ones that gave an estimated
relative vee to her "ship"—the station—a mere 2.43
meters per second.

Brun, when she looked, was staring back at her
with no recognition. Of course not—Esmay had never
changed her faceshield to allow it. Impossible now.
She had no idea what to do, but she knew one thing
not to do—let go of the gurney frame. Her suit had
the beacon.

"Lieutenant!" That loud shout in her helmet com
got her attention; she hoped it was the first call.

"Suiza here," she said, surprised that her voice
sounded as calm as it did.

"Lieutenant, have you got the gurney?"

"Yup," Esmay said. "She's alive; air's flowing."

"What about you? Somebody thought they saw a
plume."

Another look at her helmet readouts was not so
reassuring. Her own air was down, and the gauge was
sagging visibly. *I've been here before*, she thought,
remembering her first terrifying EVA from *Koskiusko*.
And I didn't like it then.

"Low," she said. "And going down."

"The blast may've pulled your airfeed loose—can
you check it?"

"Not without letting go of the gurney," Esmay said.
"And I'm not going to. What's the situation?"

"They're dead; we've got two dead, and four
tumblers, counting you and the gurney as one. Max
has you all on scan. We'll have a sled to you in less
than ten minutes."

She didn't have ten minutes.

"What is your air?" That was Meharry.

"Three minutes," Esmay said. "If it doesn't leak any faster."

"Is Brun conscious?"

"Yes. She's looking at me, but she can't see me—my helmet shield's still mirrored."

"I'm going to transmit to her, tell her to see if she can stop your leak."

"No—it's too dangerous."

"It'll be more dangerous if you pass out and can't help guide the sled in."

She could see the change in Brun's expression, though Meharry hadn't patched the transmission to her. Then Brun wriggled around, wrapping one arm in the straps waving from the gurney, and reaching around behind Esmay. Her arm wasn't long enough; she tapped Esmay's shoulder.

If Esmay let go with one hand, and turned, Brun might be able to reach whatever it was. But she might lose her grip on the gurney—they might not find her. Brun's tap the next time was a solid slug. Esmay grinned to herself. Whatever the damage, Brun hadn't changed in some essentials. Carefully, slowly, Esmay loosened her grip on the gurney frame on that side, and transferred her grip to one of the grab straps on Brun's p-suit. Brun wriggled more. The air gauge quit dropping . . . stabilized . . . at eight minutes.

"Eight minutes," Esmay reported to Meharry.

"She's got the luck, that one," Meharry said. She did not say whether eight minutes would be enough. Esmay told herself that one minute of oxygen deprivation was within anyone's capacity. Brun bumped against her, flinging out an arm and leg. What was the idiot doing—oh. Slowing rotation. Esmay extended her legs on the other side. The confusing whirl of backgrounds slowed, as they lay almost crosswise of each other, forming, with the gurney frame, a six-spoked wheel rolling slowly along.

Then Brun reached up with her webbing-wrapped

arm, and pushed up Esmay's mirrorshield before Esmay could bring an arm in to stop her. Her eyes widened. Then she grinned, as mischievous and merry a grin as Esmay had ever seen on her face. She used the same arm to work free the thermal-packed bag of IV fluids sticktaped to the gurney, and very deliberately used her glove's screwblade attachment to poke a hole in it. Then she winked at Esmay, looked past her—moved the bag around—and squeezed.

A stream of saline jetted out, instantly converted to a spray of ice crystals that glittered in the sun. Esmay wondered if Brun had just gone completely insane. Then she realized what it was. For all the good it would do, Brun was trying to use an IV as reaction mass to get them back to the station faster.

Esmay did her best to hold still, even as her air ran out, and the hunger for oxygen overtook her, urging her to run, struggle, fight her way out of the dark choking tunnel that was squeezing the life out of her.

She heard voices before she could see; the steady quiet voices of the medics, and somewhere beyond, quite a bit of cursing and yelling.

"What's her pO_2 doing?"

"Coming up. Caught it in time . . ."

"We're going to need another can of spray over here—"

"My God, what'd they do to them?"

"It was the horse, I think—" That in a tentative, soft voice.

Esmay opened her eyes to see unhelmeted faces bent over her. She wanted to ask the logical question, but she would not ask that one. One of the medics anticipated her.

"We're in the shuttle again. Our targets are alive, no wounds taken in the shootout. We lost two dead, eight with minor injuries. The station's pretty much gone and there's a fight going on upstairs somewhere. And now you're with us, we don't have to worry about you any more." The medic winked. "But I do have to do a mental status exam."

Esmay took a deep breath, and only then realized that she still had something up her nose feeding her oxygen. "I'm fine," she said. "What else is going on?" She tried to sit up, but the medic pushed her back.

"Not until we're sure of your blood gases. Your suit telemetry said you were out of air for about two and a half minutes before we got you reconnected, and that's on the edge of the bad zone."

"I'm fine," Esmay said.

"You're not," the medic said, "but you will be when we're done with you." She inserted a syringe into the IV line Esmay had not noticed until then, and a soft gauzy curtain closed between Esmay and the rest of the universe.

❖   ❖   ❖

Barin had the uncomfortable honor of observing the whole collapse of the "simple, straightforward extrication" from the bridge of *Gyrfalcon*. Most of the carnage had already happened by the time *Shrike*'s signal reached them, and his grandmother ordered the rest of the task force to jump in. They popped out less than thirty light seconds from the planet, only ten from the nearest enemy ship. *Gyrfalcon*'s first salvo took it out; the cruiser's massive energy weapons burned through its shields in less than a second.

"Not used to facing real firepower," Escovar said calmly.

"Captain—*Shrike* has recovered one shuttle—casualties . . ."

Please, please, let it not be Esmay . . . Barin clenched his hand on the ring he had bought for her.

"Firing solution on second enemy ship—RED for *Shrike*—"

"Hold!"

"Got it!" That from *Navarino*, whose clear shot at the second enemy ship had blown it as cleanly as their own had the first.

"Third target running—headed for jump point—"

That would be the job of *Applejack*, the cleanup light cruiser . . . Barin watched scan intently as the enemy ship headed toward the minefield *Applejack* had spent the past six hours sowing around the jump corridor.

❖   ❖   ❖

Hazel had seen the bulkhead peeling back, and felt a moment of complete panic—not now, not after all they'd been through—but someone's gloved hand caught the bar at the end of her gurney, and wrapped a quick line to it, then secured the line to a stick-patch. But—when she looked—she could see a tumbling, receding shape that had to be Brun and someone holding her.

She said nothing—there was enough noise on the comunits anyway—until someone asked if she was all right.

"Yes, but—what about Brun?"

"We'll get them back," a reassuring voice said. "Don't you worry. And we'll get you into a shuttle."

"Yeah, before this place breaks up completely . . ."

She was passed from one set of hands to another—each carefully attaching her to another set of secured lines before releasing the first—and then finally through the cargo hatch of a shuttle. People moved past her, all busy, all doing something she hoped would rescue Brun. She had heard of Fleet SAR all her life, but she'd never seen it in action. She'd had no idea that SAR teams wore black p-suits that looked like space armor from storycubes. She'd expected them to wear bright colors with flashers or something to make them easier to see.

"Hey there—can you tell us your name again?" That was a blonde woman with sleepy green eyes.

"Hazel Takeris," Hazel said. "Of the *Elias Madero*." Her throat closed on all the things she had meant to say, that she'd rehearsed in her head so many times.

"We're going after Brun now," the woman said. "There's a beacon on the officer with her—we can't lose her."

Hazel felt better, but she could sense more tension in the people around her. Something was still wrong.

"What is it?"

"Nothing to worry about," the woman said. "Only this was supposed to be a quick, simple extrication . . . and we didn't know about you—"

"I'm sorry," Hazel said automatically. The woman looked startled.

"Don't *you* be sorry. It's those idiots who planned it who need to be sorry."

The woman looked aside suddenly, and Hazel turned her head to see what it was. The cargo hatch gaped again, and three more black-suited figures swam in, pushing another, attached to Brun's gurney.

"Hatch closed," she heard through her com.

"Air up! Air up!"

"Patch it into the suit, dammit!"

Hazel could just see Brun's turquoise suit . . . surely she had air, from the suit tanks. The others cut off her view.

"Air pressure's nom," someone said.

Then they moved, coming past her with the black-suited figure. Two of them stripped off suit gloves, and opened the other's black suit with some tool—and it flipped back like a beetle's carapace. Hazel stared—it *was* space armor. Inside, a limp figure . . . she could see a pale face, slack-mouthed. Busy arms, hands—and then someone tapped her shoulder.

"You don't want to watch," the green-eyed woman said. "It gets messy. And since they're working on her, they asked me to do an initial assessment on you. Any trouble breathing?"

"No," Hazel said, "but—"

"Fine, then. You want to open your helmet? We can talk off the coms that way, save interference."

Hazel realized she could reach up and open her faceplate. The woman had opened hers, as well, and was folding back her gloves.

"You got any broken bones you know of?"

"No . . . is Brun all right?"

"She's fine—she's got her own team working on her."

"But who was that—"

"Lieutenant Suiza—just a little hypoxia, don't fret." She wished people would quit telling her not to worry. She glared at the green-eyed woman.

"I'm not a child, you know."

"You sure look like one."

"Well, I'm . . ." She wasn't even sure how old she was. How long had she been a captive? At least a year, because Brun had those babies. "I'm seventeen," she said.

"Mm. Well, I'm thirty-eight, and my name is Methlin Meharry. Want to tell me how you got away?"

"I was coming back from market—" Hazel began, and she'd gotten as far as cutting off their hair with the long knives when she heard someone working on the officer—on Lieutenant Suiza—let out a happy *Yes!*

"She coming around?" Meharry asked.

"Any minute now." One of the others came over to Hazel.

"All right—let us professionals at her." And to Hazel, "Let's get you out of that p-suit and see what shape you're in."

"You be gentle now," Meharry said.

"You should talk," the medic said, without rancor. "Considering your rep."

"I could get out of this myself—" Hazel started to

say, as the medic reached through the sleeves to unfasten her p-suit.

"Yes, but we want you in the tent in case the shuttle has pressure problems . . . unlikely but it's a zoo out there." The medic peeled back her pressure suit section by section; Hazel heard exclamations from those working on Brun and craned her head, trying to see, just as her attendant peeled the leg sections of the suit and the clothes underneath. "My God—what did they do to them!"

"I think it was the horses," Hazel said. "We rode horses all night."

"Horses! We send a task force halfway across the cluster, and they're getting you out on *horses*?"

"It makes you really sore," Hazel said. "And the clothes were stiff."

"Barbarians," someone muttered. "Should have spaced the lot of 'em."

Shrike scooped up the shuttle, and medics moved Hazel and Brun into the spacious sickbay. "Regen for you," said the green-coated medic when he'd peeled away the gurney's tent and draped a gown over her. "You'll feel a lot better after an hour—maybe two—in the tank." Hazel wasn't about to argue; she saw that Brun was being led to the other tank. She settled into the warm, soothing liquid, and dozed off.

✧　　✧　　✧

Brun was furious. They were talking over her head again, as if she weren't there, and no one had thought to get her a voice synthesizer. Three hours aboard, and they continued to treat her like an idiot child.

"She'll need another five hours of regen for those abrasions," one medic said. "And I still think we should order a parasite scan."

Brun reached out, caught hold of his uniform, and yanked hard. He staggered, then turned.

"Are you all right? All right?" He spoke a little too slowly, a little too loudly, as if she might be a deaf child.

Brun shook her head and mimed writing a message.

"Oh—you want to say something?"

Yes, she wanted to say something, something very firm. Instead, she smiled and nodded, and mimed writing again. Finally, someone handed her a pad.

HOW'S ESMAY? she wrote.

"Lieutenant Suiza is fine," the medic said. "Don't worry—you won't have to see her again. It was strictly against orders—"

What were they talking about? Brun grabbed the pad back. I WANT TO SEE HER.

"That's not a good idea," the medic said. "You weren't supposed to see her at all. We understand how traumatic it was—"

Brun underlined the words I WANT TO SEE HER and shoved the pad back at him.

"But it was all a mistake . . ."

SAVING MY LIFE WAS A MISTAKE? That came out in a scrawl he had to struggle to read.

"No—her being involved. Your father said, under no circumstances should you have to see her, after what she said about you."

Her father. Rage boiled up. Carefully calm, she printed her message. I DON'T CARE WHAT MY FATHER SAID. ESMAY SAVED MY LIFE. I WANT TO SEE HER. NOW.

"But you can't—you need more time in regen— and besides, what will the captain say?"

She could care what the captain said. Or her father. She had not come back to the real world to be told she couldn't talk to anyone she pleased, even if she couldn't talk.

"She's getting agitated," someone else said. "Heart rate up, respirations—maybe we should sedate—"

Brun erupted from the bed, ignoring the remaining twinges, and slapping aside the tentative grab of the first medic. The other one picked up the injector of sedative spray. With a kick she had practiced in secret for months, she smashed it from his hand; it dribbled down the bulkhead. She pointed a minatory finger at the medics, picked up the pad, and tapped the word NOW.

"Good to see you up," came a lazy voice from the entrance. Brun poised to attack, then realized it was Methlin Meharry, whose expression didn't vary as she took in the two medics, the smashed injector, and Brun with the short hospital gown flapping about her thighs. "Giving you trouble, were they? All right boys—out." The medics looked at each other, and Meharry, and wisely chose withdrawal.

Brun held out the pad.

"You want to see Suiza? Why, girl? I thought she trashed you at Copper Mountain, upset you so you ran away home."

Brun shrugged—it doesn't matter—and tapped the pad again.

"Yeah, well, she did save your life, and you saved hers I guess. Or helped. Your father thought seeing her would be a terrible trauma. If it's not—well, it's your decision." Meharry's mouth quirked. "You might want to put on some clothes, though . . . unless you want her to come down here."

Brun didn't. She was more than ready to get out of sickbay. Resourceful as ever, Meharry quickly found Brun a shipsuit that almost fit. It wasn't quite as soft as the shipsuits Hazel had found on the station, but it fitted her better.

"Now—it's customary to make a courtesy call on the captain. Since the captain told the lieutenant not to let you know she was there, and she did—this could be a bit tricky. Just so you know."

Meharry led her through a maze of corridors to

a door that had LT. E. SUIZA, EXECUTIVE OFFICER on it. Meharry knocked.

"Come in," Esmay said. When Meharry opened the door, she was half-sitting on her bunk; she looked pale and tired.

"Brun wants to see you," Meharry said. "She kind of insisted, when the medics wanted to sedate her . . ."

Brun moved past Meharry, and held out the pad on which she'd already scribbled THANK YOU.

Esmay stared at it, then at Brun, brow furrowed. "They don't have a speaker device for you! What are they thinking of!" Esmay looked almost as angry as Brun felt.

THEY'RE WORRIED ABOUT MY STABILITY.

"They ought to be worried about your voice, dammit! This is ridiculous. That should be the first thing—"

THANK YOU, Brun wrote again. MY FATHER GAVE YOU TROUBLE?

Esmay flushed. "They got the tape of what I said to you that night—and I'm sorry, it really was insulting—"

YOU WERE RIGHT.

"No—I was angry, that's what. I thought you were stealing Barin—as if he were my property, which is disgusting of me, but that's how I felt."

YOU LOVE BARIN? That was something that hadn't occurred to her, even in the months of captivity. Esmay, the cool professional, in love?

"Yes. And you had so much more time, and when I was working I knew you were spending time with him . . ."

TALKING ABOUT YOU.

"I didn't know that. Anyway—I said I'm sorry. But they think—they thought—I had something against you and your family. Your father didn't want me involved in the planning, or with the mission. But that's not the important thing—the important thing is getting you a voice." Esmay thought for a moment. Meharry. Meharry knew everyone and everything, as near as Esmay could tell. If that device on the station had survived, Meharry would know where it was, and if it hadn't, she'd know what would work.

"A speech synthesizer? Sure—I can get you one. Just don't ask where."

Ten minutes later, a young pivot, so new he squeaked, delivered a briefcase-sized box that flipped open to reveal a keyboard of preprogrammed speech tags as well as direct input.

"Here," Esmay said. "Try this."

Brun peered at it, and began tapping the buttons. "It looks like the one Lady Cecelia used on Rotterdam," said a deep bass voice.

Esmay jumped, then started laughing.

"Let's see what this one sounds like," the box said, this time in a soprano.

"I didn't like that one, let's try this . . ." came out in a mezzo; Brun shrugged. "I'll keep this one."

"I wonder why they didn't do this first," Esmay said. "If they had a speech synthesizer aboard, why not give it to you right away."

"Arrogance," Brun keyed in. "They knew what I needed; why ask me?"

"Brun, I'm so sorry—"

"Don't waste time. Thank you. You saved my life."

Esmay was trying to think how to answer that one when Brun's next message came out.

"And by the way, who's doing your hair? It looks good even after being squashed in a suit."

"Sera Saenz—Marta Saenz—took me to this place, Afino's."

"Raffaele's Aunt Marta? You must have impressed her if she took you there. Good for you."

Esmay could not believe how fast Brun was keying in the words, as if she'd used one of these for years. "You're good with that thing," she said.

"Practice," Brun keyed. "With Cecelia. And you cannot know how good it feels. Now—what's going on with Fleet and the planet? Hazel wants to get the other kids out."

"And your babies," Esmay said. "Your father's adamant about that: he's not leaving his grandchildren there."

"He can have them." Brun's expression dared Esmay to question that, and she didn't.

"I don't know what the whole situation is," Esmay said. "Because, since I'm in disgrace for letting you know I was here, they won't tell me. You're on a search-and-rescue ship; there's a task force with us, but what we're doing is microjumping around keeping out of the way of the Militia warships."

"Who can I talk to?" Brun keyed. "Who's giving the orders?"

"On this ship, Captain Solis. For the task force, Admiral Serrano."

"Good. I need to talk to her."

"Admiral Serrano?" Esmay remembered in time that Brun already knew the admiral . . . she might in fact listen. "I can get you as far as Captain Solis, but there's a blackout on communications with the task force."

"Captain Solis first," Brun keyed in. Esmay nodded and led the way without another word. Brun glanced at Esmay. Besides the more effective haircut, there was something else different. She realized, as Esmay led her through the ship and she saw others defer to her, that Esmay might indeed be in disgrace but she was far more than Brun had imagined. This was what she'd been like at Xavier, or on *Koskiusko*? Her own idiocy struck her again, the way she had condescended to this woman, the way she had assumed that Esmay was no more than any other student, no more than, for instance, herself. That man in the combat veterans' bar had been right—she had not understood at all.

They paused at a cross-corridor while what looked to Brun like huge people in armor moved past.

"Feeling better, Lieutenant?" one of them asked.

"Fine, thanks," Esmay said. She turned to Brun. "They were on the team that got you out."

"Thank you," Brun keyed quickly. She hit the controls to save that phrase; she was going to need it a lot.

Captain Solis stood as Brun came in and reached to shake her hand. "We are so glad to have you back!"

"I'm glad to be back." Brun had anticipated the need for that phrase, and had it loaded.

"Your father did not want you bothered by Lieutenant Suiza, but I understand that you wanted to see her—?"

"Yes." This had to be done word by word, carefully, and Brun took her time. "I wanted to apologize to her for my behavior on Copper Mountain. It was made clear to me during my captivity just how badly I had misjudged her. And I wanted to express my profound gratitude for her efforts on my behalf."

"You don't know most of it," Captain Solis said. "She is the one who insisted that you were probably still alive after your escape shuttle blew up—that you could have engineered that as a decoy—and said we had to go find you." He spared Esmay a glance that Brun could tell was more approving than usual. "I could almost change my mind."

"I changed mine," Brun keyed in.

"Well, now that we've got you and the other— Hazel Takeris, is that her name?—we can jump safely back to the task force and get out of here with no more disruption."

"No." Brun keyed, and switched to the masculine voice output for emphasis.

Captain Solis jumped; she bit back a grin. It would not do to laugh at the man. "But—what—?"

"We must get the other children," Brun keyed. "From the ship Hazel was on."

"I don't see how," Captain Solis began.

"We must," Brun said.

"But Hazel said they were safe—that they had adjusted to their new family—"

"We cannot leave little girls, Familias citizens by birth, to be brought up in a society where they can be muted like me for saying the wrong thing."

Solis looked at her. "You're naturally overwrought," he began.

Brun stabbed at the keyboard with such emphasis that his voice trailed away, and he waited. "I am tired, sore, hungry, and extremely tired of having no voice, but I am not overwrought. Could you define the right amount of 'wrought' for someone in my position? Those children were stolen from their families—their parents were murdered horribly—and they're in the control of people who were willing to kidnap, rape, and abuse me. How dare you suggest that they are safe enough where they are?"

"Sera—it's not my decision. It will be the admiral's, if she can make it without authorization from the Grand Council, which I doubt."

"Then I will see the admiral," Brun said.

"It will be some time before we can rendezvous safely," Solis said. He gave Esmay a long look. "And for the time being, Lieutenant, could you find quarters for our guest? I know we're crowded with extra crew, not to mention prisoners—"

"Yes, sir," Esmay said.

"Prisoners." That came out in a flat baritone, after they'd left the bridge.

"Two groups," Esmay said. "Three different shuttle loads came up to the station after you; one blew itself up, but we caught two."

She wanted to see them. She wanted to let them

see her, free and healthy and—no. She would get her voice back first, and then she would see them.

"Something to eat?" she keyed.

"Right away," Esmay said, and led her to the wardroom. Brun sat revelling in food which someone else had cooked—flavors she was used to, condiments she liked, anything she chose to drink, while watching Esmay covertly. What *had* Afino's done to her hair? And for that matter, what could she do about her own hair, which she'd hacked off so blindly with a knife?

Several days later, with her hair once more a riot of tousled curls, thanks to the crew's barber, she was ready to tackle Admiral Serrano.

"You are coming with me," Brun said. "I need you; I trust you."

"You could take Meharry—"

"Methlin is a dear person . . ." Esmay blinked, imagining what the redoubtable Meharry would think to hear herself so described. "But she is not you. I need you."

"I'm the executive officer; I can't just leave the ship."

"Well, then, the admiral can come here. Which do you think she'd like least?"

Put like that, there was no question. Esmay tracked down Captain Solis and received permission to accompany Brun to the flagship.

"And it has not escaped my notice," Solis said, "that almost two years without a voice has not begun to stop that young woman giving orders. We had better get her commissioned, so at least it's legal."

❖   ❖   ❖

Our Texas, Ranger Bowie's Household

Prima had known, from the beginning, that this was big trouble coming. She could hardly believe Patience had run off—and in fact it seemed she had been abducted. That happened sometimes, girls stolen away, but usually no one would bother a Ranger's household. And the man had said, loud enough to be heard, that he had business with Mitch.

She hadn't wanted to tell Mitch until she knew for sure what had happened. Mitch was at a meeting, an important meeting. But his younger brother Jed had stopped by, as he often did, and when Tertia came in to report that Patience had still not come home, he took it upon himself to find Mitch. He liked to give orders, Jed did, and Prima knew that his ambitions went beyond being a Ranger's brother. He wanted that star for himself, and Mitch couldn't see any danger in it.

And then Mitch had come home, in a rage with her for not supervising the girl better; it seemed the woman who'd been captured at the same time as Patience had disappeared from the Crockett Street Nursery. He'd called the older boys and they'd all gone out to search, and he'd sent for the parson to come and preach at her and the women all afternoon.

It was more than a nuisance; it was baking day, and they had to leave the dough rising to sit in silent rows and listen to Parson Wells lecture them on their laziness and sinfulness. Prima kept her eyes down, respectfully, but she did think it was a shame and a nuisance, to stop hard-working women in their work and make them listen to a scolding about their laziness. And he would go on and on about their sins tainting their children. Prima had trouble with that bit of doctrine: if, hard as she tried, her faults had made poor Sammie a cripple, and Simplicity stupid, then how could the outland women—who had arrived after lives of sin and blasphemy—bear such beautiful, healthy children?

Mitch had come home late that night, having found

not sight nor word of Patience . . . or, presumably, the other woman, the yellow-haired one. Prima wanted to ask about the yellow-hair's babies, but she knew better. He was in no mood to tolerate any forwardness, even from her. She set the house in order, and waited by the women's door, but he never came to her. Early the next morning, she heard him leave the house; when she peeked, Jed was with him. She had hardly slept. She heard the roar of a departing shuttle from the spaceport, and sometime later, another, and another.

A few hours later, a tumult from the boys' section drew her to its entrance. She could hear their tutor hollering at them, trying to quiet them . . . and then Randy, Tertia's youngest boy, shot out the door with a clatter of sandaled feet.

"Daddy's dead!" he was screaming, at the top of his lungs. Prima caught him. "Lemme go! Lemme go!" He flailed at her.

The tutor followed close behind. "Prima—put him down."

The tutor, though a man, was not Mitch, and she dared look at his face, pale as whey. "What is it?" she asked.

"That abomination," he said, through clenched teeth. "She stole a shuttle, and tried to escape. Ranger Bowie and others went after her; there's been—" Light stabbed through the windows, a quick shocking flash of blue-white. Prima whirled, suddenly aware of her heart knocking at her ribs.

The tutor had opened the window and peered out and up. Prima followed him. Outside, cars had stopped cantways, and men were looking up. Prima dared a look into the sky, and saw only patches of blue between white clouds. Ordinary. Unthreatening.

"I want to see the newsvid," she said to the tutor, and walked into the boys' part of the house without waiting for his permission.

CHAPTER TWENTY-THREE

The newsvid had two excited men yelling into the vid pickup. Prima could hardly make out what they were saying. Escape, pursuit, invasion . . . invasion? Who could be invading them? And why? Mobilization, one of the men said.

"What is it?" she asked again. The older boys were already moving toward their gunboxes.

"It's the end of the world," one of them said. Daniel, she thought. Secunda's third.

"Don't be silly," another said. "It's the heathen, come to try to enforce their dirty ways on us."

"Why?" Prima asked. In all her years, no one had ever bothered Our Texas, and she saw no reason why anyone would.

"Don't worry," Daniel said, patting her shoulder. "We'll protect you. Now you get on back to the women's side, and keep order."

Prima turned to go, still unsure what had happened, and what it could mean. In the kitchen, Secunda and Tertia were quarrelling over the meaning of the bright light, and both turned to her for an answer. "I don't know," she said. Who could know?

Temptation tickled her . . . no, she dared not risk her soul asking an outlander such questions, but . . . she made up her mind, and went out to the weaving shed.

"Miriam!" The outlander woman turned from her loom. Her face was tight with tension; she must have seen the light too. "Do you know what that light was?"

Miriam nodded.

"Was it from space? From ships?" Another nod, this time with a big grin, a triumphant grin. Miriam mimed a rocket taking off, shooting another rocket.

Invaders. There *were* invaders. "Who?" Prima asked the air. "Who would do this? Why?" She jumped when Miriam touched her arm. "What?" Miriam mimed writing. Writing . . . Mitch, she recalled, had threatened to take Miriam's right hand if she didn't quit writing; she'd hoped it wouldn't be necessary because the woman was a gifted weaver. Now she led Miriam to the kitchen and gave her the pad of paper and marker they used for keeping accounts.

Light is weapon Miriam wrote. Prima squinted, trying to read as fast as Miriam wrote. Weapon, that was clear. *Ionizing atmospheric gases.* That made no sense; she didn't know any of the words. Miriam, glancing up, seemed to guess that. *Made air glow* she wrote. Well, but how could air glow? Air was just air, clear unless there was smoke in it.

"Who?" Prima asked again. "Who would attack us?"

Miriam scribbled rapidly. *Guerni Republic, Emerald Worlds, Baltic Confederation, Familias Regnant . . .* Prima had no idea what those were, besides godless outlanders. *Battle in space, not attacking here. Someone you stole from.*

"We don't steal!" Prima said, narrowly stopping herself from slapping Miriam. "We are not thieves."

Stole me, Miriam wrote. *Stole children, women, killed men.*

"That's not true. You're lying. The children had no families, and you women were rescued from a life of degradation . . ." But her voice wavered. Miriam had been here for more than ten years; if she still believed she had been stolen, if she had not understood . . .

I can prove it. Miriam wrote. *Get to a transmitter—call—find out who that is, and ask them.*

"I can't do that! You know it's forbidden. Women do not use men's technology." But . . . if she could find out. If it was possible . . .

I know how. Miriam wrote. *It's easy.*

Forbidden knowledge. Prima glanced around, realized that the others in the kitchen were staring, trying to understand this conversation. "I—I don't know where such machines are," she said finally.

I know how to find them.

"How?"

Tall thin things sticking out the top of buildings.

"It's still forbidden." Thinking of looking up at tall thin things made her dizzy in her mind. Thinking of touching men's machines was worse.

We can look at the newsfeed. She must mean the machine kept for the women to watch religious broadcasts.

"How? I don't know how to set it up."

I do.

Miriam went to the closet where it was kept, and pulled it out. More than a little afraid, Prima helped her pull it, on its cart, into the back kitchen where there were extra electrical outlets. Miriam uncoiled the nest of wires that Mitch had left, and plugged this one and that one into the back and sides of the machine. Prima had no idea which went where, and kept expecting the machine to burst into flame. Instead, it made a faint frying noise and then a picture appeared, the same background as the one she'd seen on the boys' side. This time only one man looked back at her. Miriam kept tinkering with the machine, and suddenly it had a different picture, crisp and colorful . . . men in strange uniforms, very odd-looking.

Prima felt faint suddenly. Some of those odd-looking men in uniform were women. The view narrowed, concentrating on one of them, a woman with dark skin and eyes, and silver hair. Miriam touched one of the machine's front controls, and a voice spoke.

"—Return of children captured with the piracy of the ship *Elias Madero*. Return of infant children born to Sera Meager during captivity—" Prima felt behind her for the table and leaned against it. That yellow-hair . . . this must be about that yellow-hair. "—Ships are destroyed; your orbital station is destroyed. To avoid more damage and loss of life, you are urged to cooperate with us. This message is being transmitted on loop until we receive a reply."

Ships destroyed. Mitch's ship? Was he dead? Prima felt the weight of that loss. If Mitch was dead, someone else would be Ranger Bowie, and she—she and the rest of Mitch's wives and children—would belong to Mitch's brother Jed, if he lived. Jeffry, if Jed had died.

The sound of gunfire in the street brought her upright. "Turn that off," she said to Miriam. "Before we get in trouble. Put a—a tablecloth over it." She knew she should put it away, but if Mitch was not dead there might be more news of him, and she could not bring herself to lose that connection. "It's past lunchtime, and we haven't served," she scolded, brushing past the questions the other women wanted to ask. "Feed the children, come on now. Feed them, put the babies down for naps. What would Ranger Bowie think, if he saw us like this!"

They were washing up when Jed arrived, white-faced and barely coherent. "Prima—it's terrible news. Mitch is dead or captive; all the Rangers are. Get me food, woman! I have to—somebody has to take over—" Prima scurried out, driving the maids away; she would serve him herself. Safer. When she had piled his plate with roast and potatoes and young beans, she summoned Miriam.

"Turn it on, but keep it low. Be ready to hide it again."

The next time she came through the kitchen, all the grown women were clustered around it. This time the face on the screen was a woman in a decent dress—or at least a dress. Dark hair streaked silver—an older woman.

"She says the yellow-hair was a big man's daughter."

Oh, Mitch . . . ambition diggeth pits for the unwary . . .

"She says our men murdered people and stole things . . ."

"That's a lie," Prima said automatically. Then she gasped as the screen showed Mitch—sitting miserably at a table, not eating, with men she knew around him. Terry . . . John . . . and there was the Captain, Ranger Travis.

"—Rangers are either captive, or dead." That was the voice from the machine, with its curious clipped way of speaking. The way Patience had spoken at first.

"Prima! Get out here!" That was Jed, bellowing as usual. Prima scurried away, resenting once again that part of Scripture which would give her to this man just because he was Mitch's brother.

❖   ❖   ❖

Mitch Pardue came to in the belly of the whale, a vast shadowy cold cavern as it seemed. He blinked, and the threatening curves around him resolved into something he recognized instantly as part of a spaceship. Not the shuttle, though, and not the space station he'd been on. He looked around cautiously. There on the deck nearby were a score of his fellows, most still slackly unconsious, one or two staring at him with expressions of fright.

Where were they? He pushed himself up, and only then gathered his wits sufficiently to realize that he was dressed in a skimpy shipsuit with no boots, with plastic shackles on his ankles. He felt his heart pounding before he identified the fright that shook him. He cleared his throat . . . and stiffened in outrage and terror. No. It could not be. He tried again, forming a soft word with his mouth, and no sound emerged.

He looked around frantically—on one side of him the bodies of his own crew, men he knew well, now more of them awake, and mouthing silent protests. On the other, another clump of men he knew—Pete Robertson's bunch, he was sure—beginning to stir, to attempt speech, to show in their faces the panic and rage he felt in his own.

The troops that entered sometime later did not surprise him; he braced himself for torture or death. But after checking his shackles, they simply stood by the bulkhead, alert and dangerous, waiting for whatever would come.

He should rally his men and jump them. He knew that, as he knew every word of Scripture he'd been told to memorize. But lying there, mute and hobbled, he couldn't figure out how. He turned his head again, and saw Terry watching him. *Get ready* he tried to mouth. Terry just stared at him blankly. He nodded, sharply; Terry shook his head.

The women had been able to lipspeak to each other; some of them had a hand language too. Men should be able—he tried again, this time looking past Terry to Bob. Bob mouthed something he couldn't figure out in return, and looked scared. Mitch was plumb disgusted. Giving up this way, what were they? He rolled over to attempt something with Pete, but one of the guards had moved, and was making very clear gestures with his weapon. Mitch looked closer. *Her* weapon.

"Stop it," she said. "No whispering, no mouthing." She had a clear light voice that didn't sound dangerous, but the weapon in her hands was rock-steady. And he didn't doubt the others would get him if he tried anything with her. Down the row someone made a kiss sound, a long-drawn smooch. Mitch looked up into dark eyes like chips of obsidian and didn't make a sound. Another of the soldiers walked up to the smoocher and deliberately kicked him in the balls. He could not scream, but the rasping agonized breath was loud enough.

Another group of soldiers arrived; Mitch found himself suspended between two in space armor, propelled down a corridor to a large head. "Use it," said a voice from inside the helmet. Man's or woman's, he couldn't tell, but he had urgent need. So did the others, alongside him. From there, they were taken to a compartment with a long table set with mealpacks.

He shouldn't eat. He should starve himself, rather than eat with these infidels. He tried to signal his team, figure out a way to stop them, but four of them were already tearing open the mealpacks. He sat rigid, jaws clamped on his hunger, while the others ate. After a short time, two of them dragged him away to a small cubicle where he faced someone in a fancier uniform.

"You won't eat?"

He shook his head.

"We'll feed you, then." And in the humiliating struggle that followed, strong arms held him down while he was force-fed some thick liquid.

"You do not have the option of suicide, or resistance," the officer said coolly, when they dragged him back to the same cubicle. "You will cooperate with us, because you can do nothing else." After that, they took him back to a different compartment, a small solitary cell.

Mitch had, once or twice in his young days, travelled under a fake identity on Familias-registry ships; he had seen a few of the big commercial orbital stations. But nothing he had seen was like the interior of an elite warship. He wanted to despise it; he wanted to sneer at the exaggerated courtesy, the grave ritual, the polish and precision . . . but without a voice he could do nothing but experience it, and in that experience realize how foolishly he had misjudged his opponents. He had called down God's wrath on his people, and here was the instrument of that doom: sleek, shining, perfectly disciplined, and utterly deadly.

He wanted to defy them. He wanted to hate and defy and condemn and resist to his last breath, but he kept thinking of Prima and Secunda . . . of the smell of bread from the ovens, the bright flowers in the gardens, of the sound of children's voices echoing through the halls, the slap of the boys' sandals when they ran; the clump of the bigger boys learning to walk in boots, the soft patter of girls' feet . . . the feel of their soft little arms around his neck, the smell of their hair. His wives. His children. Who would be someone else's, who might be forced out to work in someone's fields, who might be crying, unprotected, afraid, because of him—he woke sweating, his own eyes burning.

In the empty hours, staring at the blank walls, he saw deeper into himself than he ever had, or wanted to. God was punishing him for his ambitions. That was only right, if he had done wrong. But his family—why should they be punished? His appetite disappeared, this time from no rebellion but sadness . . . and his captors did not force him to eat, this time.

Someone knocked, then entered. A man—he was grateful for that, at least—but in a uniform he had not seen before.

"I'm a chaplain," the man said. "My own beliefs are not yours, but I am assigned to help members of Fleet with matters of belief and conscience." He paused, paged through a small booklet. "I think your nearest word for me would be *pastor* or *preacher*. You are being returned to Familias space for trial, and our laws require that anyone facing charges of such gravity must be granted spiritual consolation."

What spiritual consolation could an unbeliever, a heathen, give him? Mitch turned his face to the bulkhead.

❖   ❖   ❖

"We have only the smallest chance to get those children out alive," Waltraude said. "I know you want nothing to do with this Ranger Bowie—but unless he tells his wife to give them up, she won't. And he is the only one who can influence his brother, who has now inherited responsibility for his wives and children."

"But it's ridiculous! Why can't we talk to her?" Admiral Serrano said.

"I see no reason to negotiate with him—he's our prisoner; he's going to get a good, quick, legal trial and the death sentence—"

"Do you want those children? Their families do. Their families will want to know why all these lives were expended for the Speaker's daughter . . . and children of their own family left in slavery."

"Oh—all right."

❖   ❖   ❖

Mitch had not been to the bridge of a warship of this size; he was almost drawn out of his misery by the size, the complexity, the implications of power.

His guards led him before a woman—a woman in night-dark uniform, with insignia that he recognized as an admiral's rank, and bright-colored ribbons on her chest. And he stood before her, barefoot and

voiceless, and wanted to see in her the very image
of Satan . . . but could not.

"You have a choice, Ranger Bowie," she said, in
the quick speech of these people. "Your former
prisoner, Hazel Takeris, insists that you truly love your
wives and children."

He nodded.

"We are going to retrieve the other children you
stole from the *Elias Madero* when you murdered their
parents. However, your—the other men, on the
surface—show no signs of cooperating with us. We
are concerned that harm might come to your wives
and your children, if they attempt to interfere with
us . . . and we wish no harm to them. We want no
child hurt, not so much as scratched. Do you
understand?"

He nodded again, though he wasn't sure he
believed it.

"We do not make war on children . . . though you
did. But we will have those children returned to their
families, whatever it takes, and that might endanger
other innocents. So—here is your choice. We can
restore your voice, for you to transmit a command
to your family, to release those children. Or, if you
refuse, you can remain mute until your trial—however
long that might be."

He might talk again? He might have a man's voice
again? He could hardly believe it—but all around, he
saw men and women listening as if they believed it.

"Our landing craft are ready to launch," the admiral
said. "If they are fired on, they will return fire. If
they are obstructed, they will fight through . . . and
your people, sir, have nothing capable of resisting
them. So it rests with you, how this will be." She
paused, then went on. "Will you give these orders,
or not?"

It was cooperating with the devil, to take a woman's
orders—a woman soldier, an abomination of

abominations. For a moment he thought of the weapons hidden in the city, the chance that the other men might be able to launch them. Yet—he could almost feel against his cheek the soft cheeks of his daughters, could almost hear his children's laughter. Kill them? Put them at risk? He had never killed a child in his life—he could not—but these people could, or said they could . . .

He nodded.

"You will. Good. Take him to sickbay, and have the treatment reversed, then bring him back to the bridge."

He was a traitor, a backslider . . . all the way to sickbay, he trembled with the conflict inside. His guards said nothing to him, guiding him along with impersonal efficiency.

"We have to put you to sleep briefly," the medic explained. "Just long enough to relax the throat muscles—"

He woke as from a moment of inattention, and felt a lump in his throat. When he cleared it—he could hear it. "I—can—talk . . ."

"Not to me, you can't," said one of his guards. "You can say what the admiral says you can say. Now come along."

He sat where they told him to sit, and faced the little blinking light that was a video pickup, and though his voice trembled at first, it steadied as he went along.

"Jed, you listen to me. This is Mitch, and yes, I'm a prisoner, but that doesn't matter. I want you to let the people that are landing take those outlander children with them. Prima knows which four. And send to Crockett Street Nursery for those twins, the yellow-haired sl—woman's twins. I want all six of 'em released to the people that are comin' for 'em. Prima, you get those children dressed, now . . ."

"Signal coming up, Admiral—"

"Let's see it—"

It was a vid, from his home: Jed, looking angry, with Prima, well behind him, hands clasped respectfully in front of her. They were in the small living room, the one where he'd met the others so often, with the fireplace at one end and the conference table at the other.

"Mitch, I don't believe it's you, or they've drugged you, or somethin'. It's some kind of trick. An' I'm head of the family now, and I'm not about to let any children of this house into the hands of those—those godless scum!"

Mitch felt the sweat spring out on his face, his hands. "Jed, you have to. They're comin' anyway—if you cause 'em trouble, they'll be more people dead. Children dead, most likely—"

"Then they'll go to the Lord. I'm not—"

Behind Jed, Prima had moved. Without looking up to face the vid pickup, she had stretched out her hand and touched the fireplace poker in its stand. Mitch's breath caught in his throat.

"—Not going to let the honor of our name be smirched because you got yourself caught like a weakling—"

Prima held the poker . . . she held it easily, in a grip strengthened by kneading bread dough, wringing out wet wash, lifting babies. He knew the strength of those massive shoulders, those arms.

"Jed, please . . . don't risk the other children for those few—it's not worth it—please, Jed, let 'em go." Before worse happened, before Prima did something he would have to notice. He struggled to keep his gaze on Jed.

"If they want a fight, they can have it!" Jed looked at much triumphant as angry. "The preachers have already told us to gather and fight—"

"The preachers—!" Mitch could hardly keep

talking, as he watched Prima walk softly, softly on her bare feet, coming up behind Jed, raising the poker. Horror and hope warred in him—that any woman would strike a man, let alone strike without warning—that maybe, without Jed, the children would be safe . . .

"You could stop them," Mitch went on, struggling to make Jed understand, Jed who had never understood anything he didn't want to. He should warn Jed; he should admonish Prima. But the children— "You could convince them, if you'd try—" And on the screen Prima looked up at last, straight into the vid pickup, and smiled. "Do it!" Mitch said, not entirely sure who he was talking to, and as Jed opened his mouth, the poker slammed into his head with all the strength of Prima's shoulders and arms . . . and blood spurted up, and she hit him again, and again, on the way down . . .

"Prima!" he yelled, and his throat cramped, closing on more. She looked up at the vid again, her face settling into its usual calm from an emotion he had never seen before. "Don't let them hurt the children," he said; his voice creaked like that of a young rooster learning to crow. "Don't let them hurt—" His voice failed again; tears stung his eyes.

Prima's voice on the link was far steadier than his had been. "I want to see . . . what kind of people they are, you would trust with our children."

"Be careful," he managed to whisper. "Please . . ." He was pleading with a woman . . . pleading . . . and that was wrong, but his throat hurt, and his heart, and he wanted no more pain, for him or the children. The screen in front of him blanked, and then he curled around his misery like a child around a favorite toy.

❖　　❖　　❖

"I want to go," said Hazel. "I should—the children know me; they won't be as scared. Brun would go if she could." Brun was sedated, in regen after an attempt at the delicate surgery that might restore her voice. She wouldn't be out for another three days, at the soonest.

"Not a bad idea," Waltraude Meyerson said. "And I, of course."

"You! You're not only a civilian, but you have no role in this . . ."

"I'm the resident expert you brought along—I should get to see these Texas mythologists on their own turf. And I would recommend, Admiral Serrano, that you send a member of your family— perhaps that grandson who keeps hovering around looking hopeful."

"I hardly think Barin's an appropriate choice," the admiral said.

"These people care about families. If you send a family member, you are showing that you will risk family to save family. It is also as well that he is male—that will be more acceptable, as long as there are women along."

"I see. And whom else would you recommend? Do you have the entire mission plan in mind?" Sarcasm, from Admiral Serrano, affected most people like being in close proximity to a large industrial saw, but Professor Meyerson didn't flinch.

"No, that is your area of expertise. Mine is antique studies."

❖   ❖   ❖

Hovers held position above the streets, and a mobile squad kept pace with them, helmet shields down.

"Looks kind of silly," Hazel said, "with the streets empty."

"The streets wouldn't be empty if they weren't there," Barin said. His helmet informed him of the location of hotspots in the buildings; they were clustered behind every screened window niche. He hoped none of them had weapons that could penetrate their body armor . . . he hoped even more that Ranger Bowie's transmission had convinced them not to fight. Right now the Fleet forces were on Yellow Two, which meant that even if they were fired on, they were not to return fire without authorization.

Hazel pointed out the main entrance to the house, and the side street that led to the women's entrance. "I came through this door only once, when he brought me here." Barin noticed that she did not say the man's name or title. "I used that other door to take out refuse or go to the market."

"But you think we should go in here?"

"It establishes authority," Professor Meyerson said. She had elected to wear a skirt, though she agreed to wear body armor under it, which made her look considerably bulkier.

She led the way up to the door; it swung open just before she reached it. A stout woman wearing a blue dress with a wide flounced skirt glared at them. She had a flowered kerchief tied tightly around her head.

"That's Prima," Hazel said softly. "The first wife."

"Ma'am," Professor Meyerson said. "We've come for the children."

Prima yanked the door wider. "Come in. Which one of you is the yellow-hair?"

"She couldn't come," Hazel said. "She's getting medical treatment for her voice."

"She abandoned her babies—abominations like her don't deserve children," Prima said.

"Are they here?" Hazel asked.

"Yes . . . but I'm not convinced they should go . . ."

Hazel stepped forward. "Please—Prima—let the children come."

"I'm not giving those sweet girls up to some disgusting heathen," Prima said. She had the taut look of someone willing to die for her convictions.

"It's just me," Hazel said softly. "You know me; you know I'll take care of them."

"You—you traitor!" Prima's face had gone from pale to red, and tears stood in her eyes.

"No ma'am . . . but I had my family to think of—"

"We were your family—we treated you like family—"

"Yes, ma'am, you did. As well as you could. But back home—"

"And you!" Prima turned on Professor Meyerson. "You're what—a woman *soldier*! Unnatural, disgusting—"

"Actually, I'm a historian," Meyerson said. Prima looked blank. "I study Texas history."

"You—what?"

"That's right. I came to learn about you—about what you know of Texas history."

Prima looked thoroughly confused, then focussed on Barin. "And you—who are you?"

"Admiral Serrano's grandson," Barin said. Then, when Prima seemed not to understand, he said, "The woman you may have seen in transmission—dark, like me, with silver hair? She's commanding the task force."

"A *woman*? Commanding men? Nonsense. No men would obey her—"

"I do," Barin said. "Both as admiral and as my grandmother."

"Grandmother . . ." Prima shook her head. "Still . . . do any of you have a belief in God?"

"I do," Barin said. "It is not the same as yours, but in my family we have always had believers."

"Yet you are a soldier alongside women? Commanded by women?"

"Yes, sometimes."

"How can that be? God decreed that women bear no arms, that they enter into no conflicts."

"That is not the doctrine I have been taught," Barin said.

"You are a pagan who believes in many gods?"

"No, in one only."

"I do not understand." Prima looked closely into his face. "Yet I see truth in your face; you are not a liar. Tell me, are you married?"

"Not yet, ma'am, but I plan to be."

"To a . . . another of these woman soldiers?"

"Yes." If he survived this. He wished very much Esmay were with him.

"Do you swear to me, on the holy name of God, that you are taking them to their families?"

"Yes," Barin said. Prima deflated; her face creasing into tears. Barin moved nearer. "Let me tell you about their families, ma'am, so that you will understand. Brandy and Stassi—Prudence and Serenity, as you call them—have aunts and uncles. Their dead mother's sisters and brother; their father's sister. Paolo's grandfather and uncle, and Dris's aunt and uncle. We have brought recordings of them, asking for the safe return of these children."

"They are happy here," Prima said. She looked down and away; she had the look of someone who will argue to the end but knows she cannot win. "It will hurt them to move them now."

"They are happy now," Professor Meyerson said. "They are small children, and I know—Hazel told us—that you have been kind to them. But they will grow older, and you are not, and cannot, be the same as their own family. They need to know their own flesh and blood."

"They will cry," Prima said, through her own tears.

"They may," Professor Meyerson said. "They have had a difficult few years, losing their parents and then coming to such a different place, and leaving it again. They cried when they came here, didn't they? But in the end, all children cry over something, and that is not reason enough to leave wrong as it is, and good undone."

"I am undone," Prima said, folding her apron. "But I had to try—"

"You are a loving mother," Professor Meyerson said. Barin was surprised at this; he had not thought of Meyerson as having, or caring about, families. Yet her tone of absolute approval seemed to settle Prima. "I want you to see recordings of the children's families."

"I don't have to—I believe you—"

"No, but it may help you understand." She nodded to Barin, who set up the cube reader and display screen. "We have brought our own power supply, since your electrical lines carry the wrong voltage for our equipment."

"This is men's work," Prima said.

"God gave eyes to men and women," Professor Meyerson said. She put the first cube into the reader. "This is a recording of Brandy and Stassi's parents before they were killed."

On the screen, a woman with a long dark braid over her shoulder cradled a baby in her arms. "That's when Stassi was born; their mother's name was Ghirian. Her parents were from Gilmore Colony. Brandy was a year old then." A man appeared, holding an older infant in his arms. "That's their father, Vorda. He and Ghirian had been married eight years. His family had been merchant spacers for generations."

"They—were married?"

"Oh yes. And very much in love, though I understand from Hazel that you do not value romantic love between men and women."

"It doesn't last," Prima said, as if quoting. Her eyes were fixed on the screen, where the affection between mother and father, and parents and children, was obvious. "It cannot be depended on to make a strong family."

"Not alone, no. But along with honesty and courage, it's a good start."

The screen flickered, and now showed a slightly older Brandy, stacking blocks with an unsteady hand.

Prima sucked her breath through her teeth. "Boy's toys—"

"We value all the gifts God has given a child," Professor Meyerson said. "If God did not mean her to build, why would he have given her the ability? They sent this recording to her grandparents; her mother's father was a construction engineer in Gilmore. He was pleased that his granddaughter had inherited his gift." The child pushed the blocks over, gave a dimpled grin into the camera, and stood up, dancing in a circle. Then her mother came into view, carrying Stassi, now a wiggly toddler herself. She reached out and caught Brandy to her, gave her a little hug. Professor Meyerson turned up the sound of the cube reader.

"—So we've decided to take them with us. Captain Lund says that'll be fine; there are two children about the same age, and a couple of older ones. The ship has a fully equipped nursery and playroom, with all the educational materials you could hope to see, so don't worry about them falling behind. It's as safe as being onplanet—safer, in some ways. No *bugs!*" The woman grimaced. "And no weather. I know, I know— you like the changing seasons, but with these two if it's not colds in winter it's allergies in summer."

Professor Meyerson stopped the reader. "That was made just before they rejoined the *Elias Madero*, about a year before they died."

"Was there sickness on the ship after all?"

"No." Could she not know? Was it possible? She glanced at Hazel, who shook her head. "They were killed in the capture of the ship, ma'am."

"No . . . it must have been an accident. Mitch would never kill women—"

This was farther than they'd meant to go; they'd assumed the wives knew how outworld children were taken. Professor Meyerson said nothing, clearly at a loss to think how to put it. Prima blanched.

"*You* think—you believe our men killed the parents, orphaned those children on purpose? Killed *mothers*? That's why you attacked us?"

"They considered them perverts," Professor Meyerson said. "That's what was on the recordings."

"I don't believe it! You're lying! You have no proof!" She grabbed Meyerson's arm. "Do you? Does your . . . your *device* show anything like that?"

CHAPTER TWENTY-FOUR

"Heads up—" That murmur in Barin's ear got his attention away from Prima. "May be trouble on the way—some kind of gathering across town—" A tiny picture flashed on the corner of his helmet display. Someone in a bright blue bathrobe or something similar yelling at a bunch of men.

"Excuse me, ma'am," Barin said. "Do you know what this might be?" He transferred the image to the larger screen they'd been using for the cube reader.

Prima glared at him, but turned to look. Her face paled. "It's Parson Wells—"

"A parson is a religious leader," Professor Meyerson said with renewed confidence. "Amazing—look at that garment—"

"It's a cassock," Prima said.

"No, it's not a cassock," Meyerson said, as if correcting a child. "Cassocks were narrower, black, and buttoned up the front. This is the variant of academic regalia which was popular in one branch of Christianity—"

"Professor . . . I don't think that's the most important thing."

"But look at that—those men are carrying replica Bowie knives—and that looks like a replica of an actual twenty-first-century rifle—"

"Professor—we need to get the children and get out of here," Barin said. "We don't want a conflict—we want them safe—"

"Oh. Yes, of course." Meyerson flushed slightly. "Sorry. It's just—seeing things I've only read about before—it's quite exciting. I wish I had more time—"

"Not this visit," Barin said. He turned to Prima. "Please, ma'am—the children?

"Come with me, then." She was still angry, but clearly the view on the screen meant more to her than to the professor. "I want you to see where they were housed, how they were cared for, so you can tell their families—" She led the way down the corridor to the women's wing. Through windows, Barin saw a garden brilliant with flowers, centered by a fountain—then a wall, then another garden.

"The children's garden," Hazel murmured. "The little girls were allowed to run about some there." It was empty now. The scent of warm, fresh-baked bread wafted along the corridor, as Prima opened another door. "Kitchen's down there—she's taking us to the sleeping area for the youngest—"

Another courtyard, this one paved with broad stone slabs and shaded by a central tree. Prima turned, led them down a narrow exterior hall, and into a large room. Here a dozen beds were lined up along either wall. On five of the beds, children sprawled asleep.

"Here is where they slept," Prima said. "This is the quiet time after lunch, and these younglings are napping. Prudence and Serenity are too old for naps now; they'll be in the sewing parlor." She led them on, to a room where two older women and a dozen young girls from Hazel's age down were sitting, heads bent, over their sewing. Only the women looked up; the younger one stood. "It's all right, Quarta. They do have families, real families."

Now the children looked up, shyly, staring at the intruders. Barin smiled at them; he didn't want to be a frightening memory. Two of the children stared at Hazel a long moment, then one of them said, "Patience—?" softly.

"Yes," Hazel said. "I'm back. Do you remember your Uncle Stepan?" The child nodded, her face solemn.

"He wants to see you again, and so does your aunt Jas. We can go home now, Brandy."

The girl's face lit up and she dropped her sewing— then she looked cautiously at the older women.

"You may go with Patience—Hazel—now, Prudence."

The girl ran to Hazel and hugged her. "I didn't forget, I promise I didn't forget!" She leaned back, looking up at Hazel's face. "Home to the ship? Will Mama be there? Can I use the computer again? Can I have books?"

The other child, younger and shyer, had to be led from her seat . . . but when she realized she was actually leaving, she clung to Brandy's hand and smiled.

The other girls stared, faces solemn. Clearly they had no idea what was happening.

Barin glanced at Prima, hoping she would make the necessary explanation. The older woman grimaced, but complied.

"Prudence and Serenity are going back to their own families," she said. "We wish them God's blessings in their new life."

"But who will protect them?" asked one of the other girls. "Is that man their father? Their uncle? Why are those women holding weapons?"

"We will protect them," Barin said. Shocked looks

from all of them. "In our home, women can be soldiers or work on spaceships—"

"That's wrong," said one of the older girls firmly; she picked up her sewing. "It's wrong for women to meddle in men's things."

Quarta reached out and tapped the girl lightly on the head with her thimbled finger. "It's wrong for children to instruct their elders. But I believe, Faith, that you are right and these heathens will not prosper."

The boys were in the boys' wing; Prima despatched one of the other women to fetch them, while she herself led them to the nursery to pick up Brun's twins. They seemed healthy, happy babies, scooting about on the floor in a way that suggested they would soon be crawling.

"Simplicity . . ." Hazel breathed, nodding toward a young woman who sat rocking her baby. The girl looked up with a shy smile; her eyes widened when she saw the others. Hazel picked up one twin, and Prima carried the other; by the time they were back to the front hall, the boys were there, looking worried and uncertain.

"Paolo!" Brandy said. "We're going home!" She reached out to hug him, but he moved aside.

"I don't think—"

"You need to hear this, Ensign—" That in his earplug. Automatically, he switched audio to the speakers of the cube reader.

"—Satan's snares!" the man in the blue robe was saying. "God's judgement has fallen on those Rangers, and on their families, for their sins. Suffer not the wicked to prosper, nor the ungodly woman to speak—"

"He means you," Professor Meyerson said to Prima. "You're in danger now."

"We must retake the Rangers' houses, and cleanse them of the filth of contamination—destroy the infidels with holy fire—"

"Not that there's anything really to worry about," the marine major said; his voice overrode the other man's on the com. "All they've got is old-fashioned small arms and big knives. You'll be safe enough in the ground transport—"

"No," Hazel said. "They have whatever was on *Elias Madero*. They said so, when they were talking after I was captured."

"What *was* on *Elias Madero*?" Barin asked. "Ship weapons?"

"I don't know, but something bad, something they'd stolen from Fleet."

A cold wave ran down Barin's spine, as if someone had swiped along it with a piece of ice. The Guernesi had talked about arms traffickers and stolen weapons . . . and Esmay had mentioned that her captain was concerned about missing nuclear warheads.

"Major, it could be a lot worse than that—these guys may have our missing nukes."

A pause, in which the ranting voice went on about sin and defilement and tyranny. Then: "I *knew* we shouldn't have brought a Serrano along. Things always get *interesting* with a Serrano along. All right, Ensign, suppose you tell the admiral while I see what I can do to keep these guys from using whatever it is they've got."

Barin had just presence of mind to sever the connection to the cube reader's speakers, then switched channels to contact *Navarino* in orbit.

"We're on it," he was told first. "Monitoring all local transmissions . . . and we have scan working on locating any fissionables. Get those kids out now, if you can."

"I don't want to be another man's servant," Prima said suddenly. "I don't want my children brought up in another man's house. . . ."

Barin spared her a glance, but no more; he was

trying to patch into ship's scan and see if he could spot anything. Then Prima grabbed his arm.

"You—your grandmother is really the commander? And you are a man of her family—you must give me your protection."

"I'm trying," Barin said.

"I want to go," Prima said. "Me, all my children. Take me to my husband."

Barin stared at her, startled out of his immediate concern. "Take you—? You mean, to the ship?"

"Yes. That man—" She pointed at the now-blank screen. "He will give me to someone else; he may tell them to mute me just because I have talked with you—and if he knew I had killed Jed last night, he would certainly do so." Heavily, with no grace at all, she knelt in front of Barin. "I claim you as my protector, in place of my husband."

Barin glanced around; Professor Meyerson had her usual expression of alert interest, and the guards looked frankly amused. "I—let me talk to my grandmother," he said. When in doubt, ask help.

"No—it is you I claim."

"She means it," Meyerson said. "And she'll probably do something drastic if you don't agree."

And he had always wanted command track. Well, he had it now. "Fine," he said. "You're under my protection. Get your household together—"

"I can't speak for the other wives," Prima said.

"Would he give *them* away? Mute *them*?"

"Yes . . ."

"Then you jolly well *can* speak for them, and you have. Get them together; don't bring anything but warm bodies." He chinned his comunit. "Major, we're going to be bringing out the whole household. I don't even know how many—" He looked at Hazel, who shook her head. Even she didn't know. "More transports," he said, trying to think if they'd have shuttle space. If they crammed in, if nobody blew the shuttles on the way up—

People started crowding into the front hall: women, carrying babies; girls leading younger girls, boys pushing younger boys ahead of them, and one man—a narrow, angular fellow that Barin disliked on sight. They all stared at Barin and the guards, but there was less noise than he expected. The girls were all looking silently at the floor; the boys were all staring silently, with obvious awe and longing, at the soldiers' weapons.

Prima made her way through the crowd and dipped her head to him, which made Barin acutely uncomfortable.

"May I speak?"

"Yes," he said. "Of course."

"I have sent messengers to the other Rangers' houses—by the women's doors—to their ladies."

"What? No!" But even as he said it, he realized it must be so. "You think—"

"You said I could speak for the other wives. As you are my protector, so you are theirs, through me; it is your people who killed their husbands, after all."

Barin looked over the crowd that filled the hall from side to side, and was packed into the rear passages—somewhere between fifty and a hundred people, he was sure, and made the easy calculation.

"We need more shuttles," he murmured to himself. And what of the male relatives of the other Rangers, who were surely in their houses as—what was his name? That fellow Ranger Bowie had been talking to—had been here. Wouldn't they resist? He could not possibly get that many people out of a city in riot, without casualties. A child whimpered, and someone shushed it.

"What's your situation, Ensign?"

Waiting for inspiration, he could have said. Instead, he gave his report as succinctly as possible, into the hissing void of the comunit, which hissed emptily at him for long enough to make him worry. Then his grandmother's voice in his ear.

"Am I to understand that you have undertaken the evacuation to our ships of the entire civilian population of that misbegotten excuse for a city?"

"No sir: only about five hundred of them. Rangers' households."

"And upon whose authority?"

"It . . . had become a matter of family honor, sir. And Familias honor."

"I see. In that case, I suppose we are bound to support your actions, if only to have you present and accounted for when the bill comes in." His grandmother, according to rumor which he had never cared to test, could remove a laggard officer's hide in a single spiraling strip, from crown of head to tip of toe, without raising her voice. He felt dangerously close to finding out whether she would use its full powers on a callow young descendant.

"Contact!" That was the marine major in charge of the landing party. "We arc being fired upon; say again: we are receiving hostile fire."

"Engagement code: open green." His grandmother's voice when speaking to the others was flat and edgeless. "Say again: engagement code is open green."

Open green . . . new objective, new rules of engagement. She had given it to him. Barin felt a simultaneous lift and sink of the heart which almost made him sick, then he steadied to it.

"In support of Ensign Serrano and an unknown number of civilians, in the hundreds, who will be embarking for evacuation—open green."

He could hear the suck of the major's indrawn breath: the ground support more than adequate for a small party was far from adequate to protect and escort hundreds.

"Support on the way—"

He tried to calculate how long it would take, whether they would have to draw shuttles and troops from the other cruisers, from *Shrike*. Then he shook his mind away from that, which was someone else's task, to his own, which was organizing this mass into the most protectable, in the safest possible place to await what his grandmother would send.

To Prima, still waiting before him, he said, "They will send more shuttles, but it will take time. We will keep you as safe as possible, but—" But . . . if the rioters knew where the nukes were, if they could trigger them, there was no safety. "—If you know anything of outland weapons, where they are hidden, it would help."

"I know somethin'." That was a boy, perhaps thirteen, now waving his arm.

"What?" he asked.

"Daddy gave Uncle Jed his key, an' told him right afore he left to go hunt down that runaway girlie."

Key. That would be an arming key. Barin's stomach curled into a tight cold knot.

"And where's your uncle Jed, do you think?"

"On the floor in there—" Prima waved toward a door across the hall. "I couldn't think what to do, so I left him—"

"Check it," Barin said to the guards. One of them went in, shutting the door behind him on the smell of death that had puffed out into the hall.

"Looks like an arming key, on a chain around his neck. In the pockets—another key, different—looks like he has the primary for one system, and the secondary for another."

But how many systems were there, and how many men held the keys, and did they know in what order to use them? He could not count on the other Rangers' wives to poleax their husbands' relatives.

"We have two arming keys," Barin reported to the major. "From Ranger Bowie's brother. I expect each

Ranger had one or more keys and left them with a successor."

"How many troops do you have with you?"

"Only the four, as escort."

"Damn. We need to get those keys out of those houses, before we all form a pretty fireworks display. These guys are insane—you should see how they're acting out here."

Barin could hear, in the distance, noises like those on a live-fire range.

✧   ✧   ✧

Esmay Suiza, back on the bridge of *Shrike* where she belonged, discovered that everyone aboard—including Captain Solis, who had given up the last of his doubts about her intentions—was treating her with excessive care. All the special crew borrowed from *Navarino* had gone back to their ship—Meharry, she knew, would not have treated her as if she were delicate crystal, just because she'd had a spell of hypoxia. She felt quite fit for regular duty, more than willing to go back to work rather than sit by Brun's side as she dozed in regen. If she could have been on *Gyrfalcon*, with Barin, that might've been different, but soon enough they'd be back at some base, where they could finish what they'd started.

"I'm fine," she said, to the third offer of a chance to take a break. "It's my watch—" She caught the edge of a significant glance from Solis to Chief Barlow on communications. "What? Am I making mistakes?"

"No, Lieutenant, you're doing fine. It's just that there have been . . . developments."

Something cold crawled through her chest, down toward her toes. "Developments?"

"Yes . . . while you were offwatch, the landing party went down to retrieve those children . . ."

"What's wrong?"

"There've been . . . complications. And—Admiral Serrano's grandson is down there."

Barin was down there? "Why?" came out in an accusatory tone she had not meant to use to her captain. "I mean," she said, trying to recover, "I didn't think an ensign would be chosen for such a team."

"He wasn't, originally. But he's there now, and since you and he—well, so I understand—"

"Yes," Esmay said firmly. Whatever else might be secret, that wasn't any longer.

"He's managed to get himself into a right mess, and we're supposed to help him out, but I do not think you should be on the team. You've already had your stint at suited combat—"

"I'm fine," Esmay said. "I am perfectly recovered, passed by medical, one hundred and ten percent. It is of course the captain's choice—"

Solis snorted. "Don't start *that* again. One time for each trick. Besides, he had to chew his nails over your exploits on the station; it's only fair for you to reciprocate."

"War isn't about fair," Esmay muttered. To her surprise, that got a flashing smile.

"You're right there, Suiza, and if I decide your talents are needed, be sure I'll send you. If you can assure me that being in love with the Admiral's grandson won't warp your judgement or affect your performance."

"I'm not in love with the Admiral's grandson," Esmay said. "I'm in love with Barin. Sir."

Another look between captain and chief; she felt her ears heating.

"Wonderful," Solis said, in a tone that could be taken in several ways.

❖   ❖   ❖

The crackle of gunfire was nearer, as was the *crump* and crash of Fleet light-duty guns. Barin felt he should be doing *something* with his menagerie, but he couldn't figure out what. If he took them out in the street to head for the port, they could be shot; if he kept them here, they were a grand target.

"Serrano—taxi's here, room for fifteen."

That simplified things slightly. "Sera Takeris, Professor—take the *Elias Madero* children, the babies, and—let's see—" Room for fifteen adults . . . make that two adults, four small children, and—surely he could cram in ten babies. No, another adult and ten babies. "Prima, bring eight more babies, if you have them, and a reliable woman to care for them."

That turned out to be a gray-haired woman as wrinkled as dried fruit; in less than three minutes he had ten babies, the four little children, and the adults all out the door and into the first ground transport vehicle. It clanked off noisily. Barin looked up the street, to the flower-decked park at the end of it. In the middle, a great stone star-shape. The points of the star were blunted, he noted, and seemed to have bronze plaques set on them.

Suddenly as he watched a door opened across the street, and a woman scampered toward him, eyes on the ground. When she neared him she stopped short. Behind him, Prima cried out, and the woman dashed on, brushed past him, and began chattering to Prima as fast as she could.

"An' Travis's little brother, he tooken this key and he putted it into this thing, this box thing, and then Travis's Prima she whapped him with her skillet, that she was carryin' from the kitchen all full of hot grease and fried chicken, an' that box was buzzin' and buzzin' and she said come quick tell you 'cause one-a her outland mutes she wrote BAD, BAD, BAD, GET HELP QUICK in the grease."

Prima looked over her head at Barin. "It's a bomb," he said, hoping she had that much knowledge. "The keys turn it on—"

"Like a light?" she asked. "A . . . switch?"

"Yes. If they're the bombs taken from us, it takes

at least two keys to arm them . . ." But if they'd been stolen elsewhere, he didn't know. "So no one can do it by accident," he said. "The keys have to be used in the right order."

"Where are the keys?" Prima asked the woman.

"I dunno, ma'am, she only tol' me to come tell you 'cause you'd sent word we's to get out and Ranger Travis's brother he said no, and we was all whores of Satan and deserved to die anyway."

"I'll send—" Barin said, but Prima held up her hand.

"They won't trust you; they might trust my women. You want to be sure no one uses both keys?"

"Any keys, if we're not too late."

Prima despatched another cluster of women, who followed the first back across the street. The next armored transport arrived. One baby left, then half a dozen toddlers, and women to care for them, crammed into that one. He noticed that Prima had no hesitation about which to choose, and those waiting their turn made no attempt to crowd or protest. One more would make a shuttle load—the shuttle they'd come in on.

Two sets of keys he was sure—almost sure—hadn't been used. At least three more, and he would be lucky if that was all . . .

An explosion, up the street, and a gust of acrid smoke blew past, followed by the rattle of something hard on the house walls and the street. Before he could dare a cautious look, he heard the major in his earpiece.

"Something just blew in that pretty little park up the block from you, Ensign. Looks like it took the top off that decorative star—"

Barin looked out to see, through the cloud of dust and smoke, an ominous shape rising slowly from the bright red and yellow flowerbeds.

"I think we found the nukes," he said, surprised at the even tone of his voice. "They had a silo under that thing. And somebody used both keys." For all the good it would do, he gestured to Prima to have everyone get down on the floor, and then replaced and locked his own helmet. He would like to have said goodbye to Esmay, but—

"It's not moving any more," said the major. "What's your visual on it, Serrano?"

Barin peered cautiously around the doorframe, wondering only then why he'd left the door open. "It's—about thirty feet above ground, and . . . not moving."

"Waiting an ignition signal?" asked another voice in his ear.

"Don't know. Our birds would be out and flying by now," said the major. "Is this just a way to blow up the city?"

Pleasant thought. He had not thought of that, and hoped very much that hypothesis was wrong.

The first armored transport, back for another load, ground its way around the corner, as if nothing else mattered, and paused by the door. Barin shrugged: if that thing blew where it was, it wouldn't matter whether people were in the house or the transport— they'd be safely dead. He nodded at Prima, who pointed at heads until the transport driver insisted not one more would fit in.

"Shuttles incoming—" Of course, if it blew as the shuttles were landing, all those would die too. His decision to save more lives just might be the cause of losing more lives.

And he'd asked for command track.

One after another, the shuttles left shockwaves that rattled the windows and sounded like heavier guns than any that had spoken yet. He counted—two, four, six . . . how many were they sending in one flight? Nine, ten, eleven, twelve—they must have stripped every shuttle from *Navarino*, and most from the other ships as well. Thirteen . . . the rolling thunder went on, and he lost count. Well, if you were going to commit to something, you committed in strength.

Now a nearer roar, with an unpleasant groaning whine to it.

"Troop drop." He peeked out again, to see the first shuttle doing a low flyby, its drop bay open and marines falling, then steadying on their gravpads, to form up with the others. A blinding-bright bar of blue light stabbed across, toward the north. A second shuttle, this one fatter and even slower, crawled past with its cargo bay open and disgorging dark blots he hoped were more weapons and some faster transport. A distant loud rumble suggested that other shuttles were landing.

"Equipment—" On grav sleds, big enough to hold twenty armored troops . . . steering carefully down to the wide streets around the central plaza. Once they'd gone to open green rules, attempts to match technology to that of the planet had gone by the boards. Well, it would be quicker . . .

Another distant *crump*, and another, and a column of black smoke—Barin could almost feel sympathy for the men with their rifles and their long knives. A grav sled settled outside the door, and its six occupants rolled off, leaving room for the women and children.

Prima had them ready, and sent them out the door without a word. "First shuttle's off," Barin heard in his ear. So the original mission was accomplished, if they got those safely to a ship. The grav sled took off, with a whine and a whirl of dust; the next settled in its place, and Prima directed a file out to it.

"We're loading in all the streets," Barin heard. He could see, from the door, the sleds landing and taking off in three of the streets around the plaza. He glanced around, and saw that one more sled load would do it for this house. "It's your turn," he said to Prima.

"She's not goin'," a male voice said. "She deserves

to die, the murderin' whore." The scrawny man, the one he had not liked but had ignored after the first glance, had his long knife out, and held to Prima's neck. Her eyes looked at him, a look that might have been warning, but was not fear.

Then the neuro-enhanced female marine who'd been checking the back rooms broke his arm like a soda straw, smashed him into the wall, and caught Prima before she fell. Her neck bled—but not the lethal spurt of a severed artery. The marine slapped a field dressing on it. Prima looked at Barin.

"You're a good protector," she said, then quickly lowered her eyes.

"No, she is," Barin said, nodding to the marine, who pushed up her faceplate so that Prima could see. Prima stared.

"You're . . . a woman?"

"Yup. And a mother, too. Hang in there, lady, you're gonna be fine."

The last load went quickly; Barin swung aboard the grav sled and watched others loading and taking off as they swung above the city and headed for the spaceport. There he found, instead of the chaos he expected, a perfectly ordinary Landing Force Traffic Control section. "Ah—Ensign Serrano's last load, fine. Bay 23, that'll finish that shuttle load—"

Bay 23 had a shuttle labelled R.S.S. *Shrike*. Barin helped his passengers from the grav sled to the interior with its narrow benches designed for troops in armor, not civilians in dresses. He started helping them strap in, ignoring the pounding of his heart which had speeded up at the thought of seeing Esmay again.

"Barin!"

His heart stopped completely, then raced on again. She was there, alive and well, waving from the front. He nodded, grinning but speechless with feeling, and went on with his work. He felt the shuttle lurch, then the lump-lump-lump of the wheels on the runway.

"You know her?" Prima asked him, a hand on his wrist.

"Yes. She's—" How could he say it to her? He didn't even know what words would make clear to her what his culture meant by engagement. Prima's eyes flicked to his face, then back down. She nodded.

"I will be an obedient second wife," Prima said. "After you execute my husband Mitchell."

Barin could think of nothing whatever to say to that, and the rising thunder of the shuttle engines made further conversation impossible anyway.

❖   ❖   ❖

Far below, as the last shuttles rose into the sky, the men at last made it to the Rangers' houses, the armory, the meeting hall. The houses were empty, but for a dead man or two in each; and the keys—the keys they needed so badly—were missing.

❖   ❖   ❖

Mitchell Pardue had been told that his wives and children were safe, but he hadn't believed it. Not until Prima stood before him, properly barefoot but quite improperly dressed in a bright orange shipsuit with a sheet tied around it for a skirt.

"We have a new protector," she told him. She glanced at his face, then down respectfully. "Of the Serrano family."

"Prima—you can't just—"

"I reckon you lied to me, husband," Prima said. She looked at him again, this time steadily. "You said they was all orphans. You said those outlander women was all you ever found. You never told me you *killed* parents, in front of their children, that you killed *women*, even *mothers*."

"I—"

"As far as I'm concerned, they might as well mute

you, Mitchell Pardue, because if your tongue cannot speak the truth, why speak at all?"

And after that, he found he had little need to speak, and no one to speak to. In a last act of kindness that tore his heart, his captors showed him video of his children playing in the ship's gymnasium.

✧   ✧   ✧

They were almost to the Security station at the Fleet entrance to Rockhouse Major when they spotted the crowds on the other side of the barrier. The security detail moved on ahead to take up their positions.

"Oh Lord, the media!" Brun's new voice, still furry and softer than it had been, but strengthening steadily. Esmay glanced over at her.

"You knew it would be here."

"I suppose so, but I could hope. And you know, I used to love being the top newsflash attraction."

"Well, Barin can almost top you this time," Esmay said, with a wicked smirk.

Barin flushed. "I do not really have nineteen wives—"

"No, but do you think the media cares? It's a great story."

"Esmay—"

"I wouldn't tease him," Brun said. "After all, you could be a sensation yourself—"

"Not me, I'm the plain one."

"I don't think so. Landbride Suiza in love with a man encumbered by nineteen fanatic cultists, and having gone from villainess of my abduction to hero of the rescue force? We might as well face it—we're *all* condemned to a spot on the evening news."

"So . . . what's your advice, O experienced target of the press?"

"Relax and enjoy it," Brun said. "In fact—let's give them a real show. After all, it's ours. We're heroes of the hour—let's do it right."

"I hesitate to ask," Barin said, with a glance at Esmay. "Do you know what she means?"

"No," Esmay said, "and I don't want to, but we will."

"Link arms and I'll show you," Brun said.

"We can't do that; we're sober, serious professionals, Fleet officers—" But Brun had already grabbed her arm, and they came out of the gate like a trio of chorus dancers, into the lights and hubbub.

"All we have to worry about," Brun was saying brightly, eyes sparkling, golden curls tossing, "is pirates, thieves, traitors, smugglers, assassins, and the occasional nutcase."

Esmay looked past Brun to Barin. "Do you want to duck her in the fountain, or shall I?"

"Let's do it together," Barin said, suggestively.

"Always," Esmay said.

THE SHIP WHO SANG IS NOT ALONE!

Anne McCaffrey, with Mercedes Lackey, S.M. Stirling, and Jody Lynn Nye, explores the universe she created with her ground-breaking novel, The Ship Who Sang.

THE SHIP WHO SEARCHED
by Anne McCaffrey & Mercedes Lackey
Tia, a bright and spunky seven-year-old accompanying her exo-archaeologist parents on a dig, is afflicted by a paralyzing alien virus. Tia won't be satisfied to glide through life like a ghost in a machine. Like her predecessor Helva, *The Ship Who Sang*, she would rather strap on a spaceship!

THE CITY WHO FOUGHT
by Anne McCaffrey & S.M. Stirling
Simeon was the "brain" running a peaceful space station—but when the invaders arrived, his only hope of protecting his crew and himself was to become *The City Who Fought*.

THE SHIP WHO WON
by Anne McCaffrey & Jody Lynn Nye
"The brainship Carialle and her brawn, Keff, find a habitable planet inhabited by an apparent mix of races and cultures and dominated by an elite of apparent magicians. Appearances are deceiving, however . . . a brisk, well-told often amusing tale. . . . Fans of either author, or both, will have fun with this book."
—*Booklist*

DAVID WEBER

The Honor Harrington series: *(cont.)*

Field of Dishonor

Honor goes home to Manticore—and fights for her life on a battlefield she never trained for, in a private war that offers just two choices: death—or a "victory" that can end only in dishonor and the loss of all she loves....

Flag in Exile

Hounded into retirement and disgrace by political enemies, Honor Harrington has retreated to planet Grayson, where powerful men plot to reverse the changes she has brought to their world. And for their plans to succeed, Honor Harrington must die!

Honor Among Enemies

Offered a chance to end her exile and again command a ship, Honor Harrington must use a crew drawn from the dregs of the service to stop pirates who are plundering commerce. Her enemies have chosen the mission carefully, thinking that either she will stop the raiders or they will kill her . . . and either way, her enemies will win. . . .

In Enemy Hands

After being ambushed, Honor finds herself aboard an enemy cruiser, bound for her scheduled execution. But one lesson Honor has never learned is how to give up!

Echoes of Honor

"Brilliant! Brilliant! Brilliant!"—*Anne McCaffrey*

continued